Never Everything

Caroline Ashford

Caroline Ashford Publishing

Contents

To all the women who thought they deserved better, and all the
women who thought they didn't.
You do.

Author's Note:

This book contains adult content, and is written for audiences over the age of eighteen.

Please read over the content warnings carefully. If you wish to still read, but would like to know when certain triggers will occur, please visit my website at caroline-ashfordwriting.com

Content Warnings (All content has been reviewed by a sensitivity reader):

Alcohol abuse, colorism, graphic violence, domestic violence, emotional manipulation, reference to death of spouse and children, non-con, gun violence, infidelity, depiction of panic attacks, mentions of sexual exploitation of a minor (past), neglectful and abusive parents, attempted rape, attempted assault.

"The goal, I suppose, any fiction writer has, no matter what your subject, is to hit the human heart and the tear ducts and the nape of the neck and to make a person feel something about what the characters are going through and to experience the moral paradoxes and struggles of being human."

Tim O'Brien

1

"Helena, come!" Lucio barked as he walked past Helena's desk, not even bothering to slow his step for her to catch up.

She rushed to grab her papers and laptop, banging her knee into the corner of her desk when she scrambled up after him. Stupid heels. Flats were so much better; who cared if they made her five inches shorter than the rest of the staff? At least she wouldn't have hip problems when she was older. But no, she wanted to be *sophisticated* today. Ridiculous.

Helena finally caught up to Lucio, narrowly avoiding a head-on collision with a paralegal who had their nose buried in a tablet. The office was packed—it usually was on a Monday afternoon, but for some reason, today felt especially busy. The air around her hummed with a tense energy that put her on edge.

Lucio continued walking. "Did you write up the notes from the trial yesterday?"

"Of course I did. You literally watched me do it," Helena said, attempting to dig through the multitude of files in her hands. Another one appeared on top of the stack, and she glanced up to see Dylan, another temp and her best friend, throwing her a wink as he walked past.

She mouthed "thank you," and passed Lucio the folder just as he held out his hand for it.

He barely looked at it before shoving it under his arm and walking into the kitchenette of their office.

"Great." Lucio paused at the coffee machine to prepare his third cup of the day. He ran a hand through his jet black hair, poker straight and cut in the type of style that required minimal upkeep, and opened the file, green eyes scanning over the notes, judging her work. Helena hoped he wouldn't look too closely.

He snapped it shut. "What do you think?"

Helena set the files down on the counter to take his cup, adding cream and sugar. "I think I'm tired of you constantly forcing me to do work on the cases that you already know you can win."

"Exactly why I let you work on them." He traded her the folder for the cup of coffee. "Less chance of something going wrong."

"You always say that," Helena whined as she grabbed the remaining folders followed him out.

"And yet you keep asking."

"It's so boring. Why don't you let me do something useful?"

"You are useful. You take my notes, organize my papers, and get me coffee," Lucio said, taking a sip.

It was like the paralegals and other lawyers could sense him coming; they parted like the red sea. She had to keep up, lest the waves close back in on her.

"Why can't Dylan do all that?" Helena asked, her voice nearly drowned out by a cluster of prosecutors huddled around a water cooler, speaking in hushed tones about their latest cases.

Lucio's shoes clicked against the polished linoleum as he navigated around a wheeled cart stacked high with case files. "Because I need Dylan for important cases."

"I could do important cases too, you know."

"I've tried giving you important cases." He stopped in front of the elevator, jamming his finger into the *up* button. "But they were all 'too hard' for you to understand."

"I was barely a freshman! And I'm not even in law school yet."

"A future lawyer with any real tenacity would have bit the bullet and tried it anyways."

Helena rolled her eyes, before meeting her own gaze in the reflection of the elevator doors.

Standing next to Lucio, it was easy to see why people mistook her for his biological daughter, rather than adopted. They shared the same green eyes, the same straight black hair, even the same stiff posture. But that's where the similarities ended. Helena's face was round and child-like, making her look perpetually twelve. Lucio's age was a mystery to anyone who looked at him. He had wrinkles around his eyes and mouth, which was almost always set into a frown. His jaw was sharp and angular, free of any facial hair. She was sure people thought he was handsome, but his eyes set below a deep brow likely made them hesitant to compliment him. Helena blamed him for her resting bitch face, even if she knew it wasn't possible for him to have passed it on. But there had to be some kind of explanation out there, somewhere in the nature versus nurture theory.

The dead giveaway was her complexion; she looked like a ghost standing next to him. Lucio always attributed his deep, ochre skin color to his mother's Ticuana roots. *"Dad's only claim to me is the eyes,"* Lucio would joke, but there was always an edge to it. Any attempts Helena made at asking about it were dismissed with a passive wave or an empty promise of discussion later.

"So then what am I doing here?" Helena asked, shifting the stack of manila folders she carried under her arm.

The elevator arrived with a soft ding, and they stepped inside. The small space was lined with worn wood paneling, and a motivational poster about justice hung slightly askew on the back wall.

Lucio pressed the button for the tenth floor, where his office gave him a perfect view of the city. "Keeping yourself out of trouble. And getting some experience while you're at it."

The elevator lurched as it began its ascent. Helena stared absently at the numbers, her eyes narrowing as they spotted the sixth floor button. The sixth floor was where the public defenders' offices were, her least favorite type of attorney. She was grateful she didn't have to interact with them. From what she had seen, they were underhanded and scummy, using any tactic they had to to get their clearly guilty client out of trouble.

Lucio seemed to get along with them just fine outside of the courtroom, though.

"I can keep myself out of trouble," Helena mumbled.

He shot her a stern look. "Like hell, you can."

"Oh my God, will you let that *go* already?" Helena groaned just as the elevator doors opened to reveal the executive floor, where thick carpeting covered the institutional flooring below. Oil paintings of local judges and civic leaders lined the walls, and the lighting was warmer, more subdued. Lucio's secretary, Fawziyah, looked up from her computer as they emerged, giving Helena a sympathetic smile.

Helena rolled her eyes and mimed hanging herself, but quickly schooled her face when Lucio noticed his secretary biting back a smile.

They approached Lucio's office at the end of the hall, the heavy wooden door bearing a brass nameplate that read "District Attorney Luke Torres." He opened it with little effort, breezing into the large room.

Helena shielded her eyes against the sudden transition of light from the enormous windows that lined the back of his office. Through his window, the courthouse dome was visible against the afternoon sky. She hated coming in here. A constant reminder of the future that she was destined for, but never chose.

Her eyes adjusted to the change in lighting, and she held in the sigh that always threatened to escape her here. Lucio's office was always an absolute mess. The table in the center was always covered in files, which made the four chairs surrounding it look more like decoration than functional furniture. Helena had spent hundreds of hours trying to implement a system before she realized Lucio already had one: chaos.

His desk, however, was almost bare—a small table lamp, a laptop, a Lady Justice statue, and two framed photos. One of his new family, one of his old.

The walls were much the same as his desk. Most of the space was taken up by filing cabinets—Lucio hated that so many people were trying to go digital. Helena thought it was ridiculous that he was still trying to kill so many trees. The entire place might as well have been a fire hazard.

Lucio's jaw ticked. "You beat the crap out of your classmate. That's not something I can let go."

"Only because he was bullying Gideon. Was *I* supposed to let that slide?"

"No, but you are supposed to contact the proper authorities and let them handle it." Lucio took a seat at his table.

Of course. The proper authorities, meaning the cops, or school safety, or whatever other bullshit authority figure who wouldn't actually do jack all to protect those who actually needed protecting. Lucio had tried to convince her that being a lawyer meant doing exactly that—protecting those who didn't have a voice for themselves.

Helena just thought of it as another barrier to vigilante justice.

She took a seat near Lucio, setting down her laptop and the stack of folders. "And what if they don't do anything about it?"

"Then you don't let your impulses win." Lucio pulled a folder from another seemingly random stack, shuffling through pages.

She took it from him and got out the necessary paperwork. "So lie down and let the assholes win. Got it."

"Not what I meant," he said, before beginning to prattle off information and tasks for her to do.

Helena dutifully took notes, trying her best not to let her mind wander. But when her life looked literally the same day in and day out, it was almost impossible. Luckily, Lucio's desk phone rang, giving her a much needed break from his monotone voice being directed at her. She rested her chin in her hands, looking over at his desk, her gaze resting on the frame closest to her. She knew the photo by heart—she had the same one in her bedroom. All the kids did. It was from Quinn's graduation from high school, their arms wrapped around Helena and her twin Gideon's shoulders.

It was the first and last graduation Lucio had attended for any of them.

Lucio's cellphone dinged, and Helena stretched herself at an awkward angle to try and catch a glimpse of the screen. "Who's texting you?"

Lucio reached over and clicked the lock button, then flipped it face down, not once stopping his conversation. "Yeah, alright, I'll catch you later, Morton."

Alice Morton was a detective Lucio worked closely with, and even though Helena had worked with Lucio for close to a year, she had never seen this mysterious woman. Helena wondered if she actually existed, or if Lucio was finally starting to lose it from all the late nights in the office.

"Does she need to see you?" Helena asked once Lucio had hung up.

"Yes." Lucio turned around to grab his laptop off his desk, typed in his password, and clicked away. Helena leaned back in her seat, waiting for him to continue. But much like always, the vault had sealed shut.

"About?"

"A case."

"Which one?"

"Helena," Lucio warned.

She threw up her hands. "I'm just asking a question!"

He looked back to his laptop, his eyes scanning the screen. Helena wished he wore glasses so she could at least maybe catch a peek at what he was doing, but Lucio was graced with 20/20 vision. "No, you were sniffing for information. There's a difference."

Helena huffed as she began to gather up some of the paperwork and slinked behind him. "Why are you being so secretive?"

He shut his laptop, turning to her. "Why are you so curious?"

She pushed her hair away from her face. "You tell me all the time that I'll only learn by doing. This is your fault, if anything."

"*My* fault?" Lucio raised his brows. "Fia-te na Virgem e não corras."

"What does that mean?"

"It means my daughter should have listened to me when I told her that learning Portuguese was important."

Helena rolled her eyes as she threw herself back into her chair, setting the folders back onto the table. Lucio had been pushing for all the kids to learn Portuguese from the beginning, citing how learning a second language was good for them, and how they could use it when they got to college. But Helena could count on one hand the number of people that she knew who spoke Portuguese. And it wasn't like they offered it at her school, or that Lucio was even around enough for any of what she might have picked up to stick. She knew a few curse words, mainly because they were close to Spanish, which she had all but forgotten. "Translate apps exist for a reason, you know."

"You rely way too much on technology," he grumbled, putting the stack back where they belonged, in another random spot.

She snorted. "Okay, boomer."

"That's it." Lucio stood and moved behind her. "You're out. Go get Dylan."

Helena yelped as he dumped her out of her chair, nearly tripping over her damn heels again. "Take a joke!"

"When you're DA, you can make jokes. For now, you're my glorified assistant. Go get my other glorified assistant." Lucio ushered her out the door and closed it behind her.

"Asshole," Helena mumbled. He wouldn't hear her; the door was as thick as the stick up his ass.

She headed back down to the seventh floor, once more cutting through the crowded halls of the office until she spotted Dylan at his desk, working on a case that was *actually* important. Not that Helena exactly *cared*, all this was incredibly boring. But Dylan made everything more interesting.

He finished typing something into a document before looking up at her, his deep, sepia skin all the more rich in the light from the window next to him.

"The taskmaster wants to see you," Helena said, holding out her hands as if she were a zombie.

Dylan's brown eyes crinkled in the corners as he smiled, signing, *"Seriously, Hel, you're going to get in trouble one of these days."*

"What's he going to do? Fire me?" She snorted. "He couldn't handle this place without me."

"Yes, he could. He would just dump more work on me." Dylan frowned as he stood. *"And that makes you a bad friend."*

Helena gasped, clutching her chest. "I'm a *wonderful* friend. Who saved you some lunch in Luke's office?"

Dylan lifted his chin. *"From Quinn's?"*

"Duh. You think I've got money to be ordering out for you? With the amount Luke pays me?"

"He doesn't pay you."

"You see the problem?"

Dylan just shook his head as they walked to the elevator. He had originally joined the DA's staff via an initiative for marginalized groups getting into law, and was one of the best interns Lucio had. He was nonverbal and had been for as long as Helena had known him. He spoke ASL, but most of the people in the DA's office had learned enough to understand what he was saying—courtesy of Lucio fronting the cost for a couple classes and translators.

Or, Luke, as everyone else knew him.

All of the staff knew Lucio by his government name. Helena had been introduced to him as "Luke," but when they discovered his birth name, the kids had all switched to calling him Lucio or Dad.

Helena was the only one who still held on to Luke; partly because of work, partly because she knew how much he hated it when she called him it. And she didn't care how absolutely petty it was.

Helena clasped her hands behind her back, watching the numbers on the elevator as it crawled down to them before letting her gaze casually rest on him. "So, how's the case going?"

Dylan furrowed his brows. *"Case?"*

"The one you and Luke are working on." The elevator stopped on the floor above them. "The one he refuses to tell me about."

"What are you talking about?"

Helena had no idea how he would make it in this profession; Dylan had a terrible poker face. She did too, but that was less of a problem—she didn't plan on sticking around.

"He wants to see you. He'll probably tell you all about it. Which means..." She grinned, batting her eyelashes. "You can tell me all about it."

"Not happening, Hel." The elevator doors opened in front of them, and they waited for everyone to get off before stepping on. *"If Luke doesn't want you to know something, it's for a reason."*

Helena pouted, leaning against the wall of the elevator. "Meanie."

"Hey," Dylan pouted back at her, *"let's not get too harsh with the names here."*

She pressed her lips together to suppress her smirk. "Fine, asshole."

"Much more acceptable." The elevator announced their arrival, and he again held the doors to let her off.

She thanked him, ignoring the look from Fawziyah as they started down the hall.

As bad of a liar as Dylan was, he still clearly belonged here. He looked so confident as he strode down the halls: brown monkstrap shoes, deep blue blazer and slacks, his chin held high, eyes bright. Hell, he was even smiling. Helena only smiled with him because he was always finding some way to make her laugh.

If it wasn't for Dylan, she would have tried to throw herself out a window a while ago. Alas, they were sealed shut.

They reached Lucio's door, and Dylan knocked twice before entering. Helena ducked behind his tall frame, trying her best to avoid Lucio's sight.

"Goodbye, Hel," Lucio said without looking up from his laptop.

Helena huffed, already gathering her things. "Why can't I stay?"

"Because I said so."

"That's not an answer a boss should be giving his employee."

"Fine. I'm not speaking as your employer. I'm speaking as your father. Get the hell out of my office."

"And that's certainly not how a father should speak to his daughter."

"*Goodbye*, Hel." Lucio stood, but she was out before he could get around the table.

"This is bullshit," Helena yelled, shutting the door before Lucio could scold her about her language.

Whatever, she didn't care about what was going on; it didn't matter to her that Lucio wasn't letting her in on this *one* case, even though he had let her in on every single case before this, even the super important ones that she shouldn't have been involved with. But Lucio trusted her to handle these cases with fidelity, and she always did.

Helena wasn't going to let it bother her. She wasn't going to dwell over the fact that Dylan—who was *technically* her equal—was getting to sit in on this case. It was fine. Because eventually, she'd wear Dylan down enough that he'd tell her.

And then maybe she'd care enough to make Lucio let her in on the case. If it was interesting enough, of course. Which it probably wasn't.

Helena stomped off from the doors that kept her out. Maybe she would go visit Gideon. It had been a minute, and she already finished all the work that Lucio had given her for the day.

She checked her phone, eyes catching on the photo of her, Gideon, and Quinn at the beach a few years ago. It was her favorite picture of the three of them. Quinn in the middle, towering over Helena and Gideon, all three of them looking happier than she had ever thought possible. Happier than she had felt in a long time.

Screw Lucio. She was taking off early.

C emeteries always gave Helena the creeps. Even when she was little, before everything, she hated the vibes they gave off. Maybe it was all the ghost stories Quinn had told her and Gideon, or her seeing too many scary movies, or even just instinct. Whatever it was, she hated them.

But her duty as a twin overrode all fears that would hold her back. She cursed Gideon as she continued her climb; he couldn't have chosen a nice flat piece of land to be buried in? He had to pick the hill? And worse than that, he had to be next to *them?*

Helena kept her gaze straight ahead as his headstone came into view, a smile blooming across her face. Gideon's picture smiled back at her, goofily holding up a trophy nearly half his size. First prize at Model UN. As shy as he had been, that boy knew how to work a room, and more importantly, how to get people to listen.

His small, careful voice filled every corner of a room, made people's heads turn, nod, even if they disagreed.

Helena had never been that good.

"Hey G," she said as she knelt on the grass. She reached into her backpack, pulling out a trading card. "Got something for you."

She hid it in her hand before she flipped it around. A shiny Bulbasaur. She could almost see his eyes widen, his mouth drop open as she pulled the other card out of a sleeve they had retrofitted to his headstone and replaced it with a new one. The cards were always in almost pristine condition—Helena made a point to come often enough that they never sat long enough to be damaged. Gideon would kill her if she ever did. She dug into her backpack, pulling out a cherry Coke. "I'd pour some out for you, but I don't exactly want to attract a bunch of bees."

Helena rolled her eyes as she imagined Gideon's response: *Bees are some of the most important pollinators! We should be encouraging them to come around more often. Why do you think I planted so many—*

"Fine, I'll do it after. There's already a bunch floating over by their graves." She nodded at the three plots next to her, fresh flowers laid on one, but not the others.

Her brows pulled together for a brief second. Strange; whenever Lucio came by he always left fresh flowers on all three.

Even more strange, he had left roses.

Lucio *never* got roses. He claimed they were too effortless.

Anyone can buy you roses. But someone who cares about you will put thought into each and every flower they choose for you.

Helena hadn't ever bothered to think too hard about the flowers he always bought for his past family, and she *definitely* didn't think too hard about the lilies he got her every year for her birthday. Helena shrugged it off—she was here for Gideon, anyways.

She started to absently pick at some dandelions, popping off their yellow heads and watching them fall to the ground. "Quinn's doing good. Said they're gonna stop by on Saturday."

The breeze rustled through the grass, sending the beheaded dandelions tumbling away. Gideon's voice carried with it, a million and one questions about *dad*. "Who gives a crap about Lucio?"

A bee buzzed by her ear. Helena gently swatted at it, glaring at the photo before her. "Oh, whatever."

She laid down with her head closest to the headstone, looking up at the sky above them. A few clouds dotted the sky, still blue despite it being so late in the day. July was always their favorite month, because it meant that their birthday was right around the corner. Not that Lucio would be around to celebrate it with them. Helena would probably come here and enjoy some time with Gideon, before heading to dinner with Quinn and Dylan. Like she had last year.

The bee buzzed again, and Helena sighed dramatically.

"Lucio's fine, I guess. Got a new case. Something high profile." She pursed her lips. "Well, more high profile. He won't tell me what it is, though." She let her cheek fall to the grass. "I bet he'd let you in on it."

Memories of Gideon and Lucio sitting in the home office flooded her mind. She would always try to join, desperate to be with Gideon at every waking moment, but eventually, the constant practice of Model UN debates had bored her nearly to tears. She stopped trying to worm her way in, and neither Lucio nor Gideon seemed to notice her absence.

They at least had the decency to not talk shop at the dinner table, but it was always there. Even a simple discussion about the weather could turn into a debate about the effects of climate change and which ecological solution was actually the best. Helena and Quinn would entertain themselves by seeing how long they could get away with stealing food off Gideon and Lucio's plates before they noticed. Sometimes, they never did.

Helena hated it.

Lucio stole one of the best things that she had from her, and she had let him.

If she could go back and do it all over again, she would make sure she was always by Gideon's side. She would walk with him everywhere she could, and even where she couldn't. Nothing would be able to separate them. Not even this.

Helena closed her eyes, listening to the breeze continue to shake the trees. "I miss you."

The bee buzzed by her ear again. She didn't swat it away.

"I wish it had been me."

Another buzz, louder this time.

"I'm serious, G. I mean," Helena tilted her face back to look at the photo, "I guess I wouldn't want *you* going through this either, but..." She pulled at some of the grass. "You and Quinn were so happy with Lucio."

A fresh oak leaf fell on her face from the tree nearby.

She immediately brushed it off, her anger flaring. "Don't give me that crap! You're not here to see what a huge hypocrite he is."

A squirrel chattered nearby.

"It's true. Ever since you..." Helena huffed. She sat up and brought her knees to her chest, resting her chin on them. She swallowed back the tears that threatened to burn her eyes every single time. Three years since Gideon had passed, but every time she thought too hard about it, she cried like it was just yesterday. Whoever said time healed all wounds was full of shit. Nothing would ever fill the Gideon-shaped hole in her chest. "Since you've been gone, Lucio's been different."

She closed her eyes again, breathing in deep to push back the memories: debates, practices, recitals, birthdays. Lucio had made so much time for them when Gideon was still around.

And then, he just didn't.

He retreated into his office, to his job, started telling Helena what she could and couldn't do, who she could or couldn't be. He wasn't even around half the time to make sure she was even following his rules.

Maybe that's why she had gone off the deep end. Started skipping school, staying out late. But it hadn't changed anything. It just became Quinn's problem, because they were around more often. Until she got kicked out of school.

Lucio had been pissed. He had scolded her worse than he ever had. And she had sat there and taken it, because she couldn't do it to Quinn.

I'm done, Helena. We're going to get you into a transfer school so you can still graduate on time. Then, you're going to NYU, and you're going to get your degree. End of story.

Quinn had sat right by her, holding her hand as Lucio laid into her, tried to soften the blows.

She's got a lot going on, Dad, maybe we need to get back into counseling. All of us.

Lucio had signed her and Quinn up, but he was too busy to ever attend a session.

She let out a breath, before standing and brushing herself off. "I should get outta here before it gets too late. Otherwise the buses are gonna stop running and I'm going to have to call Lucio for a ride."

Helena took a sip of her drink, before pouring out some on the grass. "Don't complain to me when you get a bunch of ants down there."

She capped the bottle, and plucked two more dandelions. "Later, G."

She set the weeds on the two remaining graves, then turned, heading back down the hill.

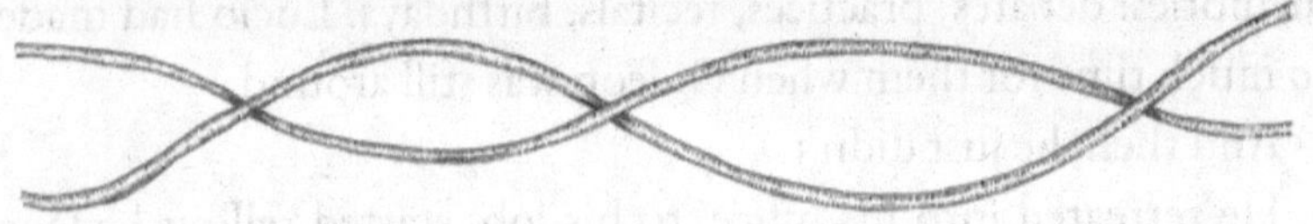

Lucio's home office door was always closed, always shutting Helena out until he found it necessary to call her in.

And it wasn't often that he did. Most of the time, he was locked away for hours, working on some case or another, only coming out to grab a snack or water, before going back in to hide away from the world again.

But there were times where she found it necessary to check in on him, like now. Dylan had texted her, asking about some document he needed for a case, it was time sensitive, blah blah blah.

She liked Dylan, but there were times where it felt like he forgot she really wasn't Lucio's secretary.

Even still, there she was, knocking at Lucio's door, waiting oh so patiently for a response. The small crack of light from the bottom of the door let her know that he was in there, but when she knocked again and still received no answer, she knew what had happened.

She sighed, opening the door and peering inside.

Lucio's office was so impressive that it was almost ridiculous. Walls covered with texts, both new and old, fiction and nonfiction, most of them being legal tomes. Awards and photos of ceremonies demonstrating his climb through the ranks from humble paralegal to District Attorney. He even had a couple of newspaper clippings hung in frames; gifts from Gideon.

Helena's eyes slid over the photos of her high school graduation, her and Quinn's smiles small and tight. Lucio hadn't even been there to snap a damn photograph.

Moonlight spilled in through the side windows, casting shadows on the areas that the lamps didn't reach. She stepped onto the hardwood floor, cool beneath her bare feet. Lucio kept his office like an ice box, said it helped to keep him awake. Which was funny, because he always seemed to fall asleep anyways.

Like right now; she saw Lucio, slumped over on his marble-topped desk, the computer screen illuminating his face. His back rose and fell evenly.

It made sense; it was past midnight, and Lucio was still working on the same case that he had been working on with Dylan earlier in the week. Helena had fought to get into the office, but Lucio had kept that door shut tight. And Dylan refused to budge—no matter how much she begged, pleaded, promised frappuccinos. No, it was only when either of them needed something that she got a slight glimpse of what it could be. And that really just meant she got to see a blank sheet of paper where everyone else saw an Andy Warhol.

Whatever. It was only one stupid case.

Helena touched Lucio's shoulder, but he didn't stir.

"Lucio," she whispered, shaking him.

He still didn't wake up.

Helena saved the document he had been working on, an older case that she already knew about, shut the computer down, and went to grab a blanket to cover him with. She looked over the desk, the photograph she had seen a million times still twisting the knife lodged deep in her chest.

Lucio stood with his wife, Elyse, a woman with long, blonde hair and deep blue eyes. Her smile was small, not showing her teeth, but it didn't affect the softness of her features. Each parent held a boy in their arms, identical twins. The boys looked like the perfect mix of their parents: Lucio's green eyes, Elyse's hair (with just a touch of curl as it started to grow out), Lucio's sharp features, softened only by the boys' young age.

Helena looked back at Lucio. She would let him sleep—to wake him now to go to an empty bed was just cruel. He might curse her out for his aching back in the morning, but she would deal with it.

Lucio's phone buzzed twice, a text message lighting up the screen.

New Signal Message from Michael Silva.

Helena's breath caught in her throat.

Michael Silva.

Her uncle.

Not that Lucio ever called him that. She only knew about Michael from when they had been cleaning out the basement a year after they first moved in, when she stumbled across an old album with some photos still in it. Helena had made the mistake of thinking it was a baby picture of Lucio, but when she had brought it to him, he crumpled it in his fist and told her to go figure out what Gideon had gotten into.

When she tried to bring it up again later, Lucio had pretended like he didn't know what the hell she was talking about.

Quinn had told her Michael's name, in an attempt to stop her from bringing it up to Lucio, and a few key details: Michael Silva was Lucio's brother, they hadn't spoken in nearly a decade, and it had something to do with Elyse.

Lucio's words echoed in her mind, firm and low. *Fia-te na Virgem e não corras.*

She nearly rolled her again in remembering. But if Michael was texting him...

This could be her chance. Michael had to be reaching out for a reason, right? Or maybe he and Lucio had been texting right along—maybe, just maybe, he was trying to reconcile whatever had broken them in the first place. Ten years was more than long enough to hate someone, wasn't it? Especially over something as frivolous as a woman. Sibling bonds went deeper than that.

Helena would know.

She tapped on the notification, entered Lucio's passcode, then again when the app opened. The text stared back at her, Portuguese mocking her monolingualism.

This was fine—Helena would just take a picture and translate it. Lucio would be none the wiser.

She hovered her phone over Lucio's and tapped the camera button. A flash lit up the room, and Helena had to suppress her gasp of terror.

Lucio stirred, grunting as the light blared in his eyes.

Helena dropped to the ground. *Shit, shit, shit!* She was such an *idiot*, why the hell hadn't she checked her flash? Lucio was going to tear her a new one for snooping. But it wasn't *her* fault. If he would just talk to her, she wouldn't care as much.

Yeah, right. Helena might as well change her name to Pandora, because she couldn't resist opening a box.

Lucio settled back down, mouth parting slightly as he mumbled, "Elyse."

Then he began to snore.

Helena released her breath into the quiet, pushing herself up off the floor.

She turned his desk lamp off, tiptoeing out as carefully as she could to avoid waking him. Once she was safely in her own room, she pulled up the photo and entered it into a translator app.

The flash had cut most of the screen, but there were a few words it was able to catch:

After so many years— come back— Try— return the favor.

Helena scowled. This didn't tell her anything. Return the favor? What favor? A "helped me fix a car" kind of favor or a "helped hide a body" kind of favor? Maybe Michael had gotten in some legal trouble once?

Damn it. She obviously couldn't let Lucio know that she had read his messages. But what if Michael was trying to reconcile?

No. Fia-te na Virgem e não corras: Trust the Virgin and don't run away.

She would do exactly that.

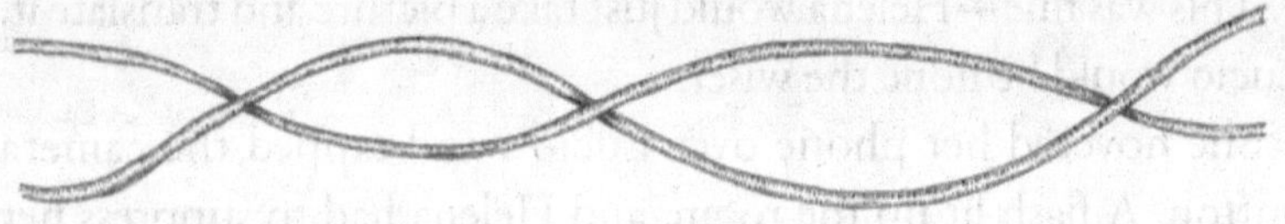

It had only taken Helena one page of LinkedIn searches to find him. She didn't know what she had expected, but she knew it wasn't what she had found.

It was strange, seeing Michael. She had expected him and Lucio to be more alike, but...no.

Michael had a smoother jaw line, accentuated by a dark beard. His nose was straight and slim; he had a heavy brow like Lucio's, but in a way that made him look more pensive than broody. He looked...*friendly,* but there was something below it that made Helena uneasy. Maybe it was his eyes.

They were a terrifying shade of blue—not the striking blue one might expect, but a deep, heavy shade. As if someone had taken the ocean during a storm and placed it in his irises.

A shiver traveled down Helena's spine as she scrolled.

Occupation: Import-Export Specialist at NomadCrate Company.

Import and Export? She had never heard of anything like that. She would look it up later.

She continued scrolling, down to his education. Helena's eyes widened. MBA at Wharton. Lucio had gone to Stanford for his JD, but both of them had found their way back to New York, and both got into top five schools.

She growled. Lucio got to go all the way to California but she had gotten stuck going to NYU? Once more Lucio proved himself to be one of the top five hypocrites.

The rest of the page was filled with boring business bullshit. It wasn't anything personal, like she wanted. Maybe he had a link to an outside profile? Helena scrolled back up to see a link for an Instagram page. She clicked on it, and immediately groaned.

No posts yet.

Of course. He was slightly older than Lucio, so it would make sense that his boomer-self *also* didn't post regularly. It was a wonder Michael even had the account in the first place.

Clicking on the tagged posts, Helena was flooded with photos. She clicked through a few of them. Most were clearly him at business dinners and events, rubbing elbows with CEOs and other higher-ups.

She clicked back to his main page, her thumb hovering over the message button. It could be that easy. She could reach out, tell him who she was, say that she found him by accident, that she wanted to connect.

But what if Michael didn't even check his messages? He clearly didn't use Instagram often, if at all.

And she was *not* reaching out to her estranged uncle on LinkedIn.

Helena groaned, clicking back to the photos, scrolling again. None of these people were accessible to her—she wasn't going to be able to waltz up to some CEO and ask if he knew her uncle.

A photo from last October gave her pause. Michael stood amongst a crowd of people, all in costume. He wore a costume too, some tacky camouflage that was clearly meant to be a hunter. A woman stood next to him, his arm wrapped around her waist, but she kept her back to the camera. Probably to show off her ass in the white lingerie that she was trying to pass off as a bunny. Michael's face was turned toward her, likely whispering in her ear, based on his smile.

Helena's eyes drifted over the photo, catching on the woman's left shoulder. There was a small tattoo, barely noticeable, in the shape of a T.

Who the hell gets a T tattooed on them?

Helena clicked the photo again, and the names of the people tagged popped up. She clicked on the woman's tag, but it led to a dead end. A private account linked to a club called Vision.

More specifically, a *gentleman's* club.

Right in the heart of the Meatpacking District.

Bingo.

3

Helena tapped her foot as the bouncer checked her fake ID. She wasn't sure what she had expected when she came to Vision, but the security guard at the front door wasn't on her list. And him actually taking his job seriously wasn't either. Each time he looked back at her, his eyes remained on her face, and only her face. Not once did his gaze stray to the fishnet shirt and black bralette combo she'd put on, nor the short-shorts that hugged her almost non-existent curves.

Her irritation worsened as he stared at the ID again. The fake would get her in—she hoped. A classmate had helped Helena get a hold of one just last week. It looked legit enough.

At least, to her it did.

Finally, the bouncer waved her in—he must have decided she wasn't worth the trouble. She didn't stick around for him to change his mind. Stepping into the club, Helena was overwhelmed by the stench of dollar store body spray, and hot garbage masquerading as bar food. Vision was something else.

Multiple stages were dotted around the floor, each surrounded by men. Helena's gaze drifted to the women, who alternated between noticing and not noticing the men who sat below them. Their bodies moved to the house music, lyricless but full of bass.

They were hypnotic. The women moved with a level of fluidity that Helena had never seen before, confident and sure of each movement. Their outfits ranged from full body suits to pieces of fabric that barely covered their breasts. A woman dropped her top, and the men below her howled. The stripper leaned down, gladly collecting bills and allowing others to be stuffed into the string Helena hesitated to call underwear.

Honestly, she didn't get how these women could be okay with this. Helena had never thought about being a stripper; the idea of men ogling her for their pleasure was nauseating. Bad enough she had to deal with the occasional cat caller.

A stripper walked past, a man in tow—an already balding thirty-something wearing a button up shirt that was way too big on him—towards a wall of alcoves. On Helena's right, other people disappeared behind closed doors. Damn, this was going to make her job a lot harder, then.

Helena walked through the maze of stages and seats, trying not to notice the way some of the men looked at her. Some strippers glanced her way, but she didn't linger long enough to let them try to stop her. The bar was empty besides a few patrons, which made it the perfect spot for her search for the stripper from the photo. Helena took a seat in the middle and cleared her throat at the bartender. "Whiskey and Coke."

He side-eyed her.

Helena rolled her own in response. "I got in, didn't I?"

The man shrugged, expertly wielding the soda gun with one hand while pouring in whiskey with the other. Helena traded a twenty dollar bill for the drink.

"Keep the change," she shouted over her shoulder and turned herself around on the bar stool.

She scanned over the bodies of the strippers, which was much harder to do, seeing as they were constantly moving. Some had longer hair, which hid their shoulders from view; others moved in such a way on the pole that their backs were never facing her, or were towards the floor. One woman spun on the pole by her thighs only. Helena rubbed her own in response.

Jeez, didn't that hurt?

Focus, Helena.

The lighting was not helping. It was almost impossible to see; the colored lights shifted and changed as it illuminated the strippers. The men were cast in shadows. The only thing visible about them was their hands as they tossed money on stage or passed it to the strippers. But maybe it was for the best. If those men looked anything like the guy Helena was sitting next to, maybe the women didn't want to see them.

Helena took a sip of her drink, cringing at the burn of cheap whiskey. Or expensive whiskey; she really didn't know the difference. Her one experience with alcohol was when she was fourteen, and that had been the last time she ever touched the stuff. She tried to suppress a cough, setting her drink down behind her.

"Too strong?"

Helena glanced over just as a man settled into the empty seat to her left. He was wearing a cheap, polyester suit, and reeked of cigarettes. The man's eyes raked over her, taking in every inch of her exposed skin.

She crossed her arm over her stomach.

"I can buy you a new drink, if you'd like. Something that's more suited for a beautiful young lady like yourself."

Screw that. Helena sneered, turning herself away from him as she went to retrieve her drink. She knew enough to not talk to strangers in a dimly lit club, especially ones as sketchy looking as this guy. And besides, the last thing she needed was some asshole distracting her.

"Hey, I'm talking to you!"

Helena yelped as she was yanked sideways, her body immediately tensing. No one had ever touched her like that before, like she was some kind of object. And now here was this absolute cretin doing exactly that. Do something, stupid!

"Pitt!" someone shouted over the music, stopping the guy just before his hand reached the edge of Helena's shorts.

A stripper cut through the small crowd with ease, her attitude communicating to all around her that she was not in the mood to be messed with. Helena took in the woman's purple outfit—although "outfit" was a generous term for the pieces of fabric she was wearing. It made Helena's clothes look like a nun's habit. Her box braids extended far past her waist, embellished with small metal pieces that glinted in the flashing lights.

The man's—Pitt—grip on Helena loosened enough for her to pull free. She kept her glass clutched in her hand just in case he decided to change his mind.

"You know the rules," the woman said as she got closer. "You can look but you can't touch."

"Mind your business, Angel," Pitt grumbled.

Angel planted her hands on either side of him, pinning him against the bar.

"You want me to get Henry to help you find your way out of here?" Angel asked.

Pitt shook his head.

"Then fuck off."

Pitt shot her a nasty look, but ducked under her arm, and the two women watched him skulk off.

Angel turned back to Helena, frowning. "Who the hell checked your ID?"

"None of your business," Helena mumbled as she went to take a sip.

"You need to learn to watch your drinks." Angel snatched the glass and dumped it behind the bar. "Your little friend over there spiked it."

"What? How can you—"

"He was pretty obvious about it. If you had been paying attention." Angel waved over the bartender and mumbled something to him, giving Helena a chance to get a good look at her.

Angel's terracotta skin was highlighted by patches of gold body glitter that normally Helena would have thought was tacky or obnoxious, but made the woman look as if she really was an angel.

She had a strong jaw, full lips, brown eyes accented by golden liner. The perfect mix of sharp and gentle. Helena struggled to keep her mouth closed. This woman was drop dead gorgeous, and she was working in a place like this? Maybe she was the reason this place was still running.

The bartender nodded once before walking over to one of the security guards.

Angel took the seat next to Helena. "First time?"

Helena blinked, coming back to her senses. "What?"

Angel motioned to the space around them. "Coming to a club alone."

"No, I come to clubs all the time."

"Really? Is that why you're so shitty at watching your drink?"

"I'm not," Helena huffed. "I just got caught off guard, is all."

Angel tapped Helena's forehead once, gently, but punctuated by a nail that would have poked Helena's eye out if she had been one inch to the left or right. "The one thing you never want to be in any kind of bar is caught off guard. That's girl code one-oh-one, kid."

Helena scowled, rubbing at the spot Angel had touched. "I'm not a kid."

"You sure as hell look like one," Angel said, catching the eye of the bartender as he returned. "Two whiskey and Cokes. Virgin."

Helena's brows furrowed. "Virgin?"

The bartender snorted out a laugh, dispensing the drinks with a shake of his head before passing the two glasses over the bar top.

Angel echoed the laughter. "Christ, kid, I'm surprised Phil even let you in the door."

Helena's cheeks burned. This wasn't helpful. She didn't need to sit here and get bullied by a woman wearing floss for clothes. She should just take her drink and go deeper into the club—her view wasn't really doing what it should—but something in Angel's smile kept her at the bar.

"What's your name?" Angel asked, picking up her drink and placing her hand over it.

Helena hesitated. There was no reason for her to be talking to this woman, except for the fact that she had just saved her from some creep twice over. And besides, what harm could it really do? Not like Helena would ever see her again. "Helena."

Angel sipped at her drink, her brows raised in amusement. "That's a weird name."

Helena crossed her arms over her chest. "At least it's unique, Angel."

"Angel's my stage name, Helena." Angel grinned. "My real name is Jay."

Helena tried to resist smiling back. "Jay, short for..."

"Just Jay. Parents wanted a boy, got me instead." Jay shrugged. "They didn't feel like changing the name, I guess."

"Yikes."

"Eh, what're you gonna do?"

Helena stirred her drink as she looked across the crowd. She shouldn't even be wasting her time talking to Jay. She was getting distracted from why she was here.

A stripper passed by, and Helena scanned her as quickly as she could, her head turning and meeting Jay's curious glance.

"Looking for something?"

Helena immediately blushed. "No—I mean, yes, but—"

"I can call her over, if you want," Jay said, already beginning to cup her hand around her mouth to shout to the other stripper.

Helena grabbed Jay's arm. "No! It's fine. Completely fine. I don't need her, I promise."

"Relax, kid, no one is going to judge you," Jay said. "We don't get girls in here often, but that doesn't mean it's a never."

"What?" Helena blanched.

Did Jay know what she was after? No, that couldn't be it; even if it was, wouldn't that technically be a good thing? Maybe Jay knew Michael, may she could—wait.

The implication slowly dawned on Helena, her face growing hot. "No! No, I'm not here for that sort of thing."

"Then why are you here?" Jay nodded towards the glass in her hand. "Cause between you and me, the drinks here are not it."

"Well, I am here for a girl—a woman, I guess—but not like that, I'm just looking to talk to someone," Helena sputtered, her mouth moving a million miles an hour while her brain tried to tell it to shut up before she said something that she absolutely shouldn't.

But luckily, Jay just found the entire thing hilarious, laughing again as she took a drink.

"Okay, okay. You're not here for the girls, or at least, 'not like that'," Jay said. "So, what are you looking for?"

Helena looked away. "To talk to someone."

"About..."

"A person."

Jay waved her hand in a "go on" motion.

"That's it."

Jay's brown eyes sparkled as a spotlight passed over her face, highlighting flecks of gold highlighter. "You're a cryptic little thing, aren't you?"

A man from across the room waved at Jay, and she took one last sip of her drink.

"Back on. Do yourself a favor, kid," she pulled a hundred dollar bill from her g-string and gave it to Helena, "get a cab and get the hell out of here. You don't belong in a place like this."

Helena gawked at the bill—she was ready to tell Jay she refused, that she didn't know where the hell this money had been, she really didn't want anything that had been that close to Jay's private area, but Jay was already gone, sauntering back to the stage. Cat calls and wolf whistles followed her, all acknowledged with a wiggle of her fingers or a toss of her hair.

Jay turned her head to the left, her hair pulling away from her left shoulder to reveal a line. The same one that Helena had seen in the photo with her uncle, Michael.

She smirked as she went to take a final drink, but something hit her lip. Said something floated in her glass. She fished it out with her finger: a small hair tie, like the one used to hold braids. Just like Jay's.

Funny.

4

Meeting Jay left Helena with more questions than answers. Why was Michael involved with a stripper of all people? Did he know? Or even care? Or worse, had they met at the club? Wasn't there some adage that you shouldn't fall in love with strippers? If they were even in love.

The sound of the office around her slowly died out as she zoomed in on the photo again, her eyes boring into the tattoo. Now that Helena was looking at it more clearly, she could tell it was really a nail. What the hell did it mean? She knew people got tattoos that meant nothing all the time, but it was just so weird. Why a nail?

Helena sighed as she lolled her head back, and nearly screamed at the sight of Dylan standing above her.

His brown eyes crinkled. "Sorry, didn't mean to scare you."

"Liar. You always make noise when you're coming up behind me." Helena turned around, setting her phone behind her.

He gave her a look. "I did. You didn't hear me?"

"No, you were dead silent."

"I think you were just a little too wrapped up in whatever you were looking at on your phone," he signed as he leaned over, reaching for it on her desk.

"Hey!" She snatched it away from him. "Don't be nosy."

His smile faded, his face only inches away from hers.

If Helena had been a different woman, she might have noticed how cute Dylan was. How his brown skin was slightly darker because of the summer sun. How he always wore his hair in locs or kept it short, because otherwise his coily hair would hang down in front of his eyes. How his lips were just the perfect amount of full, slightly pink, probably incredibly soft.

But Helena wasn't that type of woman.

And Dylan was her friend. So no, she didn't notice.

Helena raised her brows. "Can I help you?"

Dylan pointed at something over her shoulder. On instinct, she turned to look. There was nothing behind her besides a bunch of prosecutors, all doing their normal prosecutor things.

Dylan snatched her phone out of her hands, and she spun back, shooting out of her seat. "Dylan!"

He was only a few inches taller than her, but it was enough for him to be able to hold the phone over Helena's head. She grabbed at his arms, practically hanging off of him, but it was useless. He entered her passcode (his birthday), his eyes widened as he looked at the photo on the screen.

"Give me that," she growled, snatching her phone away again. "It's nothing!"

"Didn't look like nothing. Who was that?"

Helena looked around, but all the other paralegals and attorneys were busy with their work, utterly oblivious to their exchange. She pursed her lips as she set her phone down.

"Promise you won't tell," she signed. Helena's ASL on the speaking side was rusty; her motions came out stuttered and small. But Dylan was able to understand her, and would usually help her by repeating the sign back to her the correct way if she was way off base.

Dylan crossed his heart before nodding to her chair.

He leaned against the side of her desk, nudging over a small stack of paperwork as she sat down.

Helena bit her lip. "I saw a text on Luke's phone."

Dylan sucked in a breath. "You went through his phone?"

"No, I mean, kind of, but—" Helena pressed her hands against her face. "Text from my U-N-C-L-E."

"Your uncle? Luke has a brother?"

She nodded. "Haven't talked in ten years."

Dylan rubbed at the back of his neck, casting a glance out towards the window. "So, you saw a text."

"Yes," Helena signed. "Said something W-E-I-R-D. Think Michael wants to," she paused. "How do you say 'reconcile'?"

Dylan motioned, linking his hands together, one on top of the other. Helena mimicked it.

"Even if he does, I don't think that's something you want to get yourself caught up in." Dylan looked away from her again. "It's Luke's business. I don't think it's right of you to get involved."

"Luke is always in mine," she said. "Why can't I be—"

Helena yelped as heavy hands slammed on the back of her seat.

"Because my business puts food on the table and keeps a roof over your head," Lucio said, turning her around to face him. "And yours involves you talking about me behind my back."

Helena blanched. "How long have you been standing there?"

"Long enough to know you're trying to stick your nose where it doesn't belong." Lucio looked up at Dylan, jutting his chin towards the elevator. "You. Upstairs."

Dylan nodded, avoiding Helena's eyes as he headed towards the elevator.

Lucio glanced back at Helena. He had that dumb prosecutor look on his face when he was trying to intimidate her. But it never worked. She could always tell the difference between him being seriously angry and him just being miffed. Right now, he was miffed.

"What? I was just talking to Dylan." She crossed her arms over her chest. "Am I not allowed to talk to my friends?"

"Of course you are. But you might not want to talk about your boss in a place where he can catch you." Lucio straightened. "I need to borrow Dylan for a while. Can you run out and grab us some coffee?"

Her jaw nearly hit the floor. "Please tell me you're joking."

"I'm not. We're going to be here late, and I don't have the time to go get them."

"Get one of the interns to do it," she grumbled, standing up to meet him. But Lucio was close to a whole foot taller than her; she felt more like a toddler throwing a tantrum than a young woman trying to assert her place.

"The interns are not allowed to leave the building," he said. "And I also don't trust any of them not to mess up my coffee order."

"Oh, so you'll trust me with this but not a case?" Helena glared up at him. "Is this more of that sexist bullshit? Because I'm a girl? You're mandated to take that sexual harassment training, you know."

Lucio's lips twitched, just enough to cool the fire in her blood by one degree.

"This has nothing to do with you being a woman," he said. "Or even being my daughter. This case requires someone who can wait for all the information before they make a decision. And you, dear Hel, are still waiting on your prefrontal cortex to develop."

She cut her eyes over to the window. The faint outline of her reflection stared back at her. Yeah right. Woman her foot. Lucio still treated her like she was fourteen. The only difference was she got to work here. But otherwise, it was be home by eleven and text me where you're going and who you're going with. The only reason she had gotten away with last night was because Lucio hadn't been home to question why she was out.

Lucio placed a hand on her shoulder. "When you get out of undergrad, I'll let you start taking on some more complicated cases."

She shrugged it off and headed for the elevator doors. "Yeah, whatever."

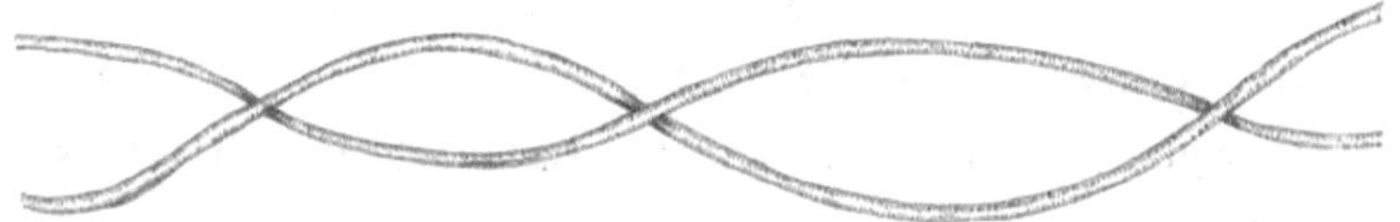

Helena let out a quiet sigh as she waited with the paralegals, their bodies too close to hers. She hated people touching her, but she especially hated it when strangers touched her.

One of the other people laughed at something, bumping into Helena and nearly knocking the coffee carrier into her. The elevators were too cramped to be up to code, but then again, the building was funded by tax payers, so maybe it was a good sign things hadn't been updated. Meant the money was going to the right places.

Hopefully.

People shuffled off around her, leaving her alone in the tiny metal box. She adjusted her grip on the carrier, making sure not to spill either drink—a mochachino with a pump of caramel and a drizzle of caramel sauce, and a black coffee.

It was a wonder Lucio didn't have diabetes from his sweets obsession.

The elevator doors opened, and Helena stepped off.

Fawziyah looked up at her from behind her secretarial desk. She at least had a nice new computer, or, newer. "Hello, Miss Torres. Mr. Torres had to step out."

"Seriously? He just asked me to bring him some coffee," Helena groaned. She looked down the hall. "Is Dylan in there?"

"Dylan is just using the restroom. He should be back in a moment." Fawziyah looked over at her phone as it started to ring. "Mr. Torres asked you to wait outside for him."

Helena rolled her eyes for the umpteenth time that day. "Outside the office?"

"Yes, Miss Torres. If you'll excuse me, I have to take this." Fawziyah picked up the phone, her voice low and steady as she spoke to whoever was on the other line.

Helena glanced down the hall, then back at Fawziyah, who was sufficiently distracted. The office was far enough away from her desk, too. Helena moved with the same casualty as a person trying to catch the last train, telling herself she was doing the perfectly legal task of dropping coffee off for the intended drinkers. Once she made it to the door, she opened it, peeking inside to make sure the coast was clear.

It was.

Helena set the coffee down at the far end of the table before scurrying over to Lucio's favorite seat. His laptop sat open, asleep. A click of the mousepad and the screen lit up.

She didn't even have to guess his password. Lucio loved to use a weird combination of his kids' birthdays: 08 for Helena and Gideon, 17 for Quinn, and 16 for his boys—month, date, year. The same one he had on his phone, too. He really should get better about that. It was a huge security risk.

A document was already pulled up on the screen:

Company Financial Statements: NomadCrate Company.

Helena's eyes narrowed. NomadCrate? As in, Michael's company?

She knew it. Michael had to be in some kind of trouble! That's why he was reaching out to Lucio. But it still didn't make any sense. Why would Lucio be acting so sketchy? She glanced at the transactions, many of them highlighted, mainly withdrawals for sums that wouldn't necessarily raise brows. Except for how many there were.

She scrolled further. There was a description of the company, nothing she cared to read. She continued onto the next page: suspect profile.

A copy of Colton Watkins' identification sheet is in the section labeled Appendix #1. Colton Watkins' W-2 for the years 2022 to

*2024 is located in Appendix #2. A complete copy of Colton Watkins'
employee file is found in Appendix #3. Copies of bank statements
from Colton Watkins' accounts at Cayman Ward Bank are included in Appendix #4.*

An embezzlement case? Was this what they were working on?
Was this what Lucio was trying so hard to hide from her? What
the hell was so dangerous about embezzlement? Why was Lucio
acting like it was the complete end of the—

"What the hell do you think you're doing?" Lucio's voice cut
through the silence.

Helena's heart leapt into her throat as her eyes met his. He stood
in the doorway, blocking her exit.

She looked down at the laptop, her fingers curling away from it
like they were atrophied. "I was just cleaning up your table."

"Bullshit." Lucio slammed the door behind him, crossing the
room in two seconds flat. He snapped the laptop shut. "You were
snooping."

Helena flinched back into the corner, trying to hide her trembling. She hated this. Years of therapy, yet she still cowered like a
terrified child every time someone moved too quick in her vicinity.
It made parties almost impossible, the train a hell-scape. But it
was worse when it was Lucio. She could count on one hand the
number of times he had ever raised his voice, ever moved in a way
that made her cower. And she still didn't need a second hand, even
now.

She took a breath in through her nose, out through her mouth,
closing her eyes as she tried to ground herself.

In through her nose, out through her mouth, again and again,
until she began to calm.

"Helena." Lucio's voice was quiet, but still held the same edge
of anger. "Are you okay?"

She kept her eyes squeezed shut as she nodded, not fully trusting
herself to speak.

"I'm sorry for scaring you. I know better than to do that." He paused, and Helena continued to count her breaths. After ten of them, he added, "Can you please look at me?"

She did. He still looked mad, but she had expected that. He remained where he was at his table, his hand pinning the laptop closed.

"Would you like to sit?"

Helena nodded.

"Can I get you a water?"

"No, I'll be okay."

"Alright." Lucio motioned towards the table. Helena took a seat across from him. "Is it okay if I talk to you?"

"Yeah." She looked down at her hands, knowing already what she was in for. They had done this dance before.

Lucio spoke first. "Why were you looking at my laptop?"

Helena counted another breath. "Because I want to know what's going on."

"And why do you want to know?"

"Because..." Another breath. "Because you've always let me in on all the other cases. What makes this one different?"

Lucio pressed his lips together as he ran his hand through his hair. "A lot."

"Like what?"

He shook his head. "You're not getting in on this case."

"Why? Is it because I don't have enough experience?" Helena hated the way her voice became whiny, desperate. "Dylan's got the same amount that I do."

"It's not about experience, Hel," Lucio said, maintaining his same level of calm.

Helena's skin flushed as heat ripped its way over her. "Then tell me what it is about! It's embezzlement, not a murder trial."

Something shifted behind Lucio's gaze, but she couldn't quite read it before it disappeared completely. "It's not."

"So?"

Lucio scrubbed at his face. "This case is complicated. I don't want you getting involved with it."

"But why?"

"Because I said so."

Helena's blood boiled. Always with the "Because I said so." A command given to a child, not to a grown adult.

"No." She pushed herself up. "You don't get to say that anymore! I'm almost nineteen, and your employee. I'm sick of you picking and choosing when I get to know things and when I don't. You didn't even tell me about Michael—"

Lucio's eyes pinned her where she stood. "What?"

Helena couldn't speak; she thought she might vomit if she opened her mouth.

"What about Michael, Helena?" Lucio stood, not menacing, but something else. His body coiled as if he might pounce on her if she said the wrong thing.

"I—" she swallowed "—he's trying to—"

"If you want to make it as a lawyer, you're going to have to do a lot better than that." His fist pressed into the table. "What is Michael trying to do?"

Helena's mind raced. Come on, Hel, think on your feet here!

"He's trying to catch this employee." She gestured at Lucio's computer. "And you're helping him, right? You guys are finally speaking again?"

Lucio's lip twitched, his teeth baring for half a second. "What led you to that conclusion?"

Shit. "I mean, this is his company, isn't it? I saw his name on the file."

"That file doesn't say anything about Michael." Lucio's voice was so low that Helena thought it might bottom out. "How do you know about him?"

The air around her suddenly became thick, and she struggled to breathe again. "Because you've told me about him, remember?"

"I have never spoken to you about Michael. Did Dylan say something to you?"

Helena's mouth went dry. "What? No, Dylan hasn't said anything about it. I swear."

"Swear all you want. It doesn't mean shit to me right now."

She winced.

"The next words out of your mouth better be the truth," he said, his eyes darkening. "Otherwise, you can kiss this job of yours goodbye."

She snorted. "I'd hardly call this a job."

"Helena."

"What? That's the truth."

Lucio stepped around the table, and she put up her hands.

"Okay! Look, I—" Deep breath in. "I saw that Michael texted you."

Lucio glared at her. "How?"

"You were in your office, asleep." She looked down at her feet, shuffling her weight from one foot to the other. "Your phone was on."

"Did you read it?"

"No! I mean, I tried, but it was in Portuguese, so I didn't understand it."

He breathed in deeply, working his hand over his jaw. "You're banned from my office from here on out."

Her cheeks burned. "Okay."

"And I don't want to hear another word about Michael from you."

Helena scowled. "Why? He's your brother, you're lucky enough to still have—"

"Don't."

Her hands balled into fists at her sides, her temper flaring. "I deserve to know about my uncle!"

"He is not your uncle."

The back of Helena's knees hit her chair.

Lucio wasn't a man of many emotions, but this one, this one she had never seen before. His skin looked flushed, his eyes wide enough to show the whites.

"He is not your uncle," Lucio repeated, baring his teeth at her. "I am your father, but that—" his shoulders shook as he took a ragged breath. "That man is not your uncle. Am I understood?"

Helena moved her eyes back to his hands. His knuckles were pale with how tight his fist was. She nodded.

"Look at me."

She did.

He hadn't lost that look, not yet. "This case, and anyone involved with it, doesn't concern you. I don't want you talking about it with anyone. Dylan included."

She pressed her lips into a line. "But Lu—"

Lucio gave her a stern look. "I mean it. If I catch wind that you're trying to involve yourself in any part of this case, or anyone who has anything to do with it, I'll fire you so quick you'll forget you ever worked here. Am I understood?"

Her nails dug into her palm. "Yes."

"Good. Now go home. Dylan and I will be working late." He straightened, unbuttoning his suit jacket and pulling it off. She watched him as he walked over to his desk, the conversation over and done with, according to him. Because Lucio always got the final say.

Helena turned on her heel and stormed out the door, taking Lucio's coffee order with her.

She nearly ran into Dylan on the way out. He was just outside the door, giving her a look. Not of pity, but of understanding.

Her cheeks burned; from embarrassment or anger, she wasn't totally sure. They would talk about it later. They always did.

5

"**H**ey, Helena!"

Helena turned to spot Brandi, one of Quinn's best bartenders, waving her over. Brandi was an easy person to find in a crowd, but Quinn's restaurant clientele made her blonde pixie cut with purple tips look like the most basic hair style. Even still, Brandi's build was enough for her to stand out in a crowd. She was all muscle—not the lean type that Helena tried to lie and say she was, but the kind that showed off long days at the gym.

"Hey!" Helena grinned as she walked over, giving a polite wave to a person dancing in a cage at the end of the bar.

"What're you doing here?" Brandi asked as she slapped a glass into a tumbler and shook it.

"Got off work early," Helena shouted back. "Quinn here?"

"Where they always are," Brandi said, nodding at the kitchen doors on the other side of the room where waitstaff dressed in bright white uniforms passed in and out. It helped them stand out in the darker restaurant, and gave them a slight glow in the colorful lighting above and around them.

Helena gave Brandi a wave of thanks as walked to the back. She weaved her way through the multitude of tables, filled with people of all gender expressions. People laughed and drank, enjoying dishes that looked more suited for a Midtown restaurant rather than the clublike atmosphere of Quinn's lower Eastside spot. But it worked, somehow. They rarely had a slow day.

She reached the kitchen, narrowly avoiding one of the waitstaff as she entered. Heat smacked Helena in the face, along with the delicious smell of chocolate, chili, and saffron. The kitchen was full of the usual sounds: plates clattering, food sizzling, washing, chopping, and, of course, the complaints of the head chef as they screamed at the exhausted wait staff.

"Where the fuck are my runners? I got plates dying up here!" Quinn threw another plate on the passthrough. Their usually unruly curls were tamed by a paisley bandana, that was a shade darker from sweat. Their chef's coat was covered with stains, as was typical during one of the restaurant's busier nights. That, or one too many arguments between the line cooks that had resulted in food fights. But they always came crawling back because no other chefs could compare to Quinn.

"We're coming! If your dishie would move faster, maybe we won't be so backed up," the head server shouted as she took a couple of plates decorated beautifully with food and garnish. Helena could see one was a plate of oysters, while another held scallops seasoned with chili.

"If your host stopped overseating we won't have this problem at all!" the dishie in question joined in, adding another plate to the dish sanitizer.

"Will you all shut the fuck up and get out of my kitchen?" Quinn yelled as they pulled another ticket.

"Wow, and you yell at me for my language?" Helena said, careful to dodge the incoming waitstaff as they gathered plates.

"Hey, Hel!" Quinn grinned. "What're you doing here? It's only," they looked at the watch tattooed on their wrist. "Six twenty-six!"

Helena scowled at them as she checked her phone. "You know that only works like, once every ten years."

"Yeah, but it's hilarious when it does." Quinn shoved another plate onto the already packed passthrough. "So why are you here?"

"Lucio sent me home," she said, dodging a server coming one way and a busboy coming another. "Mind if I crash at your place?"

They gave her a stern look over their shoulder as they began to sear a steak. "Did you tell him you were going to?"

"He's not home, so he won't care."

"Hel, you know he doesn't like it when you don't communicate with him. Runners!"

"He'll be fine. I'll help run if you let me stay."

"You touch a single Goddamn plate and I'll be calling Dad myself."

Helena rolled her eyes, her gaze drifting to the sink, plates piled high despite the dishwasher's best efforts. "What if I help clean?"

"Please!" a chorus of voices shouted.

"For fuck's sake." Quinn rubbed their forehead with their arm, wiping the sweat away from their dark brow. "Whatever, at least go put on a shirt. And some sneakers, at least. I don't need OSHA getting on my ass."

Helena grinned as one of the waitstaff handed her a spare gray shirt that the busboys wore. She went into the bathroom to change, tossing her shirt and workbag into Quinn's locker and switching out her flats for her sneakers, before going back into the kitchen.

The restaurant had been a gift from Lucio when Quinn graduated culinary school two years ago. Helena had thought the entire thing was ridiculous, since her sibling had very little training working in an actual restaurant, and Quinn was only twenty-one when they started, but Lucio had called in a favor to a friend to come help get them started. Quinn got to work with one of the best chefs in NYC, and it showed. One Michelin star later and Quinn's place became an overnight sensation.

Before the three of them had come to live with Lucio, Quinn had only ever tolerated cooking, despite their exceptional talent for it. They did it out of necessity, learning to make her and Gideon's favorites with what little they all could afford. Quinn worked like crazy, often having to miss school to pick up odd jobs, since their parents' money went to gambling and other unsavory activities. Many nights it was ramen noodles or pb&js, but on those special nights where Quinn could afford it, they would make Helena and Gideon's favorites: chicken and waffles, turkey chili, enchiladas, and on her and Gideon's birthday, pancakes with sprinkles.

Quinn always put them first, always made sure they had full stomachs. And all of them were happy. Yes, things were rough, but they had each other.

And then Lucio came along and messed all of that up.

After a few hours, service began to wind down, the pile of plates slowly lessening. Luckily, it was a Wednesday, which meant Quinn would be closing up at nine, and they both would be able to get home before the summer sun set. Maybe they'd even catch a glimpse of Manhattanhenge as they walked to Quinn's.

Quinn had an apartment only a few blocks away from the restaurant. They still spent most nights at Lucio's—"home," as they still lovingly called it—and used the apartment as a place to crash or hookup.

Helena let her hair down from her ponytail as she walked in from the back room, redressed in her work attire. "All set."

Quinn threw their dishrag over their shoulder. "Cool, now figure out how the hell you're getting home."

Her jaw dropped. "What? You said I could stay with you if I helped."

"The words 'you can stay with me' never once came out of my mouth." They dumped a load of pans into the sink, much to the dismay of the dishie. "You're just doing that annoying thing you always do where you hear what you want to hear."

She glared at them. "You're an asshole! I'm telling Brandi."

"Tell her I want her here tomorrow morning for inventory!" Quinn called as Helena pushed her way out into the dining area.

"Stop riling the boss up, they take it out on us," Brandi laughed, finishing counting her tips.

"If they do, just tell me. I'll destroy one of their eye shadow palettes for you." Helena sat at the bar and rested her chin in her hands. "Not that it'll matter much. They have a million and a half, I think."

Brandi smiled and rolled her eyes. "This is why you're such a gem."

"I do try." Helena smirked.

Brandi shook her head and closed up her register. Helena watched her as she moved behind the bar, her shorts barely falling below her ass, her top so tight, Helena thought she might have trouble breathing, all while wearing sensible black shoes. It was the standard uniform for bar staff. Quinn said it helped get more customers in the door.

If Helena worked here, Quinn wouldn't let her wear something like that. She looked down at her white button down and gray slacks, which had miraculously escaped unmarred from the evening. Quinn would stick her in a potato sack and tell her she couldn't talk to any of the customers.

Brandi finished her cleanup and came to lean on the bar in front of Helena, looking around the mostly empty restaurant. "Where's Dylan? I feel like I never see the two of you apart."

"He had to work late," Helena said.

"Damn, that's sad." Brandi winked. "I know how much you two like to spend time together."

"Well, yeah," Helena said. "He's my best friend, why wouldn't I like spending time with him?"

Brandi's head tilted as a mischievous smile crawled over her lips. "So you wouldn't be upset if I asked him out?"

Helena clenched her hands. "Aren't you like, twice his age?"

"Careful, young lady. I'm one of the only allies you got," Brandi said.

Helena glared down at the counter, ignoring the way her body grew hot. She would be lying if she told herself she hadn't caught Dylan looking at least a few times at Brandi and the other female-presenting bartenders. He was a man, after all—men were inclined to look. She tugged at the hem of her shirt, her mood souring.

"I was joking, Hel." Brandi booped Helena's nose, drawing her attention back. "I'm not gonna poach your little boyfriend."

Helena traced the reflection of light on the bar, mumbling, "He's not my boyfriend."

An arm looped around her, twisting her into a headlock. "He'd better not be. You're too young to date. You gotta wait until I'm good and dead."

"God, Lucio is bad enough, I don't need to be dealing with you, too," she said, trying to worm her way out of Quinn's grip. But it was near impossible—Helena thought there was supposed to be some rule about the first sibling being the smallest, but Quinn ignored that rule like all the other ones. Helena barely touched five three, while Quinn was pushing six feet. And they had a build that rivaled Brandi's, because what else did they have to do besides go to the gym and flirt with every person in it?

"Too bad. Dad's not here to protect you, so it becomes my responsibility." They kissed the top of her head, finally letting her go. "You ready?"

"I've been ready, jackass," she mumbled, rolling her shoulders.

She waved goodbye to Brandi and followed her sibling out, up the stairs, and onto the quiet streets of New York.

"So," Quinn began, stuffing their hands into their pockets. "Why'd Dad send you home?"

Helena huffed and picked up her pace to walk in front. "He can't just send me home?"

"He's always looking for an excuse to keep you late. So what did you do?"

"Why are you blaming me? What if he did something?"

Quinn tugged at the collar of Helena's shirt, pulling her back. "You're deflecting. That means you got in trouble, and you're trying not to talk about it."

She scowled at them. "Nuh-uh."

They rolled their eyes. "Come on, Hel, you're not a child. This whole 'teen rebellion' thing isn't cute anymore."

"It's not that." She began to walk again, this time beside Quinn. "He won't let me in on a case. And he won't tell me why."

Quinn squinted into the setting sun as they walked, their green eyes catching the light. "So?"

"So?" She raised her brows. "He always gives me shit about not caring enough about the cases, then the one that I actually want to be involved in, he shuts me out. It's bullshit."

Quinn shrugged. "Maybe he's got something better for you that he's saving up. You never know."

Helena glared at them. "What would you know? You went to culinary school, not law school. Stop acting like you know everything."

"I know that you need to stop stressing Dad out so much." They both stopped at a crosswalk, waiting with other people who were getting off late shifts or just heading in. "He's already got enough on his plate without you giving him more shit to worry about."

Many of the storefronts on the other side of the street were starting to shutter. Helena glanced through the glass of a dress shop, where a father and daughter were looking at dresses for some kind of fancy event. The girl lit up, spinning in a huge ball gown as her father beamed at her.

Follow my steps, fihla, I've got you.

This damn dress is huge, I shouldn't have let you talk me into it.

You look beautiful.

Thanks, Dad.

Helena shook the memory from her mind as the light changed, and they resumed their walk. "If he can't handle it then he shouldn't have taken on three kids."

"Better him than me. I wasn't going to deal with you two." Quinn smirked. "Once I turned eighteen, you guys were on your own."

"Not. You know you wouldn't have left us alone."

"I got close." They wrapped their arm around her neck. "So you should be grateful for Dad giving us a place to stay, at least."

"Speaking of," she said, shoving away from them. "How come you won't let me come live with you?"

Quinn laughed a lot louder than they needed to. Luckily, people didn't seem to notice. "Are you nuts?"

"Come on! I'm sick of living with Lucio, why can't I move in with you?"

"I live in a studio that might as well be a closet. Please tell me where the hell I'm supposed to put you."

"I don't take up that much space."

"You take up enough," Quinn said, gesturing for Helena to lead the way into their apartment building. The entrance was inconspicuously between a bodega and a store that had shut down shortly after Quinn moved in, and sat empty because the rent was too expensive. Helena said it was because Quinn was too loud and no one wanted to rent a place below them.

The stairwell was cramped; if anyone had been coming down at the same time, they would have either had to go back up, or the two of them would have had to leave. Moving furniture was basically impossible. It had been a hellish experience trying to get Quinn into this place—she didn't want to think about how they were going to get out.

They climbed the concrete steps, the yellow lighting above them making the entire place look like some kind of horror film. Sounds from other tenants echoed in the hall: people talking, babies crying, music blasting. Helena couldn't stand how it almost felt like everyone could hear you, even if they were a few floors away.

Quinn's apartment was on the second floor, one of two, and they were right; it was tiny. The entrance led into the kitchen, which had too little counter space, no dishwasher, appliances that made the place look like a children's play kitchen. There was a small table on the opposite side, enough to seat two people. The tile floor gave way to wood as they entered the living room, where the last few rays of sunlight were dwindling in through the back windows. On the left, a bathroom, on the right, a closet. And in between, a futon.

Quinn didn't have any photos on their walls. It made the entire place feel empty, but Helena always figured it was because they didn't want the people they were hooking up with to get attached. The less someone knew about them, the better.

Helena kicked off her shoes on the mat by the door before crossing the small space to throw herself on the futon. She sighed happily as she stretched herself out. "God, you really are an amazing sibling you know? Letting me stay here and letting me sleep on the futon?"

"Flattery doesn't work on me, you know," Quinn said as they came over, picking her off of the futon. "You get the air mattress."

"Come on," she whined. "Why do I have to sleep on the floor?"

"My apartment, my rules." They set her down on the floor before they spread themself out over the couch. "Don't like it? Go home."

She groaned again and went to the fridge. It was pretty bare outside of a couple beers, some prepared meals, and a water filter. "You know, for a chef, you have shit to eat."

"Cause I cook all my shit at home." They folded their hands over their stomach. "Where you should be."

She sighed as she closed the fridge door. "Yeah, but I'm hungry now."

"So order something." They pulled out their phone and held it out for her. "I ate at work, so I'm all set. It's on me."

Helena took the phone and sat herself down on Quinn's legs, ignoring their exaggerated groan of pain. She scrolled through the restaurants, finally settling on some Thai. A text from "Dad" appeared on the screen, but she swiped it away so she could finish her order.

"Lucio's texting you."

"Probably wants to know where the hell you are," Quinn said, already half-asleep. "Just text him back for me."

She finished her order and threw the phone on their stomach. "You do it."

"Hel."

"Nope." She went to get the air mattress from the closet. Helena avoided looking at the gun safe that was nestled in the corner. Yet another gift from Lucio—he had bought it for them just after he became a DA.

"A precaution," Lucio had said. "For emergencies only."

Helena didn't ask when she would get one of her own. She hated guns; the thought of Quinn owning one made her sick to her stomach.

She grabbed the air mattress box, wedged in between mystery shit Quinn had never bothered to unpack. "I'm not talking to him."

Quinn sighed loudly. "God, Hel, I'm not playing this game with you again."

"I'm not playing a game," Helena snarled as she continued to tug at the box. "Lucio's being a dick, and I'm done putting up with it."

"He's not being a dick. You're just a brat."

Oh, screw that. "I'm not a brat!"

"No? So all grown adults throw a temper tantrum on the daily?"

She whirled around, her anger rising at the way Quinn was still so casually sprawled out on the couch. "This is not a temper tantrum. He's always dragging me into shit I couldn't care less about, now all of a sudden I'm supposed to sit here and let him pull me off something that's actually interesting?"

"Ever think maybe it's reverse psychology?"

"It's not," Helena mumbled, going back to her previous task of trying to pull the air mattress out. "Because if it was, then he wouldn't have cared so much when I found out."

"And how did you find out?"

Helena tugged again at the box. It refused to budge. She had literally just used it last month, how the hell did it keep getting pinned in here?

"Helena."

"What?"

"Please tell me you weren't snooping."

"Fine. I wasn't snooping."

Quinn groaned from behind her. "For God's sake, Hel!"

"Shut up. You know that he wouldn't tell me otherwise."

"I know that you need to grow up," Quinn said. "Because grown adults don't snoop through their dad's shit."

Helena stepped away, huffing. "Guess it's a good thing he's not my dad then."

The closet door slammed closed. Quinn glared down at her, seething. "Take it back."

Helena crossed her arms over her chest. "No."

"Take it back," Quinn repeated, enunciating each word through clenched teeth.

Helena stepped up to Quinn, matching their energy. "He can be your dad. He's just some guy I live with. You want to think because he adopted us that makes him a dad? Bullshit. That makes him a decent human. And he's not even that sometimes."

"Why? Because he doesn't give you every single little thing you want?" Quinn's voice maintained that aggravating level of calm. They never raised their voice at her. Even in their worst fights, Quinn always kept their cool. Sometimes it made Helena want to scream. "Boo-fucking-hoo, Hel. Guess what? Sometimes you have to put aside what you want because it's what's best for someone else."

Helena pushed past them, ripping the closet door back open. She tugged at the box again, ignoring the sound of cardboard tearing. "Just because you did it doesn't mean I have to."

"No, of course not! Because why should the baby do anything but think of someone else for two seconds?"

Helena turned her head, fire licking at her throat. "Eat shit!"

"You first!"

The box came loose, and Helena flew backwards. She prepared herself for the fall, trying to drop the box to protect the back of her head from hitting the floor.

But a strong pair of arms was there to catch her, just like they always were. She looked up, trying hard to be angry, but Quinn was already putting her back up on her feet.

"I need a shower," they said, storming off towards the bathroom.

"Quinn," Helena called.

They stopped just before the door.

"I'm sorry."

Quinn's back rose and fell, before they turned around, giving her the same look they always gave her when they were trying to be mad, but had already given up a few minutes ago. "Me too. Now get the air mattress ready."

Helena nodded and did as they asked.

Their fights were always the same—a small spark, a huge blow-out, an apology.

She and Gideon never fought like this. Sure, they had spats, but it was always small things that were resolved easily. Because they understood each other. Gideon was her person, her twin, the one that she did everything with, told everything to. They were going to go to college; Gideon becoming a successful lawyer and her becoming a social worker like she always wanted. And then, Gideon got sick.

And he never got better.

Helena finished with the air mattress, letting her limbs spread out to take up every inch of space. She would have to grab the linens from the closet, too, but she would wait until after she had eaten. She didn't want to get her sheets dirty with food.

Quinn came out, dressed in the usual thread-bare tee shirt and Batman pajama pants. They scrunched their curls as they came out, dripping water onto the floor without much care. "You know I'm right."

"About what?"

Quinn flopped onto the futon, flinging water Helena's way as they did. "About Dad."

Helena turned her back to them. "When he gets the stick out of his ass, I'll be nicer."

"You promise?" Quinn's tone was teasing, but she knew them well enough to recognize the mischief that laid beneath.

Helena looked over her shoulder at them. Quinn was still giving her a wry smile, something dancing in their eyes.

"Oh God, what're you thinking?"

"I'll tell you when you're older."

"You know, I'm getting really tired of hearing that."

6

The first thing Jay noticed about him was his eyes. He had only glanced her way as he tried to choke down some overpriced drink from the bar. But she had noticed. It was almost impossible not to.

They were that color of green that stood out across a room, made you look twice, gentle enough to be inviting, but intimidating enough to make you wonder if you were the one being invited.

Jay slid down the pole, trying to keep her focus on her routine. But each time she swung around, she couldn't help but look back at him, and each time, his eyes kept meeting hers.

A clear invitation.

He was sitting next to a gorgeous looking young man, the one Jay had *really* been trying to catch the attention of. Her eyes flitted between the two. They both had a strong jaw, with cheekbones to match. A head of jet black hair, those same green eyes, only the younger one—Mr. Casual, Jay had decided to call him—had lips that were more full, a hint of boyish charm to the smile he was giving someone else across the room. The older one, The Suit, was coyly pretending not to notice her, but he was clearly failing. Jay wrapped her legs around the pole and leaned back, dangling. If she caught either of them looking at her again, she'd go over there.

She spun, counting down the seconds. *Three, two, one, bingo.*

The Suit's eyes returned to her, or maybe they never left. Either way, he was hers.

Jay's song finished, but she took her sweet time, tousling her hair, collecting some lingering bills from the clients who still sat below her, making The Suit sweat. It was a signature move: let them see how many options you had, how many others wanted you. It made the payout all the sweeter when they thought they were special.

When enough time had passed, she sauntered over, swinging her hips to the rhythm of the music. The closer she got, the more she could see the small details: a tailored suit, nice shoes, clean shaven. His olive-toned skin looked even darker in the lights, but it only made his eyes stand out all the more. His buddy was dressed much more casually: a T-shirt and jeans, stylish but comfortable sneakers, Jordans. It was almost enough. The slight flash of "I may have enough money to give you a nice tip at the end of a lap dance" almost made her take the half-step to the left instead of the right.

Mr. Casual's eyes traced over her, his body shifting in a way that screamed *try it*, but The Suit was inescapable. Even when she was pretending not to look at him, she could feel herself being pulled toward him.

Christ, Jay had to wonder who was luring who.

"Hey," she took a seat next to The Suit, "care for a private dance?"

"Oh, no, I—" he began to say, but Mr. Casual interjected, a wad of cash in his outstretched hand.

"Take him and keep him. He's got a lot of built-up tension." Mr. Casual winked, earning him a glare from The Suit.

"Quinn, don't you—"

Jay already had the cash in one hand and The Suit's hand in the other. She tugged him up with little effort, and brought her body close to his, enjoying the way he tried to keep his focus on her face. "Come on, let's go somewhere more private." She looked over at Mr. Casual, who was watching the scene play out before him. "Unless..."

"No," The Suit said quickly, his previous demeanor having completely shifted from casual interest to obvious discomfort.

Jay laughed breathlessly. "Don't like to share?"

The Suit cast a glance over his shoulder, where Mr. Casual was taking a sip of his drink. He blew a kiss at her, and Jay thought about ignoring whatever came next and grabbing him anyways.

Two were always better than one, after all.

But The Suit's voice was firm. "Not with them."

Jay shrugged, tugging on the Suit's hand while she fanned out the bills in front of him. "Your call. Think you've got more than enough here to keep us both busy, anyways."

The Suit glared one last time at Mr. Casual, but Jay pulled The Suit towards the private rooms before he could protest further.

"Have fun, Dad!" Mr. Casual called.

She quirked a brow at the man she escorted. "You came here with your kid?"

"They dragged me here," The Suit said, looking everywhere but at her.

Christ, he was going to be *easy*. "A likely story."

The private room—which was a generous term for the quiet corner of the club with a sheer curtain separating the spaces—was small, intimate, with deep red walls, a stage in the center, and long black couches. Jay set The Suit down on one of them, her touch lingering a beat longer than necessary. Not that he seemed to complain.

Jay motioned toward the bar cart. "Can I offer you a drink?"

"No, thank you. Still working on my first one." He lifted his glass, the amber liquid it held slightly watered down from the ice cubes clinking against the sides.

"Then how about you hold onto this?" She placed the cash in his free hand. "I like it when men keep their hands busy." She winked. "But not too busy."

"You don't have to do this, you know. I'll pay you and you can go," The Suit said, his gaze darting around the room.

"Relax, I'm not going to hurt you." Jay leaned over him, bringing her chest close to his face. He shifted to keep looking at her face. "And if you want to, we can even talk through the entire thing."

"I don't know if I'll be able to say much." He set the wad of cash in his breast pocket, careful to not touch her.

"Well, then I can talk and you can listen." She lifted her leg next to him. He looked away, a blush creeping up his cheeks. She suppressed her laugh of surprise. The guy had to be at least thirty, and he was acting like this? "First time getting a lap dance?"

"No, but first time in a long time." The Suit cleared his throat.

"Cute." He glared and she giggled. "Want me to walk you through what to do?"

"No, thanks."

"Okay." She removed her leg, and turned around to ghost her hips against his lap. "Why are you so stressed out?"

His voice was low, although she caught the usual lilt that men who weren't used to strangers grinding on them had. "I'm not interested in a therapy session."

Jay looked over her shoulder, a coy smile on her lips as her hair fell over her shoulder. "You can tell me things you can't tell your therapist."

The Suit's eyes rolled to the ceiling. "I have a very stressful job, is that enough for you?"

Jay's mood immediately soured, but she tried to hide it with a playful pout. "No need to be so rude."

He fell silent, choosing to take a sip of his drink rather than apologize. Typical. It was fine, actually. She got paid either way, and he hadn't even bothered to ask how much this was going to run him. She'd add a "being a dick for no clear reason" charge. And if he wanted to complain, he could take it up with Phil. But more than likely, he'd just go back out and find some other woman to be an asshole to; Jay could grab Mr. Casual and enjoy herself for the rest of her night.

"I'm sorry."

The fuck? Jay glanced back at him, trying to hide her surprise.

The Suit swallowed, his one hand gripping the glass and the other digging into the fabric of the couch. "Ask me another question. I'll answer nicely, this time."

Her lips twitched at a smile. Maybe she could turn this around, still. The corner of a bill peeked from his pocket, promising. "Okay, what do you do for work?"

He started to answer, but stopped. He relaxed into the couch. "What do you think I do?"

"Ooh, a guessing game?" Jay turned around.

She watched his eyes struggle to stay focused on hers and not dip below her collarbone to where her breasts were barely contained by her top. She had chosen this one special for the evening, a black bikini with studs along the cups. It helped to discourage the men from touching, even though she sometimes wished they would. At least, when they looked this good.

"I like guessing games."

Jay moved away from The Suit enough to get a better look, keeping up with her routine the entire time. He had on a gorgeous slate gray suit, obviously expensive. His black hair was well kept, if a little long; his face and neck were free of piercings, tattoos, and facial hair. She hummed, looking back to his face. He had dark circles, obvious signs of late nights with little sleep; wrinkles were just beginning to form, faint smile lines that she guessed were from a long time ago.

"Something corporate."

He finally surrendered to watching her body move. "You're not too far off."

"Not an accountant. You're too cool for that."

The Suit mumbled something she couldn't hear, then took a sip of his drink. His tongue touched his lips, dragging over the top one to catch every drop. Jay nearly bit her lip on instinct, but focused on bringing her body close to his again.

"Let's see…" She inhaled a faint smell of cologne. "Not a doctor. You wouldn't wear cologne if you were a doctor."

"Astute observation."

"And," she grabbed his glass, lifting it to her nose, "you like bourbon." She passed it back to him. "Lawyer, then?"

His eyebrows flicked up. "Bonus points if you can tell which type."

Jay huffed. "Prosecutor, obviously."

"You're good."

"When you spend all of your time dancing for men, you get to learn the signs."

"Even still, your ability to figure that much out is impressive, miss?"

Jay smiled. "Angel."

"Angel?" The Suit observed her. There was something about the way he looked at her, not like she was a piece of meat dangling in a butcher shop window, but like he was looking *through* her. Jay had to stop herself from crossing her arms over her body.

"That's what they call me." She straddled his hips, ghosting against him as her hands traveled up the front of his suit. It was soft, obviously wool. A nice change up from the usual cheap polyester that most men wore. "And what you're going to call me, too."

"But you're not."

She pulled away, furrowing her brows. "What?"

"Angels are intangible beings." The Suit's fingers twitched on the back of the couch. "You're right here. I could touch you if I wanted to."

She had to laugh at that one. "If you *wanted* to? Try it and see how quick you get your ass thrown out of here, buddy."

"You're a smart woman," he said, and Jay's breath caught in her throat. "You know what I meant."

She couldn't quite tell if he had meant it as an insult, or the compliment she was all too ready to take it as.

"Boneca."

She blinked. "What?"

"You're more of a boneca," The Suit said, his lips twitching.

"Boneca, like muñeca?" she asked. *Doll.* He wanted to call her *doll?* Now she really wasn't sure if he was insulting her or not. But there was something about the way he said it, a slight accent that she didn't fully recognize, but sounded just *so* familiar. Her eyes traced his face again, something nagging at the back of her mind. "Why?"

"Just fits." He shrugged.

Jay snorted. "That's a great reason."

"Would you rather I keep calling you *Angel?*"

There it was again. That accent, the way he said Angel, but almost like he was slurring the end of it. More like "anjo." It was the alcohol, she had to guess. Better make this quick, then. Before he decided that he got to start touching her, rather than just changing her name.

Before she decided she didn't really mind.

"I'd rather you pay me," Jay said, dragging her finger against the opening of his breast pocket.

The Suit pulled a bill without looking at it. "Do I just..."

"Okay, you cannot tell me that you've gotten a lap dance and then not know how to tip me," she laughed, too easily.

No, this was fine.

The Suit had money, he wasn't touching her.

Yet.

"I just don't want to be disrespectful," The Suit said, his eyes flickering to the twenty dollar bill in his hand. Smaller than she hoped, but more than she had expected. He looked at the bill as if it had personally offended him. "I'm going to kill them."

"You can be a gentleman and still have fun," Jay teased, taking his hand in hers and guiding it towards her lower half.

He slipped the cash into her g-string, hesitating for only a moment before pulling back.

"There you go. Need my help again?"

"No, I think I have the idea." The corners of his eyes crinkled. "You can continue."

She did, dragging off his lap painfully slow. "Okay. You like your job?"

"What happened to you doing all the talking?" The Suit relaxed further into the couch. He smiled without his teeth, but she knew one more drink would change that.

"Alright. Ask me if I like my job."

The Suit pulled another bill. "Do you like your job?"

Jay plucked it between two fingers, her iridescent nails catching the light and his attention. She watched him try not to follow their path as she placed it in between her breasts. "Of course I do."

"Liar."

"Hey, this is your therapy session, not mine."

He wagged his finger at her. "You said I could tell you things that I couldn't tell my therapist. I feel like that includes me being able to call you out on things I can't call my therapist out on."

"Fine. You want to know the truth?"

The Suit spread his legs wider. "Of course."

Jay placed herself between his thighs, her face close to his. His breathing stopped, his gaze flickering between her eyes and her lips, waiting. She half-closed her eyes, her lips slightly parted, her face drifting to his ear. "I hate it."

"Then why do you stay?" The Suit whispered back.

"Because I get to meet such interesting people all the time," Jay said as she pushed herself back up.

He gave her a wry smile. "Aw, you think I'm interesting?"

"You're definitely one of the more," she paused, looking him up and down, "fascinating clients I've had."

"I don't know if I should take that as a compliment or not."

"Are you still paying me?"

He slipped another bill into her G-string.

"Compliment."

"Then thank you."

"You're welcome," Jay laughed.

The Suit fell silent, just letting the music play and watching her move. She grazed him again, and she held back a giggle at his slight hiss. It was cute when they got into it, gave themselves over to her. Especially when they were clearly as uptight as he was.

He spoke up a moment later. "Why do you actually stay?"

"The money." She settled into the couch next to him as the song ended. He seemed to take the hint and passed her another few bills. "I'm sure you get it."

The Suit raised an eyebrow. "Do I?"

"You're wearing an expensive *and* tailored suit. And based on how much your kid pulled out of the bank," Jay held up one of the bills to the light, "you've clearly got money to blow."

"That's certainly presumptuous of you."

She propped her head up on her arm. "Am I wrong?"

"Well, no, but still presumptuous." He downed the rest of his drink. "Are you thirsty?"

"I'll grab it." Jay took his glass from him. "I don't allow men to make my drinks."

"Very smart. We can't be trusted."

"Nope." She walked over to the drink cart to pour him a second glass of bourbon and make herself a martini. She blocked the shaker with her body, pouring mostly water into it and just a touch of vodka. Enough that it would carry the smell, even a little of the taste, but not enough that she'd get stupid if he decided to stick around. She gave him a heavy pour, deciding to skip the ice.

"Then again, I don't know if you can be either. I've heard some horror stories about men getting drugged by dancers. How do I know you're not going to drug me and steal my wallet?"

"You're willingly passing me a bunch of twenties. I have no reason to drug you." Jay brought the drinks back over, holding his out and then pulling it back. "Unless you want me to?"

"No, thank you." He took the drink, touching it up to hers. "Cheers."

"To what?"

"To new beginnings."

Jay smirked as she took a sip. "New beginnings, huh? Does that mean I'm going to be seeing more of you?"

The Suit tapped his glass, looking up at her through his lashes. "If you'd like to."

Jay hummed, keeping her glass steady as she settled onto his lap. His breath caught, his grip on his glass tight as he moved to let her access him better.

"If you keep bringing along cash like this," she pulled another bill from his pocket, her lips ghosting his cheek, "I'd love to."

7

"Anjo!"

Jay knew that voice better than anything. She put on a smile as she turned around to see her boyfriend, Michael, sauntering through the club, his deep blue eyes tracing the curves of her body. He motioned for her to continue, slowing his pace so he could drink her in.

She amused him, dropping it low and spreading her legs for him, ignoring the men who begged for the attention below her.

None of them could come close to Michael. When he stepped into a room, it was impossible to not notice him—jet black hair and stormy blue eyes, a gorgeous smile that could light up a room if he wanted it to.

The knot in his tie was loosened just enough to signal that this was a pleasure visit, not business.

Lucky her.

She stepped to the edge of the stage and into his open arms. "Hey, baby!"

Michael spun her as he placed her on the floor, tracing a finger along her hairline. "How's my girl doing?"

"Better now that you're here," she said, looping her arms around his neck. Her head lolled to the side, enough for her to peek at Michael's associate, Colt, who was looking everywhere but at her. "I wasn't expecting to see you tonight."

"Wanted it to be a surprise." Michael pulled her closer. "Some of the guys are coming by soon, figured I should grab you while I could."

"Baby, you know you can have me whenever you want." Which was true; Michael was co-owner of Vision. If he wanted her in the middle of someone else's lap dance, she would go. And the client who she had left behind would usually be smart enough not to argue against it.

"Good girl." Michael tugged at one of her braids. "Come on, I want to get the place set up before everyone gets here."

Jay cast one last glance over her shoulder at Colt, who continued to avoid her eyes. The three of them headed into one of several larger private rooms that interspersed the alcoves. None of the gaudy print or neon was reflected in these rooms, especially this one. Michael had designed this one special for his meetings: burgundy walls, dark marble flooring, velvet couches that still looked spotless from the day that he bought them. The lighting was warm, mysterious, and most of all, flattering. The stage in the middle of the room was also kept in excellent condition, a bar cart sat on the far end, away from the couches that surrounded the main stage.

Jay and Colt took seats on opposite couches while Michael grabbed a bottle of champagne from the bar cart in the corner. It was funny how much the two men looked alike. If she hadn't known better, she would have thought they were brothers. Both had similar features: soft in the right places, hard in others. But Colt had gorgeous blond hair while Michael's was pitch black. Colt had soft, hazel eyes that felt like home, where Michael's deep blue felt like a storm at sea—exciting and terrifying at the same time. They stood out even more in the summer or when Michael went on vacation, his skin proudly displaying his Brazilian heritage, as much as he tried to deny it. He even kept Jay from going out in the sun too much. He blamed it on wanting to keep her skin from getting damaged, but she knew the real reason.

Though he'd been in this room more times than Jay could count, Colt looked determinately around, as if searching for a reason to avoid meeting Jay's eyes.

When there was nowhere else to look, Colt jutted his chin her way. "You look nice."

Jay pressed her lips together to hide her smile, instead looking down at her outfit: a gold bikini top and g string, with just enough fabric to be more on the modest side. An outfit he had seen a million times, because it was Michael's favorite. It was a safe, genuine compliment, one that Jay could accept with a simple, "Thanks."

Michael brought over two glasses, glancing between them, but Colt had gone back to averting his eyes and pretending like he was somewhere else. It was typical behavior of him. Colt knew better than to let his eyes linger too long, especially in front of Michael.

"Are we celebrating something?" Jay asked as she took the glass.

"We are." Michael handed a glass to Colt. "Colt here got promoted to director."

Jay gasped and grinned at him. "That's amazing! Congratulations. I know you've been dying to get it."

Colt mumbled a thank-you and sipped at his champagne.

"Colt." Michael spoke the same way a person might correct their dog who was misbehaving. "Jay said congratulations. You should thank her properly."

Colt forced a smile. "Thank you, Jay."

Jay tapped at her glass, the bubbles rising to the surface. "Of course. You deserve it. I know how hard you work for the company."

"As he should!" Michael pulled her onto his lap. "Isn't that right, Colt?"

"Yessir." He downed more of his drink, then got up to get himself a second glass.

Michael let his hand trail up Jay's thigh. "Everything been going okay at work, anjo?"

"Fine. Had a bit of an issue with a customer the other day, but we handled it." Jay sighed as her fingers grazed his scalp, his sides and back freshly shaved. He closed his eyes, her fingernails trailing through his dark hair.

"What kind of issue?" Colt asked as he returned.

Michael's fingers pressed harder into Jay's thigh.

"Oh, just some asshole trying to drug one of the girls." Jay waved her hand dismissively, reaching over the best she could to grab her drink. "Phil handled him."

Michael made a non-committal grunt. "As long as he's not fucking with you."

"No, one of the newbies. They just need to learn to be more careful." She took another sip of her drink, before tapping Michael's shoulder. "Listen, let me go grab some of the other girls. Your friends should be here soon, right?"

Michael nodded. "Grab a second bottle of champagne while you're out there. I have a feeling we'll need it."

He gave her a chaste kiss before sending her out. The other dancers must have seen the pair walk in, because they flocked to Jay as soon as she emerged. She had always worried that her being Michael's favorite would spell certain disaster for her time here; the other girls had been so catty when she first started here, but as soon as she and Michael became openly official, it was like a switch flipped. Every woman wanted to be Jay's best friend. She learned quick what other benefits came with dating Michael—including the lavish tips that he and his associates brought.

Soon enough, the back room was filled with dancers and businessmen alike. The girls took turns on stage, collecting tips from the men around them, who were already a few drinks deep by the time they had arrived.

"In honor of our newest director, drinks are on me tonight!" Michael shouted over the din of people speaking.

The men in the room cheered, raising already half-empty glasses that were readily refilled by the dancers next to them.

"Let Colt get 'em," someone shouted back. "He's got the fat new paycheck!"

Everyone laughed, including Jay, as she settled herself further into Michael's lap.

He wrapped his arm tight around her waist, slipping his hand under her top and teasing her nipple.

"Baby, knock it off, you're going to make your coworkers jealous," Jay whispered into his ear.

"Good, let them know what they're missing out on," Michael mumbled, slipping his hand out and moving it to her hair instead. Jay let him pull her head back to give him better access to her neck, allowing him to suck and bite at her skin, but never enough to leave a mark. She had to still look available, of course.

"When are you getting these braids out? I like it when I can run my hand through your hair," he said, looping a braid around his finger.

Jay's eyes rolled back into her head. "I have an appointment this week."

"Make sure you get it blown out or whatever. I like it when you wear it straight."

"I'd rather blow something else out," she muttered, rolling her hips into him again.

He growled against her skin, biting harder than he probably meant to. Jay let him, her gaze falling away from him and onto Colt. He sat with his shoulders slouched, elbows resting on his knees, glass gripped so tight his knuckles were pale. And still, he wouldn't look at her.

"Come on, Watkins, loosen up. You're acting like you're being tortured," a man said, elbowing Colt in the ribs.

Colt cast a glance towards Jay, ignoring the woman next to him who was whispering in his ear, her hand trailing up and down his thigh, just close enough to make Jay have to swallow down the bubble of venom that burned her throat.

These bitches needed to learn to take a hint.

Colt mumbled something, before he headed out of the room.

Michael dragged his fingers along Jay's hip. "He's never gotten over you, has he?"

She sighed. "It's a silly crush. It's hard for him, you know, seeing me all the time."

Michael's fingers dug into her side, and Jay hid her wince. "Maybe I shouldn't bring him around as much then."

"No, baby, it's okay. Plus, the girls like him. He's not as grabby as some of the other guys you have on payroll."

Michael gripped her chin gently, forcing her eyes to his. "He doesn't touch you, does he?"

"Everybody knows that I'm all yours." Jay leaned forward to nip at Michael's earlobe, earning her a slight growl as his hand went to her navel. "Want to take a trip to my room to prove it?"

"Not right now. I need to have a quick conversation with one of the guys." He patted her ass, and she shifted herself off of him so he could go sit next to a man she didn't recognize.

Jay glanced at the empty bottles on the table, then to Michael. He was busy with his conversation, so she gathered the bottles herself and went into the main room. She would be back before he even knew she was gone.

She set the empties on the bar, catching the attention of Daniel, the bartender.

"Jesus, those men can drink, can't they?" he asked, already reaching for the refills.

"They're celebrating a promotion, so expect it to be a long one," Jay said, looking around the club. Colt was nowhere to be seen, meaning he was likely in the bathroom. Or one of the girls spotted him and dragged him off for a private dance. Yeah, right.

Daniel stood, blowing out a breath. "Fuck, I'm out of this one. I need to run to the basement, want to come take a quick break?"

Jay pushed herself off the bar. "Please."

She shouldn't be sneaking off while Michael was around, but sometimes it was necessary. Especially when he kept playing the game of grabbing and touching every inch of her until she might scream. He treated her like a fucking animal at a petting zoo.

Jay followed Daniel through the outer doors, only to immediately regret her decision. The humid air stuck to her already sweaty skin. "Christ, never mind, I'm going back in."

"Suit yourself!" Daniel called as he headed down the stairs to the basement.

"Yo, Angel!"

The hairs on the back of Jay's neck stood up on instinct.

Pitt.

That scumbag. Of course he had come back, he was always trying to come back in. Multiple girls had complained about him trying to touch them, but he hadn't ever done anything enough to warrant barring him completely. Just a closer watch, waiting for him to slip up. But the other night had been far enough. Jay hadn't missed him being in the club; the fact that he was here now made the headache that had been settling behind her eyes all the worse.

She crossed her arms over her chest. "What the hell are you doing here?"

He came in too close too quick, pinning her against the brick wall of the club. The neon sign above them cast harsh shadows over his face, making him look all the more terrifying. "What's the big idea with you getting me kicked out? I didn't do anything."

"Back the fuck up," Jay spat.

He only stepped closer, nearly brushing her chest with his. "I don't appreciate getting accused of something I didn't do."

Jay nearly gagged on the stench of alcohol and cigarettes on his breath, intermingled with weed. "Christ, Pitt, did you fall into an ashtray?"

He glared at her. "Apologize."

"For what? You're out here drugging people. If anything, you should be apologizing." She tried to push him away, but Pitt's hand caught her wrist before she could. "Stop fucking touching me."

"I said, apologize." He pinned her hand near her head, his right leg holding her hips in place.

Jay's heart raced in her chest, but she adjusted her face to keep her stoic glare. "Or what?"

"Or I'll make you."

Something cold dug into her stomach. Jay looked down, the blade of a pocket knife catching the light above them. Her organs felt like they were trying to escape it through her mouth. She had this happen before, guys getting too grabby, a little confident, way too stupid. But she never had someone pull a fucking knife on her before.

"What the fuck are you doing?"

"Say it, Angel." He titled the blade so she could feel the edge of it.

"You're a fucking psycho."

"Not what I fucking meant."

Jay tried to scream, but he seemed to notice and pressed the knife into her even harder, enough to break skin. She hated the whimper that passed her lips. She wasn't a bitch, Pitt didn't get to do these kinds of things to her, he was just some dumb client. But the knife against her side said otherwise.

"I just want an apology. Say, 'I'm sorry, I promise I'll take it back'."

Jay knew better than to provoke him. But she wasn't going down without a fight. She locked her eyes to his, adrenaline coursing through her.

"Go fuck yourself," she hissed.

Pitt jerked the knife away, then dropped to the ground like a sack of hammers.

Jay finally registered someone else standing behind Pitt, twisting his arm up and back. He screamed in agony as he writhed on the ground, his face pressed on the concrete.

Colt grabbed Pitt's other wrist lifting him to his knees. "And just what the fuck to do you think you were going to do?"

"Fuck off, man! This doesn't concern you," Pitt spat, tears beginning to well up in his eyes.

Jay squeezed her own shut at the sound of Pitt's fingers breaking.

"You were going to hurt her," Colt said.

Jay glanced at him.

He was leaning down to speak right into Pitt's ear, his voice low. "That makes it my concern."

"Christ, I'm sorry, I'm sorry, I wasn't going to do anything!" Pitt whimpered, snot running down his face to mix with the tears.

Colt glanced up at Jay, his breathing almost as heavy as hers. "Are you okay?"

"Yeah." She touched her hand to her side, her knees buckling at the sight of blood. "Fuck."

"You son of a fucking bitch." Colt released one of Pitt's hands to grab his head instead. "I should fucking kill you—"

"Colt," Michael barked. He was flanked by two of the bouncers, but Jay knew he didn't need them. His presence was more than enough. There was no urgency in his pace as he observed the scene in front of him. "What's going on here?"

"He tried to fucking shank her," Colt said, not letting go of Pitt's hair.

Pitt tried to plead his innocence, but Colt corrected that with a crack of the man's wrist.

Jay looked away, bringing her non-bloody hand to her face. She couldn't get away from it all; Pitt and Colt were in front of her, the basement was to her left, Michael was to her right. She just wanted out.

Michael sighed, pulling out a cigarette and lighting up. "Let's get this over with. I've got shit to do."

Colt threw Pitt down to the ground in front of Michael, Pitt's face hitting the concrete with a loud smack.

Michael picked up the knife from where it had fallen on the ground and spun it in his hand before positioning it beneath Pitt's chin, lifting him back up to his knees with it.

Michael took a long drag, blowing the smoke directly into Pitt's face.

Pitt held back his cough, eyes watering as his Adam's apple grazed the blade.

"Now," Michael drawled, "Do you want to tell me what happened, or should I just run this sad excuse for a knife through you and call it a night?"

Pitt swallowed. "Look, man, I wasn't trying to—"

"Rhetorical question." Michael sliced the knife up Pitt's jaw, nearly nicking his eye.

Jay's blood pooled on her hip in sync with the blood spilling down Pitt's cheek. He started to scream and scramble away, but Colt shoved his foot into Pitt's back and pinned him back down to the ground.

"Please, please I'm sorry, I'm so sorry I'll never come back again if you just let me go, I promise—"

Colt's shoe connected with Pitt's teeth in a sick crack.

Michael watched on, blowing out another cloud of smoke. It curled around Jay, making her eyes burn and her lungs constrict.

"Colt please," Jay gasped, blood beginning to seep out of Pitt's mouth.

"Jay," Michael said. "Go back to your room."

Jay looked at Pitt, the acrid smell of piss drawing her eyes to the rapidly growing wet spot on his pants. "It's not that—"

Michael whistled sharply, and one of the bouncers stepped forward.

"Get her out of here," Michael said, not bothering to look Jay's way. "Colt, take him around back. We don't need the cops getting involved."

Colt said nothing as he dragged Pitt towards the side alley ignoring his begging and pleading.

Jay waved off the bouncer's attempt to physically escort her back in, heading that way on her own.

"Anjo," Michael called. She turned to see him rolling up his sleeves and slipping off his watch to expose the hammer tattoo that it hid. His gaze slid down her body, noticing the blood that had escaped her fingers.

"Stay there till I come get you." Michael dropped his cigarette, stomping it out beneath his heel, before he sauntered down the alleyway, whistling some song as he did. He wouldn't be long.

The bouncer cleared his throat, and she grit her teeth as she walked back into the club, keeping her arms crossed over her stomach as she was paraded through the crowded bar, full of patrons smart enough to keep their mouths shut and their eyes on the dancers in front of them.

8

Michael wasn't a man who liked to be interrupted, especially when he was enjoying a private dance from Jay. She had seen him lose his shit over simple phone calls, or another dancer who had just walked into the wrong room.

Which made it a surprise when Colt showed up, pale and skittish. Michael looked ready to throttle him, but Colt had spoken first: It's an emergency.

Michael scrutinized the tablet in his hand as he tightened his grip on Jay's knee. "You can't be serious."

"I am," Colt said, keeping his eyes on Michael. "If we don't do something soon, we're fucked."

With a sigh, Michael rubbed his eyes, head falling back on the velvet sofa. Jay looked at the tablet, scanning the numbers quickly. Discrepancies caught her eye at every turn, and she felt a lump rise in her throat.

Christ, emergency was an understatement.

Michael made it clear the details weren't for Jay's eyes when he clicked the lock screen button on the tablet. He threw it down on the table. "Are the executives aware?"

Colt shook his head. "Their heads are so far up their asses they only smell their own shit."

Michael let out a low growl. "Get Javier in here."

Colt nodded and stood, going to grab Vision's other owner, and Jay's technical boss.

Michael muttered something in Portuguese, rubbing at his temples. "You're not going to want to sit through this conversation, anjo."

Jay reached out to drag her fingers along the nape of his neck. It was covered in sweat, despite the air conditioning, but she resisted the urge to pull away. "You sure you don't want me to stick around?"

He hummed as he leaned into her touch, his eyes closing and a small smile tugging at his lips. "No. This isn't a talk that you need to be here for. Boring investors' speak, all that bullshit."

"I really don't mind. Especially if it'll help keep you calm."

Michael sighed, pulling her onto his lap. "And this is why you're my favorite. But really, I'd rather you save your energy for later. Go grab us a few drinks from the bar, then head back to your room. I'll get you after."

"Sounds good," Jay murmured. He gave her a quick peck as she moved off his lap to go to the door. "Your usual?"

Michael grunted the affirmative before picking the tablet back up and reviewing the numbers. Jay hesitated, curiosity nagging at her to go back in and ask about it. She could help—she had taken a couple classes at City College before she dropped out.

You're a smart woman.

Someone cleared their throat next to her, and Jay looked back over to see Colt and Javier standing in the doorway.

"Oh, shit, sorry," she mumbled, her hand brushing Colt's as she stepped out of the door. His fingers twitched against hers, until they passed one another completely, Jay heading back to the bar, Colt stepping into the back room to deal with whatever shit she couldn't and wouldn't ever know about.

It was fine, she just needed to get their drinks, and then she would—

A head of black hair and a set of green eyes caught her attention from across the room.

Jay felt her irritation spike dangerously high. "Son of a bitch."

She crossed the room, reaching the person in a few long strides and turning them around.

"Hey!" Helena shouted, immediately slapping away Jay's hands. "Oh, it's you."

Jay put her hands on her hips. "What the hell are you doing here?"

Helena crossed her arms over her chest, cheeks puffing out. "I wanted to talk with you some more. Is that so bad?"

"Kid, I'm working, I can't talk right now," Jay lied, her eyes darting towards the door to the back rooms. "So I need you to kindly get the hell out."

"Are you?" Helena tilted her head as she scanned Jay's outfit: a spaghetti strap mini dress with more cutouts than fabric. "I haven't seen you on a single stage since I got here."

"And when the hell did you get here?"

Helena shrugged. "If you had been out on the floor you would know."

"Kid." Jay scrubbed her face. "Get out."

"But I just got here." Helena took a step back. "And I wanted to talk to you."

"We're talking right now! Look how much fun we're having while we're talking. And guess what? We can also talk," Jay reached for Helena, "outside."

This time, Helena's backward step nearly had her toppling over the back of a couch. Jay grabbed for her, but Helena was quicker and ducked out of her reach, sending Jay head over heels. Two guys who were sitting on the couch quickly moved away, keeping their hands up to show their innocence.

"Okay, enough." Jay pushed herself up, fuming. She turned around, bristling at the way Helena was clearly finding the entire thing hilarious. "Time for you to go!"

"You're not my mother," Helena mocked.

"Thank God for that," Jay mumbled. She looked over Helena's head—not hard to do considering their height difference, and waved Phil over. "Now get out, I have clients waiting for me."

Helena looked back at the bouncer approaching. "Clients? Like Michael?"

Jay froze. "How the hell do you know Michael?"

"So I was right?"

"It doesn't matter if you were right or not," Jay scoffed. "I know that you're going to get the hell out of here whether you like it or not."

"No!" Helena grabbed Jay's hands. "Come on, I just want to have one conversation. One. And then I'll be out of your hair forever. I promise"

Jay got one of her hands free to stop Phil from coming any closer. "You promise?"

Helena held out her pinky.

Jay raised her brows. "Christ, what are we, in middle school?"

"Please? One conversation?" Helena begged, widening her eyes and jutting out her bottom lip.

"Kid, no, you're going to get into some—"

Michael's eyes caught Jay's from across the room. Fuck. Fuck, fuck, fuck.

"My room. Now."

Helena tilted her head. "Your room? Where's—"

"Anjo," Michael said, his eyes tracing Helena's non-existent curves as he approached. "Who's this?"

Jay's lips tugged at a snarl at the way Helena's back straightened, her crop top making the girl's small chest look bigger, probably wearing a push-up bra on top of it. Her creamy white legs caught the glow of the lights, the shorts she was wearing barely covering her ass. Helena was a child, playing dress up to be a woman. And Michael certainly wouldn't care to tell the difference.

"No one," Jay said, stepping forward to greet him. She ran her hands over his chest, nuzzling her face into his neck. "She's some kid trying to get a job here. I told her to fuck off."

Michael hummed, brushing his hands up Jay's arms. "And why did you do that?"

She stiffened at his touch. "You can't be serious."

"She's a pretty little thing." Michael pushed Jay away gently. She caught him stepping forward, his gaze resting on Helena's face. Jay had seen that look before. It was the same one he had given her the day they had met.

Helena's arms crossed over her chest.

Jay's lips twitched again.

"Michael, she's a kid. I'm pretty sure she's barely eighteen," Jay said, placing her arm across his chest, her hand cupping his cheek to move his face back to her. "And besides, she's barely got any tits or ass to speak of. You think she'd bring in any clientele?"

Michael's jaw tensed as he reached up, his finger curling under the strap of Jay's dress. "Green's an ugly color on you, anjo."

Jay's grip on his face tightened, but she tamped her anger under a dazzling smile. But even she could feel her lips were pulled back too tight, the smile not reaching her eyes. "I could say the same for you, baby."

"Find her an outfit. Javier and I will decide if she's worth keeping around or not." Michael snapped the strap, her skin stinging with the force of it. He stepped around Jay and headed out for the front doors. "Going for a smoke break."

Fucking asshole. Jay turned her attention back to Helena, who looked akin to someone who had seen a ghost.

"You going back there or what?" Jay spat.

"No, I wasn't—I didn't—" Helena stammered, rubbing at her arms. "I should go."

Jay felt herself softening, despite trying to keep her anger steady. "I thought you wanted to talk to me?"

Helena bit her lip. "I do, but—"

"Kid, if you think I'm going to actually bring you back there for him, you're wrong." Jay pointed in the direction of her dressing room. "Go wait for me in my room. I'll come get you and walk you out."

Helena looked back towards the exit, then to the dressing rooms. "You're not going to get in trouble, are you?"

Christ, she was way too young to be hanging around here. Michael was a Goddamn scumbag for even looking her way.

"No, kid, I'll be fine." Jay nodded towards the dressing rooms again. "Go."

Helena kept her arms crossed over her stomach as she walked through the stages, looking like a baby deer in a den of wolves. Lucky for her, the wolves were much more preoccupied with the meat hanging in front of their faces, all too willing to give them a taste.

Once Helena was out of sight, Jay retrieved Michael and Colt's drinks from the bar and headed back to the room.

Colt was the only one back there, the tablet in his hands as he looked up to see her coming in. His hazel eyes turned serious as he regarded her. But she could still see it there—the longing. She loved the way he looked at her, like she was the only one who existed, like he couldn't breathe without her near. Michael never looked at her like that. She never wanted him to.

Colt cleared his throat. "Hey, Michael went for a smoke."

"I know." Jay set the drinks down on the table. "Where's Javier?"

"Bathroom, I think, you know you really shouldn't be—"

Jay tore the tablet out of Colt's hands and tossed it to the side. He barely blinked before she grabbed his face and pulled him in for a kiss.

He didn't hesitate to kiss her back. His hands found the curve of her waist, his fingers warm and soft as he touched her. One hand traveled lower to her ass and squeezed it, while the other one went to her shoulder blades.

She licked along his lower lip, and he opened for her, all too happy to let his tongue mingle with hers. Jay moved her hands into his blond hair, short and freshly cut, so fucking soft and perfect and just hers.

"I missed you," Jay whispered.

He moaned as he grabbed both of her legs to lift her, then brought her over to the couch where she could be seated in his lap. He was hard already, she could feel it. And if it weren't for the chance that Michael or Javier could come in at any moment, she would be on her knees sucking Colt's cock before letting him fuck her into oblivion.

"I missed you, too," he whispered back.

She whimpered as his hands gripped her hips, pulling her down onto him.

This was how it always went with them. They had broken up the first time that she and Michael had gotten together, but eventually she and Colt found their way back to one another. Another breakup would happen, then she and Michael would fight, and it would start all over again. But it was fine; Colt was her person, he was always there for her. He was endgame, he always had been, he always would be. Fuck Michael.

Colt's lips trailed down her jaw and to her neck. She gasped as she felt his lips begin to suck.

"Baby, no," she whined, pushing him away. "Michael's going to notice."

Colt growled against her skin. "You can't rile me up like this and then tell me I can't have you. It's not fair."

Jay sighed, moving to sit next to him instead. "Yeah, but it's cute to see you all feral."

He growled again. "You're a tease."

"You love it." She giggled and pushed him away.

"I love you," he murmured, brushing a strand of hair behind her ear.

Jay smiled. God, it felt so real coming from him. She wished she could play it on repeat all the time, when she was falling asleep, when she was waking up, when Michael was on top of her and she was trying to imagine it was Colt instead. "I love you, too."

"Then stop making this harder than it has to be." He propped his head against his arm on the back of the couch. "I got my new promotion. Tell Michael it's over."

Jay resisted the urge to roll her eyes. "Babe, you know I can't. We promised to wait until you at least got an executive position."

"Director is close enough. It's a huge pay raise, and if you really wanted to, you could keep working to help us pay the bills."

"You know as soon as I tell Michael my days here are over."

"So? Not like Vision is the only club in the city."

Jay's tongue lashed behind her teeth. "It's also not the only thing I could be doing with my life."

Colt groaned, throwing his head back. "Come on, you know that's not what I meant."

"Yeah, but it's what you said, isn't it?" she asked as she stood.

He always did this. Colt never tried to give her an out, another option. And yes, it was her choice to dance, but that didn't mean it was her only choice. But maybe with him it would be.

Colt rolled his eyes, a smile tugging at his lips as he pulled her back into his lap. "Stop being a brat."

She pushed against his chest, but he wrapped his arms around her waist to keep her where she was. "I'm not a brat. You're being a dick."

"Shut up," Colt snapped. "You're the one who started it with the attitude, like you always do. I'm just trying to have a conversation, and you're out here acting like I'm keeping you prisoner."

"Yeah, because it's your fault I'm here in the first place!"

"Oh, knock it off with that shit. You're a grown woman, I couldn't make you do anything you didn't want to do."

"Let me go. Michael's going to be here in a second."

Colt only held her tighter. "Kiss me first."

"No."

"Kiss me or I'll hold you until he does come in."

Jay's skin broke out in a cold sweat. "Fuck off."

"Do it."

She tried to give him a chaste kiss, but he held the back of her head despite her protests. And God, Colt could make her weak like no one else. Her lips melted against his, her fingers in his shirt, her tongue in his mouth—

Jay moved off his lap to stand near the table, just as the door opened, Michael walking through.

He frowned. "What are you doing in here?"

She gestured with her lips towards the table with the drinks, the ice cubes beginning to melt. "You asked me to get the drinks, remember?"

Michael grunted, side-eyeing Colt, who was looking at the tablet like it was the most interesting thing in the world, before looking back to Jay. "Thanks."

"No problem."

He examined her. "You're still mad."

Jay twirled a piece of her freshly relaxed hair in her fingers. "No."

"Come on, anjo, you know you're my favorite." Michael captured her chin in between his fingers and pressed a lingering kiss on her lips. And of course, she leaned into it, wrapping her arms around his neck, making sure that Colt would see the way her foot kicked up the slightest bit, how she kissed Michael deeper.

She hummed as she pulled away. "And you're mine."

"We're almost finished here. Why don't you go back to your room and get changed. Then we'll get home and I'll make it up to you."

"Sounds good, baby," she said, letting him kiss her again. She didn't look back at Colt as she walked to her dressing room. She hoped he thought about it while he was fucking himself later. God knows she wasn't going to be around to do it.

No, she would just be stuck letting Michael shove her face into a pillow while he grunted and fucked her like she was a fucking sex doll. Maybe she could at least get him to take her out for a drink or two first, make it more bearable for herself.

Jay opened the door to her dressing room, jumping at the sight of Helena perched at her vanity, stuffing something into her pocket. Christ, she had forgotten she told Helena she could come back here.

"What were you doing?" Jay asked, scanning the room. The place was an absolute mess—her own fault, really. Jay wasn't one to clean up after herself, so clothes and bottles were strewn about on the floor and the small couch that she used as a bed for when she had to work a double shift. Or when she didn't feel like going home with Michael.

Which was becoming more and more often, lately.

"Nothing," Helena said. "Why, you think I would try to steal something?"

Jay shrugged as she walked further into the room, going to her closet. There were still a few things left in there that were fine for her to wear. But she would need to tell Michael to get the cleaners in to get her laundry done. "You might. I don't know you."

"Well, that seems kind of dumb to let me into your room then, doesn't it?"

Jay was grateful that Helena couldn't see her face. Helena was a kid, but damn, she was a little spitfire. Which made it all the more important that Michael didn't get his hands on her. Jay had been like that once. She still was, in some ways. But age does things to you. And so does letting a man dominate every single aspect of your life.

"It does. Which is why I have to kick you out. Michael's taking me home." Jay stripped off her dress, reaching for her bra. Luckily she had chosen a matching set today; Michael preferred it when she matched.

"But we haven't talked yet," Helena said.

Jay rolled her eyes as she pulled on a tee shirt. "Sorry, kid, but I don't have the time."

"So you're going home with him?"

"I don't think that's any of your business."

"Just asking."

"Yeah, well, that's my answer," Jay said as she tugged on a pair of shorts.

"Is he your boyfriend?"

Christ Almighty. Jay turned around, her hands on her hips. Helena sat with her back to Jay. "Is he your dad or something?"

The sudden thought made Jay's skin crawl. But there was a possibility. Helena had to be, what, sixteen? Seventeen? Michael was about to be forty. He'd obviously had girlfriends before, so having a few kids wasn't completely impossible. But the way Michael had been looking at Helena...Maybe he didn't even know.

"God no," Helena said as she shuddered. "He's my uncle. Sort of."

Uncle. As in, family. As in Michael had a sibling that Jay had no clue about. Why hadn't he told her?

Jay turned Helena around. She wanted to see if there was any resemblance. Any chance that the answer would be written in Helena's features, that she would somehow tell her about this family that had suddenly manifested right on the chair of her vanity. But all Jay got was a good look at Helena's face covered in a lipstick color that was all wrong for her.

Jay pressed her lips together. Helena looked like a child who had gotten into her mother's makeup bag. "You want to..."

"Maybe you shouldn't leave your makeup where just anyone could get to it," Helena mumbled, trying to wipe at her face with her hand.

Jay stopped her and grabbed a makeup wipe instead. "Maybe you shouldn't be such a snoop."

"I'm working on it."

Jay laughed breathlessly as she started on the lipstick. "So Michael's your uncle?"

"Kind of. He's technically my adopted uncle," Helena said in between swipes of the makeup wipe.

"Adopted?" Michael hadn't mentioned anything about adoption. Jay's head swam with the new information. She tried to sort through years of bullshit to remind herself of any mention of the word. But none came.

"Yeah, my dad and him are siblings, and my dad adopted me and my siblings," Helena said.

Jay finished with the wipe and threw it in the garbage. Some of the color was still stained into Helena's pale skin. Poor thing was damn near translucent. She would need some concealer; Jay didn't want to send her out looking like she was having an allergic reaction or something.

"I'll be right back."

Before Helena could protest, Jay was out the door and passing into another dancer's room. Okay, so Michael had a brother. That was fine. It was fine that Jay didn't know that the guy she had been seeing for the last six years had a brother who had adopted a bunch of kids. It was fine that Michael had told her he was an only child. All of this was fine.

So why did it feel like it wasn't?

Jay found a few colors that could be a match, and went back to her room. She held one up to Helena's face.

Helena flinched. "What are you doing?"

"It's concealer, you have a little staining. This'll help cover it up," Jay pulled Helena's head back towards her. She found a color that was close enough, putting some on the back of her hand before retrieving a clean makeup brush. "You don't wear makeup?"

A silly question, really, considering how bad Helena had fucked up with the lipstick. But still, at her age, Jay was wearing a full face almost every day.

"No, no one ever taught me how to," Helena mumbled, trying her best not to move her mouth too much.

Jay furrowed her brows. "No mom?"

"No." Helena averted her gaze. "L—Dad's wife passed away before we got there. And my mom was..."

"A shitty excuse for a parent?"

"Yeah."

"Been there, done that one," Jay sighed.

"So, how do you and Michael know each other?"

"He's a client."

"You let all your clients touch you like that?"

"Just him." Jay turned Helena back towards the mirror. Jay felt the tension leave the girl's shoulders as she looked at herself, the red stain around her mouth gone. "Now listen, I have to go. Do me a favor and wait a few minutes before coming out."

"I thought you were going to walk me out?" Helena asked, meeting Jay's gaze in the mirror.

"Change of plans." Jay straightened and went for her shoes. "Unless you want to run into your uncle who doesn't seem to know he's your uncle, again."

"No, that's okay," Helena said, folding her hands in her lap.

A distant feeling tugged at Jay's heart, pulling her back her back to the vanity, where her fingers sifted through the multitude of unused lipsticks, and found the perfect one. She lifted one of Helena's hands and pressed the tube into her palm.

Helena looked at it, confused. "What's this?"

"A lipstick that's actually your shade. Go watch a YouTube tutorial on how to apply it." Jay gave her a gentle smile as she went back to the door. "Give us a few minutes to leave before you come out. It should be clear in about ten. And, kid?"

"Yeah?"

"Don't come around here again. You'll be safer if Michael forgets you ever existed."

9

It was an unusually slow night at the club. Jay had done a couple lap dances, but the tips were small and not worth her time. Even the stage had proven to be less busy than she would have liked.

Maybe it was because Javier had hired on some new blood. Pretty little things that still had a bright sparkle in their eyes, skin that was still soft, youth that didn't have to work so hard to keep their bodies tight and perky.

Christ, twenty-five and Jay was already looking at the twenty year olds like they were about to put her out of business. Not that Michael would ever let that happen. He had seen enough girls come and go, but he made sure she was well taken care of. And she would make sure that it would stay that way, as long as she needed it to.

Jay sucked down more of her water, her irritation growing as she watched one of the new dancers up on the stage. She had talent, Jay could give her that, and the men below her didn't seem to mind too much that her feet stuttered and her grip faltered, the way her body tightened too much when she spun around the pole.

She would warm up eventually. It would become a habit, almost, the same thing day in and day out. After so long, Jay didn't even need to think about her routine anymore. And maybe that was the problem—maybe she needed to change it up. She could practice some of her moves on Michael; he always liked getting to see her new stuff first.

"Evening, boneca."

Jay held in her sigh as she pasted on her pretty smile. Only took thinking Michael's name twice, this time. She would have to be more careful.

"Since when do you call me—" Jay startled, looking to her left to see The Suit. Although, The Suit no longer felt applicable. He wore a deep gray sport coat and black tee shirt, with dark jeans to match. There was an air to him that he hadn't had a week ago.

Jay repressed a genuine smile with the one she reserved for clientele.

"Hey…" she trailed off, going through the list of names her long list of clients had let slip at some point or another.

"Luke," he said. "I guess I never introduced myself."

"It's fine," Jay said. "I didn't expect to see you back." She flashed him a smile as she ran her finger along the hem of her top. "Especially not so soon."

Luke tilted his head in a way that felt too familiar. "I told you I'd like to see you again."

Jay's stomach fluttered. It was a line. She knew that. Maybe he was hoping that by buttering her up he'd get some kind of discount. That's what people always did—call her sexy, or gorgeous, or ask her if she'd ever considered modeling because they have a friend who—

"And I thought you were joking." Jay poked at the ice in her drink.

"I'm a man who keeps to his word." Luke smiled as he took her in. "You look nice."

She turned to face him fully, the lights catching the green metallic fabric of her wrap top. "Keep complimenting me. You're not getting a cheaper dance."

"I mean it. Green looks good on you. Brings out your eyes." His lips twitched. "Doesn't hurt that it's my favorite color."

Jay's real smile broke through before she could catch it. "Thank you."

Luke returned it, his eyes slowly tracing the contours of her body, then frowned. "What happened there?"

She looked down. The cut Pitt had given her was peeking out of her bottoms. She had chosen high-waisted specifically because of this, but apparently, they had rolled down. Jay waved her hand dismissively. "Nothing, walked into the corner of a table, caught my hip."

"Odd angle for it to be a table." Luke reached out.

Jay took a large step back. The clients were not allowed to touch. Especially not her. Michael had made that more than clear when he came back with split knuckles, blood spattered over his shirt, and taken out whatever lingering aggression he had out by fucking her senseless. She hated to admit that it had been the best sex that they had ever had—the way he kept whispering to her how she was his, he would do anything to keep her, no one would touch her like that again. Not if he could help it.

It was the closest she had ever felt to making love with him.

Jay cleared her throat and crossed her arms over her stomach. "I was bending down."

Luke placed his hands on the bar, folding them in front of him. "I thought you said you were walking."

"I don't see why it matters," she said. "It happened, I'm fine."

Never mind the fact that Jay still struggled to be around Michael right after he smoked, how she had actually talked to him about changing her stage name.

Something about hearing "Angel" now made her heart race.

But Michael had patted her head and told her she would be fine, so she would.

"You don't seem fine," Luke said, his hands appearing to struggle with staying on the bar. "You've got a weird cut and you're changing your answer. You don't have to lie to me, you know."

Jay's long nails dug into her side. Who the fuck did this guy think he was, saying she was lying? If she said that's what happened, it's what happened. She had walked into plenty of tables before, tripped over herself a few times when she was still getting used to the heels, dealt with more than enough small accidents. It wasn't the first time, it wasn't the last. "And you don't have to interrogate me. Now, are you going to buy me a drink or what?"

"Got it. Conversation over." He waved down the bartender.

It was a new guy; after the incident with Pitt, Daniel had been "let go." Jay had fought for him to stay, since it hadn't been his fault, but there was only so much she could do before Michael would start asking questions. There hadn't been anything to question, but if he looked hard enough, he'd find something, and then Jay would have to deal with the fall out. And no one was worth that.

"Bourbon on the rocks and whatever the lady would like, please." Luke winked.

"Make his a double," Jay said as she batted her eyelashes at the bartender.

Luke's smile dropped. "A single's more than fine."

She placed her hand on his wrist, running her thumb over the faceted crystal of his watch. "Don't worry about it. The owner and I are close, he won't mind me slipping a loyal customer a little extra."

Luke cleared his throat, his fingers twitching when Jay's ran over the back of his hand. "Really, it's fine."

The bartender gave him a double anyway, before pushing the martini glass towards Jay. Luke passed over his card, picking up his drink.

Jay lifted her glass as well. "Cheers."

"Cheers." He took a sip, attempting to hold her gaze, but failing as he started to cough.

"I know the shit here is usually cheap, but that's top shelf," she said, nodding at his glass.

"Out of practice," Luke said, coughing again. "I don't drink often. Not good for me."

Jay narrowed her eyes. "Didn't seem to have a problem last week."

"That was a special occasion." He swirled his drink, watching the way the ice cubes spun.

"I would figure with your job you'd be drinking all the time."

"Exactly why I don't. I prefer to relieve my stress in other ways."

"That why you're here? To relieve some stress?"

"That..." Luke said, turning himself more to face her. His jacket was open, showing off his tee shirt—and the small amount of skin peeking out beneath the hem. "And I wanted to see you."

Jay took a large sip to coat her suddenly dry mouth. "Well, here I am."

"Here you are," he echoed, twisting the glass in his hand. "Are you working?"

She shot him a bored look while he flashed her that gorgeous smile of his.

"You know what I mean."

She checked his watch, her fingers hot against his skin. "Just finished my break."

He frowned. "Damn, wish I had come in sooner. It would be nice to talk to you off the clock."

"Even off the clock, I'd still charge you," Jay said, her thumb brushing over the back of his hand. "Why do you think I made you buy me a drink?"

"You didn't make me do anything, boneca." Luke's hand moved beneath hers. "I never do anything I don't want to."

"So they always say." She moved her grip back to her glass, then looked around the room, registering that he was alone. "Your son isn't with you?"

"My kid? They're home," Luke said. "But I didn't want to miss our therapy session."

Jay's lips spread into a wide grin before she could stop herself. "I thought you said it was because you wanted to see me?"

He shrugged. "Can't it be both?"

"*Wanting* to see your therapist?" she teased as she took a step towards him. "You got something you need to get off your chest?"

Luke brought his glass to his lips, mumbling something behind it. She was about to call him out on it, but he pulled out a wad of cash, smaller than the one from his first night, but still big enough that she wouldn't be able to turn him away. "Ready when you are."

"Private dance?" Jay plucked a bill from the stack, tucking it into her top.

"Of course," he said, placing the rest back in his pocket. "I don't like to share."

She hummed, eyeing the wall of partitions. "Come on. We'll do an alcove—"

"Does it have a curtain?"

She paused, casting him a sideways glance. "Yeah? Why, you wanna do a room instead?"

"No, an alcove is fine," he said, stepping so close to her that she could feel the heat rolling off of him. "I just like my privacy."

Jay was grateful she was holding onto the bar, because otherwise, her knees might have given out. The new guy had made her drink too strong; she was feeling the alcohol quicker than usual.

She hadn't slept very well last night—so it made sense.

"You're in the wrong place, then." Jay crooked her finger before starting towards the alcoves. "But what is it you guys call it? Attorney-client privilege?" She opened the curtain, allowing him to step in before her. "I feel like I can give you the same."

"I'd appreciate that." Luke settled into the couch. The space was smaller than a room, more intimate. She couldn't move much without bumping into him, which was kind of the point. But there was something about his energy that made Jay think maybe she should have pushed for the room.

No, it was nothing. She was being paranoid, especially after the whole Pitt fiasco. It was fine.

She breathed in deep, the scent of Luke's cologne reaching her nose. Not overpowering, but comforting. A nice change up from the usual stench of stale cigarettes and alcohol that most men had.

Luke's fingers moved on his glass, following along to the music playing.

"You a musician?"

"Sorry?"

"Your hand." She gestured with her lips. "You were playing keys."

"Right. I play a little."

"Of?"

"Guitar. It's been a few years though." Luke held out his hand, inviting Jay to take it in her own. She ran her thumb over his palm. His fingertips were free of calluses, as was the rest of his hand. To be expected, since he was a lawyer. Michael's were pretty similar, outside of scarred knuckles from too many fights—or more accurately, beatings.

"But I've been thinking about picking it up again," Luke said.

"Were you in a band or something?" Good. This was safe. Keep it on him, make him feel good. That was all she was doing.

"When I was way younger, yes. And no, I won't show you pictures."

"You're no fun." Jay pouted. She started into her routine, letting the slow music flow through her, the bass matching her heartbeat.

She liked it when she got to take her sweet time. It meant she could usually get a few extra bucks out of whatever client she was working. Maybe she'd pick herself up a nice new bag, on her own dime. Not Michael's.

"What about you? What does a woman like yourself spend her free time doing?" Luke asked.

An innocent enough question. One Jay could answer honestly—shopping, traveling, sleeping, occasionally spending time with the one person she called a best friend—but she chose not to. Because this is how it started: make small talk, which led to light conversation, then to sharing. And from there it was all downhill. The client gets attached, thinks you're something more, starts wanting things from you, expecting. And she knew where that led, too.

"Why, you trying to ask me out?"

Luke's taps on his glass paused, fingers suspended in midair. "Just making conversation, is all."

Jay suppressed the urge to snort. "Good. Because we're not allowed to date the clientele."

"And why's that?" Luke asked. He moved his free arm to rest behind his head, relaxing into the couch more.

"Because then you always know where to find me if we broke up. It's a safety risk."

"Don't I know where to find you anyways?"

Something about the way he said it made Jay's stomach twist. The smell of cigarettes and alcohol permeated her nostrils, making her aware of just how close they were. Her hand brushed over her hip, just above the cut.

Say it. Angel.

Luke must have noticed, because he sat up straighter and ran a hand over his pants leg. "Sorry, I didn't mean for that to come off as creepy as it did. I just meant you must be worried about your safety a lot, as a dancer. Guys must come in and request you often."

Jay shrugged, trying to regain her focus, breathing in deep. Luke's cologne slowly overtook her again, and she relaxed into it. She was here, giving a guy a lap dance, her typical Thursday night. Nothing out of the ordinary. "Not really. Every once in a while they do, but it's not as often as you think."

Luke flashed a smile. "Ah. So I'm one of the few, then?"

"You are," Jay said.

It was true. She had plenty of clients who liked to say they would be back, and then ditched her for the next pretty face that stepped onto the stage. It was fine, of course. She didn't like it when the clients got too attached to her. But when they were high rollers like Luke, she couldn't help but feel pissed.

"Lovely, I won't have to share my time with you, then." He winked.

The fluttering in her stomach was a coincidence. She was hungry, she'd skipped dinner—since Michael had decided stuffing her face into a pillow after work was more important than letting her choke down some food before a long shift.

"Do you plan on coming here more often?"

"Not necessarily. But when I do choose to come in, I would like to ask for you. Would that be alright?"

Christ, he was really laying it on thick. He *must* be lonely if he was practically begging to see her again. But was that really such a bad thing? *Yes. It is.*

"Let's see how this dance goes and I'll let you know." Jay gestured at the bills in his pocket.

"Right." He pulled out a ten dollar bill and slipped it into her bottoms on the right side. "Still getting used to this."

"You seemed to be pretty confident that time."

"Just because you make it easy. You're a very calming person, boneca. I like being around you."

"Thanks." Jay turned around, rolling her hips into his and working her hands into her hair.

Boneca. Jay had looked it up—it meant doll, as she had expected, but it was the fact that it was Portuguese that had given her pause. Helena's words still rang in her mind. Helena's dad and Michael were brothers. And technically, Michael was Brazilian, or, at least, half. Not that you could tell by looking at him—he easily passed for white. He always said that if they had kids, hopefully they'd be light like him.

Jay would rather drop dead than have his babies.

"What does your tattoo mean?"

Jay stiffened, looking back. "What?"

"That tattoo on your shoulder." Luke nodded towards her left shoulder. "I've never seen one like it before."

Jay tilted her chin up. "Nothing."

"You got a tattoo that means 'nothing'?"

"It was a gift."

"Strange gift."

Jay's nails dug into her palm, attempting to relieve some of the venom that was pulsing in her veins. Better not to snap at the clients twice. "No one's given you a tattoo as a gift before?"

"Yeah, actually." He undid the strap of his watch on his left wrist to reveal a small tattoo that read *Papai*. "I got this for Father's Day one year."

No fucking way. Jay held his wrist to read the writing better. Her eyes traced the shaky lettering, clearly the work of a very, very young child. Jay tried to swallow past the tightness in her throat. "Cute."

"One of my kids did it."

"*Kids?*"

"I have five. You met the oldest."

Jay's eyes flicked to Luke's ring finger, where a gold band with filigree etched into it sat. *Mother fucker.* She didn't know how she missed it before; she was always good at spotting the assholes who didn't bother slipping their wedding bands into their pockets before they stepped in the door. And even those that did usually had a tan line to show where one would usually be. She had fucked up by not seeing it sooner. "Your poor wife."

"Not all of them are by her."

Jay shot him a dirty look. "Your poor wife."

Luke didn't seem to register the fact that she was trying to murder him with her gaze, instead choosing to take his wrist back and put his watch back on. "Two were ours. The others are adopted."

What, didn't want to fuck around with a side-chick and have some more of your own? "Really?"

"I always wanted a big family," Luke said, his voice too fucking light and happy for the conversation they were currently having.

Jay had known it was too good to be true, that she would have *one* normal client. But here Luke was, flaunting the fact that he was married and had *multiple* kids. She imagined his wife waiting for her *lovely* husband to come home after a long day at work, enjoy a nice, homecooked meal, and then fuck her until he was exhausted. Jay wondered who Luke thought of while she did it. Then again, he wouldn't exactly be here if he was content with his wife, would he?

"So, the tattoo? It really means 'nothing'?" Luke asked, sipping at his bourbon.

Jay had half a mind to dump it in his lap. "It's a nail."

"So who's the hammer?"

Jay ignored him.

"Breakup, then?

Her fingers twitched, anger rolling off of her as she rolled her body against him. Luke had some fucking nerve asking her about her love life in any capacity. She lowered herself between his thighs, trying to keep her face neutral.

He pulled a bill from his pocket and handed it to her, rather than trying to tuck it away. "How long have you been dancing?"

Jay snatched it away from him and stuffed it in her bra. "Since I was nineteen."

He examined her, probably trying to figure how old she was. Asshole. "That's young. You never wanted to do anything else?"

"Already told you..." She hesitated, her routine interrupted. Fuck. She didn't get tripped up like this. But her clients also usually weren't this nosy. "I like the money."

"That doesn't mean you didn't have dreams."

"I *chose* this."

"But you're not happy with it." Luke's voice was soft, which made Jay all the more pissed. She didn't need his pity. This was her job, and whether she liked it or not was solidly none of his Goddamn business.

"So? What do you care? You're here to get a lap dance, aren't you?" Jay slammed her hand into the couch near his head, but he didn't flinch. "So why don't you shut up and enjoy it?"

Luke tilted his head as his eyes met hers, speaking gently. "Am I upsetting you?"

She looked away from him. "No."

"You don't have to dance for me if it's too much."

"It's not too much. You're just asking some deep questions." Jay tried to meet his eyes again, but he was giving her that same stupid look he had been giving her before. She felt a slight pang of guilt for having snapped at him.

"I'm sorry," he said.

Jay didn't acknowledge him. The moment had been lost, the beat floating somewhere that she couldn't reach. She shouldn't have been talking to him, she knew better; get too familiar with the clients and it causes trouble. Familiarity breeds comfort. And comfort meant men who thought they could come to see her whenever they liked and touch her in ways that would land them both in serious trouble. Whatever, she would finish her dance and then go. Maybe she could ask to get off early tonight. She could call Colt to come get her, and they could salvage some of the evening.

Luke's voice pulled her back from where she had been lost in her thoughts. "Ask me something."

Jay eyed him. He sat with his hands in his lap, fingers wrapped around the still full glass of bourbon that the melted ice had watered down. She kept her feet planted, rather than putting them where she would have liked, and making his poor wife pick glass out of his limp dick. "Like what?"

"Something that you think would make me uncomfortable."

"Fine." Jay crossed her arms, her hip swinging out to the side as she widened her stance. "Does your wife know you're here?"

It wasn't anything new: married men coming in here and getting a dance. But she was pleased by the guilt in his eyes. "No."

"And how do you think she would feel if she knew you were here?"

"Honestly?"

Jay sneered. "Brutally."

Luke's voice was barely audible over the sound of the music pulsing over them. "Pissed beyond all reason."

"Then why are you here?"

"I already told you. I wanted to see you."

Jay bit the inside of her cheek. There was no denying it—Luke was hot. And the compliment tucked into his desire to see her again was something that was hard to ignore. But that didn't matter. What mattered was that this man was married, and had five kids waiting for him at home.

Luke was a scumbag. And she didn't need another one of those in her life.

"She's not going to come in here and try to fight me, is she?"

He shook his head. "No, she won't."

"Good." Jay sat beside him, keeping a safe distance between them. "Cause you're not worth the fight."

"Ouch." Luke pressed a hand to his chest, turning toward her. "Tell me how you really feel."

"Look, I have enough bullshit in my life without you coming in here and dragging me into your unhappy marriage. So, how about we do this?" Jay brought her face close to his. "How about you go home to your pretty little wife and your precious little family, and stay the hell away from here?"

He had the fucking nerve to look wounded. "And if I don't want to?"

"I'll make you."

Luke's laugh came out choked. "I'd like to see you try."

"Okay." Jay dug the bills out of his pocket, counted her payment plus a hefty tip, before shoving the rest back in. "You have five minutes to get the fuck out before I call security. Your time starts," she pulled up his wrist to glance at his watch, "now."

Jay dropped his arm into his lap as she stood and sauntered away, her hips swinging as if counting the seconds. She had meant it; it was better this way. He got to remain faithful to his wife, and Jay to keep her job. God only knew it was one of the only things she *could* keep.

10

Helena checked the time again, pushing herself off the metal bench from where she had spent the last hour. It was getting dangerously late—close to three AM—and it wouldn't be long before Quinn or Lucio realized she wasn't home and started blowing up her phone. She should have asked Dylan to come wait with her. But then again, he would have told Lucio as soon as he found out she was sneaking into a strip club.

Or maybe he wouldn't have. Either way, Helena wouldn't have felt great about keeping Dylan out this late—he turned into a pumpkin if he wasn't in bed by ten.

She yawned, rolling her shoulders. Was Jay even working tonight? Helena had no idea—there was literally no way for her to check—she couldn't exactly go into the club and ask.

While Helena was in the habit of ignoring Lucio's rules, there was something about Jay's warning that made her pause. It was silly. Jay was just exaggerating, there had to be some other reason that she wanted Helena to keep away from the club.

Not that she minded. Helena didn't want to risk running into Michael again. But she needed answers, so Jay would have to be the one to give them.

Helena fiddled with the tube of lipstick in her jacket pocket. She had followed Jay's advice and practiced a little, but she still wasn't bold enough to wear it in public.

"Night, Angel!" a woman's voice called.

Helena looked to the exit to see Jay stepping out. It was weird seeing her dressed in a tee shirt and shorts, her heels traded out for more comfortable, but still clearly expensive, sneakers.

"Jay!" Helena shouted, bounding up from the bench where she sat.

Jay looked up from her phone, first right, then left, her face settling into a look that clearly read *You've got to be kidding me.*

"Seriously?" Jay set her hands on her hips as Helena approached her. "How many times do I have to tell you to stop coming around here?"

"You told me I couldn't come *into* the club anymore," Helena said, ignoring Jay's obvious displeasure. "You never said I couldn't come *around* the club."

"Whatever I said, I meant it. Now beat it." Jay glanced back down at her phone. "My ride's gonna be here in a minute."

Helena sucked in a breath. She had to work quick, then. "Wanna grab dinner?"

Jay's eyebrows shot up. "*Dinner?* It's three—"

"My treat." Helena bounced on her toes. "I know a cool little diner that's open all night."

Jay scoffed. "It's three AM. Don't you have school tomorrow?"

Helena scowled. "First of all, it's summer. Second of all, I'm in college."

Jay eyed her skeptically. "No way you're in college."

"Sophomore year! Come on, free food or what?"

An Uber pulled up next to them, flashers illuminating Jay in a yellowish tint. "What's stopping me from stuffing you in this car and dragging your ass home?"

"Well, one, you don't know where I live," Helena said, counting off on her fingers. "And two, I bet you're *starving* after working so hard all night. Wouldn't you like to go home feeling at least a little satisfied?"

Jay pulled a face. "Don't say it like that."

"Come on, one meal, then I'll let you go."

Jay's gaze flicked between the car and Helena. Helena started to think of another reason, another excuse for Jay to come with her, but luckily, it wasn't needed.

"Fine. But you try anything funny, I'm kicking your ass."

"That's assuming you could catch me."

"Kid—"

"Joking! No funny business, promise." Helena crossed her heart, biting back her smile.

"You and these damn promises. You're like a fucking twelve year old," Jay grumbled, tapping something on her screen. The car rolled away, leaving them standing in the glow of the streetlights and neon signs from the club.

Helena grinned. "Ready?"

Jay just nodded, and they began walking down the street.

It was eerily quiet, but Helena had to guess that many of the bars and restaurants that existed in the Meatpacking district were closed by now. Luckily she had scouted a twenty-four hour diner in the hours that she had been waiting.

"So, do you always work this late?" Helena asked after a few minutes of silence.

"Pretty much," Jay said.

More silence.

Helena kicked at a piece of garbage near her shoe. "Do you like working there?"

"Pays the bills."

Helena pursed her lips. Jay wasn't giving her much to work with, but she didn't exactly want to interrogate Jay about Michael when Jay could so easily walk away. And the last thing Helena wanted to do was walk herself to the subway at this time of night.

Something rustled near a pile of trash bags, causing Helena to jump in Jay's direction, and nearly knocking both of them over in the process.

"Christ, kid, it's a rat," Jay said, a hint of irritation lacing her voice. "You never been in the city before?"

Helena scowled up at her. "I come here all the time. Just not this late."

And not alone.

Helena kept her eyes glued to the ground as they resumed walking, trying hard to force the embarrassment heating her cheeks anywhere less visible.

"You take classes in the city?" Jay asked.

"Yeah. NYU," Helena said, trying to hide her distaste.

"Lot's of cute guys there. Smart ones, too. Bet they keep you real busy."

Helena ducked her head, keeping her eyes forward. "I don't have a boyfriend."

"Bullshit." Jay's tone wasn't insulting, more, disbelieving?

"No. I don't have time to date."

It was a half-truth. Helena had boyfriends throughout high school under Lucio's nose, but none of them ever lasted long. Same with friends. Before Gideon, people only hung around her because they knew she was smart, and would help them with cheating on homework or essays. And after Gideon...She had left that school.

Or, flunked out, would be a better way to put it. So all those people that Helena might have dared to at one point call friends disappeared. And those that she met at her new school never got close enough to even be called acquaintances.

But it hadn't mattered. She had Quinn, then she met Dylan. And they were more than enough as far as friends were concerned.

"That sucks. You're a pretty girl."

Helena stumbled as looked up at Jay, who was a downright *goddess* as far as Helena was concerned. Jay thought *she* was pretty? "I'm okay."

"I mean it. You just don't dress yourself right to show it off."

"What?"

"Like—oh, perfect." Jay stopped in front of a mirror that someone had left out for trash day, holding Helena by the shoulders in front of it. "So, look at yourself here."

Helena did, unsure of what she was supposed to really see. Her long black hair sat limp around her shoulders. It was always too damn difficult to do anything with outside of a ponytail; curls fell out the second anyone tried. She was wearing a light gray tee shirt and jean shorts that almost touched her knees, although she wished she had brought along a hoodie since the temperature was dropping. "Yeah?"

"You're washing yourself out. Girls with your complexion should wear dark colors. It'll make your eyes stand out even more."

Ugh, her *eyes*. Helena hated her stupid green eyes. Every time she looked at them, she felt like she saw Lucio staring back at her. Or, sometimes worse, Gideon.

"And these shorts are not doing you any favors." Jay squatted down, pushing down the sides of Helena's shorts. "I know you're gen z, but these things are so damn baggy."

Helena rolled her eyes. "I like these clothes."

"And that's fine. But you're hiding yourself, kiddo." Jay stood back up and started walking away. "You're pretty. That's not something to be scared of."

Helena quickened her pace to catch up with Jay. "I'm not scared of it. I just...don't know how to do it."

"You certainly did when you came into the club the other day."

"Yeah, and look what it got me. My uncle offering me a job at his strip club."

Jay fell silent. It was fine, Helena wasn't too sure she was in the mood to talk, anyways. That entire night had been a disaster. Helena had gone home after, taken a shower to try and scrub the feeling off. But it had seeped into her skin, making her feel disgusting.

She's a pretty little thing.

"Michael's an asshole."

Helena cast a glance at Jay.

"You looked…fine. He's just always looking for fresh blood, and you happened to be there. It wasn't your fault," Jay said.

"Thanks," Helena muttered, tucking a strand of hair behind her ear. She still couldn't shake the sticky feeling of the memory, but it felt a little less, now. Like Jay had scraped some of the gunk off of it. Jay had been the one to defend her, anyhow. And that was kind of nice. "The restaurant's right up here."

The hostess looked a mix of annoyed and passively relieved to see the two of them walking into the diner. Helena wondered if it had anything to do with the rowdy crowd of drunken patrons that filled the booths on the right side. Helena shifted uncomfortably. The group was laughing too loud and yelling, and a part of her itched to call the whole thing off. This was dumb, anyways, she should be home, or at Quinn's, anywhere that wasn't—

"Can we have that corner booth?" Jay asked, gesturing with her lips at the booth farthest away from the group. It was one of those circle booths, meant for families or big parties.

The hostess nodded, grabbed two menus, and led them over to their seats.

One of the men whistled in their direction.

Helena shot them a dirty look. There wasn't anything she could do besides that.

"Eyes forward, kid," Jay said, stepping into Helena's line of sight. "You don't fuck with drunk people."

"You want to just let them get away with cat-calling you?" Helena asked as they settled into opposite sides of the booth.

"I want to get out of here without worrying about getting followed." Jay glanced down at the menu.

"You think they would?"

Jay didn't respond.

Helena kept looking up, but Jay made it seem like the laminated sheet of paper in front of her was a first edition *Jane Eyre*. How long could you read over the same menu? It wasn't very extensive; this place had a late night menu of burgers, fries, wings, and chicken fingers. The same shit someone could get at any old diner. Helena huffed, having decided before they even walked in what she wanted. She got the same thing at every new restaurant: Burger. It was extremely hard to fuck up a burger. Even though she knew it was possible. Quinn had burned a couple of their meals before, but usually it was because her and Gideon were distracting them with homework.

Helena had always been shit at school.

The server finally came over, managing to smile despite looking like she'd rather scream. "Hello, ladies. Can I get you started with something to drink?"

"Water for me, and for her, a virgin whiskey and Coke," Jay said.

Helena shot her a look that she hoped would signal for Jay to shut up.

"We don't serve alcohol," the server deadpanned.

"Damn. Just two waters then." Jay grinned, relaxing her arms on the back of the booth.

The server let out a sigh through her nose. "Do we know what we would like to eat? Or do we need a few more minutes with the menu?"

"I'll have a burger. No cheese," Helena said.

Jay hummed. "Make it two. Mine without tomato."

The server collected the menus and walked off.

Helena poked at her cutlery. Now was her chance. She didn't know how quick it would be for the cooks to drop two burgers, but she knew it wouldn't be very long. If she was going to get what she wanted out of Jay, she needed to move quick. Straight to the point. No messing around. "So, how was work?"

Jay barked out a laugh. "Are you seriously asking me how work was?"

Helena glared at her in response. "Forgive me for trying to make conversation."

"Work was, well, work," Jay waved her hand, her long nails shimmering in the light. "Same shit day in and day out."

"Sounds like my job," Helena grumbled.

"What do you do?"

"Oh, uhm..." Helena swallowed. There was no harm in telling Jay the truth, right? Besides, it wasn't like she knew who Helena was, or who her dad was, or how any of them were connected to Michael, outside of him being her uncle. "I work with my dad."

"Doing what?"

You're my glorified assistant. "Secretarial work. Taking notes. It's an internship thing."

"Nepo baby?"

"What?"

"You're a nepo baby." Jay's lips tugged at a smirk. "Daddy got you the internship?"

"If I was a nepo baby I would actually be doing shit that mattered," Helena said, pulling apart the paper that held her flatware together.

The server returned with their drinks, giving Helena a welcome pause. She didn't want the focus to be on her, she was here to talk to Jay about Michael.

"And you work for Michael, right?" Helena asked.

Jay's lips hovered at her straw. "Sort of."

"But, you went *home* with him?"

"I didn't tell you I went home with him." Jay took a sip. "I told you I got a ride."

"From Michael?"

"I don't think that's any of your damn business." Jay crossed her arms over her chest.

"Sorry." Helena pushed her hair behind her ear. *Don't piss her off. Ask the right type of questions.*

Too bad Helena spent more time doodling than she did actually taking notes on Lucio's tactics. She could use one or two of them right now. He got people to tell him anything he wanted in the courtroom—and he could smell bullshit from a mile away. But she still couldn't tell how he did it.

"Is there a reason you're asking me and not your dad these questions?" Jay finally asked.

Helena chewed on her straw. "Sort of."

"Which is?"

"My dad won't talk to me about Michael, and every time I try to he tells me," Helena put on her best Lucio voice as she said, "'it's none of your business'."

Jay huffed out a laugh. "Yeah, they're brothers alright."

"Why do you say that?"

"Michael never tells me shit. Didn't even know he had a brother," Jay said. "I always figured it was a 'parents are dead and I'm an only child' situation."

Helena winced at Jay's casual tone. "That's a little dark, don't you think?"

"People don't tell you things, you fill in the blanks. That's what you're doing now, right?"

"I mean, I guess," Helena said. "But, you didn't ask about it?"

Jay narrowed her eyes. "About what?"

"You know, his family. Like, you never asked to meet his parents, or where he grew up, or..."

It was subtle. Subtle enough that Helena couldn't read it, but she had noticed it, at least. Jay's tongue darted out to touch the tip of her teeth, her eyes leaving Helena's to look over at the rest of the patrons.

"When you dance for as long as I have, you learn not to ask dumb questions," Jay said.

Helena's brows furrowed. "Asking about someone's family is a dumb question?"

"It is when you're not interested in knowing that person long term."

"How long have you known Michael?"

Jay's throat bobbed. "Six years."

There was something in Jay's voice that made Helena uneasy. The way it dropped, like she was trying to let it be swallowed up by the sound of rowdy drunk people. Helena looked at Jay's ring finger. It sat empty, which was...surprising? Unsurprising? Helena had no intention of ever getting married, but she knew most people got at least engaged around Jay's age. And if she was as involved with Michael as Helena *thought* she was, six years was a long time to go without commitment.

"That's a lot of time to not know something about someone," Helena hedged. "You sure he's just a client?"

Wrong question.

Jay sneered, her nails sinking into the back of the booth. "Pot, meet kettle."

Helena sat up. "L—My dad not telling me things is different."

"Wrong. Because Michael's a client. He chooses what to tell me or what not to tell me. And I don't ask about things that I don't care to know. He comes in, gets what he wants, gets out. That's how it works," Jay said, her words punctuated by her hand cutting through the air, stiff and sharp, until she rested it against her head.

Helena started to speak, but then thought better of it. She didn't need to upset Jay any more than she already had. And besides, it was useless. If Jay didn't know about Lucio, then there was no way in hell she knew about what happened with Michael. Helena was back at square one. She almost thought about telling Jay that she had changed her mind, that it was late and she really should be getting home. But that meant she would have to call Quinn, which meant letting them know that she had snuck out of the apartment, if they hadn't figured it out already. Then again, her phone wasn't blowing up—*shit*.

Helena let out an audible groan as she pulled her phone from her backpack.

"You good?" Jay asked, her tone free of the previous irritation it had carried.

"Yeah, my phone's dead," Helena sighed. "I don't know how the hell I'm gonna get home."

Jay waved her off. "Don't worry about it. I'll get a ride with you."

Helena eyed her curiously. "Why?"

"The fuck you mean, why?"

Helena fiddled with her fingers, looking down at the table. "I just figured you wouldn't want to."

"Girl code," Jay said, each word punctuated with a tap of her nail against the table. "You don't let women in a sketchy area go home alone. Especially when they're scared of things as small as rats."

"I wasn't scared!" Helena huffed.

"Oh, no, you just got 'caught off guard,'" Jay teased, putting air quotes around the last phrase. "You're gonna get yourself in a load of trouble."

Helena's lips thinned as she sulked back into her seat. She didn't need someone watching over her. She was eighteen, she could handle herself just fine. Okay, maybe she hadn't thought about bringing a charger with her when she knew she might be out late, and she wasn't used to being in Manhattan alone at night, but that was beside the point. She was an adult. "I can handle it."

"Sure. If I don't let the newbies get in a cab alone, I'm not letting your ass walk around Manhattan alone."

"I—"

"Not a discussion." Jay frowned. "I'm taking you home. Don't like it? Tough shit."

The server set their burgers down in front of them, before walking off to handle one of the rowdy patrons who had begun shouting for her attention. Helena grit her teeth at the sight of cheese on her burger. She turned around, ready to flag down the server, but the sound of plates stopped her.

Jay swapped their burgers.

"Why did you do that?" Helena asked. "I would have just called her over."

"Why are you gonna bother her over something so small?" Jay asked. "Mine doesn't have cheese. It's fine."

"They messed up, they should know—"

"Let it go." Jay took a bite of her burger, nodding at Helena's. "Eat."

"My sibling works in a kitchen. I know it's not that hard to remake a burger," Helena said as she began to eat. The burger was awful, but it was so late, and she hadn't eaten anything since she had caught dinner with Dylan after work.

Jay covered her mouth with her napkin as she swallowed down a bite. "Oh yeah? Where do they work?"

"The Pink Port. They're head chef."

"Head chef? Are they single?"

"You're not allowed to date them," Helena said, taking a big bite of her burger.

"I think that's for them and me to decide isn't it?" Jay wiggled her brows.

Helena shoved her plate away from herself. "I've lost my appetite."

"Nope, eat." Jay shoved the plate back in Helena's direction. "I'm not leaving this table until you do."

God, it was like having Quinn sitting across from her, forcing her to eat whatever God awful concoction they had come up with for dinner on the nights things were really scarce. She always would, of course, but it took a while for her to understand: either eat the shit you were given, or starve. And going to bed hungry made it hard for her to sleep, which made it hard for her to concentrate in school, which always drew the attention of teachers.

And that attention meant calls home.

The food in front of Helena looked even worse, but her stomach wasn't nearly full enough. "Are you going to stop making jokes about dating my sibling?"

Jay made a cross over her heart with a french fry. It was enough. Helena felt her lips split into a wide grin, and she picked up her burger again. It still tasted awful, but the company was nice, at least.

And maybe that was enough.

11

"**M**ake sure it's coconut milk!" Helena shouted, to which Lucio held up an "okay" symbol over his shoulder as he walked to the counter to order.

It was Helena's favorite part of errand day—the mid-afternoon coffee break. Helena used to enjoy their little day trips together. She and Gideon would always tag along wherever Lucio went, desperate to escape the horrible stuck-up rich kids of Scarsdale. It was bad enough she had to be neighbors with them, but trying to build any semblance of a friendship was entirely out of the question.

But now, it was more of a chore than ever. Lucio was always dragging her along, saying how they never spent time together anymore, but really it was just a way for him to grill her about herself or Quinn. She had grown to hate the sound of his keys, because it meant that just a moment later, he would be calling her downstairs to go for a ride, as if she were some sort of dog. And here she was getting her treat for being a good little girl.

Today was especially torturous as she had only gotten a few hours of sleep at Quinn's place before Lucio called her. Jay had brought her there, as promised, and Quinn was out cold when she got in, thankfully. But that also meant that Lucio had no clue how exhausted she was. As far as he knew, she had caught a movie with some college friends in the city; it was easier for her to crash at Quinn's place.

Lucio returned to their table, taking a seat across from her. "How was the movie last night?"

"Fine."

"What'd you go see?"

"Why does it matter?" Helena set her head in her hand, glaring at the door. He was so irritating sometimes. To anyone else, he was trying to make small talk, but Helena knew better. Lucio hadn't trusted her in years, outside of some minor work-related cases. The only time she managed to have any semblance of a social life was when she hung out with Dylan.

Lucio leaned back in his seat. "I'm just asking a question. No need to bite my head off."

"I don't know, some action movie. It was fine."

She could feel Lucio examining her. Sometimes she wished he would just look anywhere *but* at her.

"Everything okay?" he asked, concern lacing his tone.

"Yes, God! It's fine, I'm tired, I just want to get this shit over with and go home."

"You didn't have to come with me."

Helena snorted. "Yes, I did. You literally never give me a choice of whether or not I come with you."

"Name one time I've forced you to come with me."

She tried to dig her nails into the laminated wood, but it was impossible to do.

Lucio's voice remained calm as he spoke. "Helena."

"What?" she snapped, glaring at him.

He didn't look at all fazed, which was typical. The guy was basically a statue; Helena could count on one hand the number of times she had seen him smile in the past two years.

Then again, she had said the same thing about him being as angry as he was when he caught her snooping. And it was still true. Helena drummed three of her fingers on the table. One for each time he had ever raised his voice at or near her.

"You can talk to me, you know," Lucio said, playing with the strap of his watch. Helena, Gideon, and Quinn had gotten him it for father's day one year, their names and date he adopted them engraved on the underside of the golden face; the leather strap was new, though. Lucio had worn it so often that the old one had begun to give out.

"Yeah, 'to' you, not *with* you." Helena kept drumming her fingers on the table.

"Fine, with me then."

"You're just gonna hide more shit from me, so why should I?"

"What do you think I'm hiding from you?"

Helena shot him an exasperated look. "Stop bullshitting me."

"About what, Hel?" Lucio gestured outwards. "Tell me *one* thing you think I'm not telling you about."

"Why you and Michael don't talk anymore."

The switch in Lucio's demeanor was immediate. He visibly tensed, his eyes narrowing and lips pressing into a thin line.

"Well?"

"It's a long story," Lucio said, flexing his fingers. "And one I'm not going to tell you about here."

"Or at all," Helena grumbled.

"Hel—"

"It's fine. Be a hypocrite."

"Order for Luke!" The barista shouted over the din of customers talking.

Lucio breathed in deep as Helena continued to avoid looking at him. Finally, he seemed to give up continuing their conversation and left her to sulk in her chair.

She scanned the relatively thin crowd of the cafe, which was surprising for being right by Central Park. Then again, it was pretty late in the afternoon. Most people getting coffee at this point probably worked nights like Jay, which—oh my God, is that Jay? Don't lock eyes with her, Hel!

"Everything okay?" Lucio asked, placing her coffee down.

She looked up, fighting to remain calm. "Yeah, I just thought I—"

"Helena?"

Of course.

Jay stood in a pretty sundress, light fabric flaring to compliment her fantastic figure, hair pulled back in a high ponytail to show off her shoulders.

Helena's temper flared at how damn perky Jay seemed—she must have gotten to sleep in as late as she wanted.

Jay smiled warmly, not seeming to register that Lucio was standing there. Helena wished she could melt into the damn floor.

"Wasn't expecting to see you here after—"

Jay's smile faltered. It was only a flash, so quick Helena almost missed it. But she had seen that look before. She had just hoped Jay would be different.

"Hello," Lucio said, setting down his drink. "You are?"

For once, Helena was actually quick enough to think on her feet. She shot Jay a pleading look as she said, "This is Jay, one of my classmates."

"Jay, what a gorgeous name for a gorgeous woman." He grinned.

Helena's heart was beating in her throat, but from irritation or fear, she wasn't sure.

Jay's smile tightened as she looked at Helena. "Is this your dad?"

"I am. Luke. Pleasure to make your acquaintance." Lucio held a hand for Jay to take, but she just stared down at it, her nostrils flaring.

"Well, this was lovely, but I'm sure Jay has places to be, don't you?" Helena said through her teeth, trying even harder to get the woman's attention.

"Helena, don't be rude," Lucio chastised.

"Yeah, actually," Jay said, pulling out her phone. "I'm meeting a friend. It was nice to see you, Helena."

"A friend?" Lucio tilted his head. "Or boyfriend?"

Helena tried to kick him from where she sat at the table

"Friend," Jay repeated. "My *boyfriend* is at work."

"Shame. Would love to meet him."

"No you would not," Helena grumbled into her drink, then took a long sip to avoid the glance Lucio sent her way.

"Well, at least allow me to grab you a drink to make up for my daughter's brusqueness," Lucio offered as he turned to Jay.

Helena shook her head behind his back, trying to motion for Jay to leave.

Jay shifted the purse on her shoulder. "I'm fine. I can get one myself."

"I'm sure you can." He took a slight step towards her, and Jay stiffened in response. His voice was so low Helena strained to hear him. "But consider it me paying for some of your time."

Something that looked like annoyance crossed Jay's face before it relaxed again. "Fine. A grande caramel macchiato."

"Lovely." Lucio said, pulling out a chair for Jay. She looked between it and him, but when he motioned for her to sit, she did.

Helena wanted to gag at the way his hands lingered too long on the back of the chair. God, she knew it had been a while but did he have to be so *obvious*?

"Be right back," he said, finally walking away.

Helena's face immediately fell once he was out of earshot. "What the absolute hell was that?"

"What was what?" Jay asked, twirling the end of her ponytail.

"You and—my dad." Lucio's name almost slipped past Helena's lips too easily. But Jay didn't seem to catch it.

"I wasn't doing anything. Your dad was the one being pushy," Jay said. "Might as well get something out of it."

"Don't encourage him." Helena grimaced. "He might get ideas."

Jay looked back to where Lucio stood. He didn't seem to be paying them any mind, but Helena knew better.

"Hey, didn't you say your dad's wife died before you came along?"

"Yeah, why?"

"No reason," Jay said, turning her attention back to Helena. "Now, want to tell me what 'classes' you and I have together?"

Helena barely looked at her. Lucio was just getting up to the counter. Luckily, a crowd had come in just as he was getting to the counter, leaving them plenty of time. "I'm doing my undergrad in Poli Sci."

"Poli Sci?" Jay raised her brows. "For *what?*"

"Dad wants me to become a lawyer, like him."

Jay snorted slightly. "Nepo baby."

"Oh shut up," Helena snarled. "I'll make more money in my sleep than you do in an entire week stripping."

Jay's face fell, her tone becoming icy. "Says the girl who thinks street smarts means looking both ways."

Helena's eyes cut to where Lucio was still waiting in line, watching the two of them carefully. She gave him a half-hearted wave as she pretended to laugh off the comment Jay had just made.

"He's not going to buy it," Jay said, casting a look over her shoulder at Lucio, who had gone back to his phone.

"You could always just be doing some classes in business," Helena said. "Isn't that what Michael does?"

"Import and export, yes," Jay said carefully.

It was Helena's turn to raise her brows. "Import and export of what?"

"Nunya."

"Nunya?"

"Nunya business."

"For God's," Helena scrubbed at her face. "If he asks, we're taking some finance classes together. You're brushing up on some skills that you need for your job. And as far as he knows," she leaned over the table, locking her eyes with Jay's, "you and Michael don't have any association."

Jay mocked zipping her lips and locking them. "But you owe me big time, kid."

"Promise," Helena said before sitting back in her seat.

Lucio returned with Jay's drink, setting it down before her. "Well, you ladies looked like you were in quite a serious conversation," he said, sitting next to Helena. "Everything alright?"

"Of course, we were talking about an upcoming project." Jay tapped her manicured nails on her coffee cup. "Helena's been a huge help."

"Forgive me if I seem forward, but you don't seem like a traditional student," Lucio's eyes wandered over Jay. "Is this a recent life change?"

"I'm getting tired of my current line of work. So I've been taking classes to help me get my degree and become a CPA."

"Ambitious. I like that in a woman."

Helena rolled her eyes.

"Well, I like to keep it interesting." Jay looked up at him through her lashes. "Life can get boring when you stick with one thing for too long."

"I wouldn't know." He sipped his coffee. "I'm a man who likes routines."

Jay's eyes flashed. "Routines, huh?"

"I would figure someone in your field could appreciate that."

"We also appreciate transparency," Jay said, taking the top off her drink and blowing on it. "Which I think you can understand. Attorney-client privilege and all that."

Lucio sucked in a breath beside Helena. He tried to cover it up with a cough, then a sip. A reddish-tint touched his cheeks. Was he...*No freaking way.*

"I'm surprised you're choosing accounting. You seem like you're better suited for a people-facing role," he said. God, they were *seriously* doing this? Helena was sitting *right* there!

Jay flinched, hissing as the coffee spilled slightly over the side of her cup. Helena reached for a napkin, but Jay beat her to it. Her lips struggled to stay locked together as she held the paper to her hand, staring daggers at Lucio all the while.

He just continued to drink his coffee. "You know, psychology, or something like that."

"I work enough with people as it is right now. It gets annoying." The table suddenly shifted, *hard*. Lucio's eyes went wide, and he tried to cover whatever painful sound he had made with another cough.

"Especially when people lie straight to your face," Jay hissed.

"I can understand that." Lucio cleared his throat, his teeth clenched together as he spoke. "My job is literally poking holes in people's stories. It can get...interesting."

"Ahem! Am I interrupting something?" Someone chimed in.

Helena looked up to see a woman standing behind Jay: umber skin, black hair pulled into a bun, about Jay's height. There was something vaguely familiar about her, but Helena couldn't place what.

"Not at all!" Jay said as she stood and pulled the woman into a hug.

The woman looked over Jay's shoulder to Lucio, shock immediately setting in over her features. "Luke?"

"Hey, Morton," Lucio said, raising his cup to her. "Funny running into you here."

Shit. Morton. As in, Alice Morton, the detective that Lucio had been working with.

This wasn't going to be good.

"I could say the same," Alice looked between Jay and Lucio. "How do you know each other?"

"We don't," Jay said, motioning towards Helena, who gave a half-hearted wave. "This is Helena, my classmate."

"Classmate?" Alice's brows raised.

This was it; Alice was unknowingly going to blow this entire secret up, and they were going to watch in real time as Lucio murdered Helena for thinking that there had even been a slight possibility she would get away with this.

"Yeah, decided to get back into it." Jay grabbed her purse and drink. "I'll tell you more about it over our coffee." She looked at Helena, shooting her a wink. "See you in class."

"Pleasure meeting you, Jay," Lucio called, as the pair walked away but only Alice turned around to acknowledge that he had spoken.

Helena sighed heavily and rubbed at her temples. God, she just wanted to go home. Watching that whole display had made her nauseous. But she wasn't sure if it was more from the flirting, or the fear. Maybe a little of both. "I would appreciate it if you didn't flirt with my classmates."

He frowned at her. "I wasn't flirting."

"You clearly were," she said, glaring. "You two acted like I wasn't even here!"

"I was simply getting to know Jay." Lucio turned to face Helena, quiet rage building in his eyes. "And find out how my daughter knows my brother's hookup."

Helena struggled to breathe under the weight of his stare. "What are you—"

"Her tattoo," he said. "Michael's got the other half of the set."

Lucio might as well have shot her dead with the way he was looking at her. She would certainly be better off, because whatever was going to come next was about to be hell on earth.

"Now, would you like to tell me how you and Jay *actually* met?"

12

Dylan

Helena stuffed her phone into her pocket, face growing hot despite the cool evening breeze. She had expected Lucio to blow her off for her birthday, but *Dylan*? That was Lucio twisting the damn knife. Dylan hadn't missed a single special occasion since they started hanging out. It was basically tradition at this point; she would spend her afternoon with Gideon, go home to get ready, then go to the Pink Port for dinner with Dylan, or, if the restaurant was closed or Quinn had the day off, they'd all get together and go see a movie. Sometimes, Lucio could be bothered to force his way into their plans. Other times, he couldn't. It never made a difference to her one way or another.

Whatever. She tugged at her ponytail, grateful to have her hair off her back. Her and Gideon's birthday was the one excuse a year she had to dress up in an actually fun outfit. And Jay had been right—the purple satin top Helena had borrowed from Quinn made her entire complexion seem...*brighter.* She didn't look so pasty. And the lipstick Jay had picked out was also a huge upgrade. Too bad it was going to just get wasted on dinner alone.

The train announced her stop, and she clamored off with the rest of the commuters. Quinn's place was on the lower east side, a few blocks away from their apartment. Helena would probably crash there; tomorrow was Saturday, meaning she could hang out with them most of the day, then again Sunday. It would be nice, getting a weekend away from Lucio.

The walk to the Pink Port was quick, but with each step, Helena felt her legs growing heavier. This was dumb. She should just go home. The whole reason she was coming to Quinn's was so she didn't have to be alone, but Quinn was going to be working, anyway.

Even still, she walked until she saw the neon sign illuminating the concrete steps that would lead into the restaurant. Some people came up, laughing and stumbling over themselves, earning glares from the patrons entering the higher-end "Silk Room."

They were just mad that their place didn't have the Michelin star that Quinn's did.

Helena took the stairs two at a time, greeted at the bottom by a steel door covered in graffiti and stickers. Her eyes quickly adjusted to the blacklight-only lighting in the small vestibule, the hostess's voice only slightly louder than the music.

"Miss, I do apologize, but unless you have a reservation, I'm afraid we'll have to turn you away tonight," Winter, the hostess, said. But Helena had heard it often enough to know that she was getting more pissed by the second.

The woman Winter was speaking to threw her hands up. "I'm *one* person! And besides, I can just sit at the bar. I'm just looking for—"

"Jay?" Helena called.

Jay turned around, squinting in the low lighting. Helena almost laughed; she would have figured that Jay would be used to lower lighting since she worked at Vision.

"Helena!" Jay said. "Hey, I was hoping I would see you here tonight."

"What're you doing here?" Helena took in Jay's outfit: a crop top that barely hid the lacy red bra she wore, and a mini-skirt. Helena almost wanted to ask if she was going to work after, but that seemed like a bad idea.

"You told me your sibling worked here." Jay jutted her thumb over her shoulder. "So I figured you'd come hang around here too, right?"

"I mean, I guess, but—" Helena shifted. "Why did you come by?"

Jay's grin was too wide. "I wanted to come hang, is that cool?"

Winter and Helena exchanged a glance, Winter's hand already on the phone. Helena shook her head. "Yeah, that's cool."

"Awesome." Jay spun around, resting her elbows on the host stand. "Table for two, then."

Winter pressed her lips into a thin, tight smile. "Wonderful. Follow me."

Jay motioned for Helena to go first, and they were led through a second door. Sound blasted as soon as it opened, a testament to the level of soundproofing that had gone into making sure the restaurant could function as it did. The tables were filled with patrons—some with interesting looking drinks, others with large and complicated plates of food, while bartenders who were dressed in leather and lace uniforms made a show of serving drinks; a perfect complement to the cage dancers at each end.

They reached a back room, which was separated only by a heavy black curtain, but was much more private. The music was dampened significantly, the intimately lit space a far cry from the colorful lighting outside.

Quinn kept this room for special events, and Helena's birthday obviously qualified as one of those events to them, at least. But she was grateful they had forgone the usual decorations. It was only her nineteenth—hardly a big deal.

Despite there being multiple other tables, only one was clearly set for guests. Another tradition of Quinn's—they always joked about giving Helena the "VIP" treatment, but she knew it had really been so she and Gideon could celebrate their birthday and not disrupt the paying customers. Even still, it had been nice while it lasted.

"This place is a lot different than what I expected." Jay took a seat at the table.

"What were you expecting?" Helena asked as she sat down as well.

"I don't know, like," Jay motioned around her. "Not a *sex* club."

"It's not a sex club. It's just got a lot of sex elements."

"So is being sex-obsessed a familial trait?"

Helena tilted her head. "What?"

"Nothing," Jay said, looking down at the table. "Is there a reason we don't have any menus?"

"Oh, yeah. Quinn's got a special menu picked out for tonight."

"Is that a usual thing?"

"Not really." Helena rubbed at her arms. "It's kind of my birthday."

"No shit!" Jay lit up, her smile absolutely contagious. "Happy birthday, kid. How old are you now?"

"Nineteen."

Jay whistled. "Nineteen, big deal. You can drink in Canada. *Legally.*"

Helena rolled her eyes, laughing breathlessly. "I'm not going all the way to Canada to drink."

"Gonna keep sneakin' into clubs, then?"

"No," Helena grumbled, then added under her breath, "maybe."

"Trust me, kid, worth the wait." Jay leaned back in her chair, taking in the room. "So, just you tonight?"

"Yeah. Usually my best friend will come with me, but they got suckered into working late with Lucio," Helena said, then bit her tongue. *Shit.*

"Who?" Jay asked.

Helena averted her eyes. "What about you? You're not working tonight?"

Jay put up a hand. "Back up, who's Lucio?"

"I meant Luke." *No! Why the hell did you do that?*

Jay narrowed her gaze. "Is Luke's name 'Lucio'?"

"I mean, sort of, but, it's not—"

"Then why the hell has he been telling me it's Luke?"

"Telling you?" It was Helena's turn to be suspicious. "You only met him once."

"Yeah but he introduced himself as Luke," Jay said. "If you're calling him Lucio—"

Helena breathed a sigh of relief as a server walked into the room. Alcohol was just what they needed. Not for her, of course, but for Jay. Maybe she would get drunk enough that she wouldn't remember the night at all, and Helena could go back to what she *should* be calling her father-figure around strangers.

Not that she wanted to.

Jay ordered a vodka tea, and Helena was grateful to avoid a crack about virgin whiskey and Cokes. She ordered herself a strawberry daiquiri—a sweet treat she only allowed herself on special occasions.

"Your sibling lets you drink?" Jay asked as the server left.

"No, Lucio would kill them if they did." Helena absently played with the silverware on the table. "It's non-alcoholic."

"How come you call him Lucio?"

GOD—

"Cause that's his name." Helena tried to shrug, but her shoulders were so tense that it probably looked more like a turtle trying to retreat back into its shell.

"Most people I know call their parents 'dad,' or 'mom.'" Jay leaned forward, holding her face in her hands. "Is it 'cause he adopted you?"

"No." Helena dug her fingers into the fabric of her jeans. Did Jay even have to ask? It seemed like a ridiculously obvious question. *Do you see him here? Did you hear him at the coffee shop? If I told you that the last time he told me he loved me was when I was sixteen, would that explain it?* "I just don't."

The server came back with their drinks, placing them on the table before disappearing again. Helena smiled softly at the little "Happy Birthday" flags that Brandi had clearly put in along with a huge chocolate covered strawberry. She pulled each one out and placed them on her napkin.

"Hey," Jay said as Helena went to take a sip. "Cheers."

"To what?" Helena asked, touching her glass to Jay's all the same.

"Your birthday, duh."

Helena smiled. "Thanks, Jay."

"Alright! Where's the birthday girl?" Quinn shouted as they threw the curtain open. They had traded out their usually disgusting chef's coat for a crisp, clean one, their hair was free of its bandana, falling in loose curls that framed their face. It took all of .02 seconds for Quinn to notice Jay sitting in the other seat.

Helena's blood immediately boiled. "Quinn—"

"Oh, *Helena*, you didn't tell me you were going to have a *guest*," Quinn said, pressing a hand to their chest as another server brought in the food cart behind them.

Jay's jaw was practically on the floor, and if Helena hadn't been worried she might have gotten *drooled* on, she would have shut it for her. "Hello..."

"Heya," Quinn grinned, holding out their hand for Jay to shake. "Quinn, Helena's sibling. Nice to finally get a chance to talk to you, Jay."

"Have we met before?" Jay asked, taking Quinn's hand.

Quinn kissed the back of hers. "We have, but you were a little distracted last time."

Helena thought she might actually vomit.

The server chuckled as they began to set down a plate of ceviche, and Helena wasted no time dipping her fork into the mix and picking out a huge shrimp.

"Well, I'm not distracted now," Jay said, batting her eyelashes.

"Wish I could say the same." Quinn leaned forward, their lips slightly parted as they moved closer to Jay.

Helena launched the shrimp at the side of Quinn's head. Both Jay and Quinn turned to look, Jay biting her lip to suppress her smile.

"That could have *blinded* me!" Quinn shouted.

"Oh shut up! Don't you have food to cook?" Helena dipped her fork back into the ceviche, popping some into her mouth.

"I've got time." Quinn glanced back at Jay, smirking. "Especially for someone as beautiful as this."

Helena lobbed another shrimp at them.

Quinn walked over and put her in a headlock. "Do you know how much that shit costs to make? Stop wasting food!"

"Stop flirting with Jay!" Helena tried to push them away as they tugged on her ponytail.

"I let you come eat at *my* restaurant for free *with* a guest, and you've got the balls to talk back to me?" Helena bit back a giggle as they lifted her up, wrapping an arm around her waist and turned her upside down with ease. "Too bad your skinny ass doesn't have enough meat for me to cook with, maybe I can use your bones to make a stock."

Helena and Jay laughed as Helena tried to wriggle out of Quinn's grasp. "You're an ass!"

"I am what I eat," Quinn said, putting Helena upside down in her chair.

"So, you're Quinn?" Jay asked, her laughter subsiding.

"The one and only. Favorite sibling, most talented chef, they/he, sex icon."

Helena righted herself, kicking in Quinn's direction as she did, but they dodged her long legs with ease. "Most annoying sibling ever to exist."

"And you two are blood related?" Jay's eyes flickered between them, and Helena could almost see the wheels turning in her mind.

"Yes, unfortunately," Quinn sighed, kissing the top of Helena's head. "God didn't want to have too much good in this world, so He unleashed this demon spawn upon it."

"Ass," Helena grumbled, pushing them away.

"Brat." Quinn grinned as they headed towards the curtain. "Enjoy your dinner, ladies. When you're ready for dessert, just let Rex know."

Helena stuck her tongue out at Quinn as they left, then refocused on the table. Quinn had gone all out, as they always did. Ceviche, oysters, salmon, and some kind of lobster salad were spread out in colorful plates across the table, all made to be enjoyed like finger foods. Quinn always liked to make her seafood for her birthday, since it was something they didn't get to enjoy growing up.

"Wow, they really know how to cook, huh?" Jay said, eyeing the plates.

"They've always been great at it." Helena picked a couple of items and loaded them onto her plate, before motioning for Jay to do the same. "But they've gotten really good in recent years."

"Are they your only sibling?"

Helena's hand hovered over her plate, the once delicious food in front of her suddenly looking a lot more like garbage.

Jay continued, seemingly unaware of Helena's composure shifting. "Luke mentioned having five kids, so—"

"Two," Helena bit out.

"What?"

"I have two siblings. One is Quinn, and the other is Gideon." Helena stabbed her fork into some of the salmon, hoping the taste of whatever seasonings Quinn had laid on there would distract her. But it didn't taste like anything.

"So, the other two are your *adopted* siblings?" Jay pressed.

"Gideon and Quinn are my only siblings." Helena willed herself to breathe evenly. This was her and Gideon's day, it was meant to be—who was she kidding? This day was going to be shit anyways. There wasn't going to be any way that this day would have worked out to be anything less than fine; none of her birthdays had been since Gideon. This one was just worse because Dylan wasn't here. He knew better than to ask prying questions.

Then again, Jay didn't really know the difference, yet.

"You're lucky."

Helena looked up, blinking back her tears.

Jay was serving herself some ceviche and lobster salad. "I'm an only child."

"I thought you said your parents wanted a boy," Helena sniffled.

"They did. But, they only ever had me." Jay huffed out a laugh. "I think they just didn't want to risk another disappointment."

"That's harsh."

"They weren't always the kindest people." Jay popped a piece of avocado into her mouth. "But I turned out alright."

"That's debatable."

"Hey! I could have been a lot worse!" Jay said, pointing her fork in Helena's direction. "I could have ended up a *nepo* baby."

"You're a sugar baby, is that really any different?" Helena's tone was teasing, but she could see something akin to pain flicker across Jay's face. *Shit.* "Sorry, I didn't mean to—"

"I'm not a sugar baby," Jay said, scooping lobster salad onto her fork. "Michael's my boyfriend."

Boyfriend. So it was what Helena had expected. "I thought he was a client, or your boss, or whatever?"

"Eh, client, boss, boyfriend." Jay shrugged. "Lines blur together at some point. I'm sure you get it, working with your dad and all."

"Yeah, I guess I do." Helena picked up an oyster, staring at it. Lucio had given them their first introduction to real seafood during a trip to the beach, and she loved oysters from there on out. She set it back down on her plate. "Can I ask you something?"

Jay hummed around the fork in her mouth. "Hm?"

"You didn't know it was my birthday. And I doubt you *chose* to come here." Helena pushed her food around her plate. "So, why are you here?"

Jay set her fork down, relaxing back in her seat. "I told you earlier I wanted to come hang with you."

"But, why?"

"Do I need a reason?"

"Kind of. Lucio chewed me out pretty bad when he found out that I was hanging around you in the first place."

"Why did he chew you out? Over the club thing?"

"Yeah," Helena lied. "He wasn't exactly thrilled over the whole situation of me hanging out with a stripper."

Jay's face soured. "You could be doing a lot worse. When I was your age I was working at the club. You were just sneaking in."

"Exactly!" Helena said. "I was just trying to find out about this freaking uncle that he's told me—" she finally registered Jay's comment, and scowled. "Rude."

"It's true, kid," Jay laughed. "And I still don't get why you care so much in the first place."

"About Michael?"

"Yeah."

Careful. "It's like I've said. Lucio never told me about him."

"So? I have family that I haven't seen in decades. You don't see me sneaking into strip clubs to find out about them," Jay said, adding some hot sauce to an oyster.

"I…" Helena rubbed her arms. "Well, you and I aren't the same person."

"We're not. But you're avoiding my question." Jay pointed her fork at Helena. "What do you want to know, and why do you want to know?"

Helena's lips thinned. "I guess, I'm just sick of secrets."

"You ever think that he's hiding things from you for a reason?"

"But why hide the fact that he had a brother? Why wouldn't he tell me that I have a whole freaking uncle out there?"

Jay said nothing, so Helena continued.

"He's always pushing this agenda that family's so important, yet he's got a brother he hasn't spoken to in a freaking *decade*? I've lived with him for six years, but I feel like I still barely know him. And yet he knows everything about me—or, thinks he does. And then he holds it all over me and treats me like a child. Meanwhile, I'm supposed to be training to become a big lawyer like him. I'm tired of it! Why should I always be the one who has to be so open and honest with him when he's *never* given me that same energy back?"

"Helena," Jay said, drawing Helena's eyes to her. "I think this is one time you need to let it go."

Helena's brows shot up. "What? You *cannot* be serious! Weren't you the one telling me that Michael lied to you, too? You're fine with your boyfriend hiding something *that* big from you? You've been together *how* long?"

"If there's anything that I've learned," Jay said, her voice careful and measured. "It's that blood means fuck all."

Helena reeled back. *"What?"*

"I haven't spoken to my parents in," Jay paused, "almost eight years. And I don't plan to ever again."

"But...why?"

"Because they stood between me and what I wanted," Jay said. "Maybe that's what happened between Michael and Luke."

Helena mulled the idea over in her mind. But it still didn't make sense. Why wouldn't Lucio just *tell* her that? Why was he so desperate to cut Michael out of his life completely, pretend like he didn't exist? And why did it seem like Michael was all too happy to do the exact same thing?

"I don't know..." Helena stirred her drink, which had begun to separate.

"Kid," Jay started. "I meant what I said before. Michael's not the type of guy you want to get caught up with."

"But you're *dating* him."

"Exactly." Jay's nails tapped the table. "So you should listen to me. Stop snooping around before someone gets hurt."

Helena scowled. "No one's going to get hurt."

"Can you promise that?" Jay asked, her brows raised.

Helena opened her mouth to speak, but stopped herself. Because if there was anything *she* had learned, it was not to make promises that she couldn't keep.

"I'm just trying to look out for you," Jay said. "Now eat."

They spent the rest of the meal enjoying the food and swapping stories of birthdays past. Helena recalled hers and Gideon's thirteenth fondly: it had been their first one with Lucio, who had gone all out trying to make it the most special occasion he possibly could. He had a huge itinerary planned for the entire day in the city, including museums, a trip to Coney Island, ending with a Broadway show. But Quinn had ended up stepping on a jellyfish at the beach, and they had to stay home for the show. Helena had felt bad leaving them behind, but she enjoyed only having to get to share Gideon with one other person, instead of two.

And Lucio had made it all the better by letting them sit in front of him, rather than with him in the private suite. Her and Gideon had cracked jokes about being Edwardian play-goers, putting on God awful accents the entire time.

And Lucio had just laughed. He used to laugh a lot, before everything.

"My favorite was my twenty-first," Jay said, wiping carefully at her mouth. "My best friend and I went barhopping. People kept buying us drinks, so we got absolutely *smashed* at the first bar. It was so bad." Her face lit up with a smile. "We got kicked out when I tried to dance on a bar."

"You did *not*," Helnea gasped.

"We barely made it home," Jay laughed, wiping tears out of her eyes at the memory. "I had to call my boyfriend to pick us up and he was so pissed. Alice threw up in the backseat of his car. We both felt like shit the next day and went to this little diner up in Harlem for breakfast. Pancakes as big as your face, and bacon that's just," she gestured a kiss with her hand.

"I don't know if I could do anything like that for my twenty-first," Helena said. "I've never drank like that before."

"Well, when you turn twenty-one, I'll take you out." Jay flashed her pretty smile. "I promise, I'll be sober as a stone."

"Yeah, we'll see." The thought of getting to spend more time with Jay was nice, but Helena wasn't about to get her hopes up. This whole thing wasn't going to last, anyways. "Are you ready for dessert?"

Jay groaned, placing her hands on her stomach. "I think I can make some room. But only if Quinn and I get to sing you 'Happy Birthday'."

Helena covered her face. "It doesn't matter what I say, does it?"

"Not at all!" Quinn shouted as they burst through the curtain, then launched into the loudest and possibly worst rendition of "Happy Birthday" to ever be sung in history.

Jay joined in, as did half the staff, and Helena sunk lower into her chair as a cake was placed in front of her. It was the same one every year: pink and white, covered in little rosettes. A one and a nine candle had been stuck in it, flickering faintly as the singing mercifully ended.

"Make a wish, birthday girl!" Quinn said, placing their hands on her shoulders.

She looked up at them, her expression serious as she said, "I want a new sibling."

Quinn frowned down at her. "Now it'll never come true. You've just doomed us forever."

"Whatever. Not like any of our wishes come true anyway," she said, and blew out her candles.

"Oh, boo! No killing the vibe on your birthday!" Jay dipped her finger in the frosting and smeared it on her nose.

"Shut up!" Helena laughed, wiping the frosting off with her napkin. "I can do whatever I want!"

"Keep telling yourself that, kid." Jay smiled. "Happy birthday."

13

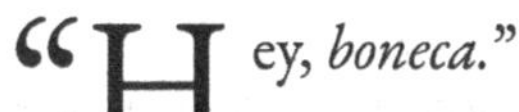

"Hey, *boneca*."

The voice was wrong. The accent missing, the sultry ring that Jay hated to admit that she craved absent. But the visceral reaction was still immediate.

Jay turned, seething as she set her eyes on Penelope, one of the other dancers, who was cowering in fear at what Jay assumed was the murderous look written on her face. "The fuck did you just call me?"

"Damn, chill!" Penelope put up her hands in mock surrender, her blue eyes wide with fear. "That's what the clients started calling, isn't it?"

Jay relaxed, but only slightly. "Who told you that?"

"That one guy, you know..." Penelope smirked as she made a lewd motion with her hands. "Tall, dark, and fuckable?"

That mother fucker. It had been a solid month since she had last seen Lucio at the coffee shop, but her anger hadn't dissipated from him choosing to miss Helena's birthday two weeks ago. And now he had the nerve to show his damn face around here?

She was going to enjoy making him regret it. "Where is he?"

Penelope looked her up and down. "If I tell you, are you going to kill him?"

"Pen—"

"All I'm saying is if you don't want him, let me take him!"

Jay growled, storming off onto the main floor and scanning for that frustratingly gorgeous combination of green eyes and ochre skin.

Nothing.

She went to the alcoves next, ignoring the shouts of surprise and aggravation as she tore open one curtain after another. And with each passing moment, she felt her anger rising. He was playing with her. Making her chase his dumb ass around the fucking club. Knowing him, he was watching her from some corner, a stupidly handsome grin on that smug face of his. She couldn't wait to knock his lights out.

There was only one other place left to look: the champagne room. It could be reserved ahead of time, or on demand. Jay should have suspected he'd be there.

I'm a private person.

Yeah, she'd see how private he was when she got his ass thrown out. Men. They always thought they could do whatever the hell they wanted, and for what? Because he could flaunt a little cash her way and make her feel special? She didn't need to feel special. What she *needed* was to get Lucio's ass out of the damn club before she did something stupid. She liked this job—and Michael and Javier would certainly have something to say about her assaulting a customer.

Jay threw open the door to the champagne room, the music and vibe completely different from out on the floor. It was quieter, allowing for more intimate conversation. Unlike the other rooms, the walls were a gorgeous purple, highlighted by the wall sconces that lit the room. No touch of the neon and colored lights from the main floor.

And also, no *Lucio*.

"Good. Must've gotten his sorry ass out of here before—*Jesus!*" Jay screamed at the sight of Lucio standing behind her.

His hand lifted, but he stopped midway. "Sorry, didn't mean to scare you."

"Yeah, I find that one hard to believe," Jay pressed her hand to her chest, trying to steady her heartbeat. "What the fuck are you doing here?"

"I'm here for our appointment," Lucio said. He was dressed casually again, only a black tee shirt and jeans. His wrist was free of a watch, and Jay could clearly see the "Papai" tattoo on his wrist. He had a lot of fucking nerve showing that thing off.

Jay scoffed, crossing her arms over her chest. "I told you to fuck off."

Lucio smiled in that way that made her knees feel weak. "And I told you that I didn't want to stay away."

She should have called security. She should have sat back and helped herself to the champagne chilling in the corner while Lucio got his ass absolutely handed to him. But that would be letting him get off easily.

No. Jay had a much better idea.

"Fine." She sneered. "You want to tell your wife, or would you rather I call her?"

He toed the dark marble tile with his shoe, not meeting Jay's eyes. "If you can get a hold of her, let me know."

"I forgot, kind of hard to do when she's dead, right?"

The look on Lucio's face was absolutely priceless. A mixture of shock and a touch of pain, as if his heart was still breaking inside his chest. "How did you—"

"Your daughter told me," Jay snarled. "At her birthday that *you* couldn't be bothered to make it to, *Lucio.*"

Lucio rolled his tongue over his teeth. "I was working."

"Heard that one before." Jay pointed a finger as she walked closer to him. "You know, you're a real piece of shit for leaving her high and dry like that. What kind of father just doesn't show up to his daughter's birthday? And then, comes to a fucking strip club, wearing his wedding band, when he *could* be home spending time with his family?"

"Are you defending Helena, or getting out some of your own pent up anger here?" he asked, shoving his hands into his pockets. The wedding ring still stuck out, mocking her.

Jay sneered, finally chest to chest with him. In her heels she was *almost* taller than him. It gave her just enough height to look him in the eye and feel like she could still be looking down at him. "Fuck off. You don't know shit about me. Go home and spend some time with your kids."

"She didn't want me there."

Jay's jaw fell open. "You have to be joking."

He had already lied to her about everything else. And now he was trying to lie to her about this, too? Jay wasn't stupid. She had seen enough people who clearly needed a parental figure and didn't have one in their life. She knew what it did to people. And Helena was still young enough that that could change.

"Helena doesn't like to spend her birthday with me. It's," he rubbed the back of his neck, "a rough subject."

"Why? Because she knows that you put your fucking job over her?"

Lucio winced. Because it was true—from what Jay had heard, from what she had seen, there was clearly a hierarchy. He was one of those men who tried to say they were noble because they worked long hours to "support their family," and then turned around and ignored every other aspect. They put neglect in a pretty little bow and called it the gift of providing.

"Because her twin brother died. And she blames me for it."

Jay's arms, still across her chest, slackened, and she had to correct it before Lucio thought maybe this was her showing him pity. Because Helena had said she had two siblings, and Lucio said he had five kids—

"Hold on." Jay pressed her hand to her forehead, closing her eyes, as if somehow that would make all the pieces swirling in her head fall into place. "Why does she blame you?"

"It's a long story," Lucio said. Jay opened her eyes, watching as he struggled to meet her gaze, his fingers playing with that damn wedding band of his.

"Then you'd better talk quick, 'cause you're paying for this room by the hour." She pointed to the couch. "Sit."

He did. Lucio rested his elbows on his knees, locked in a staring match with the floor. The only reason she was doing this was for Helena. Jay wanted to make sure this man understood that Helena *needed* him, and that after this, they were done. Jay didn't care if she ever saw him again. She didn't want to.

Lucio didn't look up as she settled into the seat next to him. "Your wife and Gideon died at the same time?"

"No." He finally met her eyes. There was a slight sheen to them. He pressed his lips together, breathing in before he spoke again. "I lost my wife, and two of my kids, first. Then Gideon, a few years later."

Jay's heart leapt into her throat. Christ. She had lost people before, sure, but most of them were back in Puerto Rico, or had moved out of state. She hadn't seen a lot of her family growing up outside of mom and dad. And even now, she wouldn't care too much if they dropped dead.

And people lost spouses all the time. Yes, it was painful, but people found ways to get over it. Most often, they let themselves get lost between the legs of someone else. Jay had worked with plenty of widowers, and the occasional widow. People who just needed to pretend like there was someone who was happy to see them, who wouldn't remind them that there was a cold and empty bed waiting for them back home.

But *kids*—kids were different. Parents weren't supposed to bury their children. There was no remedy for that. Only people who tried to come in and dull the ache with her only to suddenly say "She would be your age now" or "you remind me of her" and "I'm sorry I just can't do this". Tears that never fully dried and hearts that never fully mended.

"I'm so sorry," she muttered, her hand searching for his on instinct.

He took it easily, using the other one to rub at his eyes. "Not your fault."

"No, but," she squeezed his hand, as if that would somehow ease the ache that was likely blooming throughout his chest, "that's a lot to lose."

"Gideon got sick a few years after I adopted the kids. Brain cancer. Stage four by the time we found out. There was nothing we could do." Lucio swallowed. "But, she blames me for not fighting for more. For better treatments, better solutions."

Fuck, it just kept getting worse. Jay pressed her lips into a thin line. "She can't hold that over you. When it's that bad, it's..."

He shrugged. "She needed someone to be angry at. So I let her be angry at me."

Jay felt herself softening. She might not have liked her dad, but that was for completely different reasons. Her father had been selfish and cruel; Lucio was literally acting as a martyr for his daughter. "And what about your boys?"

"Car accident."

Jay gasped. "Christ—"

"That one was actually my fault." Lucio squeezed her hand tightly. "She and I had gotten into an argument, she had packed up her stuff and the kids to go stay at her mother's." He quickly swiped away a tear that had begun to roll down his cheek. "I didn't stop her."

"Lucio..." Jay sat with everything that he had told her, still squeezing his hand tightly. She resisted the urge to hug him, even their hands touching was too much, too familiar, but Jay couldn't let go now, not when Lucio was cracking apart in front of her.

"I'm sorry." He sniffled, attempting to smile. "I shouldn't have just dumped all that on you like that."

"Don't be sorry." Jay shook her head. "Have you talked to anyone about this?"

"Yeah, I uh." He wiped at his eyes again. "I did therapy for a little while, after my first family died, and then we did it again after Gideon died."

"And?"

"And you can see what good it did us." He chuckled, but it was empty of humor.

"So what are you going to do about it now?"

Lucio looked at her, confused. "What?"

"Helena," Jay said pointedly. "You're letting her call the shots on what your relationship is. And you're cool with that?"

"I mean," Lucio rubbed at his leg. "It is what it is. Any time I've tried talking to her, it just ends up with her screaming at me that it's all my fault in the end anyways. She doesn't listen to me."

Jay breathed in deep. She knew all about shitty parental relationships. She had decided to go no contact with her family the day she turned eighteen, but they had problems before that, much different from what Helena had been going through. Helena had a dad that cared about her, wanted what was best for her. Jay's parents had tried to separate her from Colt, the love of her life, saying that he was only going to ruin her, that she was throwing her life away for some man. They didn't see what she saw, that he was willing to give her the world if she asked for it.

And she only needed to give a little back in return.

"Do you want me to talk to her?" Jay offered, rubbing her thumb over the back of Lucio's hand.

He smirked. "Helena's a stubborn little thing. You sure you can handle her?"

"I was a teenage girl, not too long ago," Jay said. "I think I can relate."

"Yeah, maybe you can," he said, running a hand through his dark hair. He made a move like he was going to get up, but still held onto her hand. "I should—"

"Stay."

Lucio settled back into the couch, watching Jay carefully. "I thought I should go home and talk to my daughter."

"If you try and go home to talk to her now, it's not going to go how you want it to." Jay moved to straddle him, releasing his hand to lay her palms flat on his chest. "We need to leave you off on a good note."

Watching Lucio's pupils blow out might have been the sexiest thing Jay had ever seen in her life.

"Do we now?" he asked, his voice taking on a gravely sound as she settled further into his lap.

"Mhm." Jay leaned down, brushing her lips against his cheek. "Now relax, and let me do what I do best."

And she would. She would work her magic, let him forget about who he was, what the world outside was like for him, just for a while. Lucio deserved it. She couldn't take the burden off his shoulders completely, but if she could let him focus the pressure somewhere else. If only for a moment, she could leave him better than she found him. Jay rolled her hips into his, relishing in the groan he probably didn't mean to let her hear. His hands lifted, ghosting her waist.

"Remember," she teased, grabbing his wrists. "No touching. Now be a good boy and keep these," she placed his arms spread eagle on the back of the couch, "right here for me."

"Yes, ma'am," Lucio mumbled.

Jay giggled, letting her chest brush his, wondering if he could feel the way her heart was racing, if his was doing the same. She let her hair fall around them, his green eyes capturing hers. Christ, they were haunting, like a forest she could get lost in. But she wasn't sure she would ever want to be found.

Focus, Jay, she reminded herself. She was here to make *him* feel good, not think about how drop dead gorgeous he was. How his cheekbones were so perfect, just sharp enough to give him the right amount of definition, his jaw line etched from stone, his nose a gentle slope than she wanted just *so* badly to run her finger along.

It was hard to believe he and Michael were brothers—they looked so wildly different. Michael's features were soft, not in a way that made him look young, but just more...*gentle*. Lucio had a face built for the court room.

Enough. Jay dipped low, positioning herself between his legs and pushing them further apart. Lucio's breath audibly hitched.

"That's it," she said, trying to keep her own voice steady as she spoke. "Focus on me." She placed her hands on his knees, and pulled herself up, letting her breasts graze his pants.

"Kind of impossible not to," he grunted, his face turning to the ceiling.

"Eyes on me, Lucio."

He looked back down at her, and *fuck*, she would have gladly stayed down there all day if she could. His chest rising and falling, his cock straining against his pants, like he was going to snap at any moment and take her the way she had dreamed he would. "I'd prefer to have you back up here."

Jay hummed. "You want me close?"

"Fuck," he muttered. "I can't say what I want."

"Why can't you?" She brought herself back up, settling into his lap. "Attorney-client privilege, remember?"

His lips parted, and his cock twitched beneath her, sending a shiver up her spine. It took all of her power not to grind deeper against him, to give into that need that was so badly building between her own legs. Normally, she was able to turn this part of her off, let herself go anywhere else but here. But with Lucio, there was nowhere else she wanted to be. It took all of her not to let her mind wander off to where she *really* wanted it to go.

Lucio's reply came out strangled. "What I want is a lot more than you're willing to give."

Jay crossed her arms over her chest, and fingering the hem of her top, lifted it painfully slow, her nipples peaking at the feel of the chilly air around her. "Try me."

Lucio's fingers dug into the fabric of the couch, his jaw struggling to stay attached as it fell open. "Fuck, Jay..."

Watching him react this way was everything. Lucio looked at her like she was the first woman he ever saw, and was the last one he ever would. He looked at her like she was *real*. Like he would touch her and it would be soft and warm and gentle caresses that made her skin tingle. But she could touch him all she wanted. She leaned back to give him a full view of her as she ran her hand down his chest, lingering on his stomach.

"Jay, I—"

She sat back up, rolling her hips into his. And oh fuck did it feel so good to feel him between her legs, it took everything in her not to whimper, to say fuck it all and give in because she knew it would feel so—

"Fuck, I—I need you to stop."

Jay snapped back, immediately moving off his lap. "Are you okay?"

Lucio sat up, his elbows resting on his knees and his hands in his hair. His back rose and fell, breathing unsteady as he spoke quickly in Portuguese, too low for her to catch anything.

Jay's stomach flipped. *Fuck.* She'd gone too far—Michael always acted this way when he was pissed at her, and she felt herself shrinking back away from Lucio, steeling herself for the onslaught of insults and criticism he was for sure thinking of.

"If you stayed on me one more minute, I would have—" He took a breath, before getting up and going to the bottle of champagne. He tore off the foil, and uncorked it, not bothering to be gentle with it. Foam rose over the rim, soaking his hand in white. He brought it to his lips, sucking the dripping liquid before it could fall, and his tongue lapping up what his lips couldn't catch.

Jay had to rub her legs together to distract herself from the image. "Would have..."

"I would have violated our little agreement," Lucio said, pouring a heavy glass of champagne.

"Agreement?"

"'Dancer to client,' 'therapist to client'..." He poured a second glass and turned to her. "Take your pick."

Jay crossed her arms over her chest, heat rising to her cheeks. "I'm sorry."

"Jesus Christ, don't be. It's my fault." He brought the glasses back to the couch, handing one to her. "As embarrassing as it is to admit, I don't find myself in these situations very often."

"What, with a stripper?" Jay asked as she sipped at her champagne. At least if she drank she would have an excuse for why she felt so flushed.

"With a woman as gorgeous as yourself having total control over me." Lucio brought the glass to his mouth, mumbling, "It was...different."

"You seemed to do pretty fine with it," Jay said, still not looking at him.

"I never said I didn't like it." Lucio sat down beside her, pressing the sweating glass to his brow. It did nothing to hide that expression Jay had seen so many times before. "Just that it was different."

Jay's arm relaxed from her front, but she kept herself covered.

Lucio reached down to get her top. "I'm sorry. I didn't mean to scare you."

"You didn't scare me," Jay said as she put her top back on.

"You sure? You flinched pretty hard back there when I asked you to stop."

"Oh." Jay took a swig of champagne. "Yeah."

"You want to talk about that?"

"Nothing to talk about."

His lips twitched. "You're cute when you try to lie."

"Too bad I can't say the same about you," Jay teased.

"When did I lie to you?"

"Your name? Having a wife?" Jay raised her brows. "Being my boyfriend's brother?"

"Luke is my name, I did have a wife," Lucio leaned in, "and I didn't know you were my brother's girlfriend until right this moment."

"You're so full of shit."

"I mean it." Lucio lowered his glass to rest in between them. "Michael doesn't usually put a label on these things."

"What's the story with you two, anyways?" Jay asked, rubbing absently at her shoulder. She knew it was useless to try and ask Michael. She had to guess that there was a reason why he hadn't mentioned Lucio before, and if she told him that his estranged brother was getting a pretty hot and heavy lap dance from her, she had to guess it wouldn't help anything.

"We don't exactly have the best relationship," Lucio said. "Lots of bad blood."

"Over a woman?" she guessed. That's how these things usually went, anyways. It was always two men thinking with their *heads* rather than their heads.

Lucio grinned. "You really don't miss, do you?"

"Told you I'm observant." Jay leaned in closer, her lips twitching. "You men are so easy to read."

"Are we?" he asked, matching her energy. "Then what am I thinking?"

She knew exactly what he was thinking. But she didn't want to admit it to herself. Because somehow, saying that she knew how he wanted to touch her, how he would be willing to do anything for just a—

"—go in there!" A woman's voice came crashing through as the door flew open, and the two of them looked up to see Colt standing in the doorway.

"Colt! Jesus Christ, what are you doing?" Jay scrambled to shield Lucio. "I'm with a client!"

Colt ignored her, looking past her and straight at Lucio. He crossed the room, his face growing red. "You better the fuck out of here before I take you out myself."

"Colt, stop!" Jay pressed her hands against his chest, blocking him from going any further.

What the hell was his problem? He *never* busted in on her when she was with someone—that was a privilege reserved only for Michael. *Michael.* Was he with Colt? Did he send him in ahead to get Lucio out? She tried to look over Colt's shoulder, but Lucio's voice stopped her.

"Relax, boneca." She looked behind her to see his eyes locked on Colt. "I'm not afraid of my brother's lap dog."

"Lap dog? Fuck you!" Colt spat, and he stepped forward despite Jay being in front of him. "You're the one out here going after your brother's scraps."

Jay flinched. "Colt—"

"Move, Angel." He didn't even look at her.

"Colt, enough," she said, trying to hide the wavering in her voice. "He's a client."

Colt's lips pulled back in an ugly snarl. "Is that what he told you?"

"Careful, Colton," Lucio said. "Don't want to let your 'daddy' know you've got a big mouth."

Colt shoved Jay to the side, and she barely caught herself on the couch. Out of the corner of her eye, she could see Colt swinging at Lucio. *"Don't!"*

The next thing she knew, Colt was on the ground, holding the side of his face.

Lucio loomed over him. "You don't put your hands on her. Ever."

"Fuck you. She's not your fucking problem," Colt said, struggling to get up.

Lucio shoved his foot into Colt's chest, pinning him to the ground. "She is when you start touching her."

"Lucio, let him get up," Jay said, but her voice didn't hold the authority she wished it had. "He didn't mean it, it's fine."

"Didn't mean it?" Lucio turned to look at her, his face a mixture of shock and fury. "He just shoved you, and he didn't mean it?"

It was enough of a distraction for Colt to push Lucio's foot off him, and stand up. But instead of throwing another punch, or doing anything that Jay had dreaded him doing to Lucio, Colt glared at her, his finger raised in warning. "Get out."

"Colt, let me just get security, and they'll—"

"Like hell you will," he snapped. "You think I can't fucking handle this?"

"No, that's not what—"

"No, it absolutely is! You think I can't protect you? Who took out that piece of shit who was harassing you the other day when you were stupid enough to go outside without protection?"

A lump formed in Jay's throat. "I—"

"Or are you just spreading your legs for anyone who's got a couple fucking bands in their pocket these days?" Colt moved around Lucio, continuing to yell. Jay tried to back away, but she was stuck by the couch, and Colt kept closing in on her. *Nowhere to go*. "I'm sure Michael would love to know that you're whoring yourself out to—"

Lucio's arm was around Colt's neck in a second. "Enough."

Colt slapped Lucio's arm, but he ignored it, kicking out the back of Colt's knees instead and dropping him to the ground.

"Stop!" Jay cried, her hands flying to her mouth. "You're going to hurt him!"

"He'd be lucky if that's all I did," Lucio grumbled, not letting go of Colt's neck. The veins in his forearm bulged a little with his tightening grip. "Are you going to apologize?"

Colt's eyes started to flutter closed.

Before Jay knew what she was doing, her hand was on the bottle of champagne, smashing it against the table, champagne pouring over her hand. The alcohol burned as it seeped into the small cuts she got from the broken glass, but she ignored it. She stepped forward, her teeth clenched so tight she might break a tooth. "Let. Him. Go."

Lucio raised his brows. "Look at you. You do this for all the men who treat you like garbage?"

Jay's grip tightened. "You fucking hear me?"

Lucio grunted, but released Colt. He gasped for air as he fell to the floor, landing on the ground with a hard thud. Jay moved to his side, reaching for him with her free hand. "Are you okay?"

He slapped her away as he got up to all fours. Jay remained where she was by his side, ignoring the sting of rejection. He gasped again, looking up at Lucio. "That was a dirty fucking move."

Lucio shrugged. "You'll live."

"Fuck you," Jay spat, resting her hand on Colt's shoulder. He didn't shrug it off, but she could still feel the way his muscles tensed under her touch. "Get the hell out."

"And leave you here alone with him?" Lucio shook his head. "You go first."

Jay scoffed. "Are you actually insane? You think I'm going to leave you here after you just attacked my—"

Colt shot her a look that chilled her blood. "Leave. Now. I can handle this."

"You clearly can't!" Jay gestured with the bottle in Lucio's direction. "He just fucking sucker punched you and then nearly choked you out, come—"

Colt shot up to his knees, grabbing the wrist that was holding the bottle so hard she dropped it. It shattered against the floor, broken glass gathering near them. "Go."

"Hands off, Colton," Lucio warned, and Colt's grip released a second later. "Don't worry, boneca. As long as he behaves, I won't hurt him."

Jay glared up at Lucio, rubbing her wrist. "You're full of shit. How do I know you're not going to—"

Colt stood, forcing Jay back on her haunches. His hazel eyes were almost black as he looked down on her. "Leave or I'll tell Michael."

Jay shrank back, glancing between Colt and Lucio. Lucio's face was a perfect mask of calm as he continued to watch Colt, his body tense as if ready to pounce on him if he tried to touch her again.

"You won't hurt him?"

Lucio looked at Jay, his mask slipping, if only for a second. "As long as you go, no."

Jay brought herself up, the adrenaline beginning to wear off. Every part of her screamed to stay, that there was no reason for her to trust Lucio. But she wasn't sure she could fully trust Colt, either.

She walked over to the door, casting one glance back at the two of them. Colt was looking at the ground, but Lucio's green eyes were pinned on her.

He winked. "Until next time."

14

J ay wasn't used to getting calls from Michael inviting her to his office. Actually, in all the years they'd been together, she couldn't remember a single moment where he'd welcomed her into his space, outside of his bedroom. The one place she was useful, apparently.

The huge building towered above her, windows covering every possible inch and reflecting the early afternoon sunlight. She had to blink a few times to clear the spots in her eyes. It was a standard building, one that held a multitude of companies; it took her a second to find Michael's. Twentieth floor. Of course. Michael had a weird thing about being high up.

A receptionist greeted her from where he sat behind a massive desk, covered in the latest tech.

"Hi, I'm here to see Mr. Silva?" Jay said, pulling her purse closer to herself.

"Yes! You must be Jay," the man said brightly. "Mr. Silva is just finishing up a meeting, but asked that I bring you to his office. Follow me."

The office itself felt like a typical corporate space that was trying too hard to be cozy. The windows let in a lot of natural light, but the steel gray carpet and white walls littered with random pieces of art and motivational posters made it clear it was still a place where dreams went to die. There were too many desks and tables, spread out in a way that she had to guess was strategic, but just felt cluttered to her. Jay glanced down at her lavender midi dress, and wished she would have chosen something more appropriate. She stuck out like a sore thumb amongst the suits and blouses of grays, whites, and blues.

She spotted Colt, who was sitting on the edge of a desk and giving that all-too-gorgeous smile of his. She couldn't see exactly who he was talking to, but she felt a slight pang of jealousy for whoever it was. He looked a lot better than he had two days ago, but the bruise across his cheek was still clear as day. Jay snorted. She never understood what the point of fighting was, especially when it meant that both you and the other guy looked like shit afterward.

"Mr. Silva will be right with you," the young man said, opening the door to Michael's office.

Jay nodded politely, walking in.

The office was large, made to appear larger from the windows all along the back wall. It gave a perfect view of the city. Two modern couches sat in the middle of the room, a glass coffee table in between them.

The walls were standard, covered with art that Michael himself had curated—she recognized a few of the pieces—all tasteful and using only a few colors. He had his own drink station near his desk, which was a gorgeous dark red wood. Jay wondered how many interns Michael had bent over it, but shook the thought from her mind, something else catching her attention.

A notebook, small and thin, placed on the middle of his desk. The aged, light brown leather was soft as she ran her fingers over it. She toyed with the string that bound it closed, curious, but the door opened, interrupting her before she could pry further.

"Hey, you must be Jay."

Jay turned, smiling as Michael walked into the room and closed the office door behind him. He was still dressed up, a light gray suit complementing his fair skin and deep blue eyes. His stubble was darker, giving his usually soft features a more mature edge. She wondered if Michael let himself get tan enough, if he'd look more like Lucio. "And you must be Mr. Silva."

"Please, my father is Mr. Silva." Michael grinned as he came in further, meeting her in the middle of the room. "Call me Michael." He motioned for her to sit on one of the couches. "Would you like a drink?"

Jay sat. "Sure, you know me."

Michael nodded. "Vodka or gin?"

"Vodka, please." She didn't care that it was barely noon; she needed a drink if she was going to ask what she was going to. "You know we've been together almost six years and I've never seen your office?"

"Really?" Michael said, finishing their drinks. "I swore you and I have had at least a couple times here."

She shook her head. "No, baby, I've never been here."

Michael grunted, muttering something beneath his breath. A nasty habit the brothers shared, apparently. "Well, either way you're here now. What do you think?"

"It's nice, seeing where you work," Jay said. "I feel like I'm getting to see a side of you that I don't know about."

He smiled as he walked back over with their drinks. "You know everything about me, anjo."

"Oh come on." She took hers from him. He settled into the couch next to her, and she closed the distance between them. "You're telling me there's *no* secrets between us? I know everything about you?"

Michael's smile started to drop. "Is there something you want to talk about?"

"No, baby," Jay said. "I just like feeling close to you. Sometimes I feel like there's more to you that you're hiding."

He leaned away from her, the cords in his neck tightening. "I'm not hiding anything from you."

"Of course not," she laughed weakly. "I'm sorry, I was just being silly."

Michael's lip pulled at a snarl, but appeared to take that as enough of an admonishment. "I wanted to talk to you about Vision."

Another sip, this one much bigger. "What about it? If you're worried about that guy, he hasn't been back since you handled him."

"What guy?"

"Pitt? You know, the one who..." Jay motioned to her stomach. The cut had long since healed, not even leaving a scar like she had worried that it would. At least, not a physical one. She had started carrying her pepper spray in her hand as she left the club, and part of her sometimes hoped Helena would pop up out of nowhere. Then again, Jay didn't exactly want Helena putting herself in that kind of situation, either.

"Oh, him? Yeah, he's not going to be coming back." Michael waved his hand dismissively, taking a long sip of his drink. He rested his arm around the back of the couch, the storm in his eyes brewing. "I heard there was a pretty serious incident involving Colt and one of your...clients."

"Oh..." Jay gripped the stem of her glass so tight she thought it might snap. "Yeah."

"He come around a lot?" Michael pretended to be interested in his drink, but Jay knew better. She could tell when he was watching her, waiting for her to slip up. She had learned a while ago that Michael would look for the usual tells—a twitch of the lip, a tapping of the fingers. So she practiced, working them into her everyday habits, leave him guessing what was a truth and what was a lie. Soon enough, he accepted everything she said.

"He might have. The guys all start to look the same after a while." Jay leaned in close, her lips parted as she went in for a kiss. "And none of them get my attention like you can."

Michael took another sip from his drink instead. "Well, either way. I know Colt handled him."

She resisted the urge to roll her eyes. Of fucking course he said he won; Colt *always* won. He never apologized, never tried to make it up to her. Because he was always right. Just like Michael.

"And it got me thinking." He reached up and twirled a strand of Jay's hair around his finger. "I think it's time you moved on from Vision."

Michael was obviously kidding. He had to be. Jay had worked at Vision for as long as she had known him. He liked keeping her there, he said, because he always knew where to find her. Really, it was probably that he liked getting to see all the men fawn over her, and thinking she was still coming home with him instead. Which she did, most nights, if Colt wasn't there first.

But, if she didn't work at Vision, then what? Jay had some money saved up. Enough to let her buy herself small gifts: a new purse, a new pair of shoes. But if Michael became her only source of income, that money would need to be for emergencies. It would mean if she wanted something, it would have to be through him.

"But, why? Because of some guy?" Jay tried to smile. "It was nothing, baby, I promise."

"It wasn't nothing." The finger twirling her hair tugged, and she winced. "I know that guy, Jay. He's a snake. And once he sinks his teeth into you, you won't even know you're dying until it's too Goddamn late."

She reached up to hold Michael's hand, hoping it would be enough to trigger him to know he was hurting her. Apparently, it wasn't. His hold remained tight around the lock of hair. "Okay, baby, I get it. But..."

The finger loosened. "But what?"

Jay swallowed, weighing out her words carefully. "I don't want to be a *burden*."

Michael's eyes softened, his hand shifting to cup her face. "Anjo, you're *never* a burden. You know that whatever you want, you get, because you're my favorite."

Jay closed her eyes as his thumb caressed her cheek. His palms were soft, lacking calluses that she had been dreaming about. "And you're mine."

"What if you came to work here?" Michael asked, lifting her face to draw her attention.

Christ, he was throwing her all kinds of curve balls.

"I just had to fire my last secretary," he said. "She was constantly fucking up. Couldn't keep a single thing about me straight. But you? You know me better than anyone."

Jay bit her tongue, nearly drawing blood. *One cage for another, what did you expect?* "So you want me to..."

"Be my new secretary. It would be easy work. Schedule meetings, coffee runs, take notes." Michael chuckled. "Nothing complicated."

Nothing that would let her actually *help* in a way that mattered. She would still be his bitch, still beneath his thumb, worse now, even. She would be at his beck and call, and he'd try to domesticate her even more than he already was. Toting her to and from work like an accessory. More nights at his place, more mornings stuck with his needs.

"Of course, baby, that sounds great," Jay said, putting on her best smile. She leaned in to kiss him, but he pulled away.

"There's one little complication."

"Which is?"

"People here can't know we're dating."

Jay huffed out a laugh. "Doesn't half your male staff already know?"

"No, they don't." Michael set his drink down on the table. "They just think you're a stripper who works really hard for tips. And they also know that what happens at Vision, stays there."

She swallowed down the sting with a sip of martini. "Got it."

"And besides, the women here can be so bitchy. You really want them to know that you're dating the Manager?" Michael frowned. "I'm just trying to protect you, anjo."

"No, of course, I understand." She did, truly. And it wasn't like it was anything new, anyways. She was good at keeping secrets.

"This'll be good, baby. You get a new job, and I get to see more of you. It's a win-win."

"If you wanted to see more of me, you could just move me into your place," Jay teased as she took a sip. When Michael didn't say anything, she looked up at him, confused.

"That was going to be my next topic, but it seems you beat me to the punch." He picked his drink back up. "It would be nice to be able to have you whenever I want."

It was the wrong place and the wrong time to ask all the questions that were barreling through Jay's mind. And it was useless, anyways.

She had learned a long time ago that whatever Michael said, went.

"Of course, baby, that all sounds wonderful."

He grinned. "Great, I'll get some movers over to your place later this month."

"You already have most of my stuff anyway," she laughed, effortlessly hiding her sigh. "Shouldn't be too hard."

Michael brought his glass to hers. "Cheers to new beginnings."

"Cheers." Jay smiled back, downing the rest of her drink in one go.

He did the same, before giving her a long kiss. "You're my favorite, Jay."

"And you're mine."

15

"**C**ome on, Helena! It's Halloween," Quinn whined, throwing themself onto Helena's bed. "You *have* to come out with me."

"I don't *have* to do anything." She clapped her hands over her ears, staring harder at her textbook. "Now leave me alone."

Helena had been attempting to study for midterms for the past hour, but Quinn seemed to think that it was the perfect time to come bother her and lament.

"But Helena," they continued to whine, dragging out her name until she couldn't take it anymore.

"Get out of my room!" Helena snapped as she turned around, only to find Quinn pouting at her with big eyes.

"Please? No one else is going out tonight, and I'm going to be so lonely."

"You're so full of shit," she said. "You know you're going to find someone to go home with and then I'm going to get stuck downtown by myself."

"Nuh-uh. I promise, I'll stick with you all night. We can even invite Dylan out. I'm sure he would have a great time."

"I don't know, Quinn, Dylan isn't the type to, you know, go out," Helena said. At least, she thought he wasn't. But Lucio kept them both so busy that she wasn't sure that Dylan even had a social life.

"I'm sure if you told him you were going he'd be down." They flopped back onto her bed. "What if we invited Jay?"

Helena raised her brows at Quinn. "And what's going to stop you from going home with her instead?"

"Whatever," they groaned. "Just hit her up. It'll at least make me feel like I'm not the third wheel between you and Dylan."

"Shut up, you wouldn't be a third wheel," Helena said, already reaching for her phone. She and Jay had been texting on and off for a few weeks, but it was mostly Helena texting *at* Jay, with Jay giving the occasional response, or sometimes just reacting with an emoji. Which was fine. She was a woman with a life, and a boyfriend—she didn't have a ton of time to answer Helena's stupid ass questions about which pair of jeans looked better on her, or what top she should wear, or if this lipstick color looked good on her. That's what friends were for. And Helena *had* friends. Just...not those kinds of friends.

She bit her lip. "If we invite her out, you can't tell Lucio."

"Promise," Quinn grinned, holding out their pinky to link it with Helena's.

"Great. Now go find me a costume to wear," she said as she began to text Jay. "But nothing slutty!"

"Can't promise that." Quinn was already in her closet, digging through power suits and blouses to try and find some clothes that they could manipulate.

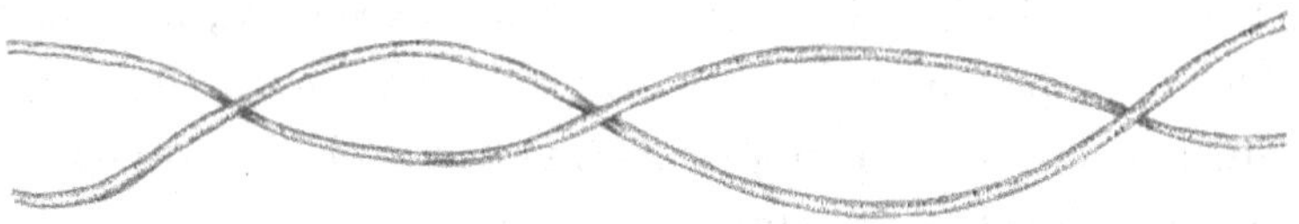

"Jay said she's pulling up now," Helena said, standing on her tiptoes to see over the crowd.

The line to get in the club was nearly around the block, but Helena and the crew stood to one side.

We don't wait in lines, Quinn had said, proudly waving the VIP tickets on their phone. Having a sibling with connections definitely had its perks.

"Awesome, I'm excited to see her costume." Quinn checked their appearance in their pocket mirror, spreading a bit more lipstick on their cheek like blood.

It had been Jay's idea to do a group costume. She had chosen zombies, as it was simple enough to put together so last minute.

For Quinn, simple was an understatement. It only took them a single 30-second makeup tutorial before they were replicating it, giving her and Dylan the full treatment. But Helena couldn't lie; they looked *awesome.*

She adjusted her top, making sure the holes Quinn had cut in it weren't landing anywhere she didn't want them to.

Quinn had tried to convince her to wear shorts, but she shot them down. It was cold enough outside; she wasn't about to catch pneumonia. And she didn't want to hear any lip from Lucio, either. He was already against them going out.

"Hey!" Jay called, and the three turned to look at her. Helena thought she could hear Quinn's and Dylan's jaws drop behind her, in perfect sync with every person in line who was even remotely attracted to women. Jay's jeans had more holes than fabric, and her top looked like it was hanging together by threads. She was wearing heels that Helena would immediately break her neck in.

"God, Jay, did you just grab some thread from a sewing kit?" Helena asked, looking Jay over again. She looked great, and a part of Helena wished she had gone for the shorts like Quinn suggested.

She felt completely frumpy standing next to Jay. And Dylan's attention seemed to be completely diverted.

"It's Halloween," Jay said. "This is the one night I get to dress like a slut and not get judged for it."

"Amen to that," Quinn mumbled. "Good to see you again, Jay."

Jay looked up, giving them a wry smile. "Good to see you too. I didn't get a chance to thank you for dinner."

"Well, I can think of a few ways you can thank me."

Helena elbowed Quinn in the ribs, ignoring their curses as she gestured to Dylan. "Jay, this is Dylan, my best friend."

"*Our* best friend!" Quinn chimed in, dodging Helena's second attempt to elbow them in the ribs.

"Nice to meet you." Jay waved hello. "Your costume looks sick."

He signed a quick thank you, earning him a curious look from Jay.

"Dylan is nonverbal. He communicates through sign. I'll translate for you when I can, or you guys can text."

Jay shrugged. "That's cool. We won't be doing much talking in there anyways."

"Not if we do this night right, we won't!" Quinn stepped around Helena, holding out their arm for Jay to take. She smiled as she did, walking ahead of Helena and Dylan, who jokingly mimicked their motions.

"This is my friend's place, so drinks are on the house tonight. Just mention my name," Quinn said, pushing open the large glass doors. The group was engulfed in darkness, before walking into a room illuminated by black lights. Quinn flashed their invites to the bouncer, who quickly checked IDs before allowing them all in.

Helena rolled her eyes. The only difference between this place and Quinn's was that it was more bar than restaurant, with a huge dance floor in the center. People dressed up in costumes, both complicated, simple, and clothing that was more normal club attire filled the space, and more people stood at the part of the bar that flanked the dancefloor on three sides.

Jay shouted loud enough for Helena to hear, "Wow, I expected this place to be more packed."

"Cyberspace is pretty exclusive. You have to know someone to get in." Quinn led them over to the bar.

Jay gave Quinn a smile that could only be described as flirty, ignoring the daggers Helena was sending her way. "Well, lucky me."

Helena sneered as Quinn rested their hand against the small of Jay's back. "I'd say I'm the real lucky one, here."

Quinn ordered Jay and them shots, and Dylan and Helena some non-alcoholic drinks.

"Come on, you dragged me out here, you can at least let me drink," Helena protested.

"Sorry," Quinn said. "But I'm not getting in double trouble for you by bringing you home drunk."

Helena huffed. "This is such bullshit."

"Hey, you can still have a great time and not drink!" Jay smirked. "I'll show you."

Helena half-yelled as she was pulled towards the dance floor, trying to wrench her arm from Jay's grip. "Hell no! I don't dance."

"Oh, bullshit. Everyone dances," Jay shouted back, pulling her deeper into the crowd.

"I'm not good at it!" Helena protested again as they came to a stop near the center.

Jay placed her hands on Helena's hips. "You don't have to be good, you just have to be moving."

Whatever beat Jay was moving Helena's hips to, they couldn't follow it. She felt like everyone's eyes were on her. "This is weird."

"Only because you're not letting go," Jay said. "No one here cares, you won't even see them again after tonight. So let loose, and enjoy yourself."

"Easier said than done," Helena grumbled, trying to do as Jay said.

Follow my steps, fihla.

Helena rolled her eyes so hard she thought they might fall out of her head. She did *not* need that memory popping up for her. This was a completely different type of dance. The dance that Lucio and she had danced was formal, the box step and two-step she had learned had no place in the music that was currently playing. It was some kind of electronic hip-hop, nothing that Helena would be caught dead listening to. And yet, the longer she did, the more she felt her feet moving naturally.

"There you go, kid!" Jay beamed. "Just like that."

Helena smiled despite herself. "Shut up."

Jay just laughed, letting Helena's hips go and holding her free hand instead. "Now put your arms into it."

Helena let Jay lift her hand, moving their arms in circles, and pulling her into a spin. "I still think this is weird!"

"I think *you* don't know how to have fun!" Jay let Helena go and moved herself freely, dropping low and coming back up with ease, clearly comfortable in the space despite the number of bodies pressing against them.

Quinn and Dylan found them in the crowd, and Quinn clutched their chest. "My sister? Dancing? Is that top cutting off circulation to your brain?"

Helena flipped them off as she continued to move to the music, becoming more comfortable by the minute.

Dylan smiled as he just shifted his weight from one foot to another, doing his best to avoid bumping into the other people. Quinn, in the meantime, moved themself behind Jay, their hands going to her hips.

Jay wasted no time starting to grind on Quinn, much to Helena's disgust.

She turned to Dylan, mocking a vomiting motion.

"Let them have some fun," Dylan signed, giving a gentle smile.

"Have fun without," she signed back, motioning towards the pair, *"that."*

"It's harmless. Do you want to try?"

Helena was grateful for the dark lighting to hide her blush. *"What?"*

"It's just dancing. It's seriously not hard to do."

"I," Helena averted her eyes but didn't move away from him. "Quinn is there."

"Doesn't seem like they care too much," Dylan joked, looking back over at the pair.

He wasn't wrong. Quinn and Jay looked like they had forgotten where they were as they danced. Helena was surprised Quinn hadn't shoved their tongue down Jay's throat yet.

Dylan tapped Helena and motioned over his shoulder. *"Come on, let's head back to the bar."*

She nodded, holding on to his sleeve as they weaved their way through the crowd.

Helena slid into a miraculously empty seat, keeping her back to the bar. Dylan settled himself in front of her, still moving slightly to the music. The bar stool was the perfect height to make them eye level, allowing her to notice how the low lights made his eyes sparkle. His deep brown skin shifted with all the colors; purples, blues, reds, all more rich as they danced across him.

"You can go back if you want," she said, nodding towards Jay and Quinn. "I didn't mean to take you away from a good time."

"You're a good time," Dylan signed, then seemed to register what he had said. His hands moved quickly, oblivious to the people who were all standing close to him. *"I mean, a good time in the sense of I like hanging out with you, not in a sexual sense!"*

Helena giggled and poked his shoulder. "You're such a goof."

"Only around you." He winked, and nodded towards the bar. *"You want another drink?"*

"I wish I could get an *actual* drink," she sighed, turning to the bar all the same. "Promise that when you're twenty-one you'll buy me alcohol."

He settled behind her, resting his hands on the bar so his arms would prevent anyone from bumping into her, before finger spelling "No."

She rested her head against his shoulder to speak into his ear. "Some friend you are."

The bartender came back over, and she ordered two virgin whiskey and Cokes.

The bartender raised a brow. *"Virgin* whiskey and Cokes?"

She gave him an incredulous look. "Yeah, I've gotten it at another bar and had no problem."

"Virgin *whiskey* and Cokes?" he repeated.

Dylan's chest shook with laughter as he rested his chin on her shoulder.

She turned to meet his eyes, their faces only a breath away from each other. "What the hell is so funny?"

"There's no such thing as a virgin whiskey and Coke." He bit back his smile. *"Virgin means no alcohol. It's literally just Coke."*

God, it was hot in this bar. Really hot. Like, impossibly hot. Which was totally the reason Helena felt like her entire body was on fire, it wasn't the absolute embarrassment. She glanced at the bartender, who looked exasperated.

"Two Cokes, please," she mumbled.

The bartender passed them their drinks, and Helena covered hers with her hand as she turned back out to the crowd.

Helena and Dylan spent most of the evening on the fringes of the dance floor, only going up when a song Dylan *swore* was his favorite came on. It turned out, he had a lot of favorite songs. But Helena had a good time, even when people kept bumping her into Dylan, who didn't seem to mind wrapping his arms around her to keep people from stepping on her. She appreciated having a friend like him. Unlike *Jay*, who Helena had seen drink multiple shots and spent the entire night dancing with Quinn.

Helena pulled out her phone to check the time, and saw multiple missed calls and texts from Lucio. "God, I go out for one night and he acts like the world is ending."

"He's a dad," Dylan signed. *"It's what they're supposed to do."*

"If you do this to your kids I'm going to fight you," she said. "I'm an adult, and I'm out with you for God's sake. What does he think is going to happen?"

Dylan shrugged. *"I stopped trying to figure Luke out a while ago."*

"Lucky you," Helena mumbled. "Come on, let's get beauty and the beast off the dance floor before Luke decides to come down here himself."

She took Dylan's hand as they walked through the crowd, which had declined drastically as the night wore on. They found Quinn and Jay at the other bar, Jay looking *sloppy* drunk.

Her grin widened as she noticed Helena and Dylan walking over. "There she is! We thought you and Dylan had snuck off to go fuck around."

Helena shot Quinn a look, ignoring the way her cheeks flushed at the accusation as she pulled her hand out of Dylan's. "How much did you let her have to drink?"

"She's a big girl! I thought she could handle it," Quinn said, throwing their hands up in mock defense.

"I'm fine, kid," Jay giggled. "What's up?"

"Time to go. Lucio's blowing up my phone." Helena held up the offending item, a new text from Lucio flashing on screen as she spoke. Sometimes, she wished he had a normal sleep schedule—maybe then he'd be too busy sleeping to worry about where the hell she was.

"Boo! Give me your phone, I wanna tell him what an asshole he is." Jay reached out, but the motion caused her to completely slide off the bar stool. Quinn reached out to steady her.

"I got ya," Quinn said, wrapping one arm around her waist and slinging her arm over their shoulder. Jay hummed as she leaned into them, closing her eyes.

"The subway is gonna be fun," Quinn chuckled.

"Why can't we get a ride?" Helena asked as they headed to the exit.

Quinn gave Helena a look over their shoulder. "You got money for the cleanup fee if she throws up?"

"I'm *fine!*" Jay stumbled over her heels. "You guys are so *dramatic.*"

"You're trashed," Quinn laughed. "How far are you from here? Might be easier to carry you home."

"Only like, ten blocks," Jay said.

Helena grit her teeth. She didn't have a ton of experience with drunk people—Quinn had only ever had one house party (that she knew of), and she didn't go to parties. Well, more accurately, she didn't get *invited* to parties. And she didn't want to. The thought of standing around with a bunch of people she barely knew while getting drunk out of her mind sounded like the least fun thing she could do with her brain cells. And if Jay was any indication of what her behavior *could* be, Helena never wanted to know.

They made it outside, and while Jay immediately breathed a sigh of relief, it took all of Helena's strength not to go running back. The temperature must have dropped at least ten degrees when they were inside. "It's freezing! I'm not walking ten blocks."

Something warm and heavy landed on Helena's shoulders.

Dylan had taken off his flannel to place on her, returning the smile that quickly spread over her lips.

"Look how fuckin' cute you two are," Jay gushed, drawing Helena's glare. "Wish I had a boyfriend that would do that."

"I'd like to apply for the position," Quinn teased, squeezing her waist.

"Position is filled," Helena yelled.

Jay pouted, before loudly whispering, "She's so *serious.*"

"Kind of her thing," Quinn said. "That's why she's got me to balance her out."

Helena was about to throw out an insult at Quinn, but someone shouting over the din of the crowded streets stopped her.

"Jay!"

Jay's posture immediately changed, and the little that Helena could see of her face paled. She tried to distance herself from Quinn, but Quinn kept their grip around her waist tight.

A man, tall, blond, and utterly unexceptional, outside of the rage he seemed to carry approached.

Helena's body tensed. There was something about this guy she didn't like, and she really didn't like that he seemed to know Jay.

"Hey, sweetheart," Jay said, clearly struggling to smile. "What are you doing here?"

Sweetheart? Who the hell was Jay calling "sweetheart?" She must have drank more than Helena thought she did, if she thought this guy was—*oh, shit.*

"We had plans, remember?" the man said through clenched teeth. "And then I see on your Instagram story you're out?" His eyes locked on Quinn. "Who the fuck is this?"

Helena's instinct screamed at her to protect Quinn, even though she knew damn well they could take care of themself. She didn't need to get in the way, but she also didn't know what this guy was capable of.

Quinn didn't hesitate to put themself in front of Jay. "Better question is who the fuck are you?"

"Quinn, don't." Jay put her hand on their chest. Her face was etched with fear.

The anxiety gripping Helena only worsened. She tried to move, but Dylan's arm around her shoulders kept her back.

Jay turned back to the man. "Colt, I'm sorry, I didn't have any service—"

"Bullshit!" He grabbed her wrist and yanked her forward. "We're going home."

Helena surged forward, but Dylan wrapped his arms around her waist to stop her from going any further. She fought him, screaming, "Keep your hands off of her!"

Three sets of eyes locked on her, Jay's filled with immediate terror. For herself, or Helena, it wasn't clear.

Jay shook her head, trying to step in front of Colt, maybe to block his line of sight. "Stay out of—"

"Who the fuck is that? You out here hanging around with kids?" Colt mocked. "You're getting more desperate by the day, aren't you?"

Helena seethed, ready to just jump this asshole herself, but Quinn beat her to it. Their hand grabbed a fistful of Colt's cheap-looking shirt, forcing Colt's attention to them. "First of all, take your fucking hands off of her. Second of all, this is between you and me, don't you mind the audience."

Helena looked around, her stomach dropping to see people were beginning to stop and stare, but those that had any sense kept it moving. They needed to get the hell out of here before someone called the cops. But, by looking at this situation, maybe the cops wouldn't be such a bad thing.

"Quinn, please I can handle this," Jay said, trying to loosen Quinn's grip on Colt.

Quinn didn't look at her as they spoke. "While he's putting hands on you? Hard fucking pass."

"I'll be fine, I just need you to please stop provoking him."

"Provoking *him?* He comes up and starts screaming, *grabbing* you, and I'm provoking him?"

"He doesn't mean it, you're just—"

"You know what? You want her so bad? Take her. I'm fucking done." Colt pushed off of Quinn, sending them stumbling back. But they quickly righted themself.

Good. Now that this asshole was going, they could get Jay home, far away from this guy.

Only Jay wasn't coming back to them. She was on Colt, her entire body trembling, and Helena swore she saw a tear glistening on Jay's cheek.

"No, no come on baby, I'm sorry, don't be that way," Jay begged. "I'm sorry I didn't call you, come on, let's talk about this at home."

"Home?" Colt barked out a laugh. "Fuck that. I'm done. Call Michael to pick you up." His cold eyes scanned over the group, and Dylan's grip around Helena's waist tightened.

"Or have these assholes take you. I don't give a shit what you do anymore," Colt said as he shoved his hands into his pockets.

"Colt don't—" Jay tried to reach after him, but he turned away, ignoring her begging and pleading as they walked away from the club. She stumbled after him, catching herself on the wall just before she could hit the ground. "Colt!"

It was strange, seeing someone so put together falter. Like the curtain forgot to fall on cue. But watching Jay continue to tremble, Helena's body moved automatically.

She tore out of Dylan's arms to run straight to Jay, placing Dylan's shirt on Jay's shoulders.

She barely seemed to register it. Her eyes still fixed on the Colt-shaped hole that had been burned through the crowd.

"Come on, Jay," Helena murmured, placing her hand into Jay's. "Let's get you home."

16

"Why does it bother you so much?" Dylan's hands moved freely in the open space of the park, and Helena rolled her eyes at his blasé tone. *"Jay's an adult. It's not like she's cheating on you or anything."*

"It's not the cheating," Helena said. "It's the way he *talked* to her. He was a complete asshole, but Jay was *still* begging for him to come back. It was so screwed up."

Helena looked up at the trees, watching some of the leaves flutter down towards them. They were strolling through the park near Lucio's office, enjoying the warmer weather that the gorgeous November day had to offer. People walked around by themselves or with friends, others playing with their kids on the playground. She and Dylan found a bench to sit on, and Helena blew on the hot chocolate that he had bought her.

Despite the whole incident having happened almost a week ago, Helena couldn't get it out of her head. Colt screaming at Jay. Jay begging him not to go. And Helena absolutely helpless to stop it. She wished she would have decked Colt. Maybe it would have made her feel at least a little better. Let Jay see that he's a complete and utter loser, and she shouldn't be hanging around people like that.

"And Michael did the *exact* same shit to her. Like what gives them the right to talk to her like that?"

"I mean, nothing does, but..."

"It's so aggravating! I would *never* let a guy do that to me," Helena sipped at her hot chocolate, enjoying the way it burned down her throat. "And I don't know what the hell Jay's thinking, letting them do that. She needs to get away from those douchebags."

"I mean, things aren't always so simple, Hel."

"Excuse me? Colt grabbed her and threw her around like she was a rag doll, how is it not simple to see how completely wrong that is?"

"That's not what I'm talking about," Dylan signed, keeping his motions slow. *"You and I both know better than anyone that it's hard getting out of these kinds of things. That, after a while, you..."*

He didn't need to continue. Helena looked away, struggling to keep her thoughts on the here and now, rather than back there. That part of her life was over with. The questions, the stares, the visits from CPS and just enough covered up to let it be thought that maybe things were getting blown out of proportion.

The phone call that her parents weren't coming home.

The fear that they were going to be separated, the attempts to keep them together, Quinn being completely and utterly out of control.

He keeps sneaking out and lying about where he's been, I think he's—

We don't think we're a good fit for all three of them, maybe the twins but—

They have young children in the house already, around your age, and Quinn can always come—

I met a guy today. He's a lawyer, a really good one. He says he wants to meet us, all of us. And he's got this huge house, out of the city. He's great, Hel, you're gonna—

They had made it out. Miraculously. And Helena had Quinn and Gideon to share some of the burden, to help understand what had happened to them back then. To help them realize it wasn't their fault their parents were the way they were. To help see that sometimes, shit happens, but you get through it anyways. And they had turned out okay, for the most part. Until they weren't. Until the world fell out from beneath Helena's feet, and she nearly lost herself completely. If it hadn't been for Quinn, she didn't think she would have come back at all.

But Dylan hadn't been so lucky.

He hadn't told her about what he had gone through, what had made him the way he was. He said he had worked it out in therapy; he wasn't going to drag up the past even more than he already had. But she knew that whatever it was, he hadn't had anyone to experience it with him. Dylan had to go through what he had gone through on his own, had learned to cope with it on his own, and a part of her felt guilty that she was constantly dumping on him, constantly turning to him for comfort, but he never seemed to do the same for her.

"She doesn't deserve it," Helena whispered, kicking at the leaves by her feet. Hesitantly, she put her hand on Dylan's knee. "And you didn't either."

He placed his hand over hers, warm and soft and so effortlessly comforting. He squeezed her hand, getting her to look up at him. *"Jay will be okay. You'll there for her."*

Easier said than done. Helena hadn't heard from Jay since Halloween. They had dropped her off at her apartment, having decided to just grab a ride anyways. The charge had been outrageous, but Quinn waved it off, putting it on their card. And Helena had been grateful, since Jay had remained painfully silent the rest of the way home. Even when she got there, all she had managed was a quick "thanks." But, it had been more than Helena had expected.

She and Dylan settled into a quiet moment. Tourists wandered around, smiling and laughing as they pointed out the gorgeous colors above them. The parks were some of the only places they could actually enjoy the changing seasons in the city, which was why they were always packed with people who didn't belong.

Helena couldn't wait until she could get out of here. Once she was out of college, she was going to law school where *she* wanted. If she wanted. Maybe she would say screw it entirely and go back to school for her degree in Social Work. But as long as she was living under Lucio's roof, she had to play by *his* rules.

"Do you think you're ever going to get out of here?" Helena asked.

Dylan thought it over a minute before signing back to her. *"Honestly, probably not. I don't know many other places where I'll find this many people who know ASL."*

"That's understandable," Helena mumbled, sipping at her drink. It had gotten slightly too cold for her liking.

"What about you? You planning on sticking around?"

"Hell no. As soon as I'm done with my undergrad I'm getting the hell out of here. I want to go as far as possible."

"Why didn't you go away for your undergrad?"

"Luke told me the only way he would pay for my college was if I stayed in the city." Helena sighed. "And NYU gave me the best scholarship."

"Yeah. That's how they get ya." Dylan held out his hands, making a scary face at her. *"Take the scholarship or fall victim to decades of student loan debt!"*

Helena laughed, nudging him with her elbow. "You're ridiculous."

"I'm just glad to know I at least get a few more years with you before you bounce."

Her smile fell. She hadn't thought about how leaving the city meant leaving Dylan behind. They had been basically inseparable since they had met, and, for some strange reason, she had felt like he would have come with her, no matter where she went. But Dylan was his own person, why the hell would he follow her like he wasn't?

"I'll still come visit."

"I can feel it now. Once you escape the grasp of the city, you won't be looking back." Dylan smiled at her. *"And that's fine! You should*

want to clear out of here. You're gonna do all these amazing things. We're just going to hold you back if you stay."

"You wouldn't hold me back," she said, pouting. "You're the only one who's actually supportive of me."

"I'm all for people getting to explore their dreams. I got the opportunity to, so I think everyone else should too."

"Getting to be a prosecutor was your dream?"

"Yeah. I figure I'll do a little prosecution, a little defense, maybe I'll land somewhere I like in the end. I don't like limiting myself to one option for too long."

"Your girlfriends must love that," Helena teased.

Dylan's eyes widened. *"Oh, no, I don't mean like that. I just meant more in a job sense. When it comes to women I am* fully *committed!"*

Helena laughed, and grabbed one of his hands, holding it to still his frantic signing. "Dyl, it's okay. I knew what you meant."

Dylan licked his lips, slowly removing his hand from her grip. *"You know, Helena, there's something I've been meaning to ask—"*

"Dylan!"

They looked up to see a young woman, about their age, bounding over. Her curly hair was pulled back into a ponytail, a cute plaid scarf loosely wrapped over a tan leather jacket that complimented her ochre-brown skin.

Dylan smiled in a way Helena didn't recognize, his hands moving in a way that Helena wasn't familiar with. The young woman's hands moved in a similar motion, and Helena looked between the two of them, watching as the conversation played out before her.

The young woman smiled in Helena's direction.

"Hey, I'm," she put her hands up to her chin, curling her fingers inward and then pulling down.

Helena immediately looked to Dylan for clarification.

"This is A-Z-I-Z-I. Her sign name is A-P-R-E-C-I-O-U-S."

Helena smiled, signing back to Azizi. *"Nice to meet you, I'm Helena."*

Azizi smirked at the sign Helena gave for her name, casting a look at Dylan.

What the hell was that about? It was her name, did she think it was funny or something? Or maybe it was a weird sign? Helena knew that her sign language wasn't that good, but had she done something offensive?

Azizi again signed unfamiliarly to Dylan, who scowled as he signed back at her in a similar fashion.

Helena watched them, trying to figure out any part of what they were saying. But their hands moved so quickly, their motions were so different from what she had seen before. Whenever Helena and Dylan talked, he always moved slower; watching him now was like watching a foreign film at two times speed and no captions.

A knot began to tighten in Helena's stomach as Azizi laughed at something Dylan said. She had a pretty laugh. And a pretty smile.

And Dylan was smiling right back.

Helena stood up, which seemed to be enough to draw Dylan's attention away from Azizi. "Hey, I'm gonna go."

"Sorry Hel, I promise we can leave in a second," Dylan signed, then signed to Azizi again.

She nodded, giving Helena another friendly smile. *"It was nice meeting you! You should come around sometime, D-calm has told us a lot about you, so I know everyone is dying to meet you."*

The knot in Helena's stomach eased, if only a fraction. "Yeah, that would be cool."

Again, Dylan and Azizi exchanged gestures, and he stood to walk back to the office with Helena. They walked in silence for most of the way, Dylan making attempts at conversation, but Helena giving him one word answers the entire time.

When they reached the entrance to the office, Dylan pulled Helena to the side, giving her a confused look. *"Everything okay?"*

"Yeah." She shrugged.

"What's wrong?"

Damn her terrible poker face. She glanced down at her feet, her cheeks heating up. "It's stupid."

He waved in her eyeline. *"Not if it's upsetting you."*

Helena bit her lip. Dylan wasn't going to let this go, she knew that well enough. It was the one thing that she loved and hated about him. "How come I couldn't understand you guys?"

"What do you mean?"

"You and Azizi. You guys were signing, and I know I'm not fluent, but it was almost like I was speaking Spanish and you guys were speaking Portuguese."

Dylan pressed his lips together, clearly trying to hide a smile. *"You didn't understand because we weren't speaking ASL."*

Helena's brows furrowed. "But you guys were—"

"It's not ASL. It's BASL."

"What?"

His smile broke free. *"Black American Sign Language."*

Helena started to speak but then realized. "Oh..."

"Yeah. It's sign, but just a different dialect. And you're still learning ASL, so it makes sense that you wouldn't be able to understand us."

The knot in Helena's stomach eased completely, but a feeling of embarrassment washed over her. She had been a total bitch to Azizi for what? Because she was signing in a way that had been *comfortable* for them? Because Helena hadn't been privy to a conversation that she hadn't needed to be involved in? Dylan was allowed to have friends, especially friends that were able to speak to him in a way that he preferred. It was fine.

"Well, now I feel like an ass."

Dylan laughed, *"You're not an ass, you didn't know."*

"Let's just go up, please," she muttered, wanting to just crawl in a hole and die.

"Whatever you say, Hel."

17

Taking one last breath of freedom, Jay closed the door to Michael's apartment behind her, and looked out over the space. There was no question in her mind that it was Michael's. Everything felt so much like him. The living room had a long, black, L-shaped leather couch, with two arm chairs facing it, turned away from the electric fireplace, above which hung one of those expensive flat screens that was as thin as a credit card, and looked like a painting until you turned it on. The living room was separated from the rest of the apartment by a cream rug, which covered dark hardwood that carried through the rest of the apartment.

The kitchen looked out over the living room, a breakfast bar built into the black marble island, white cabinets that she had to imagine were a pain in the ass to clean. A six burner stove and dual ovens on one end, a fridge stuffed with everything she could imagine and more. And along the back wall, floor to ceiling windows that looked out over Central Park.

Jay fixed her gaze on what was in front of her. There was only one small box sitting in the living room; all the others had been carried into the bedroom, holding purses and shoes and clothes that hadn't yet found their way to Michael's or Colt's apartments. Michael's place was so orderly and pristine it felt wrong to clutter it up with random trinkets and tchotchkes, so Jay only packed what mattered most, leaving the rest of it in a storage unit instead. She would decide what to do with it later down the line.

Jay kneeled in front of the box marked "fragile." There wasn't much in it: her jewelry tray; a couple frames with photos of her and Alice, or her and Michael wrapped carefully in bubble wrap; and her most treasured possession. So precious it was still tucked safely in the box it had come in. Clear glass surrounded an engraved blue jay—a gift from Alice for Jay's twenty-fourth birthday.

Alice had actually made it herself. They had gone up to the Corning museum of glass, agreeing to make each other a gift for their respective birthdays. Jay had struggled with an idea for Alice. Everything seemed cheesy, even though that was kind of the point. She finally settled on making Alice a windchime; Alice's apartment had a lot of sunlight, and she always loved having her windows open in the summer. The experience had been fun. Jay never thought of herself as a person who liked to work with her hands—she always was so scared of doing something that could jeopardize her career in dancing.

Alice had chosen the more difficult activities. She had never been scared of danger—that was the whole reason she became a cop. Even when she was in college, Alice was always sticking her nose where it didn't belong. Jay had always tried to pull her out, tried to convince her it wasn't worth it.

Alice always ignored her.

"Everything all set, anjo?"

Jay jumped when Michael's hands pressed on her shoulders, but she quickly settled back into him, tilting her head up. He was dressed in sweats and a tee-shirt, more casual than she was used to seeing him. Her visits had previously been kept to seeing him after work, still dressed in one of his suits, or at least a nice shirt or a polo. Seeing him in anything less felt like an invasion of his privacy. "Yeah. Now it's just the fun of unpacking all this crap."

Michael hummed as he rubbed her shoulders. "Why don't we start with the clothes? I already made some room for you in the walk-in."

Jay set the gift back into the box, then stood. "I feel like you're just trying to get me to go to bed with you."

"Is sex the only thing ever on your mind?" His hand shifted to her stomach, slipping his thumbs under the hem of her tee shirt. She resisted the urge to recoil at his touch.

"Not always. Sometimes I think about food."

He chuckled, kissing her forehead. "You're terrible."

They went into the bedroom and began unpacking the multitude of boxes. Michael had a huge closet, much larger than the one she had at her last place. And even with the space that he had made for her, most of it was taken up by his clothes. He clearly preferred muted tones, but there were a couple of brighter suits and sportscoats for the summer months. Jay ran her hand absently over the fabric, loving how soft it felt beneath her fingers. A fleeting thought about a certain green-eyed man wearing suits of similar quality ran through her mind, but she pushed it away.

"You have a lot of suits," Jay said, still fiddling with the material. "I don't think I've seen you wear the same one twice."

"I didn't know you were paying attention," Michael said. He pulled out his pocket knife and cut the tape on one of the boxes.

"It's kind of crazy to me that you can afford all of these." She pulled open one jacket, looking at the label. It was one she didn't recognize, which was unsurprising. She knew women's labels like the back of her hand, but she hadn't ever had a need to bother with men's. Fabric and cut were always the focus—hallmarks of tailoring, which meant fat wallets. "A lot of these must have cost you thousands."

"They did." Michael opened up a box of hangers, brand new. Her old ones would have clashed with the whole aesthetic his closet had. And it was never any problem for him. Michael had money for days: fancy dinners, fancy cars, this place itself likely cost a couple million. But Jay hadn't been able to shake that night in the back of the club. The numbers that hadn't made sense. Him shutting her out instead of letting her in.

Jay watched him reach for one of her shirts. "I know you do really well at your job, but how much do you make?"

Michael stiffened. "Don't you know it's rude to ask a man his salary?"

"I thought that only applies to strangers." Jay reached into the box to help him, keeping her own tone light. She met his gaze. "And we're not strangers, are we?"

"According to you, we might as well be," he chuckled, but Jay knew his laughs well enough to know when he was annoyed.

"Only because you're always so secretive." She placed one of her favorite tops on the hanger. A gift from Michael, just because.

"I already told you, I don't keep secrets." He set the shirt he had been working with in the closet. "I don't have time for petty games like that."

"So then why won't you tell me how much you make?"

Michael's lip pulled back in a snarl, but he tried to correct it. "Is there something you want? You know money's no object, anjo."

"No, I just..." Jay knew she should shut up. She could tell his temper was beginning to flare, and that was dangerous.

"Just what?"

She licked her lips. "What was that whole thing at the club about?"

"What thing?"

"The numbers. You being worried about the investors." Jay reached for another top. "Are you doing something shady?"

Michael slammed the wooden hanger onto the bar so hard the hook broke. "It's not your business where my money comes from. And I haven't heard you complain about all the pretty things I buy you."

"I'm not complaining," she said, her nails digging into the fabric of the shirt she held—nails he had paid for.

"Then stop asking stupid questions. If I don't tell you something, it's for a Goddamn reason."

"So what was all that bullshit about 'you know me'?"

"Yeah, *me*. Unless I'm mistaken, my money and I are not the same thing."

"You're not but—"

Michael's voice rose, drowning Jay's out. "So let it go. I don't feel like dealing with putting away *your* shit all day."

Her tongue lashed behind her teeth, desperate to let him just fucking *have* it. To tell him how she was so sick of his games, how she was tired of walking on eggshells that were hiding landmines. Michael had been practically *begging* her to move in with him, and now he was going to give her attitude?

"Then don't. I can handle this myself. Like I *always* do." Jay grabbed for another hanger, aggressively pulling out a shift dress.

"You don't do shit for yourself!" he yelled. "I have to do everything for you, pay for everything for you, even had to get you a fucking job because *you* didn't want to do what you needed to and find a new one!"

Jay spun on him. "Are you fucking kidding me? I got that job *way* before I met you, and the only reason I left was because *you* wanted me to."

"Don't put words in my mouth," Michael growled, towering over her.

She glared up at him, hardening her gaze. "If I was putting words in your mouth, I wouldn't be hearing you constantly spew bullshit at me."

"Name one fucking time I've lied to you."

She could name hundreds. "It's not the lying, Michael, it's you hiding shit! You know I didn't even know you had a brother?"

Michael's eyes bore into her. "What?"

She held his stare. She couldn't look away. If she did, she wasn't sure what he would do. At least this way, she could watch him. Prepare.

"What the fuck did you say?"

"Nothing, I didn't say—"

"Don't you *dare* lie to me." Pain shot up Jay's arms. Michael's hand was wrapped around her bicep so tight she could see it starting to turn red. "Who told you I had a brother?"

Lie. "You did."

"Like fuck I did." Michael shook her, forcing her to look at him. "Did he tell you?"

Jay spoke calmly, biting back the cry that threatened to tear its way through her throat. "Michael, you're hurting me."

His grip on her tightened, and the pain was so bad Jay swore light flashed across her vision. Michael grabbed her other arm, and she swallowed her whimper. "What else did he say to you? What did he tell you?"

"Michael, let *go* of me!" A mistake.

He yanked her so close to him that all she could smell was the cigarette he had smoked earlier, and suddenly there was a knife against her side and her back against a wall—

Say it, Angel.

"He's a liar, you can't believe a word that—"

Jay drove her knee into Michael's groin.

He let her go, doubling over in pain as she stumbled backwards, falling into the rack of his suits, his cologne overwhelming her, choking her out. She gasped for air as she pushed herself away from it, her mind dizzy as she finally steadied herself against the doorframe.

The only sound in the room was their breathing, harsh and uneven, even as Jay tried to understand what the fuck had just happened.

"Anjo," Michael called, and her head jerked up to see him straightening. Terror raced through her as he took an uncertain step in her direction. "Anjo, I didn't mean it. I didn't mean to get so upset."

Jay stepped back.

Michael noticed. "It was an accident, anjo, I didn't hurt you."

Pain radiated up her arms, pulsing slowly and steadily. A warning. Every fiber of her being screamed at her to run. But where was she going to go?

"Anjo?" His voice was barely a whisper. And his eyes, God his eyes, those violent oceans that she had come to know so well, had settled into a placid pool. "Talk to me."

"I need a minute," Jay said, struggling to keep her voice steady. "I'm going to go out."

"No, anjo, come on, don't do that." Michael stepped forward, hand outstretched. "Let's talk about this. We need to talk about this."

"I need a minute," she said again, her voice more firm.

His hand dropped, his lips pressing into a thin line. "Okay."

She turned, walking without really seeing. But somehow, she made it outside, ignoring the way the cold air touched everything but where Michael had held her a little too tight.

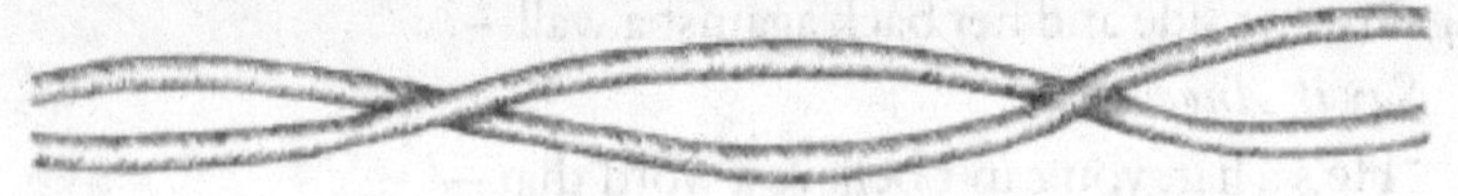

Jay thanked the server as she took a sip of her amaretto sour. She didn't care that she hadn't eaten dinner; Michael had gotten her so shaken up that she needed something to take the edge off.

She wasn't hungry, anyways.

And Jay was only a few blocks away from his place. A small bar slash restaurant that lacked enough zeroes on the menu to fly under Michael's radar. Another good thing for her to keep in mind in case she needed to get away from him for a minute.

She rested her chin in her hand as she looked out the window. Her phone sat on the table, quiet. Michael hadn't even bothered to try and call her, which was probably for the best. She didn't want to talk to him.

Helena had texted her a few hours ago, trying to find another reason for the two of them to get together. Jay had been dodging her since Halloween—partially because she didn't want to risk getting grilled over what happened with Colt. Her lips twitched. Helena was cute, a little naive, but cute. Jay wished she had been more like her when she was nineteen.

But where Helena had chosen ambition and education, Jay had chosen love and security. A part of her wondered why those things had been mutually exclusive for her.

And why one suddenly felt like it wasn't so certain, now.

"Hey!" Alice called, and a wave of relief washed over Jay as she spotted her best friend walking in. They hadn't seen each other since the coffee shop a few weeks ago, both busy with work. But they had the type of friendship where they could go months without talking and fall right back into place.

Alice smiled as she hugged her best friend hello. "Something must be up if you're calling me."

"I don't just call you when something is wrong, you know." Jay pouted, settling back into her seat.

Alice gave her a serious look. "But something is up."

Jay rubbed at her arms, still slightly sore. There was no need to tell Alice. No need to worry her over an argument that had gotten too heated. And Alice would blow it out of proportion, call it something it wasn't, offer to go over there and handle it.

And besides, it was an accident.

"Come on, spill. What did Colt do now?"

As far as Alice knew, Colt was the only man in Jay's life—Alice wouldn't understand the dynamic with Michael. Hell, even though she tried to deny it, Alice definitely judged Jay for dancing. If Jay told Alice that she was dating Colt and Michael at the same time? Jay might never hear from Alice again. So she slid the blame from Michael to Colt—Halloween, the argument, even some minor shit that had been building up from too many snide comments from Michael.

In the end, it was all Colt's fault anyways.

Alice's jaw remained slack as she listened. "And he didn't apologize?"

"Nope. And I can guarantee he's not going to." Jay sipped on her drink again, moving her straw to get every last drop. The server returned with the olive and cheese plate Alice had ordered when Jay had ordered a second drink.

"Seriously, Jay, don't just give into him. He owes you an apology." Alice leaned over the table, pressing her finger into the laminated wood. "A real one."

Jay shook her head. "I know, and I promise, I'll get one."

Alice looked skeptical. "Do you want to come stay with me tonight? We can do a movie night, popcorn and everything."

The thought was tempting. Let Michael stew on it for a while, think about what he had done. But she knew how he got after most of their arguments: the longer they went without talking about it, the worse *he* got. "No, I need to go back and deal with this. Especially since I'm going to be seeing him at work all week."

Alice's brows raised. "Colt's coming to the club all week?"

Jay immediately lit up. "I didn't tell you? I got a new job."

"You're kidding! Where are you working?"

"NomadCrate. It's an import slash export company."

"Oh?" Alice rolled her shoulders. "How did you swing that?"

"Colt got me the job." Jay beamed, the lie rolling off her tongue effortlessly. "He said he wanted me to be closer to him."

"Oh."

"What?"

"It's just," Alice played with a stray olive, "I'm surprised you want to work there. Like, do you know what you're going to be doing?"

"Just secretary work," Jay said. Her mood began to fall. "I figured you would be happy for me."

"No, I am! I'm so happy you're getting out of dancing, but I haven't heard the best things about that place. Michael Silva is infamous." Alice rolled the olive on her plate, laughing humorlessly as she added, "And we know your track record with those kinds of people."

Jay tried to hide her bristling. "What're you implying?"

"Nothing about you, I just want to make sure you're okay." Alice stabbed the olive. "You seem to attract that type of guy, unfortunately."

Jay's palms pressed into the table, and it wobbled beneath her weight. "Colt's not one."

"You literally just sat here and told me that he just screamed at you over nothing, does that not make him a scumbag?"

"No, that makes him an asshole."

Alice set down her fork. "Is he like that often?"

"It was literally just this time," Jay said, turning her face toward the window. It was just starting to drizzle. And of course, she hadn't grabbed an umbrella or a coat. Her hair was going to be fucked.

"I have a lot of calls and texts that say otherwise."

"Oh what, so now you're keeping tabs on my boyfriend?"

"Look." Alice leaned forward, holding Jay's gaze. "I'm just trying to make sure you're safe, I've heard really shady things about NomadCrate, I don't think it's a good idea for you to get involved in that."

Jay swallowed, the numbers flashing behind her eyes. If Alice knew something—

"I'm just trying to protect you," Alice said.

"Protect me?" Jay raised her brows. "So you'd rather I keep dancing? You'd seriously rather me deal with men who grope at me and try to assault me? Some dickhead literally pulled a knife on me the other day—"

"You didn't tell me that," Alice said, her face falling into concern. "Why didn't—"

"Because it doesn't matter now, does it? I'm getting out of Vision, but all you can focus on is some stupid rumor that has literally *no* basis."

Alice kept her voice irritatingly calm. "Jay, please, you're putting words in my mouth."

A dull ache radiated through Jay's arms, and she shoved herself away from the table. "I'm done. I don't need to listen to you spew bullshit at me. You know you've *always* needed to be better than me. You can't let me have this *one* thing!"

Alice's eyes hardened. "That's not what this is about—"

"Then what is it, Alice? Because from where I am, you're out here hiding shit from me. I'm your *best* friend. And you're making it seem like you can't trust me."

"It's not a trust thing, it's a—"

"No, it's fine. You get to keep your big secrets and judge people from your ivory tower." Jay pulled a couple bills from her purse and threw them on the table. "Just don't expect me to be praising you from the bottom of it anymore."

"Jay, don't do that..." Alice tried to reach out over the table to grab Jay's hand.

Jay flinched away.

A beat. A pause that lingered a little too long, and Jay thought for a second that maybe Alice would see it, would catch that something had happened, something was different.

Jay spoke quickly, moving back to hide the way she had stiffened. "Do what? We're not kids anymore. I don't have to listen to you all the time."

"I know that, I'm just trying to look out for you," Alice said. "I'm serious, you going there is a bad idea."

"Well you know what, you don't have to worry about it. You don't have to concern yourself with anything that has to do with me anymore."

"Jay!"

Jay ignored her, slamming the door open with more force than she needed to. She didn't need Alice. She didn't need anyone.

The last thing Jay wanted to do was go back to Michael's place. But it was beginning to get late, and she didn't want to be on the streets alone at night, especially not when it was raining.

So she took the elevator back up, readying herself for a fight as she stepped into the apartment.

The first thing that Jay noticed was the lack of boxes. She looked around, slightly terrified that Michael had chucked them out the window, but she hadn't seen them when she was walking in the building.

What Jay did see was her photos sitting on the TV console. Her little trinkets were placed below, arranged with care and precision, like they had been there all this time. She walked over, stooping down to look at them better. Her blue jay was carefully displayed, and Jay had to stop herself from throwing it across the room.

"I hope you don't mind," Michael said.

Jay looked over to see him leaning against the hallway wall, still looking wounded. *Good.*

"You didn't have to do this." She stood. "I would have handled it."

"Yeah, but I also wanted to make you feel like this is your home, too." He moved slowly toward her.

She didn't flinch, but she was hyper aware of the fact that the windows were at her back and she could dodge to the right if she needed to.

"I put your clothes away for you."

Jay forced herself to smile as he continued to close the distance between them. He had put on some cologne, her favorite, and she could see that his hair was slightly wet from a shower he must have taken. "Thank you, Michael."

"You're my favorite, Jay, and I want you to remember that." Michael tucked a stray strand of hair behind her ear, then tilted her chin to meet his eyes.

"And you're mine," Jay said.

He kissed her—gentle, real, and she remembered back when he first kissed her in the back of the club, trying some cheesy line on her about the champagne she had been drinking probably tasting much sweeter on her lips.

She had let herself go, then. Forgotten why she had been letting him kiss her in the first place. And she did the same thing now.

"It's late. We should get to bed," he mumbled against her lips, his hands traveling up her sides and rolling her shirt up.

"We should." She trapped his bottom lip between her teeth. "So what're you waiting for?"

Michael smiled, then lifted her with ease to carry her back to their bedroom.

18

"Just wear the one I bought you a few months ago," Michael shouted to Jay from where he was fixing his tie in the mirror.

"Babe, this is an *indoor* cocktail event in the middle of November, if I wear that I'll look ridiculous," Jay said back, still looking through the dresses that Michael hadn't already voiced his approval of.

"Yeah but you know you look prettier in the lighter colors."

Jay was grateful for the wall separating them—she could roll her eyes without worrying about Michael getting upset at her.

She just grabbed a muted green dress, the best she could do given what she had. Michael hadn't cared as much before, but since she was going to be starting with him next week, he wanted her to make a good impression. She threw on the dress, her new red sole heels, and paired it with a set of gold hoops and a few gold rings to match.

She looked at herself in the mirror of the closet, smoothing out the dress.

Doesn't hurt that it's my favorite color.

Jay chased the thought out of her mind. She had been so good about forgetting Lucio, about forgetting everything, and just settling into her life here. It was bad enough that she was *still* waiting on Colt to call or text.

They had never gone this long without talking. But it was fine. He would get over it. Just like he always had. It wasn't even that big of a deal, he was so dramatic sometimes.

Tonight would be fine.

Michael would be satisfied, and Jay would grit her teeth and bear this for the time that she had to. At least Colt would be there. He would be forced to interact with her, maybe they could sneak off and actually talk about this whole thing.

"Ready," Jay sighed as she stepped back into the bedroom, smoothing out the fabric of her dress.

Michael sucked in a breath, and she readied herself for yet another comment about how she needed to change this, or how he didn't like that, and she made sure to fix her face before looking up at him. But to say he was looking at her with anything less than pure adoration would have been a lie. "Jesus, Jay, you look gorgeous."

Jay tilted her chin up, a smile tugging at her lips. "Thank you."

"If I had it my way I would say fuck this thing, and just stay home with you instead," Michael said, wrapping an arm around her waist and kissing her shoulder just above her tattoo.

"As much as I would love that, baby, tonight's kind of important," she said.

"You're right," he mumbled. He trailed kisses up her shoulder and neck, before reaching her ear, his breath hot against her skin. "But I still can't wait to get back home already."

Jay kept her face tilted toward the ceiling, ignoring the sparks lighting up her spine. "Me neither."

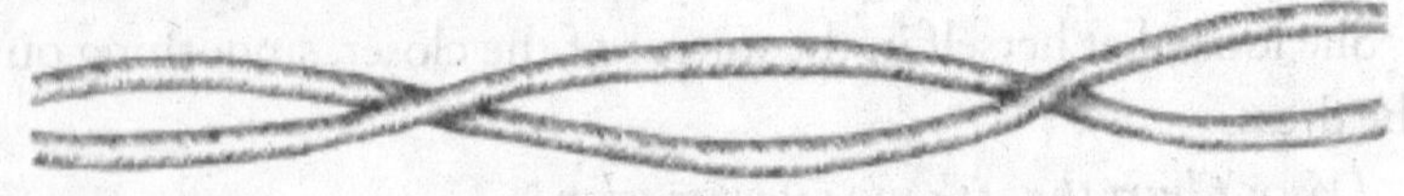

"You're not worried people are going to notice us coming in together?" Jay asked as they pulled up to the venue.

Michael snorted, flicking his cigarette out the window. Never mind that it was a hired car—if Michael wanted a smoke, he got one. "They're not gonna say shit to you. Besides, Colt's meeting us out front. So as far as anyone knows, we all came together."

And just as Michael said, Colt was waiting for them out front, talking with a woman. She was wearing a black dress with large, printed flowers, one that hugged curves that were almost non-existent. Colt was just entertaining her. But there was that smile again, the one that Jay had always thought was only reserved for her. He laughed, loudly, his hand reaching out in the direction of the woman. But upon seeing Jay and Michael approach, he pulled back, the smile fading and his laughter dying out. Jay tried to get a good look at the woman, but she had waved goodbye and headed into the building by the time Jay and Michael approached.

"Delilah?" Michael asked, nodding in the direction of the doors.

"Yeah. She said she'd meet us up there. Had to run ahead," Colt said, speaking directly to Michael as if Jay wasn't standing right next to him.

Michael grunted his approval, gesturing for Jay to start walking. She lingered for a moment, trying to catch Colt's eye, but he was back to his usual: looking everywhere but at her.

The minutes moved slower than Jay could have thought possible. She knew the evening was going to be painfully boring: a ton of hand shaking, pretty smiles, and dodged glances from those who looked a little too close and realized just where they knew Jay from. But Michael must have warned the guys—say anything, and it'll be the last thing you do.

"Lovely party isn't it?" Michael said absently. He touched the small of her back.

Jay took the signal to step closer to him.

Colt nodded, keeping his eyes on the paintings around them. "Gorgeous. It would be a great place for a wedding."

He wasn't wrong—the venue was a gallery, where Michael and the client had met, both big art collectors. The white walls were lit from above to create the illusion of a warmer atmosphere, focusing the attention on the paintings. A good excuse as to why Colt had seemed to be dodging Jay's glances and nods. He looked distracted, his attention flirting to any brunette that walked near him.

Jay tightened her grip on her glass.

"Now, there's certainly an idea," Michael chuckled. "Speaking of, when are you going to find someone and settle down?"

Jay did her best to hide her stiffness with a shiver, rubbing absently at the arm that wasn't close to Michael. He swept her a little closer to him. A dangerous thing to do considering the crowd, but it was so packed that really, it could have easily just been her attempting to stay in the conversation.

"Maybe when you decide to stop riding me so hard with work," Colt said, his tone humorless. "I barely see daylight by the time I get out."

Michael smiled too tightly as he looked back at Jay. "Well, maybe Jay can set you up with one of her little friends. Maybe that girl that you went out to lunch with the other day. What was her name again? Alice?"

"Alice works just as much as Colt does," Jay said, flashing teeth. "I don't think it would work."

"Besides, I'm already involved with someone." Colt spoke with the confidence of a man who didn't mind dying. The only question was who was going to kill him first: Jay or Michael.

"Oh really? Why haven't you introduced us yet, then?" Michael gestured, as if she would miraculously appear.

Jay tried to shoot Colt a look of pleading, but he continued to look through her.

"She wants to keep things private, at least for right now," he said. "But when she decides she's ready, you'll be one of the first to know."

Jay struggled to catch her breath in the suddenly thin air. She took a sip of her drink, the watered down vodka doing nothing to help. But at least it was something else to focus on besides the horrible tightness in her chest.

"Well, I'm looking forward to it," Michael said, finishing off his drink. "Shit, I'm out. You need a top-up, anjo?"

"I'll get 'em," Colt said quickly, taking Jay and Michael's empty glasses. "I'll be right back."

Jay swallowed as she watched him go, before turning to Michael. "He's right, you know. You really do work him too much."

Michael looked down his nose at her. "Maybe I don't work him enough, by the looks of it. He's still got enough energy to keep sniffing around you all night."

She held back her sigh, opting for a batting of her eyelashes instead. "Michael, please, not this again."

It didn't do much to quell the anger in Michael's tone. "It's pretty hard to ignore."

Jay's lips thinned, as did her patience. "He's not doing anything. You're being paranoid."

Michael's fingers pressed into Jay's wrist. Not enough to leave a mark, she knew, but just enough to get her to wince. "I am not paranoid. If I say he's doing something, he's doing something. Maybe it's time for him to move on."

The fear charged its way up Jay's throat, constricting the air even more. No, no, Colt *needed* this job, without it, he was fucked. *They* were fucked. She looked over her shoulder at the bar, where Colt was still waiting for drinks. He hadn't looked at her all night, and right now, she wasn't sure if she was grateful, or angry.

Don't make a scene.

Jay glanced back up at Michael, using her free hand to trace the veins that were bulging against the skin of his hand. "Would you like me to talk to him?"

He snarled, but quickly corrected it. "And say what?"

"I'll tell Colt to back off. He needs to understand that he and I aren't together anymore," Jay said. "And I think if it comes from me, it'll be better."

"Maybe I should just beat it into him."

"No, baby, you do that and you look like an out of control, jealous asshole. If it comes from me, it'll mean more. He'll understand that it's really over."

Michael watched her, blue eyes carefully searching her brown ones. She held his gaze, steady and strong, braving the storm that raged. He released her wrist. "Fine, but if you're gone for too long, I'm coming after you."

"Deal," Jay said, absently rubbing at her wrist as she walked toward the bar where Colt was.

He was just about to turn around when Jay grabbed him by the arm. "You and I need to talk."

Colt blinked at her. "About what?"

"Not here," Jay snapped, motioning towards the balcony. "Outside. Now."

Jay went first, fighting her way through the sea of bodies to get to the balcony. It wasn't much, really only enough to fit a few tables, with a glass and metal banister surrounding the entire area. There were a few people, mostly smokers braving the cold for a hit of nicotine. She would have to work fast, before Michael started fiending for one and found her and Colt out there.

Luckily Colt came out a moment after her, looking bored. She waited until he walked over to her completely, hands in his pockets and shoulders slumped forward. She wanted to fucking deck him. But she knew she needed to still apologize for Halloween, for not going home with him, for blowing him off entirely in the first place.

One thing at a time.

She squared her shoulders. "Why did you say that to Michael?"

"Say what?" Colt shrugged.

"Colt," Jay said carefully. "You made a comment about a 'private relationship,' and you *know* that Michael is suspicious of us. You don't think that saying something like that isn't going to cause problems?"

"Why would it?" Colt looked out over the balcony at the night that had settled in. "Not like you and I are involved."

Jay choked on the lump in her throat. "That's not funny. I know you're still mad about Halloween, but you can't be saying things like that."

"I'm serious."

She was grateful for the railing to grab onto. "Stop it."

"Stop what? Pretending like you hanging all over Michael doesn't kill me? Acting like everything is okay when it's not? Like this entire relationship isn't a complete and utter embarrassment?" He finally turned to her as he spoke, his voice rising in tone but not in volume, each word coming out more desperate and choked. She couldn't touch him, not with Michael so close. It would only make things worse.

"Baby, no, come on, you know that I love you, that I'm doing this for you, for *us*," Jay said, her body beginning to tremble with the weight of his words. "It's just until—"

"Until what? He's moved you into his place, he's got you working with him, what's next? You have his fucking kids?"

Jay shook her head. "No, Colt, you know I would never do that to you."

"You already *have*, Jay." He met her eyes, and she saw it. How broken he was, how much she had fucked up, how hurt was and how long he had been holding everything in.

It was her fault.

"You have said yes to everything. You could have told him no, told him to wait, told him that you weren't ready. You could have told him back when I got the manager position that—" Colt licked his lips, kicking at the ground a moment before meeting her eyes again. "I got a new job."

She felt herself trying to smile. "You're *leaving*?"

"Yeah. An old friend of mine told me he'd let me come work for his new company, a start-up. Wants me on as CFO."

CFO. Chief Financial Officer. Leagues above manager, more money than she could imagine, just as much as—

"Baby! That's amazing! Why didn't you tell me sooner? When do you start?" Jay squealed, reaching out to hug Colt. "I'll need to—"

He gripped her wrists, stopping her dead in her tracks. "You're not coming with me."

The words hit her like a slap in the face. "What?"

"You're not coming with me." Colt pursed his lips. "I already told you. We're done."

He was kidding. Obviously. He was playing some sick prank on her, he couldn't leave her behind, not when she had done this, *all* of this, for him.

"This is goodbye, Jay. I start at the new firm in two weeks." He dropped her wrists to hold the railing instead. His lip trembled. "And after that, I never want to see you again."

The feelings crashed into her like a tidal wave. Terror. Dread. Denial. Hope. Anger. But what finally settled heavy in Jay's chest was anguish. She tried to reach out to steady herself on Colt, but he stepped away from her, leaving her hand to catch air.

Her voice was barely a whisper as she said, "Please, don't leave me."

But Colt said nothing, not even goodbye, as he walked away from her, leaving her utterly alone on a crowded balcony.

She leaned on the railing, trying to focus her blurry vision on the lights before her. No. She couldn't cry. Wouldn't cry. Because if she cried, Michael would know, and that was the last thing she needed. If she had any chance of getting Colt back, she needed to make sure Michael remained ignorant to the entire thing. She could hold it together. She could do this, she could—

"Well, there's certainly a view if I've ever seen one," a dangerously familiar voice echoed through the space, encircling her through the haze of cigarettes and vape smoke.

No. Christ, out of all the people that could possibly come out here, not *him*.

"Get away from me."

Lucio chuckled behind her, heat radiating off of him as he came close. "So harsh, boneca! I thought we were past this. What happened?"

"You happened. You beating the shit out of my boyfriend happened. You being a stalker happened, you risking both of us getting killed by just being here happened," Jay snapped, turning around.

Lucio was dressed in a navy blue suit that brought out his stupid green eyes with a shit-eating grin on his face. And she hated how stupid she felt for wanting to just collapse in his arms. Not because he was anything special, but because he was *there*.

"Boyfriend? I thought Michael was your boyfriend?" Lucio asked, his head tilting.

Jay felt her cheeks flare, and she tried to move away from him, but he had her pinned against the railing. "Just leave me alone."

"Hey," Lucio shifted enough to give her space. "Are you alright?"

"Fantastic. Wonderful. I was having the time of my fucking life before you showed up." A sob threatened to wrack through her. She hid it behind cold eyes and a set jaw, desperate for him to leave, hopeful that he wouldn't.

Lucio matched her stare. "If you're trying to get me to leave, it's not working."

"Boo. I'll have to try harder."

"Do you want me to leave you alone?"

Jay's eyes stung. "Yes."

He examined her. "You're lying."

"What do you care?" She dabbed at her face with her fingertips. "I haven't even seen you since..."

"Since I 'beat the shit out of your boyfriend'?" Lucio's voice was light. He moved next to her, leaning against the railing instead of blocking her path. "Did you miss me?"

"Why would I miss you? You're literally just a client. There were a million of you coming in and out of that place every day."

And yet. Jay wouldn't admit that all she had hoped for the week she left, and the nights before that, was that someone with green eyes and a sultry voice would request her back into the champagne room, whispering her name. He would ask to touch, and she would let him this time, run his hands across her skin, her breasts, her thighs, her—

She cleared her throat. "You weren't special."

"And there were dozens of pretty girls in there that I could have asked for," Lucio said. "But I asked for you."

"Oh, don't feed me that shit. You just figured out that I was dating your brother and wanted to rub it in his face that I was giving you a lap dance. News flash, Lucio, I do that for lots of guys who are willing to throw money at me."

"And why do you?" Lucio asked.

She wished he would touch her. Something, besides just standing here next to her. She just wanted to feel something, anything, besides the Goddamn cold that seemed to be biting into every single part of her, and the absolute heartache that was seeping out of her every pore.

"You don't really need the money, do you? Michael takes care of you."

Jay pressed her lips into a thin line. "I don't want Michael's money. I want to have my own."

"Independent woman," Lucio mumbled. "I like that."

"I don't care what you like," she sniffled. A mistake. He was wearing that cologne she loved so much. The one that drifted into her dreams, where she was lost in a forest and only had that smell to lead her out, but she never found it—the land would give way to a sea that she sank into until she woke up nearly screaming. Luckily, Michael was a heavy sleeper.

"You did when I was slipping twenties into your g-string," Lucio teased.

"Yeah, because I liked the money. I never said I liked you."

"You're right." Lucio leaned down to whisper in her ear. "I just figured it out."

She shoved his arm, pushing him away from her. Her hand burned from where she touched him, but not as badly as the fire burning deep in her belly with need. "Fuck you."

Lucio slinked back to where he had been standing, but kept some distance between them. "Something tells me Michael and Colt wouldn't like that very much."

Jay rubbed her arms as she struggled to hold herself together. She didn't need to say it. Lucio didn't need to know, didn't care. He was cracking jokes. And she deserved it. It was her fault in the first place.

"Jay," Lucio said, drawing her gaze to his. His green eyes sparkled in the light, and Christ, she hated how beautiful he looked right then. "What's wrong?"

Jay shook her head. She shouldn't be talking to him, of all people, about her cheating on his brother with someone else. For all she knew, Lucio was recording this entire thing, and he was going to go back and tell Michael. But the words were out of her mouth before she could stop herself.

"Colt and I broke up."

Lucio hummed. "And that's a problem because...?"

"It's not."

"But you're still upset."

A single tear slipped out. She quickly brushed it away.

"Talk to me, Jay."

"I didn't mean to hurt him," she whispered, her body beginning to tremble. "I didn't want it to be like this."

And before she knew it, she was grabbing Lucio by the lapels, hiding her face in his shoulder, and sobbing. Loud, ugly sounds that made her chest heave and her eyes hurt. She was embarrassing the absolute fuck out of herself. But Christ, for one minute she just didn't care. It felt *good*.

Jay could register him stiffening, before slowly, his arms closed around her, one around her waist, the other holding the back of her head, enveloping her in a warmth she didn't think was physically possible. She couldn't find the strength to stop. Her knees felt weak, and she gripped the front of his jacket like it was the one thing that was going to keep her from sinking into her grief.

"It's okay."

"It's not," she whimpered. "All I do is hurt or use people."

"It's human. People hurt each other and use each other all the time." Lucio shook with a laugh. "I used you, didn't I?"

"No, you paid me." Jay sniffled. "That's different."

"How so?"

"Because we both got something out of it. Didn't we?"

He dropped his hand from the back of her head, prompting her to look at him. He tried a smile, but she could read that it was shaky. "Yeah. I guess we did."

Jay dabbed at her eyes, sniffling again. She probably looked a complete mess; her mascara wasn't waterproof, and she likely had huge streaks from where her makeup was coming off. She needed to fix her face before she went back in.

A soft cloth touched her cheek, catching the tears still falling.

She reached up, her fingers brushing Lucio's as she took the handkerchief from him. "Thank you."

"Of course," Lucio said, resting his hands on her waist before moving them to the small of her back.

She stopped herself from trying to encourage them lower. "Did you talk to Helena?"

"Honestly? I haven't had a chance." Lucio looked toward the city. "Work's been a lot lately."

Jay huffed. "You're always making an excuse, you know that?"

"Hey, this is *your* therapy session," he said, glancing back down at her. "Let's keep this focused on you."

Jay pressed her lips together, wiping at her eyes. "I don't want to focus on me. I want to go home. I want to forget that this night ever fucking happened at all."

"So go."

"I can't."

"Come on. Tell Michael you don't feel well and catch a cab with me. We'll grab a bite, then I'll take you home." Lucio gave her a wry smile. "We haven't completed our therapy session anyway."

Jay giggled through her remaining tears, smoothing out his jacket. "Are you going to give me a lap dance?"

"Only if you promise not to make fun of me. I might not be as good as you."

She laughed again, resting her head on his shoulder. She has expected hard muscle, or bones with how tall and thin he was. But Lucio was soft in the places he needed to be, the places where it mattered when you hugged a person. And God, he was *warm*, as if he had been bathing in sunlight all day and was radiating heat off of him.

His breath rustled some of her hair as he spoke. "You're better off, you know."

"Hm?"

"Colt. He's an asshole."

Jay pushed away from Lucio's chest, enough to look him square on, but not enough to fully break the spell, not just yet. "Don't do that."

"I'm serious." He frowned. "I shouldn't have let you talk me out of beating the shit out of him. Especially now."

She stepped away fully, Lucio's arms falling from around her waist, the warmth falling with it. "He didn't do anything wrong."

"Screaming at you in front of a complete stranger wasn't doing anything wrong? Putting you down wasn't doing anything wrong? What does he say to you behind closed doors?"

"He was upset," Jay said. "And you didn't help."

"Being upset doesn't mean he gets to yell at you," Lucio said. "Does Michael do that to you?"

Jay swallowed hard, rubbing at her arms again. *It was an accident. I didn't mean it. We need to talk about this.* "No."

"You don't have to lie to me." Lucio's voice was low with warning. "I know what he's capable of."

"Capable of?" Her brows furrowed. "You think you know him? When's the last time you even *talked* to Michael?"

"I grew up with him." Lucio held her gaze. "I know him."

He's a liar, you can't believe a word that he says.

"People change, Lucio." Jay turned, looking back toward the doors.

"Did Colt?"

She didn't look at Lucio. He would probably be able to read the answer written all over her face, and she knew he wouldn't like what he saw. "I need to go."

"Offer still stands," Lucio said.

"Don't want it." She stalked toward the door, ignoring the way her body screamed at her to stay, how she wasn't ready to go back in and face Colt. She wasn't ready to pretend like everything was okay yet.

"Jay," Lucio called, just as her hand touched the handle. "I'm serious."

She breathed in deep. She needed to go. The longer she stayed, the more his voice wrapped around her, pulling her back to him.

"Michael isn't who you think he is."

"And you are?"

"I don't lie to you. I have no reason to."

"Bullshit." She began to pull at the door, but her phone buzzed from where it sat in her purse. Christ, probably Michael calling her to see where she was. She knew it had been too long, that he was—

Unknown number

"For when you figure it out," Lucio said from where he still stood against the railing.

Jay's brows furrowed, and she allowed herself to look over at him. "How did you—"

He smirked. "I have my ways."

She returned it. "Is one of them getting it off of Helena's phone?"

He leaned back, nose crinkling in a way that made him look painfully adorable. "You're killing the mystery here."

Let it be the only thing I kill tonight. Jay tossed Lucio a smile as she walked back into the venue, allowing the crowd to swallow her whole.

It was a battle, but eventually Jay found her way back to Michael and Colt, who were enjoying the company of the woman Jay had seen before. She watched in fury as the woman laughed a little too freely, touching Colt's arm. And there was that *fucking* smile. He looked over, seeing Jay, but the smile didn't fade. It twisted, turning into a sick grin that made Jay's heart drop into her stomach.

All she wanted to do was run. Lucio was probably still out on the balcony. She could go to him, and he would take her home like he had promised. And maybe they could do more. For a moment, she could lose herself with him, forget about this fucking party, and Colt, Michael, everything that was making her feel like she was so completely and utterly worthless.

But there Lucio was, shooting Jay a wink as he slipped out the door, right under Michael's nose. She had to stop herself from calling out. It wouldn't do anything but make this awful night even worse. No. She would do what she always did. She would put on her pretty smile, and go back to sit on Michael's arm.

Jay sidled up to him, digging her nails into his arm in an attempt to stop her from clawing the other woman's eyes out. "Hello."

"Hey, Jay!" Michael didn't react to how deeply her nails had sunk into him. He clearly had been drinking in her absence. "This is Delilah, she's one of the other managers."

"Lovely to meet you. Michael was just telling me about him bringing on a new assistant." Delilah gave her a genuine smile. "Hopefully you're better than the last one."

"Now, don't be too hard on Katie. She was a sweetheart," Michael said.

"Oh she was something alright," Colt said. "She must not have been very good if you kept calling her into your office for private meetings, Michael."

"Colt," Delilah chided. She glanced at Jay, her smile tighter now. "Just ignore him. Colt's always been such a joker."

Jay was slightly grateful for the fabric of Michael's suit. If she gripped any tighter, she might break skin. Michael would fucking deserve it. He was no better than Colt. Why would he be? He didn't care about her. She was nothing but a piece of ass to him.

But she would make herself useful.

Jay smiled up at Michael. "Of course, I know Michael's going to be a wonderful boss."

Michael frowned at her. "Where's your drink?"

"Huh?" Jay glanced down at her empty hands. "Oh, the bar line was so long, I got impatient."

He grunted, stealing a drink off a tray for her. "You were waiting in line that entire time?"

"Yeah."

"Well, you missed quite the story. Delilah was just telling us about this crazy meeting she had with a client the other day."

Jay mumbled a response as she took a large sip of her drink. She was going to need a lot more alcohol.

19

"So where'd you go last night?"

Lucio didn't bother looking up at Helena as he continued to dig through his stacks of files. They had multiplied over the last few weeks, and the chaotic order that Lucio always had appeared to be deteriorating. Even still, he was able to find whatever the hell he was looking for. "I told you that I had an event to go to."

Helena tilted her head, narrowing her eyes at him. "Oh really? Who was it for?"

He finally looked up at her, raising a brow. "Since when do I have to answer to you?"

She smirked, leaning her elbows on the table. "Just asking a simple question, no need to bite my head off."

Lucio sighed through his nose as he passed another case file to Helena. His office was stifling hot—the heat cranked up even though it was barely below fifty degrees outside—and she resisted the urge to fan herself with the file. She didn't know how the hell he wasn't struggling to breathe in his suit and tie.

There was something off with him lately. He was more frayed at the edges, coming home later and later, not eating, and if the dark circles beneath his eyes were any indication, he wasn't sleeping, either. He had even changed the passcode on his phone. Helena hadn't been snooping this time. She had been checking something for him while he was driving, and when she entered his usual code, it remained locked. He had used his fingerprint, instead.

Lucio blamed the change on a security issue and shot her a look that meant it was her fault.

"So, an event?" Helena pressed.

He turned his attention to his laptop, fingers flying over the keys as he continued to ignore her. She pursed her lips, deciding to lean back in her chair instead. She looked out the window, the sun beginning to set even though it was barely four. Winter in New York sucked. At least in the summer, she could get a sliver of sunshine after working in the damn office all day. But between this and classes, Helena's only time outside was spent waiting for the train.

"How was it?"

Lucio slammed his laptop closed, scrubbing at his face. "Helena, I am not in the mood today."

Helena's brows furrowed. "Oh? Am I supposed to just put up with your shitty attitude, then?"

"Don't like it? Go home," he said, beginning to go to the door. "I don't need anything else from you today anyways."

She licked her teeth, turning towards him. "You're full of shit, you know that?"

"Excuse me?" He turned around, eyes dark.

Helena knew better. She knew that she was pushing it, that Lucio was already on the brink. But so was she. "You want to constantly bitch at me that I'm not involved enough in your cases, that I don't care. And the *one* time I try to show genuine interest, you shut me out. Do you not hear how messed up that is?"

Lucio's grip on the door handle tightened. "I have my reasons."

"You always have your reasons." Helena slumped down in her chair. "You have a reason for everything. What you *don't* have is a real explanation."

"I don't have to explain myself to you." Lucio stepped away from the door, his posture shifting. "We are not equals, I don't know why the hell you think we are, but I don't have to tell you anything."

Helena stiffened. She crossed her arms over her chest, fear slowly creeping into her gut. But right alongside it, a heat that flushed over her skin and tugged her lip into a snarl. "It's not about being equal, Lucio. It's about you being *honest* with me. It's about you not being a hypocrite."

"I'm a hypocrite?" Lucio's brows shot up, his voice rising in volume. "You think you know everything, you think you know how the world works, and you don't. You're still a child, as much as you think you're not. Because an adult knows when something isn't their business, and they're fine with that. They know when to let things go." Lucio turned away from her again. "Go home. I'll be keeping Dylan late."

"Fuck you."

Lucio whipped around so fast Helena was surprised he didn't break his neck. "What did you just say?"

Helena knew she shouldn't repeat it. She had *never* sworn at Lucio, at least, not like that. But listening to him dismiss her so easily, speak down to her like he was, like he always had, she had snapped. She stood, her arms dropping to her sides and her hands setting into fists. "Fuck. You."

Lucio's jaw slackened. "Who do you think you're talking to right now?"

"Don't try and lecture me!" Helena pointed her finger at him. "I'm sick of this. I'm sick of you deciding what I know and what I don't for me, when I'm expected to tell you everything. You've been acting like a dick for weeks now, and I don't understand why. And I shouldn't have to put up with it. If this was me, you'd have chewed me out and told me to get over it. So explain to me why *I* have to sit here and take this shit from you!"

"You're going to watch how you speak to me," Lucio said, stalking towards her. But Helena refused to back down. "I am your boss and your father, you—"

"You're *not* my father."

It was enough to knock Lucio back on his heels. Helena felt a twinge of pleasure as she watched the way he blinked twice, his throat bobbing. She pushed forward, closing the distance between them. She ignored the way her chest felt like it was going to explode, like a hand was wrapping itself around her throat, the way her vision was blurring at the edges. She was going to say what she wanted to say, what she had been meaning to say for a long time now. And he was going to listen. After all these years, *he* was going to listen to *her*.

"You think just because you signed a little sheet of paper, that you get to call yourself my dad? That only lasted until I was eighteen. And guess what? I haven't been eighteen for sixteen months. You haven't been my dad for three years. A dad talks to his daughter. A dad answers her questions, tells her the truth, is there for her when she needs him. A dad doesn't turn his back on his daughter when she feels like she's lost literally everything! You?" Helena laughed breathlessly, "You were the shittiest excuse for a father I've ever had."

The room chilled. The weight that had been sitting in Helena's chest remained, but she wasn't sure why. She had thought that after she had told Lucio off, told him how she really felt, she would feel better. But now, she only felt an ache that seemed worse than before. And Lucio...

Lucio didn't look hurt. He didn't look angry, or upset, or any of the emotions that she had expected from him. He looked...*indifferent.*

And for some reason that made the ache all the worse.

"You don't want to be my daughter anymore? Fine." He shrugged, and Helena's heart shot its way into her throat. "From here on out you're a tenant and employee. Rent is due on the first of the month."

And that was it. Said with such a finality that Helena wasn't even really sure what had happened. But the ache dissipated, settling into her bones with a numbness she knew she wouldn't be able to place.

She swallowed, squaring her shoulders as she met his cold stare. "And pay is due on the fifteenth."

Lucio opened his mouth to speak again, but a knock at the door interrupted him.

Dylan walked in, holding a stack of files. His mood shift was immediate as he registered the energy of the room. He tried to catch Helena's eyes, but she looked down toward the table.

"Ah, perfect. Are those for the Barker case?" Lucio asked, his previous demeanor completely dissolved. Typical.

Dylan nodded as he set them down on the table. His hand brushed Helena's, but she ignored him, gripping the back of the chair in front of her instead.

"Helena, you're dismissed. Dylan, please bring detective Morton in," Lucio said as he walked back to his desk.

Dylan waited for Helena, but she didn't move. She kept her eyes on the table, scared to look at anything else. Especially Lucio.

"Did you hear me? You're dismissed," Lucio repeated. "Take the files Dylan just brought in and start drafting up notes and questions."

Neither Dylan nor Helena moved. She knew she should go with him, but she couldn't get her legs to move. It was as if she was rooted to the spot, and to remove herself from it would be to admit something she wasn't ready to name yet.

Lucio let out a hard breath through his nose. "Dylan, Helena will be out in just a moment."

Dylan hesitated beside her.

"Dylan." Lucio's voice lowered. An order, not a request. "Go get Detective Morton as I asked."

Helena felt Dylan's hand on her arm, but she shrugged him off. "I'll be there in a second, Dyl."

Another moment of hesitation, before footsteps retreated out the door, and the temperature of the room dropped by ten degrees.

Lucio spoke, keeping the same tone that he had with Dylan. "Take the files, and leave."

Helena finally let herself look at Lucio. "I'm not going anywhere until you let me in on this case."

"You are on this case." He motioned to the files in front of her. "Now go."

"No." Helena tightened her grip on the chair. "I'm your employee. You have no reason to shut me out anymore, now tell me what's going on."

"Helena," Lucio warned, stepping up to meet her. "Either you take those files and get out, or you're fired."

"You promise?" She met his eyes, a small part of her hoping that she would see some flicker of emotion, of regret, of red rimming the green that showed he was just as hurt as she was.

But his eyes were clear. "Going to be *really* hard for you to pay rent without a job, now isn't it?"

Helena grabbed the files and stormed towards the door, almost crashing into Dylan and Alice as she left. The phone rang, drawing Lucio's attention long enough for Helena to quickly pull the door shut behind her.

"Hey, Alice, right? Jay's friend."

"Yeah. You're Helena, Luke's daughter?" Alice asked, giving her a smile that reeked of earnestness.

Helena's jaw clenched, but she still managed a tight smile and a nod of affirmation. "Employee, when we're working here, of course."

"Oh, well, it's nice to see you again, either way," Alice said absently, reaching for the door.

Helena placed herself in between Alice's hand and the knob. "Wait, Luke's just on a call. He said he'll be out in a moment, but I know he wanted me to grab some notes on the case before you went in."

"Okay..." Alice looked towards the office. "But I don't think we should—"

"Come, we'll go to the meeting room. That's where he wanted to talk with you anyways." Helena said as she led Alice away from Lucio's office.

Dylan fell into step beside her, keeping his signing small. *"Are you okay? What happened in there?"*

"Luke's tied up at the moment. He asked me to take Detective Morton down to the meeting room. You know how he *hates* having people in his messy office."

Dylan looked back over his shoulder towards the office in question. He tried to sign to her, but she passed him the files.

"Hold these, would you?" She smiled tight, signing to him, *"Please. Will tell you later."*

Dylan shook his head, but his arms were full of the case files, so Helena turned her attention back to the elevator, jamming the button. The doors opened before them, and Helena motioned for Alice and Dylan to step on first. They did. Helena cast one last glance back at Lucio's office, the door sealed shut.

Fia-te na Virgem e não corras, asshole.

Helena led the way to a meeting room. It was standard fare, a long table with chairs set up on either side, beige walls, some windows along the back wall. The sun had almost completely gone down by now, and the harsh lights from overhead were giving Helena a headache. She motioned for everyone to sit: her and Dylan on one side, Alice on the other.

"Luke just asked me to get any updates from you," Helena said, pulling out a pen and her notepad. Dylan tried to sign something to her, but she pretended not to notice. "About the case."

"Sure," Alice said, pulling out her own set of notes. It was full of detailed scribbles, and it took her a moment to find the correct page. Helena wondered absently what else was written in there. "There's two whistleblowers at the company, although they'd like to remain anonymous."

Helena pressed her tongue into her cheek. "That won't work. If we want this trial to run smoothly, they'll need to testify."

"That's where I'm hoping Luke can help out. He has a way of getting people to open up to him."

Dylan moved his hand to Helena's leg, just above her knee, finger spelling, *"W-H-A-T D-O?"*

She moved her leg away, shooting him a look as she continued to jot down her notes. "And obviously our defendant is none the wiser, correct?"

"No, seems like he's been keeping a pretty low profile due to all the shit getting stirred up. But we want to make sure that he doesn't catch wind." Alice flipped to another page of her notebook.

Helena nodded, continuing to write. Jay flashed to the forefront of her mind. If this case involved Colt, that meant that Jay could be caught up in this somehow. There was no way she knew about the embezzlement, right? Jay didn't seem like the type who would get herself caught up in this sort of thing. And besides, she wouldn't have been dancing as long as she had if Colt was making bank. Unless....he wasn't giving her a cut? Maybe she knew, but he was the one pulling the strings on everything. If Halloween was any indication of how their relationship worked, it wouldn't be too far-fetched. But there was always a chance. Maybe Jay was doing all this as a cover-up, she was hiding behind dancing to keep the suspicion off of her. She made most of her money in tips—Helena was sure Jay wasn't above lying and saying she made less than she actually did—but this? There had to be a line somewhere. Right?

Dylan touched her leg again. *"S-T-O-P. D-A-N-G—"*

Helena crossed her legs, moving as far as she could from him. She kept her eyes on Alice, who didn't seem in the least bit bothered. Fury boiled over in Helena's veins. Jay mentioned that they were close, best friends, even. And best friends told each other everything. But did they tell each other something like this? And if Alice didn't know, she would want to, wouldn't she? She would want to protect Jay just as much as Helena did?

She cleared her throat, meeting Alice's deep brown eyes. "And obviously, Jay won't be affected by this, correct?"

Alice's eyes darkened. "Jay's a big girl. If she wants to get caught up with a guy like Silva, that's her choice."

"Helena!"

There was no time to process the pit that opened in Helena's stomach. She looked up to see Lucio bursting in, absolute fury rolling off of him as he took in the sight: Alice, shocked at his entrance, Dylan, cowering in fear, and Helena, pen poised over the page as realization slowly flooded her.

Lucio didn't even attempt a smile. "Just what the hell do you think you're doing?"

"Talking with the detective like you asked me to," Helena said, standing on wobbly legs. It took all of her strength not to let her knees knock together.

He looked to Dylan, saying one thing but signing another. "I'm sorry, Dylan, I didn't think about you needing a translator." *"You didn't try to stop her?"*

"I tried to, sir. But there wasn't much I could do." Dylan trailed off, his hands falling into his lap.

Lucio avoided looking at Helena like the coward he was, but she could clearly read the anger coursing through him. "Thank you for stepping in, Helena. Now, you're dismissed."

"Detective Morton gave me a brief rundown of the case. Here are the notes," Helena said, half-shoving them at him.

"Perfect. I couldn't ask for a better assistant. Now, do us all a favor and go out for some coffee, will you?"

Helena smiled up at him, matching his all too sweet tone. "Of course, sir. Same as always?"

Lucio returned it with a smile that more resembled him baring his teeth at her. "Of course."

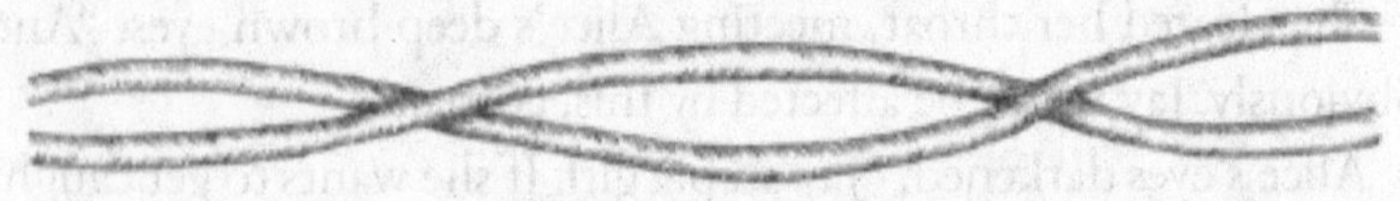

Helena glared out the window of Lucio's office, the night beginning to settle in completely, now. It would be freezing outside, she knew that. But as of right now it didn't matter. The office was still stifling hot. Whether from the anger rolling off of Helena's body or the bullshit furnace, she wasn't sure.

A burst of air came through as the door to the office flew open, and just as quickly left as it slammed shut. Helena turned around in Lucio's chair, staring him down as he stalked across the floor.

She didn't hesitate. "Are you insane?"

"No, you are *not* talking right now," Lucio said, slamming his hands on the desk.

She didn't flinch.

"Move. Now."

"Soak it up, Lucio, you're not going to be telling me what to do after you get *disbarred* for prosecuting your brother!"

Lucio bared his teeth at her. "I'm not going to get disbarred."

"You're going to get caught, Lucio. And then what?" She stood, calm and collected despite how badly she wanted to throw the desk at him. "You've worked so hard to get here, and you're going to throw it away for what? Why are you so obsessed with Michael?"

"You don't get to ask me questions," Lucio hissed. "You're the one who snuck into a meeting that you had *no* business being in. This is data misuse, I could lose this case."

"You *should* lose this case!" Helena turned from him, throwing her hands up. "You're going to lose a lot more if someone finds out about this."

"No one is going to find out because *you're* not going to say anything."

Helena barked out a laugh. He was so sure of himself, so sure that everyone around him was just going to give into his every little whim. Not her. Not anymore. She would be all too happy to watch everything around him go down in flames.

"Give me one damn good reason as to why I shouldn't? If you do this, you're going to lose *everything!*"

"I already have!"

She froze, meeting Lucio's eyes in the reflection of the window. She didn't recognize the man looking back at her. Hunched over his desk, arms stiff and long as he struggled to keep his head up.

Broken.

She had never seen him broken.

"Michael took everything from me."

Everything. The word stuck itself in Helena's mind, lodged itself so deep in her psyche she knew she would never be able to dig it out.

"What are you—"

"Michael is the reason my family isn't here anymore."

She turned to face Lucio, her eyes widening. "What?"

"They said it was an accident." His head fell, his shoulders trembling slightly. "That she fell asleep at the wheel."

The story Helena had been told. The one Lucio shared with her when she saw the photo of him and his family. His *real* family, she had tried to call them. But Lucio had corrected her, ever so gently. *You're my real family too, Hel.*

It was the first time she hadn't corrected him using her nickname.

"But I know. I know he did something. He always hated us together." Lucio's voice cracked, a sob replacing his breath. Tears dropped onto the desk. One right after the other, his body trembling as he spoke. "He didn't want me to have her. I had everything he wanted, and he *hated* it. He took them from me. Elyse, my boys, everything. I can't let him get away with this, Hel. He's already taken so much from me. I *need* to do this, for their sake."

Everything.

He took everything from me.

Helena took a step back. A dangerous thing to do, since she wasn't sure the floor was beneath her anymore. "And what about us?"

Lucio looked up, blinking at her as a tear rolled down his cheek. "What?"

"Me, and Quinn," she whispered, struggling to raise her voice. But she couldn't get enough air, something was sitting on her chest and she couldn't breathe. "Are we *nothing* to you?"

"No, Hel, that's not what I—" Lucio reached out across the expanse of desk.

She took another step backwards, her back hitting the window. "Don't call me that," she spat, but it was wounded and hollow of the anger that she tried to fill it with. "You don't get to call me that."

"Helena—"

She crossed her arms in a desperate attempt to stop herself from shaking. "What, we were just a surrogate for you? A band-aid?"

"Helena, please, you're taking this the wrong way."

"How am I supposed to take this?" Her voice broke as she swallowed back a sob. "You're sitting here crying over your family that's been dead for *years*. You didn't even cry at Gideon's *funeral*."

"Because—"

"Don't try to make up some stupid excuse! You had your chance." Helena blinked back her tears as she stared daggers across the space between them. "You could have been there for us when we lost Gideon, but you *weren't*. You shut yourself up in your stupid office and pretended like he didn't even exist! I lost the one person I cared about most, and all I needed was my dad to show me that he cared too, and you *didn't*. Because we're nothing to you, right? You already lost everything years ago."

Lucio shook his head, his breathing unsteady. "No, that's not—"

"No, it's fine. I get it. You never wanted us in the first place. So I'll make this easier on you." She crossed the room, ignoring his pleas for her to stop, wait, let him explain. "I'm not your daughter, and you're not my father. And from here on out, I'm not your employee. I quit."

Helena slammed the door behind her, wiping the tears from her eyes as she walked as calmly as she could manage towards the stairs, not wanting to give him a chance to catch her on the elevator. She would have Dylan collect her things, and she would go stay at Quinn's until she could find her own place.

She didn't need Lucio. And he didn't need her, either.

20

"**H**ey, Jay, right?"

Jay looked up from her new desk to see Delilah smiling at her. Her straight brown hair was pulled back into a low bun, perfect for showing off the crisp white blouse she wore, a few buttons undone towards the top—enough to show off a small, heart-shaped silver locket. Her honey brown eyes popped against her fair pink skin, making her look like one of those corporate stock photos, but much prettier.

Jay wanted to rip her fucking face off.

She returned Delilah's smile, smoothing out the dull gray dress that Michael had insisted she wear. He didn't want the other women to be jealous—better to dress more conservative on the first day. A part of Jay missed the freedom of her old outfits. She might not have loved the attention, but at least she felt like she could *breathe*.

"Yes, Delilah, right?"

"Yes! We met the other day at the event," Delilah said. "I wanted to come check in on you and see how you're doing."

Fucking fake ass bitch.

Jay shrugged. "It's going. Mr. Silva is busy, so I'm trying to make sure I keep everything straight."

"Don't worry, you'll get the hang of it. Has Michael given you a tour of the office yet?" Delilah asked, to which Jay shook her head.

"Well then, let me do the honors. Come on, I'll fill you in on all the juicy gossip while we walk."

Delilah introduced her to some of the people that she would need to be in contact with because they worked closely with Michael. Everyone seemed nice enough, but Jay could tell that they all had a guard up. To them, she was an outsider.

And maybe she was.

Colt certainly seemed to look at her like she was a complete and utter stranger as Delilah happily reintroduced them, oblivious to their history. But Delilah might as well have been the fucking sun with the way he looked at her. The way that he used to look at Jay.

And Jay smiled and pretended like her heart wasn't breaking inside of her chest.

Over coffee in the high-tech break room, Delilah said, "I know it might be difficult, considering how good-looking he is, but don't get caught up with Michael."

Jay blew on her americano, feigning surprise. "I thought you said Colt was joking the other day."

"I mean, he was, but he wasn't." Delilah sighed, dragging her finger around the rim of her coffee cup. "Michael can be a bit of a flirt. Sometimes the girls get caught up in the moment, if you catch my drift."

Jay shifted, forcing a smile. "That doesn't seem appropriate."

"Well, nothing happens. Or I mean, if anything does, no one comes forward about it."

"But you know something does?"

"I don't know anything. All I know is that that man goes through women like they're water. I don't think he's had an assistant that's lasted longer than a few months." Delilah stirred a packet of splenda into her coffee. "But I hope that you're different. You seem like you're going to fit in well here."

"Hah, I hope so. I'm not exactly in a position to leave. And he was nice enough to offer me this job," Jay said. "But you don't have to worry about me. I'm just getting out of something, so I'm not really looking to get involved in anything new."

Delilah's eyes softened, but Jay had seen the look often enough to know when a woman was fishing for more information. "Oh, I'm sorry. Was it a really bad breakup?"

"Is there such a thing as a *good* breakup?" Jay asked, and Delilah laughed just like she had with Colt at the event, when her hand had lingered on his arm for a second too long to be anything less than friendly.

Jay's smile tightened. "What about you? Are you seeing anyone?"

Delilah bit her lip, but the corners of her mouth did nothing to fight the smile blooming across her face. "Sort of."

Jay gripped her coffee cup to stop herself from clawing Delilah's eyes out. "Does he work here?"

"Oh, God no," Delilah said. She took a sip of her drink, her pink lipstick staining the white porcelain. "I know better than to get involved with people at work. Makes breakups *so* awkward, you know?"

"Yeah." Jay looked back down at her coffee.

It was fine. This wasn't a breakup. Not really. This was her and Colt going through one of their rough patches, like they usually did. Maybe being so close, seeing her all the time, it would help Colt realize that they *were* meant to be together. And maybe she could help him with his work, get to the top a little faster. It wouldn't be that hard to—

No. He was leaving. In two weeks, he would be gone, walking out of her life forever.

Delilah's phone buzzed from where it sat on the table. She glanced at it, a flash of excitement crossing her features before settling back into boredom. "Crap, I got a meeting. But this was nice, Jay. I hope we get to do it again soon."

The rest of the day was uneventful. Jay learned the ropes rather quickly, setting up meetings for Michael and scheduling events. She wondered how he was able to get any work done—it seemed like his schedule was constantly packed. But it made things easier for her. She didn't have to worry so much about putting on a brave face for him, especially while listening to Delilah and Colt chat from across the room.

As if he knew she was thinking about him, her desk phone rang. Jay answered in her most professional tone. "Yes, Mr. Silva?"

"Come into my office."

Jay grabbed the tablet she'd been issued, which had access to his calendar and other work-relevant things. She glanced one last time towards Colt, but he was too caught up in Delilah to notice her going anywhere.

Michael was seated behind his desk, hair slightly disheveled from the long day. Before she had moved in with him, Jay couldn't recall a time in the past six years she had seen him like that; he made sure he was always put together, except when he was freshly woken up. And even then he looked painfully good. But now that they were living together, there were more times like this. More moments where she began to see the other sides of him.

Some that she liked, and some that she didn't.

It all was the same in the end.

He gave her a rare smile as she came in. "Hey, how was the day?"

"Great. Delilah showed me around the office and introduced me to some people," Jay said, languidly walking to his desk. He turned himself in such a way that invited her to sit in his lap, and she didn't hesitate.

"Delilah's a good friend to have here. You'd do well to get on her good side," Michael said, wrapping an arm around Jay's waist.

Jay bit back her comment. It was nothing. It was a passing thought, nothing of substance, coming from him. And it was quickly forgotten as he put his hand on her thigh, and moved it below the hem of her dress.

"I have to say, I've always loved seeing you with nothing on, but this...This is a very different sight."

Jay tilted her head back as he kissed her neck, needle-like pangs shooting through her with each touch of his lips to her skin. She laced a hand in his hair, desperate to suppress the feeling. "Funny, I was going to say the same to you."

He hummed against her throat while he settled his hand between her legs. More needles. Jay closed her eyes, trying to imagine Colt moving her panties to the side instead, pressing his fingers inside of her.

But the image shifted to him and Delilah. Her hair loose and lips parted as he fingered her in the break room.

Jay's grip on Michael's hair tightened enough to elicit a hiss from him.

He pressed his thumb against her clit. "Christ, anjo."

Jay dipped her head down to meet his lips, shifting so she could straddle him. He welcomed it, hiking her dress up further as she ran her tongue along his bottom lip. Michael's lips parted, and she moved into his mouth, focusing on his moans, his movements, his cock hard as she grinded deeper in his lap.

Michael was hers. He would fuck her, and her alone. Jay would make sure of it. She didn't need Colt; he was a lousy fuck anyways.

Michael's hands shifted to grip her ass and hold her, moving her to the desk instead. "You're in a mood today."

"Don't you like it when I want you?" Jay batted her lashes at him, before leaning in for another kiss.

He wrapped a hand around her throat, pushing her back. "I do."

"So what's the problem?"

His eyes searched hers. She did her best to hold his gaze, but Michael had a way of making it feel as if he could look straight through her.

Jay tried to swallow past his grip. "Baby?"

Michael pulled her in, kissing her so hard she thought she might bruise. He ripped her panties off, and Jay moved herself closer to try and grind on him, desperate to get something.

But Colt kept coming back, memories of him gently running fingers up and down her back, holding her thighs, kissing her breasts, calling her beautiful. Laying beneath her as she rode his cock, moaning her name as he came inside of her.

She needed to forget.

"Michael," Jay whispered over the sound of his belt buckle coming undone. "Get on the desk."

He pulled away from her, his brows furrowing. "What did you just say?"

She licked her lips, reaching up to hold his face. "Get on the desk."

The storm was building in his eyes, pupils showing only the slightest hint of blue. "I fuck you the way I want to, not the other way around."

"You're right." Jay reached into his pants, sliding her hand to his hard cock. Michael groaned at the touch, his hand gripping her thigh. "But this is different, baby. This isn't a boss fucking his secretary, or a client fucking a stripper." She stroked him, slow and hard. "This is you and me."

Michael went rigid, but Jay ignored it.

"You always tell me I'm your favorite," she whispered. She pressed her lips to the corner of his mouth. "Let me show you why."

It was only a moment of hesitation. A moment where Jay remembered who she was. That it was *her* choice to be here, with or without Colt. She was staying because *she* wanted to. She was fucking Michael because *she* wanted to. It was her choice. It was

always her choice. Michael was *hers,* she was the one in control,
here. Not him.

Michael's hand gripped her hair, and he pulled her off the desk,
throwing her towards the window. He pulled her head back just
before it slammed into the glass, like he knew it would bruise.

He pressed himself up against her, his dick at her back. "You are
my favorite, anjo. But it would be best for you to remember your
place."

Jay kept her eyes on the skyline, trying her best to fake moans of
pleasure as he fucked her, concerned only with his own.

21

Helena breathed out a heavy puff of air as she walked out of the lecture hall, her eyes having to adjust from the sterile lighting of the building to the warm streetlights around her.

December was officially upon them, and of course, she hadn't dressed properly for the weather. Quinn hadn't grabbed much for her from Lucio's place—stating that if she wanted anything specific, she would have to go get it herself.

Helena had said that she would rather stab her own eyes out than go back to that hell hole.

She and Dylan hadn't really talked—he had tried to defend Lucio again, saying that she didn't get it; he hadn't meant what he said, blah blah blah.

Dylan had apologized the next day, but she was still pissed at him. She couldn't stay mad at him for long, of course. But for some reason, she felt his loyalty to her was slipping. Even tonight, he had to miss class because Lucio needed him for some last minute emergency.

Which meant Helena was stuck walking to the train alone. She hated this damn city. She should have tried to go somewhere upstate like she wanted. At least then she wouldn't be wandering around the dark streets alone.

Helena's mind drifted to Jay. It had been weeks since they had last talked, despite Helena reaching out multiple times.

It made sense why Jay hadn't responded. What the hell would Jay want to do with Helena, anyways? They were living two completely different lives.

Them being friends was never going to happen.

"Hey, Helena!"

Helena looked back towards the doors to see one of her classmates approaching her. "Hey, Christine."

Helena didn't know Christine very well. They had a couple classes together, had gotten paired for a few assignments, but their interactions outside of that had been limited.

But she was nice enough from what Helena knew. She had pretty blonde hair and blue eyes, with a face and body that made her closer to model status than future politician, like she said she wanted to be. But who was Helena to judge?

"A bunch of us are heading to a party at Harry's place to celebrate midterms being over," Christine said. "You wanna join us?"

Helena looked at her phone. It was late enough already, and she knew if she didn't catch the train at the right time, she'd be screwed. "I don't know..."

"It'll be fun, I promise. We're literally just going to sit around and drink. And if you don't want to drink, no biggie. We've got some other stuff you can do."

It could be fun. Helena didn't go out often, except with Quinn during Halloween, and that one time she had snuck into Vision. But otherwise, she was always home right after class, unless her and Dylan were hanging out. A party with people her age could be cool—maybe she could make some friends. Or maybe this could be a complete and utter shit show, and she'd get stranded somewhere standing with a bunch of people that she really didn't know or care about. The wind blew, causing her to shiver.

"Look, I really appreciate it, but I really should get home," she said. "But, maybe next time."

"Okay, I guess we'll catch you later," Christine said, heading off in the direction of the train.

Helena sighed, rechecking her phone.

A text from Quinn letting her know they were working late, and Lucio, checking in with her. Her blood boiled.

He had some nerve, texting her after what he had done. She didn't care what Quinn said; her, Quinn, and Gideon were nothing but a replacement to Lucio, something to distract him from the pain of losing everything that he always wanted.

Helena walking out of his life didn't matter. And besides, she was an adult. So she was going to do what adults do.

Whatever she wanted.

When Christine had said they were having a get together, this was not what Helena had in mind.

The apartment was crammed, and Helena was stuffed into a too small kitchen with people that she didn't know well, if at all. Some faces she had seen in lecture halls, or in passing, but most of them were complete strangers, with smiles too wide and pupils blown from one substance or another. She kept trying to drink to help ease her nerves, but each one just made the knot in her stomach even worse. She should have just gone back to Quinn's. They didn't even know she was out, but the room was spinning too much for her to worry about anything else.

Helena grabbed herself another drink, some weird mix that someone had filled in a Gatorade cooler jug. She knew better, but she didn't give a shit. All that mattered was letting loose, and not letting Lucio get to her any more than he already had.

And after three jungle juices and a few shots, Helena had reached that point. The apartment had become unbearably hot, and the noise was too much. She stumbled through the crowd, until she noticed an open window that visibly led out onto a fire escape.

Maybe people were going out there to smoke. But since everyone around her was already smoking in the apartment, that didn't seem very likely. The fresh air that blew in was enough of a sign.

She crawled out, gripping the rusty metal as she moved away from the window, the sound of the party dying down significantly.

Helena looked down at the unusually quiet streets; a small benefit to being on the Lower West Side. It was pretty. Maybe when she could afford her own place she would get one here.

She rested her head against the brick of the building. Yeah, her own place, where she could do whatever she wanted, whenever she wanted. No one to question her or tell her to be home at a decent hour, or annoying siblings constantly walking in on her. Just her.

Helena's phone buzzed. The world spun, and it took all of her focus to pull out her phone from her back pocket and look at the name on the screen. *Lucio.* Helena scowled, hanging up on him. He had probably checked her location and seen that she wasn't at Quinn's or at school.

God, Lucio was such an *ass.* She had told him to leave her alone, but all he had done in the week that she had been gone was bother her. He hadn't even tried to apologize. He kept telling her to come home, that they needed to talk, but Helena had ignored him. If her brain had been working, she would have blocked him. Or turned off her location. But as of now, all she could do was continue swiping at her screen, rejecting the call each time.

He finally seemed to get the hint and stopped calling. But then her phone buzzed again, and she groaned as she had to once more exert mental energy to look at it.

Lucio

Where are you? Are you okay?

Helena just swiped the message away, not even bothering to open it. Her eyes burned, and she wiped at them, sniffling. She didn't get it. Three years of him basically ignoring her, but now that she told him she wanted nothing to do with him, he wanted to have a relationship with her? Typical. People always wanted what they couldn't have. Well, too bad for him. She was done. She didn't need him. She didn't need a dad. She had Quinn, who had been more of a parent to her than Lucio had *ever* been.

Quinn had taken care of her, taken her to doctor's appointments, made her breakfast, went to open school nights and helped her with her homework. And yeah, maybe Lucio had tried to do those things too when he came into the picture. Maybe he took them on vacations, taught her how to look for sea glass, brought them to museums and the aquarium and taught her all these useless facts that she sometimes liked to flex on other people. Maybe he was there for her when she had a really bad nightmare and needed to talk when Quinn was out working late.

But Lucio wasn't there for her when Helena needed him most. And she couldn't forgive him for that.

"Kid? What's going on?"

Helena blinked away the bleariness in her eyes, pulling her phone away. When the hell had she called Jay?

"Kid?"

"Sorry, didn't mean to call you," Helena slurred. God, her body felt *heavy*.

Jay paused. "Are you drunk?"

"No."

"Say 'She sells seashells by the seashore.'"

"Why?"

"Do it."

"I'm not gonna do that," Helena mumbled. "So stop askin'."

"Drunk. Where are you?"

Helena breathed in the cool night air, filling her lungs and letting it out as she spoke. "Some party. Sucks. Don't know anybody."

"I thought we talked about you going out?"

"What are you, my dad?"

"No, I'm a concerned citizen wondering where the hell there's a party with underage drinking."

Helena had to giggle at that one. "Shut up."

Jay's smile was clear in her voice. "You need a ride home?"

Helena pressed her foot against the metal of the railing before her. "I'm not going home."

"Then where are you going to spend the night?"

"Quinn's."

"Okay, how are you going to get there?"

"I can order a ride."

"By yourself?"

Helena huffed, stamping her foot against the bars. "I'm not a child."

"You're not."

"So stop treating me like one."

"Hel, you remember when I didn't let you get a ride to Quinn's when you were stone cold sober?"

Helena realized Jay couldn't see her nodding, so she hummed her affirmation.

"So what makes you think in that pretty little brain of yours that I'm going to let your drunk ass get a ride home alone?"

"You and your dumb girl code," Helena mumbled.

"You don't get to make fun of girl code when you're still out here making pinky promises. Can you tell me where you are?"

"I told you, a party."

"Christ Almighty," Jay sighed. "Okay, are you at least sober enough to send me your location?"

Helena opened her eyes enough to do as Jay asked, but it felt like she was moving through water. God, she had drunk *way* too much. But she hadn't ever been drunk—the one party Quinn held she tried a sip of alcohol, thought it was the most disgusting thing on the planet, and then never tried it again.

And Lucio wasn't a very big drinker. She thought they had a wine cellar thing, but she couldn't remember the last time he'd had a drink with dinner. Or a drink period.

Fuck him. This was his fault. Maybe if he had drank around her, she would have—

The sound of beer cans being shoved into garbage bags.

A glass bottle—the glass ones were always the prettiest, but her parents usually bought the stuff in plastic bottles, cheaper, easier to recycle, and they hurt a hell of a lot less when—

"Helena, sweetheart?" Jay's voice drawing her back.

"Sorry."

"You feeling okay?"

"I want to take a nap."

"Who made your drinks?"

"Myself."

"And you—"

"Yes, mother, I watched my cup too." Helena rolled her eyes, which was a huge mistake, because it sent the world tumbling with it. She leaned her head against the brick, listening to the sound of Jay getting in a car and saying hello to the driver.

"Good girl. Think you got twenty minutes in you?"

"I think so," Helena mumbled.

Jay sighed again. "You want to tell me what happened?"

"With what?"

"With you. What made you go out drinking tonight?"

"Why do you care?"

"Because it's a Thursday night and you're trashed out of your mind at a party alone."

"I'm not alone." Helena turned her face toward the window, where a faint smell of someone's vape climbed out to meet her. "There are people inside."

"Friends?"

"People."

"So you're alone."

"Not."

"Come on, kid. Talk to me," Jay said, and maybe it was the alcohol, or maybe it was Jay's voice having that genuine tone to it, or maybe Helena was just tired of holding everything in.

"Lucio and I got into a fight," Helena said, gripping the metal bars beneath her. "Well, not a fight, maybe, but..."

"About what?"

Michael took everything from me.

"Nothing."

"Kiddo."

Helena sniffled. "I don't wanna talk about it."

"Okay," Jay said, final and clear.

Helena blinked, pulling the phone away from her ear to make sure the call hadn't disconnected. "Okay?"

"You don't want to talk about it, fine. But you gotta talk to me about something."

Helena pursed her lips, gazing at the building across from her. She could see a Christmas tree in the window, or at least what she thought might be a Christmas tree. Shit was pretty blurry, still. She liked Christmas. Or used to. It was the one holiday Lucio was forced to take off, and actually spend time with them. But she wasn't sure how it would look this year.

"I'm tired."

"I know, you told me you—"

"No, I mean I'm tired of being treated like a child."

Jay hummed. "So what are you going to do about it?"

"I've tried doing something about it," Helena said, bringing her knees to her chest. "I've tried talking to Lucio, I've tried showing him that I can handle more, and he *still* makes me feel like I'm thirteen and can break at any moment. It's annoying. Like, I didn't even want to go to NYU. *He* told me that's where I had to go. And I didn't even get to choose my program. He's all 'you're going to be a prosecutor and that's final' and shit. He doesn't know anything about me. He thinks that *just* because Gideon wanted to be a lawyer, that means I must have too. Just because Gideon wanted to stay close to home and work with him, *I* must have too. And just because Gideon got sick out of nowhere then I must—"

Shit. Shit, shit, shit. The words caught in her throat worse than a razor blade, cutting the sob that tore through her and rocked her forward. *Don't cry. Don't you dare cry. Not when he never did.*

"Kiddo," Jay's concern reached through the phone, wrapping around Helena like a hug .

"I'm my own person." Helena sniffled. "And I just want to be treated like one."

"And what does Lucio say?"

I've already lost everything.

"He hasn't said shit to me in three years." Helena wiped at her eyes. A breeze ripped through the street, nearly blowing her over, but she pressed her free hand against the fire escape. "He doesn't care about me."

"That's not true," Jay said.

"What do you know?" Helena snapped. "Not like you two are friends. He flirted with you once in a coffee shop. Don't act like you're some all seeing being or some shit."

"I know your dad a lot better than you think I do."

"Yeah right." Helena snorted. "What, did he start coming into the club or some shit like that?"

Jay's silence was deafening.

"Did he?"

"I can't talk about—"

"Oh my *God!*" Helena screeched, wanting to hurl at the mere thought. "Did he see you naked? No, wait, don't answer that, I don't want to know. Oh my God I think I'm going to throw up. Or die. I might choke on my own vomit right here."

Jay laughed quietly, and Helena realized that maybe the driver could hear their entire conversation. Great, now everyone knew her dad was hooking up with a stripper. No, not hooking up. Right? Oh God, Helena wasn't sure if she could handle the thought of—

"Relax, Hel," Jay said, clearing her throat to hide a giggle. "You're spiraling."

"Don't talk to me. You gave my dad a—" Helena covered her mouth to keep from actually throwing up. She didn't know what the penalty was for vomiting on a fire escape, but she had to imagine it wasn't something she could afford. "Why didn't you tell me?"

"You see how you're acting right now? Why the hell would I?"

Helena groaned. "I knew something was going on. I can't believe you."

"Relax. It was before I knew he was even your dad. And as soon as I found out, I chewed his ass out for you."

"You did?" Helena furrowed her brows. "Why?"

"Cause he was being an asshole. You wanted me to be *nice* to him for missing your birthday?"

"I mean..." Helena played with the laces of her shoes. "He didn't exactly miss it."

"What do you mean?"

A helicopter passed overhead, its lights blinking into the empty sky. Helena hated how you couldn't see the stars in New York. It wasn't as bad in Scarsdale, since there wasn't as much light pollution, but one time for her and Gideon's birthday Lucio had taken them camping, and the four of them laid beneath the stars for hours, pointing out constellations with Lucio's help, and making up their own. Gideon had called his "Acer Stella." It was just an amalgamation of stars, random ones that he had selected because they were the brightest.

"Why would you try to make a tree constellation?" Helena asked, *squinting as she tried to follow Gideon's finger.*

"Because trees live for a really long time. There are some trees that are hundreds of years old, thousands, even! How cool would it be to think about a tree that is made of stars, that are billions *of years old?"*

"I think it's a great idea, G," Lucio said, pressing a marshmallow into a s'more. "That constellation will be here long after any of us."

Gideon smiled as he adjusted his glasses. "And if I go before you, Hel, you can always look at the stars and know that I'm up there too. Looking down on you."

"Shut up. You and I promised that if you go, I go, remember?" Helena said, flicking him in the forehead.

"Neither of you is allowed to go anywhere!" Quinn shouted from where they were throwing more wood on the fire. "I'm the oldest, I get to go before all of you!"

Lucio chuckled. "Alright, enough. Come make your last s'mores of the night before bed."

Her birthday gift this year had been a star map, the constellation traced out for her. Acer Stella.

"Hel?"

Jay's voice pulled Helena out of her thoughts, and she looked back down toward the city streets. "Yeah?"

"I'm here, can you come down?"

Helena squinted between the bars of the fire escape, spotting Jay stepping out of a car, her bright pink jacket making her easy to see. "Yeah, I'm coming. See you in a second."

The party had died down enough that Helena had a much easier time leaving than she had coming, but the alcohol had had more time to settle in her veins. She gripped the railing for dear life, carefully counting each of the steps as she walked down from the fourth floor.

Finally, she was out of the building, and she half-smiled at the sight of Jay walking to meet her.

Jay's coat did nothing to hide her bright blue pajama bottoms, hilariously matched with a pair of boots that were likely as much as Lucio brought home in a month. Helena collapsed into Jay's arms, smiling at the feeling of her warmth.

"Christ, you reek of alcohol," Jay said, using one hand to wave at her nose as she put the other around Helena's shoulders.

"Shut up about it," Helena slurred, leaning further into Jay.

"You got a key for Quinn's place?"

Helena dug through her pockets, but they came up empty. She could have sworn she—"Shit."

"Kid, you're killing me here," Jay groaned.

"I must have left it at Quinn's. We left together this morning."

Jay sighed loudly, loading Helena in the back of the car. The driver must have asked about her, because Jay mentioned something about just cracking the window open.

"Where are we going?" Helena mumbled, resting her forehead against the cold glass of the window. The breeze came through, the cold December air tickling her nose. The snow would be coming soon, she could feel it. She liked the snow.

"My place," Jay said. "And I need you to be very, very careful."

Helena just mumbled in agreement, her eyelids heavy as the car began to drive.

Someone was shaking the crap out of Helena, which was a risky thing to do. She wasn't too sure she wasn't about to throw up, even though it sounded like a very good idea at that moment.

But instead, Helena snapped awake, her surroundings spinning in a blur of light.

Oof, they *hurt*. Who the hell turned all the lights on? And where the hell was she?

She groaned and placed her hands over her eyes. "Where?"

"My place," a voice that sounded an awful lot like Jay's said.

Right. Jay.

Jay had picked Helena up from...somewhere.

Where had Helena been? Why couldn't she remember?

Cool air kissed her face, but *oh God more lights turn off the Goddamn—*

"Christ, kiddo, we need to build up your tolerance." Jay put one arm around Helena's waist, and put Helena's arm over her shoulders as she helped her out of what Helena realized was a car.

She tried to tell Jay that she didn't need a tolerance, that what she needed was a really good taco, Quinn made the best tacos, but she wanted one with a lot of grease and maybe some hot sauce, but her lips felt like they weighed a ton, so it just came out in a string of likely incoherent grumbling as they moved away from the car.

Helena kept her eyes half-closed, which helped to alleviate the way that the world continued to spin around her. The only steady thing was Jay. And that was enough, for now. But soon, Helena was going to need a bed. A nice, cozy bed where she could sleep this off.

"Hey, Chris," Jay said, her voice echoing through the space. The foyer of a very fancy and probably very expensive apartment building, Helena had to guess. The floors were certainly fancy. And looked cold. Ooh, cold sounded good. Helena tried to reach for them, suddenly feeling very hot, but Jay kept her upright.

Jay adjusted her grip on Helena's waist. "Had to go pick up my little cousin."

Helena registered a man sitting behind a fancy marble counter looking between them, eyes full of suspicion. She had half a mind to flip him off, but that required effort, and also meant letting go of Jay.

And Jay was *so* comfy.

"I can see that," Chris said. "Will you need any assistance bringing her up?"

"No, we should be okay, but, if you could do me a favor, and not let Michael know, I would seriously appreciate it." Jay covered Helena's ears, and she scowled as she escaped one of Jay's hands. "These two don't get along very well, and it's always a huge headache whenever I bring her around."

Chris smiled and nodded. "Of course, I completely understand. Have a good night."

"You too," Jay said. They continued to move, and Helena recognized the familiar whoosh and ding of an elevator. Jay pulled out her keys, holding them up to a sensor before pressing a button. "Now, don't throw up in the elevator, okay?"

Helena nodded slowly, leaning on Jay as she closed her eyes again. The motion made her stomach wrench, but she knew it was only a matter of time before they got to the room.

But a ding and the sound of keys jingling told her they finally did.

"Okay, kiddo, let's get you to bed."

The next thing she knew, her body was hitting possibly one of the comfiest mattresses she had ever laid on. She smiled as she was rolled onto her side, her feet lifted and freed from their shoe prisons, before dropping back onto the soft cloud of a mattress.

"I've got a bucket right here for you, okay?"

"Thanks," Helena finally muttered, feeling a hand push back her hair, while her body sank into darkness.

22

J ay settled herself into a huge armchair near the window, the perfect place to keep an eye on Helena for the night. The risk of alcohol poisoning was low, but never zero. Jay wasn't a person who took chances. And besides, Helena looked kind of cute with her hair pushed back away from her face, which was free of her usual scowl. She really was a pretty girl. And smart, too. A little headstrong, maybe too opinionated, but if she was going to go for law like she said she was, it was important for her not to let people push her around. Jay had been like that once. Hell, she still kind of was. But Jay had enough experience to know when to bite her tongue and when to talk back.

And sometimes it was easier to just swallow your pride. You catch more flies with honey than with vinegar, after all. Jay's new boots were proof of that enough.

A few long buzzes came from Jay's pocket, and she pulled out her phone, not needing to look at the screen to know who was calling her at this hour. "She's safe and sound."

Lucio let out a heavy sigh. "She'd better be. I'm going to kick her ass when she gets home."

Jay rolled her eyes. He was so dramatic. Now she knew where Helena got it from. "Lucio."

"I'm serious. This is what I get for letting her do what she wants. I give her an inch and she takes a mile."

"An *inch?*" Jay raised her brows. "I can smell that lie from all the way down here."

"I'm not lying. I don't lie to you."

She snorted and sank a little further into the chair. "Heard that one before."

"Look, Helena's my daughter," Lucio said. "I know how to handle her."

"Do you? Is that why she called me instead of you?"

Lucio went silent. Jay almost pulled the phone away from her ear to make sure the call didn't disconnect, but he spoke up a moment later. "She called you?"

He actually sounded hurt. Served him right, if what Helena said was true.

"Mhm. Told me all your dirty little secrets, too." Jay kicked the side of her chair. "You're going for 'Dad of the Year', aren't you?"

"Watch it," Lucio growled.

"You first," Jay shot back.

She could practically hear his jaw ticking on the other end.

Jay twirled a piece of her hair between her fingers. She needed to get it pressed again soon, maybe she'd drag Helena along with her—they could make a day out of it. "You do realize she's an adult, right?"

"She's my child," Lucio said. "And when she makes stupid decisions like this, she only proves my point."

"Proves your point? Girl's got oxygen deprivation from you choking her out on that tight ass leash. Of course she's not making smart decisions."

"I'm keeping her safe."

"Safe, or sheltered?"

Silence.

Jay sighed and got up to check on Helena one last time. Her breathing was completely even, but just to be safe, Jay stacked some pillows behind Helena's back to guarantee that she wouldn't shift during the night. She seemed to be good, and if Jay was going to be talking to Lucio, she didn't want to risk waking Helena up.

"She's her own person," Jay said, softening her voice. "You can't treat her like she's not."

"I know she is, but—"

"Excuse."

Lucio huffed. "Alright, I'm not paying for therapy right now."

"Yeah, you still owe me for the last one." Jay flicked off the lamp and tiptoed out of the room, closing the door gently behind her.

"I thought we called it even when you fell to pieces on the balcony over your ex-sidepiece?"

Jay scrunched her nose over the thought of it. God, she had been so *stupid*. Colt had planned to leave her behind, and she had been completely oblivious. After everything she had done for him, he'd just tossed her aside. Maybe if she had told Michael earlier, they would still be together.

But it didn't matter, now. Not much mattered anymore.

"How can we call that even? You left me all emotionally fucked," Jay said, staring at a painting in the hall. It was some hideous modern piece that Michael had picked out from an art show he had dragged her to. She had made some vague comment about it and he had taken that as a sign that she loved it. He was so annoying with that shit.

"And whose fault is that? I told you to come home with me."

"Yeah? And then what? You were gonna make me feel better?"

Lucio went quiet. The air around Jay suddenly felt thick, as if it would be hard to move if she tried.

"That's how this works, doesn't it?"

She didn't miss the way Lucio's voice gained a slight edge. Like he was trying hard not to let his thoughts meander the same way that hers were beginning to.

Jay bit her lip. "Is it?"

"I've been following your lead the entire time." A shift, a creak of a chair, a tapping of—fingers?—against something solid. "And so far, that seems to be our routine."

"I forgot, you like routines, don't you?" Jay said, holding onto the wall as she walked toward Michael's bedroom.

"I do. Especially yours."

The door handle was ice beneath her burning palm. "You've only seen me dance a few times."

He chuckled, a low, sultry sound that rumbled through the phone, danced down her spine, and settled between her legs. "You're less observant than you think."

Jay immediately sorted through her memories, struggling to search crowds of blurry faces, looking for that dark skin and those stunning green eyes. Impossible to miss. "You've only been to the club twice."

"Would it make you feel better to think that was true?"

She didn't know how to answer that question. "What are you doing?"

"Me?" Lucio asked, faux innocence lacing his tone. "Sitting here. Talking to you."

"Not what I meant," Jay said. She had to clear her throat to hide the way that it almost cracked. "You're playing with me."

Lucio's voice lowered. "Trust me, boneca, if I was playing with you, you'd know."

Jay opened the door to the bedroom. It was large, the type that people often wanted on those home improvement shows. A pair of chairs with a small area rug looking over at the bed, a small table between them. The bed itself was a California king, which should have been more than enough for Jay to be able to find her own space during the night. But every morning, she woke up to Michael's arms around her, or his lips trailing across her neck, his dick hard at her back, expecting her to roll over for him. Beyond that, the city. A storm was moving in, drowning out any semblance of a night sky. A perfect view from her ivory tower.

"Then what are you doing?" she asked.

"I already told you," Lucio purred. "Sitting here. Thinking about you."

She crossed the threshold, shutting the door behind her. "Thinking of me how?"

"You're asking a lot of questions." Jay could hear another creak, like Lucio was leaning back in his chair, probably with a cocky smirk playing on his lips. "And ones I think you already know the answer to."

"I don't, actually."

"Liar."

She needed to stop. This was crazy, ridiculous, insane, and if Michael found out, he'd kill her.

But there was something in Lucio's voice that made Jay's hand trace the skin where her tee shirt had rolled up just enough.

"No, I'm serious. I want to know what you want from me." She walked over to the bed, crawling across the deep blue bedspread until she was in the center, burying herself between the pillows, her finger playing with the hem of her pants.

"You mean you haven't figured it out yet?" Lucio's voice was like honey, and Christ, Jay was so grateful that he couldn't see her right now. She didn't think she could handle it. She couldn't bear those eyes meeting hers from across the room, watching her as her fingers slid into her panties.

The memory of when things had gone too far, when she had wanted him too much, and he had wanted her too, waltzed into her mind. The burning desire to have him touch her, to run his hands over her breasts, kiss her skin, slip a hand between her thighs, all of it cascaded back over her.

"Say, it, Lucio," Jay said, surprising herself with how demanding she was. Not a whine, or even a plea, but an order.

"Fine," Lucio said. "I want you to close your eyes."

"What, you think you can make me come just from talking to me?" Jay asked, but her voice shook slightly as she ghosted her finger over her clit.

Lucio's hum rumbled through the phone and down her body. "Close your eyes."

She did.

"You're just outside my office door," he began. "Wearing a shirt that's too low cut and a skirt that's too short."

Jay could imagine herself as he spoke, painting a picture in her mind. Of course, men were all the same. But even still, she pictured herself reaching for the door, opening it, and walking inside.

Lucio was sitting at a desk, not like Michael's glass one, but solid oak. And Lucio was wearing that gorgeous suit of his; the one that brought out his eyes.

She stood in the doorway a moment, taking it all in. Lucio behind his desk, slowly moving away from his computer. And she could see it: he wanted her, needed her. And she would let him have her.

But on her terms.

Jay strode in; slow, deliberate steps, her heels echoing in the space. His eyes continued to trace every curve of her body as he turned away from his desk, but Jay stopped him from getting up. Instead, she straddled him and lowered her lips to his. She could imagine his cologne—she had finally found it: orris and leather and lemon, with a hint of tobacco flower—infiltrating every single part of her.

Lucio moved his hands up her thighs, fingers just barely grazing her ass. She went without panties.

"They'd only get in the way," Jay whispered, and Lucio finally let out a small moan. It's a delicious sound; not that strangled growl of a man holding back. He was giving in, completely, utterly, and she would take him. She would have all of him that he would give.

She pulled him in by his tie, kissed him hard, deep, hungry. And he kissed her right back. God, his lips were soft, as soft as she imagined, and when his tongue slid past her teeth, she couldn't wait to know what it would feel like between her legs.

Lucio ripped her shirt off, and Jay wasn't quick enough to stop herself from gasping. Either he didn't notice or didn't care, because he was too focused on her body, looking at her, oh fuck she loved when he *looked*—no. When he saw her.

All of her. All the parts that she loved, that she brought out because they made her feel a little more like herself; all the parts she hated, that she had tried to hide because Michael had made them ugly and wrong and Colt had never argued.

Lucio saw all of it. He drank her in like he was drowning in the ocean and she was his last breath of air. And he was hers.

His lips trailed down her skin, working slowly down her neck to her chest. His hands caressed her breasts and waist, exploring every inch of her that he could reach. Featherlight touches that lingered, held her tighter for just a moment, then resumed their journey. Jay's hips begged to roll into him at the touch, for some kind of relief for the ache building between her legs.

"If you're trying to hold back, you're not going to enjoy this as much," Lucio mumbled against her. He cupped her breasts, his left thumb brushing over her nipple, while his right fingers pinched her bud.

"I'm not," Jay whispered, letting herself give in, grinding against him so his hard cock sent shockwaves of pleasure up her spine. God, she could ride him just like this and not care if he was ever inside her. Her clit brushed against the fabric of his pants, and she expected him to stop her.

"Fuck, quierda," Lucio moaned. *Quierda. Quierda, quierda, quierda.* Jay savored the way the nickname tumbled out of his mouth so easily. "You're making it hard to focus."

"Come on," Jay teased.

His fingers pressed into her hips.

"You can do better than this."

Lucio brought his mouth to her breast. His tongue swirled around her nipple, before his lips closed around it. His bite was gentle but firm, not enough to hurt, but enough to make Jay's eyes flutter as her hand worked its way into his hair.

His hand on her other breast continued to pleasure her, gentle brushes and squeezing in direct contrast to his mouth continuing to suck.

Jay thought she might come just from this. And she could, fuck, she could let herself go and moan his name as she rode out her high. But she couldn't, not yet. So she switched her focus to him, pushing Lucio back against the chair so she could work his tie off of his neck.

"Off," she ordered.

His eyes darkened, and Jay readied herself for retribution, terror replacing bliss.

But Lucio kept one hand on her stomach, the other pulling off his tie. He kept their eyes locked, lips parted and his breathing labored.

Jay could feel his cock straining against his pants.

"Is this what you want, quierda?" His hand moved down to her thigh so he could drag his finger up her pussy. It came away wet, and he placed it in his mouth, sucking the taste of her off of it. Jay's breathing grew heavier, the hand resting against his chest gripping his shirt. "I can do more. Just say the word."

She pulled his hair back so he looked up at her.

Another twitch of his cock.

She breathed out a laugh. "You like being told what to do?"

"I like it when you show me what you're really made of." He teased her clit. "When you don't hold back. Don't hide who you are. There's a reason I came back for you."

Jay moaned as Lucio pressed a finger inside of her; her toes curled in pleasure.

"Tell me what you want." His tone was closer to begging than a command.

"I want your face buried between my legs."

He didn't need to be told twice. He lifted her, sitting her gently on the edge of his desk, sliding her skirt the rest of the way off. Jay was still wearing her heels, but she didn't care. It made the image of Lucio tearing off his jacket, kneeling before her, and swinging her legs on his shoulders all the more sensational.

Jay moaned louder than she meant to as he licked straight up her center. "Christ."

"Say my name, quierda," Lucio muttered, making a slow circle around her clit.

"Lucio," she whimpered, and he rewarded her with his tongue sliding into her.

"You have no idea how good you taste." He licked her again, his hands gripping her thighs.

She pulled his hair to force him away from her, desperate for his lips on hers. She jutted her chin up. "Then show me."

A low rumble from his throat made her legs twitch. He glanced back down at her pussy, reluctance clear as day.

"Lucio," Jay demanded, but he remained where he was. His lips were slick with her wet, his pupils blown. He was a fucking *sight*.

Lucio slid a finger into her, crooking it against her and causing her back to arch in absolute fucking need.

"Lucio," Jay begged, tightening around his finger as he pulled it out of her and brought it to her mouth.

His finger rested against her tongue just as he helped himself back to her.

They were playing a game, and Jay was losing, *hard*. But she knew how to handle him. Her lips closed around his finger. She could taste herself, and more than that, she could taste him. She could feel the pad of his finger, the slight roughness of it; he'd been playing guitar again, she could tell, because there was the start of a callus forming. She let the tip of her tongue glide over it, and she was rewarded with a light moan against her. She gripped his wrist, adjusting to put a second finger in her mouth. Lucio moaned again, louder this time.

Jay held his hand steady as she began to suck, moving her mouth up and down agonizingly slow on his fingers. Her mind traveled back to the champagne dripping down his hand, the way his mouth sounded and looked as the white foam trickling down the same skin that she was tasting now. She wanted him to think about her every time he looked at his fingers, she wanted him to remember her mouth every time he brushed something soft, every time he wrapped his own hand around his cock.

She wanted to make him come just by doing this.

Lucio snatched his fingers out of her mouth and nipped at her thigh as he spoke. "Not too much on me."

"Please, Lucio, I need you," she whimpered.

He looked up at her, pumping his fingers in her agonizingly slow. "You gotta be more specific than that."

Jay gripped his face in her hand, locking their eyes. "Fuck me. Fuck me like it's the last night you'll have me."

"Don't make threats like that." He stood, keeping his fingers inside of her as his other hand undid his pants. "I'm not through with you yet."

"I know," she said, whimpering at the loss of his fingers. "You still need to come."

Lucio grunted as he pushed himself inside of her. God, he was *perfect*.

Jay wrapped her legs around him to pull him closer. She wanted him so deep that she forgot where he ended and she began.

"Lay back, quierda. I want to see all of you."

She did, her skin lighting up as he placed his hands on her hips, holding her steady so he could pump into her.

Jay wasn't sure if she had ever been fucked like this before. She couldn't remember a moment where every single movement of a lover's hips made her stomach coil. Her fingers gripped his arms, desperate to ground herself. Her senses were overwhelmed with him.

Lucio's cologne mixed with the sweet smell of sex.

His voice coaxing her in between moans, praise of "yes, quierda," and "God you feel so good," broken only by her begging for more, harder, faster, "please Lucio I want you to make me come."

The taste of her and him on her tongue.

Him looking down at her, green eyes almost completely overtaken by the black of his pupils, his hair mused from her hands in it and his body backlit by the moon pouring in the window behind them.

His cock, perfect as it pushed inside of her. It was like she was sinking, and despite trying to hold on, trying to outlast him, it was useless.

Lucio cupped her face. "Come for me, Jay."

And she did.

He followed a moment after, a string of curses and words that she didn't understand talking her down from her high.

The moment didn't last. Her eyes fluttered open to the bedroom, Lucio's scent dissipating and his warmth leaving her. Her grip on his arm revealed itself to be just her phone. She was alone, again.

But she could still hear Lucio, his breathing heavy and shaky as he came down with her.

Thunder rumbled in the distance, and she looked over to see the rain battering the window, as if it were trying to break through the glass and reach her.

"I meant it," Lucio said, his breathing beginning to steady.

"Meant what?" Jay asked, pushing her hair back.

"I'm not through with you yet."

She laughed. "Well, I'm through with you. Goodnight, Lucio."

She hung up the phone before he could speak, before he could pull her back into his world and make her come again. She went to turn off her light, but hesitated.

Fuck.

Heaving a sigh, she padded into the walk-in, pulling out a shoe box, and retrieving her vibrator. Sleep wouldn't be coming for her anytime soon.

23

Helena woke up to her stomach trying to fight its way into her throat to join the headache that was building behind her eyes. It felt like someone had thrown her body into a meat grinder, then run it over with an eighteen-wheeler. She groaned as she turned over, which immediately made her nauseous.

"Easy, kid. I got a bucket right here if you need it," a voice cooed, gentle and quiet, helping soothe a tiny bit of the ache. It sounded like Jay, but that was impossible, right?

Helena wondered if she was hallucinating. How the hell did Jay get into Helena's bedroom? Wasn't that where she was?

But then why did her sheets smell funny? And why was she still wearing her jeans?

Helena opened her eyes as much as she could to see Jay kneeling by her side. Jay looked so different without makeup on. Still painfully beautiful, though. "Where am I?"

"My place. You got way too drunk last night, and I had to come get your ass."

The thought of alcohol was enough to put Helena over the edge. She was grateful for Jay holding her hair back as she vomited into the bucket, which made the headache worse, which in turn made the nausea worse.

"There you go. You're not going to be feeling very good today," Jay said, rubbing Helena's back.

Helena shook her head, but that made her feel nauseous again, so she stopped and laid back down. "I want to die."

"Yep, that's a hangover for you."

Helena placed her hand over her eyes. She was on fire, but her forehead felt cold and clammy under her palm. The events of last night were a blur: she remembered class, a text, Christine, and then the train, but that's where things ended. Why did she go with Christine? Lucio had texted her, and then—*shit.* "Did Lucio call you?"

"Yes. Did I tell him that all this was his fault? Yes," Jay called from the hall.

"And?"

"Move your hand," Jay said quietly, and Helena did, cringing at the light bleeding through her terribly thin eyelids. Something wet and cold settled on Helena's eyes, and she reached up to touch a soft washcloth.

"You're still in trouble, but I think I knocked a few years off your sentence."

Helena pressed the cold cloth, savoring it as a little water dripped down to her temples. "Thank you."

Jay brushed some of Helena's hair back. "Anything for you, Hel."

"I'm sorry."

"Sorry for what?"

"Constantly getting you caught up in my bullshit."

"You're not getting me caught up in anything," Jay said. "I could have hung up that phone last night. But we're friends. I'm not going to leave you hanging."

Helena peeked an eye out from under the washcloth. "We're friends?"

"I hope we are. Otherwise, I just put myself into a very shitty situation for an acquaintance."

Helena laughed, which was enough to prompt her to vomit again. She groaned, "Why do people do this?"

"Because it's fun," Jay sighed as she rubbed Helena's arm. "Or to forget why they weren't having fun in the first place."

"Hey, Jay?"

"Yes?"

"As my friend, please never let me drink again."

"Okay, you got it."

Helena rolled onto her back. This sucked. But at least Jay had been the one to get her. Lucio would have scolded her, and Quinn would have been passive aggressive and banged around a bunch of pots and pans as they made her breakfast.

But Jay was calm, quiet. She knew how to take care of people when they needed it. Helena's thoughts drifted to Halloween. She doubted that Colt would have been this nice to Jay the day after, and a small spark of anger lit up in Helena at the thought of him being a dick. Jay had probably felt just as shitty as Helena did, maybe even worse. And he wanted to blame her for what? Having *fun?* "You're too good for him, you know."

"Who?" Jay asked.

Helena pressed the washcloth into her eyes. "Colt. Michael. Lucio. Take your pick."

Jay let out a laugh, but it sounded humorless. "Don't need to list them all out like that, you know."

"Sorry," Helena grumbled. She moved the cloth off her to look at Jay. She was sitting on the floor, somehow unbothered by the lingering smell of vomit. Maybe it was because of too many drunk nights of her own. "But I mean it. They all suck. And you're way too good for any of them. Like, why are you even with Michael?"

Jay's brows furrowed. "Why does it matter?"

Helena was way too hungover to be doing this. And honestly, she still hadn't learned much from Lucio, or Jay, or really anyone, for that matter. But there was still something nagging at the back of Helena's mind. The way Michael had looked at her in the club. Jay's warning to stay away from him. And Lucio's breakdown in his office. There was something wrong there. Helena just couldn't name it.

"He just...doesn't seem like a great guy, is all," Helena said, moving to sit up. "I mean—"

"Where'd you get that idea?" Jay said, her tone going flat. "Your dad?"

"I mean, sort of, but—"

Jay snorted. "Try someone who's not so biased, kid."

Helena clenched the sheets in her fists. "He's right, though."

"You've met Michael once, and I get it, he didn't make the best impression on you. But that doesn't mean he's a bad guy." Jay crossed her arms over her chest. "So drop it."

"Look, I heard something from Lucio the other day that I think you should know."

"I think it's best you keep it to yourself." Jay stood, and walked out into the hallway. "I'll run out and grab us some breakfast."

"I'm serious," Helena said, scrambling as best she could out of the huge bed. She was a lot slower than Jay, mainly because the room spun if she moved her head too quick, but Jay deserved to know. Helena made it to the door, and held on to the frame to keep herself steady. "Lucio told me about what happened to his wife."

Jay froze just before she walked out into the living room. "What?"

"He told me that Michael is the reason that his family is gone." Helena leaned against the wall behind her. The room kept spinning, and she wanted to sit down more than anything.

"What do you mean, 'Michael is the reason'?" Jay's tone was harsh, cutting. "Like Lucio is trying to say *Michael* did something?"

"I mean, I think so." Helena rubbed at her temples. "I don't know how true it is, but—"

"If you don't know if it's true then why the hell would you say it?"

Helena glanced up too fast, and had to steady herself on the wall with her hands. Her vision was too blurry to focus on anything, her pulse behind her eyes trying to force them to close. But she could just make out Jay's silhouette, her arms were locked at her sides. "I'm just trying to warn you. I think there's a lot more to Michael than you know."

"*Warn* me?" Jay scoffed. "I don't need a *child* warning me about my boyfriend."

The blood that had previously been building behind Helena's eyes rushed to her cheeks. "I'm not a child. I'm an adult, like you. And more than that, I'm your friend."

"If you were really my friend you'd keep your nose out of my Goddamn business."

Helena stepped forward, trying to reach Jay. "You don't know this guy like you think you do."

"And you don't know him at all." Jay continued down the hallway. "He hasn't been in your life. He's not even your uncle, not really. So why the fuck do you even care?"

A lump formed in Helena's throat. Jay wasn't serious, right? This was some kind of joke or something. Or maybe Helena was just having some kind of terrible nightmare. She was going to wake up in her own room, and everything would be fine. And then she could call Jay, and she'd actually believe her, and she'd get the hell away from Michael. "I'm just trying to help you."

"I don't need your help!" Jay turned back around, eyes blazing. "I've been helping myself for the past six years. Not all of us can be nepo babies."

"I'm not a nepo baby. I've had to fight for everything I have." Helena's lip curled. "Unlike you."

"You have *no* idea what I've been through." Jay pointed at her own chest. "What shit *I've* had to deal with."

"Oh yes, it must be *so* hard being with a guy who literally gives you everything," Helena snapped. "You throw one little temper tantrum and he buys you the whole store."

"You'd know all about temper tantrums, wouldn't you?" Jay raised her chin. "Now I get why Lucio keeps you on such a tight leash. You might run into traffic if he doesn't keep an eye on you."

Helena inhaled sharply. "I can handle myself."

"Can you? That little stunt you pulled last night doesn't exactly scream 'I can make responsible choices.'"

"Yeah, and neither does getting drunk and almost getting my sibling into a fist fight on Halloween, because your *sidepiece* came looking for you."

Jay stepped forward. "Colt's not my sidepiece."

"Oh, is he the actual boyfriend? What's Michael, then, your Sugar Daddy?"

"Michael is my *partner*," Jay snarled. "If I wanted a Sugar Daddy I would have just kept going after your dad."

Helena's chest heaved, her anger rising into her throat and barreling out of her. "Does your 'partner' know you're cheating on him? Or does he not care that he's a cuck?"

Jay slammed her hand next to Helena's head. The sound vibrated through the wall and into Helena's skull, and she had to swallow down the urge to hurl as Jay glared down at her. "Fuck you. Get out of my apartment."

Helena hid her trembling, shoving off the wall to bring her face only inches from Jay's. "Don't you mean *Michael's* apartment?"

"I said *leave!*"

"Fine." Helena stormed towards the bedroom, her head pounding.

Of course. Jay was just like everyone else. She didn't want to listen because to her, Helena was just a *kid*.

It didn't matter that she was just trying to keep Jay safe, that she was trying to save her from getting screwed over not just by Michael, but by Lucio too. Because after all, what did Helena know?

She could say whatever she wanted, and it wouldn't matter, because no one was going to listen to her anyways.

"But when the police come busting in here, don't come crying to me!"

Helena's skin chilled as she grabbed her shoes, turning to try and run out the door before Jay could register what she had just said. But it was too late.

Jay gripped the frame of the door in her claw-like fingers. "The fuck did you just say?"

"I didn't say anything," Helena said, trying to push her way past Jay. But Jay held firm.

"Fuck you didn't. What the hell do you mean 'cops'?"

Helena backed off, avoiding Jay's eyes.

"What *cops*, Helena?"

She could only watch in horror as Jay put the pieces together.

"Is Lucio trying to do something to Michael?"

Helena couldn't get her voice much past a whisper. "I need to go home."

"You need to tell me what the hell you're talking about," Jay stepped into the room, looming over Helena. "Is that why you started coming around? You were using me?"

"No, no, I promise that—" Helena felt the room closing in on her. Her chest was tight, her vision blurry. *No, breathe. In, out. In*—"I mean—it wasn't always—"

"You fucking *bitch*." Jay ran a hand through her hair. "I trusted you."

Helena's lips trembled as she desperately shook her head. This wasn't supposed to go like this. She would explain—she *could* explain, Jay would believe her, right? They were friends—friends believed each other, friends *forgave* each other. "Please, I'm sorry, I didn't mean to—"

"Fuck you. I never want to see you again, do you understand me?"

"Jay—"

Jay pointed harshly down the hall, no longer blocking Helena's exit. "Get out before I call the cops myself."

Helena reached for Jay's arm, desperate to make her understand, for her to know that it was a mistake, that Helena hadn't meant for any of this to happen. She hadn't meant to jeopardize one of the few people who had ever called her "friend." "I'm—"

"Get *out!*" Jay screeched.

Helena ripped her eyes away from Jay's.

Gripping her arms, she left the apartment, her vision watery as she called the elevator, grateful that it was waiting for her. She didn't bother looking back, not even as she jammed the first floor button, tears already beginning to spill down her cheeks.

She collapsed just as the elevator began to descend. Heavy sobs wracked her body as hot tears rolled down her cheeks. Everything was too close, too tight. Her head throbbed. She couldn't get off the elevator fast enough.

People in the lobby might have looked at her, they might not have. Helena didn't care. She walked out of the front door, her phone in her hand before she knew what she was doing.

He picked up on the third ring. "You better have a damn good excuse as to why—"

"Lucio, please hold the lecture," Helena sniffled, wiping at her face.

His voice dropped an octave. "What happened?"

"I fucked up, I fucked up so bad, I'm so sorry."

"I'm coming to get you."

"No, please, I'll just meet you at the office."

Lucio was silent, and she could tell he was checking her location. "You'll meet me halfway. I'll see you at Union Square."

He hung up before Helena could continue to argue. She wiped at her eyes, pulling her jacket close to her as she walked to the nearest station.

Helena sat on a bench, a cup of coffee the only thing making her feel like she was alive. It wasn't helping anything—the headache, the nausea, and certainly not the hollow feeling in her chest. The market buzzed around her, people shopping and pushing into one another for the opening weekend of the Christmas Markets.

"Helena!"

She looked up to see Lucio running toward her, scanning over her as he approached. He crouched down in front of her. "Are you okay? What happened?"

"I—" Helena looked away from him. "Jay and I got into a fight."

"A fight? What do you mean by a fight?"

She sniffled. "I was just trying to warn her about Michael, and..."

"Helena," Lucio prodded. "What happened?"

"I told her. I'm so, so sorry, I was just so angry and..."

"Told her what, fihla?"

Helena nearly fell to pieces again. All she wanted in that moment was to go home, for things to be back to the way that they were. But Lucio was looking up at her, his green eyes searching hers. Helena soaked it in, knowing it may be the last time he ever looked at her like that again.

"About the case."

She closed her eyes to avoid looking at the anger she knew she would find all over his face.

"You didn't."

"I'm so sorry."

Lucio didn't say anything. Helena opened her eyes; he was standing now, running a hand over his chin, eyes unfocused as he looked off in the distance. He was in his lawyer mode, likely trying to figure out how to get them out of the situation that she had put them in. Again. The same way he reacted when he found out about her fighting at school, when the school told her that because of the days she had missed, she wouldn't be able to graduate on time, and would need to go to a transfer school or get her GED. He had been disappointed then, too.

And it was all her fault.

She switched her focus to trying to burn a hole in the side of her cup.

"Will you be okay going home alone?"

Helena gripped the cup so tight she almost crushed it. Of course, he would dismiss her, send her off where she couldn't do more damage. "Where are you going?"

Lucio placed a warm, firm hand on her head.

She looked up hesitantly, a small part of her terrified that she would find him still looking at her with contempt, with disappointment, with anything other than the gentle gaze of the dad she needed right then.

But what she found was Lucio trying to smile down at her. "I need to clean up your mess."

24

Jay didn't know how long she sat there for. It could have been minutes, hours, or only a few seconds. Lucio was investigating Michael. That meant whatever Michael had been trying to hide from her, whatever he had decided was so unimportant for her to get involved in, it was already out there. And she had just let the Devil's spawn into the house. Had she—no. Helena was so drunk last night that it was absolutely impossible for her to have gotten up without Jay knowing.

But then the call with Lucio.

Christ, how could she be so fucking *stupid?*

Helena had been faking it. The little sneak. She was working for her dad right along, she must have, why else would she be *so* desperate to get to Jay and know about Michael?

Jay bolted upright, going to the guest room. Technically, it also served as a home office for Michael; nothing extravagant, just a small desk with a few drawers, enough space for him to get some work done when he needed to. Jay ripped open one of the drawers, looking over it. Nothing seemed out of place—it was filled with notebooks and old papers, but she had to guess that Helena wouldn't have been stupid enough to make it look like she snooped.

Jay quickly skimmed through one notebook, but it was empty. The second was also empty. Maybe Michael just had these here just in case? As a decoy or something? She let out a frustrated groan, switching to the other side and pulling open the drawer.

Another Goddamn notebook. But Jay recognized this one. It was the same one that Michael had in his office, with the aged brown leather and string to hold it closed. Except the string was undone. Fuck. Had he left it that way? Or was it always open? She picked it up, hoping that there would be some kind of sign that Helena had messed with it, giving a clue as to whether Jay needed to retie it or leave it be.

She opened it up, scanning the pages quickly.

Sketches.

She found sketches, dozens of them, of a woman. A woman who wasn't *her*. All of them were in pen or pencil, some sketched out quickly, probably hastily done in between meetings or phone calls, while others looked like they must have taken hours, visited and revisited again and again.

Some of the drawings showed the woman laughing, smiling, lost in thought, while others showed her only in pieces: hands, eyes, lips, her elbow, a leg, hair tucked behind her ear.

And every page she turned, Jay could see more and more of the woman. How fucking *gorgeous* she was. Her cheekbones, her lips, her jaw, all soft, angelic. The only thing sharp about her were her eyes. Jay couldn't tell the color, but she could tell that Michael had captured the emotion that burned behind them—not a quiet, demure, peaceful energy, but an unwavering one. Like she'd take out anyone who'd get in her way, and not even stop to worry about the consequences.

"Jay!"

Fuck. Michael was home. And by the sound of it, he was fucking pissed. Jay quickly redid the string on the notebook, slammed the drawer shut, and rushed into the hall, trying to compose herself as she walked out.

"Hey, baby, I wasn't expecting you home so—" Her heart leapt into her throat. "How the fuck—"

Lucio stood in the apartment, the front door slamming shut behind him as he crossed the room in two seconds flat, forcing her back against the wall.

Jay froze under him, struggling not to tremble as the memory of cigarettes and alcohol washed over her.

Lucio didn't notice. Or didn't care. "What the hell were you thinking?"

"Get out," she tried to yell, but her voice came out small, strangled. "Get out before I call the cops."

"Do it. What're they going to do to me?" Lucio lifted his hand, keys catching the light. "I have a key."

Jay's eyes widened. "How the fuck—"

"Why did you bring Helena here?"

Jay looked back at him, trying to steady her breathing. "What?"

"My *daughter*," Lucio growled. "Why did you bring her here?"

Jay swallowed, her anger overtaking her fear, replacing her wobbly knees with strong legs that wanted nothing more than to kick his ass. "Like you don't fucking know."

"No, Jay, I actually *don't* know why the hell you would bring Helena to the mouth of a Goddamn lion!" Lucio yelled. "Do you know how incredibly stupid that was? How much danger you've put her in?"

"*I* put her in?" Jay repeated. "You're the one who told her to call me. You knew that I would help her out, and I would bring her here, don't act like this wasn't all part of your sick little plan!"

Lucio gave her an incredulous look. "Excuse me?"

"Stop playing stupid." Jay stabbed her finger into Lucio's chest, forcing him backwards. "It's all just one big fucking coincidence that your daughter sneaks into my club, asking about Michael, and then you just *happen* to show up a few nights later? You just *happen* to start requesting me, and showing up where I am? And then your daughter just *happens* to get drunk the night Michael is out of town, and you call me and start playing your little fucking game with me?" Jay shook her head, snorting. "You've got *some* nerve using your kid like that."

Lucio stopped dead, and she almost ran straight into his wall of a chest. His face twisted, confusion giving way to a rage she was all too familiar with.

"I have *never* used my daughter. I would *never* put her in danger. And I would *never* willingly allow her to associate with someone like you."

The words struck Jay like a slap in the face, the sting making her skin itch.

"My children are everything to me. I would kill for them. I would happily die for them. And if I *ever* suspect that you tell Michael about Helena being here, I'll show you just how serious I am."

Jay swallowed. "You're full of shit."

"Am I?" Lucio pulled out his phone. "Try me. I'll call him right now. I'll tell him everything. I'd be more than happy to let my brother know I got his precious anjo to come without even touching her."

"And then what?"

Lucio stood there, his green eyes boring into hers. "You know exactly what."

"Do I?" Jay smirked. "You really think I'm *scared* of Michael? Why should I be? He's done nothing but take care of me for years. And besides, you really think he's going to believe you over me?"

Lucio sneered. "And you think he's just going to brush over the little affair you and Colt have been carrying on with?"

"What affair?" Jay said, motioning outwards. "You've got any proof? Or just a fuck ton more lies?"

"Don't test me, boneca."

"Then call him." Jay stepped forward, her face only inches from Lucio's. She could smell his cologne, and the memory of the night before threatened to overtake her again. But she shook it off, wrapping her hand around his tie instead. "But just know that he's never going to believe a single thing out of your fucking mouth. Because I am *everything* to him, Lucio. That man worships the ground I walk on."

Lucio chuckled. "That's what Elyse said about him, too."

The floor gave out from underneath Jay's feet. Elyse. Lucio's wife. But there was no—

"Oh, he didn't tell you?" Lucio tilted his head, a sick smile too wide on his face. "Michael didn't mention his pretty little fiancée before you came along?"

Elyse. Fiancée.

"Told her he loved her, couldn't wait to spend the rest of his life with her, until she left him." Lucio slowly loosened Jay's grip from his tie, but she could barely register it. "He was so heartbroken. And then she died, and I thought maybe he'd never get over her. That is, until he found you."

The only thing holding Jay up was an arm snaking around her waist, slow and deliberate, pulling her close to Lucio's chest.

"And sure, he might care about you. Might buy you all the nice fancy clothes, take you on these gorgeous trips. But let me tell you a secret, boneca." He brought his lips to her ear, his breath hot against her skin. "*She* was everything you'll *never* be."

Jay gasped as she collapsed on the floor, Lucio letting go of her.

Her chest heaved as she tried to breathe in too deep, too quick. Her vision tunneled, and she tried to grip her hair, to feel something, to bring herself back to the world. But everything was going black, and all she could see was Lucio, all she could smell was him, hear him, taste him. She wanted to throw up.

"I meant what I said, Jay. If you ever interact with my daughter again, or even try to tell Michael about this, I'll expose you," Lucio said, before turning on his heel and walking back to the door. "Oh, and he can have his key back." The object clattered across the hardwood floors. "Elyse certainly doesn't need it anymore."

25

To say that Jay's life was falling apart was an understatement. It had been two weeks since Lucio had ambushed her in the apartment, but she felt anxious at every turn, constantly waiting for the other shoe to drop. She was surprised her hair hadn't started to fall out, although according to Michael, she was due for another trip to the salon soon. Her nails were way overdue for a touch up, and her hair was beginning to curl again. But lately, keeping up with appearances was starting to feel like too much.

Jay sighed as she glanced at the clock. It was nearly eight, much later than she would usually be at work. Everyone else had already left, but she still sat at her desk, waiting for Michael to leave. The sun had gone down a few hours ago; she wasn't about to take the subway by herself in the freezing cold.

Her stomach growled. Jay hadn't eaten since breakfast, when she managed to choke down a granola bar, and she knew Michael would probably be starving. Or maybe he wouldn't. She'd been having trouble reading him ever since he got back from his trip two weeks ago. According to him, they were getting close to the end of the quarter, which meant long nights with the office door shut tight. Only Delilah would be permitted in until the office had emptied out. Then he would call Jay in and fuck her until he was satisfied. And on the days where it was too much and he couldn't get it up, she would dance for him like she used to, or sit with him while he got drunk enough to make a half-hearted pass at her.

Usually he just passed out on the couch, and she would cover him with a blanket and head home alone.

She was grateful for those days. Every time Michael touched her, she imagined it was Lucio, and her chest ached. Sometimes, she could blame her lack of libido on a headache. Other times, Michael wouldn't let her.

Jay's desk phone rang; she picked it up without bothering to read the number. "NomadCrate Company, how many I direct your call?"

"Michael Silva, please," a woman's voice said. A jolt of jealousy shot through Jay. It was late for Michael to be getting calls. She cut her eyes to his door, still sealed shut. There wasn't anyone else. Just her.

"Hold, please." Jay pressed the proper buttons, Michael picking up a moment later.

"What?" he snapped.

She sank her nails into her palm. "Call for you."

He heaved an aggravated sigh.

Jay nearly wanted to curse him out. This was literally her fucking job, and he wanted to have an attitude with her?

"Who is it?"

"They didn't say."

"Jesus Christ, did you even ask?" he growled, mumbling something else beneath his breath. "Just put them through."

Jay pressed the transfer button, holding a moment to make sure the call connected.

Michael spoke first, his tone still holding a hint of aggravation but much lighter. "Silva."

She moved to hang up, but the voice purring through the phone stopped her. "No hello? That's bad for business, *Michele*."

Jay clasped her hand over the speaker, which was unnecessary considering she wasn't breathing.

"Lucio?" Michael asked.

A beat, one that Jay couldn't follow.

Michael spoke again, his voice returning to peak aggravation. "What the hell do you want?"

"Just calling to catch up on old times," Lucio said. "Check in on business."

"You know exactly how business is going," Michael said. Jay could hear him shift in his chair. "So talk."

"Never were one for conversation, were you?" Lucio sighed. "Well, since you're so desperate to know: I wanted to give you a second chance."

"A second chance?" Michael barked out a laugh. "A second chance for what?"

"To come forward."

Lucio couldn't be serious. He had just laid into her about making sure Michael didn't find out anything about this, now Lucio was just calling him up like they were going to talk shop?

"Come *forward*?" Michael repeated.

"Exactly. If you turn yourself in, I'll go easy on you," Lucio said. "We can offer a plea deal. Maybe you'll only do fourteen years instead of fifteen."

"Shove it up your ass," Michael snapped. The sound of something slamming down on his desk could be heard through the door. "You're not going to get me for shit because you know you don't have anything."

"I don't?" Lucio asked. "It's cute that you think so many people are so loyal to you."

Jay's skin turned to ice. He wouldn't. She hadn't done anything, she had kept her mouth shut about the whole Helena thing, just like Lucio told her to. Not because she had been scared, but because it had been easier to deny that the whole incident had ever happened. Because nothing *had* happened. Nothing that could be proven, anyways.

"Because they are," Michael said. Jay caught the slightest hesitation in his voice.

"Are you willing to bet on that?" She imagined Lucio leaning forward, smirking. "I know you've never played it safe, but this seems stupid, even for you."

"Shut the fuck up," Michael said. "You've got nothing on me, you're only calling to try and trip me up."

"Maybe I am, maybe I'm not," Lucio hummed. "I just wanted to give you the chance to come to your senses. But it seems like you're still the same old Mickey."

"You haven't spoken to me in close to a decade!" Michael shouted. "And you think you still know me? I've changed, Lucio. What the hell have you done?"

"You've *changed?* People like you don't change. You're the same piece of shit you always were, always will be."

"What the fuck did I ever do to you?" Anyone else would have missed the break in Michael's voice. But not Jay. "You were always the one taking from me. And even now, you're still trying."

"I didn't take anything from you. Dad and your mom *gave* me your hand me downs, your scraps," Lucio shouted back. "You think I wanted what was yours?"

"Don't give me that!" Something slammed against the wall near the door. "Dad always liked you better. You and your mother were given whatever the hell you wanted, whatever you needed, while I watched *my* mother struggle to put food on our table. We were never good enough for him, and then you come along and suddenly we're less than dog shit."

"Do you know how much he put *my* mother through? The only reason I got anything is because he wanted to make up for what he did to her. Don't you *dare* say it was our fault!"

"Maybe your whore of a mother should have kept her legs closed."

"And maybe yours should have opened hers more often. Maybe she would have had a child that wasn't a huge fuck up."

Michael laughed harshly. "Real fucking original, Luci. Get some new Goddamn material."

"Like Elyse?"

Jay's heart stopped. She had learned too much about Elyse in the last few weeks. Nothing from Michael, of course, but one quick search had pulled up a LinkedIn page full of awards, degrees, and a job at one of the best accounting firms. A woman who was determined, gorgeous, loved by many, and worst of all, who had broken Michael's heart.

And had taken pieces of it with her to the grave.

"Don't you dare say her name. It doesn't belong in your fucking mouth," Michael growled, his voice regaining its steady candence.

Lucio snorted. "You're just upset because she made the right choice. Her leaving you was the best thing she ever did for herself."

"Is that why she came crawling back to me?" Michael's words landed like a bomb.

What the fuck was he talking about? Lucio and her had gotten married, had kids. Michael and Elyse were—

Lucio breathed in sharply. "Fuck you."

"What's the matter? Still upset over the fact that the last thing your pretty little wife did was suck my dick?"

Jay's stomach turned at the sound of Michael's condescending tone. This wasn't something she knew. Was something she was *never* supposed to know, and now regretted that she would never be able to forget.

"I forgot how good she looked on her knees. And that mouth of hers," he chuckled, "I haven't had anything close to it since."

Jay hated the way the words stung. She needed to hang up. She couldn't listen to this anymore. She shouldn't have been listening in the first place. But she was frozen. This was her punishment. She deserved this for what she had done to Michael.

"This is why she left you," Lucio hissed. "Because you *only* ever saw her as a fucking object. You're a pig."

"I saw her for what she was, Luci," Michael said, dragging out his name with a low growl. "Not a mother, not a person, but a woman. A woman with needs. You know what she told me? That you hadn't fucked her since she had the kids. Oh, sure, you 'made love' to her, made her feel precious and special and delicate. But you didn't satisfy her. You couldn't. Because how could you do all the dirty things that she liked? Call her a whore, a good little bitch, bend her over a table and fuck her until she was begging for mercy. She *loved* it. But you couldn't do that to her, not the mother of your little angels."

"You shut the fuck up," Lucio spat. His voice trembled, Jay could picture him shaking. "All she ever got from you was sex. That wasn't enough for her. She needed more, and I *gave* her that. A career *and* a family, like she always wanted. If you had it your way she would have been barefoot and pregnant, waiting on you hand and fucking foot."

"You're so Goddamn *delusional!*" Michael laughed. "Elyse only married you because you knocked her up. Don't pretend like she actually wanted you."

A clattering sound on the other end of the line. "We loved each other, which is a hell of a lot more I can say for you! She only wanted you because she thought you would help her get ahead. And look at what you did."

"What I did? If she had stayed with me she would still be alive. *You* killed her, Lucio. She was going to leave you and you couldn't handle that. You couldn't let me have her, let her be happy. You've always been a selfish piece of shit." Michael's voice cracked, but he quickly corrected it. "This whole thing is just your sick little way of trying to get revenge for her cheating on you with me. She *chose* me, Lucio. Not you. Get the fuck over it, and stay the fuck away before you get someone else killed."

Michael's line clicked, followed by things breaking on the other side of the door. She slowly let her hand move from the receiver, letting out a shallow breath.

"Hope you enjoyed the show," Lucio said before the line went completely dead.

It was close to an hour before things finally settled down in Michael's office. From what Jay had heard, it was going to be a mess.

She didn't bother knocking—she wasn't sure if Michael was even awake. Maybe he had gotten drunk, or simply passed out from the adrenaline rush that he had given himself. But Jay spotted him sitting on the couch with half a bottle of scotch on the table, and a glass pressed against his forehead.

The moonlight spilling through the windows wasn't much, but it was enough to let her see him, just for a moment. Real, and broken. Dark circles rimmed his puffy eyes, his beard was scruffier, his back hunched. His tie was absent from his neck, the first few buttons on his shirt were undone, and the sleeves rolled up. His hammer tattoo was visible even from where she stood, but she didn't allow herself to linger on it.

The office was as bad as she had thought it would be. His desk was completely cleared, all of the things that had once been on it now scattered across the floor. Jay stepped in, glass crunching beneath her shoes.

Michael looked up, his eyes rimmed with red. "Hey, you're still here?"

"I thought we were going home together." She walked in, each step careful and deliberate. "Are you okay?"

He nodded, taking a long sip of his drink. Some of it dribbled down and caught itself in the stubble along his jaw.

"You can tell me if you're not, Michael," she said, sitting down next to him. "It's—"

"Jesus Christ, if I tell you I'm okay, I mean it," he snapped, slamming the glass down on his coffee table.

"Okay, I'm sorry," Jay said, flinching away from him.

Michael sucked in a breath, pressing the heels of his hands to his eyes. They sat there in silence for a moment. Jay locked her gaze on her hands, anchored to her knees to keep her legs from bouncing.

He sighed. "I shouldn't snap at you like I do."

Jay just reached out and placed her hand on his knee, ready to pull it back at the first sign that the touch was unwelcome.

He put his hand on top of hers, squeezing it tight. "My brother and I were never close."

She looked up, trying to read him, to see if Michael was telling her this because he knew she had been listening. But his eyes were glued to their hands.

"Our dad had an affair when I was three. Mom had no clue until I was ten, eleven. When suddenly my dad brings home another kid and says that this is his other son, and his mom died so we're taking care of him now." He cleared his throat. "Son of a bitch just told her this is what we were doing. And from there on, it was all about him. I don't know if it was pity, or guilt, or what, but I was second best, and Lucio was the golden child. Even with my own mother."

Jay pulled Michael to her chest, trying to ignore the aching feeling building there. He wrapped his arms around her, hiding his face in her neck.

"And every single fucking girlfriend I had went to him. It was like he was magnetic. They couldn't help it, but I knew. I knew what kind of guy he was. He's the biggest manipulator. He would make people pity him, and they gave him everything. I was always the villain, always the antagonist." Michael trembled in her arms. "I didn't want to be, I don't want to be."

"You're not, baby, you're not," she cooed, stroking his hair.

"I need you." He pulled away, holding her face in his hands. His eyes were so beautiful, a shade of blue that she had never seen before. She could drown in those eyes. "You're the one thing I know he'll never have, he can't."

"Michael," Jay whispered. It was too much. The wave of guilt, of knowing, of what she had done to him—Colt, Lucio—all came crashing over her. The words rushed forward, bubbling up her throat, desperate to escape. She had to tell him. She couldn't keep carrying all this inside of her.

Michael pressed his forehead to hers. "I love you, Jay."

She didn't answer him. She couldn't. Jay closed the distance between them, kissing him like she meant it. She couldn't speak, words would only taint the moment. She would say everything she wanted to, everything she couldn't. And it didn't matter anymore. She would prove to him that she could be everything he wanted, everything he needed. For this moment, and every other.

She was his.

26

You up for drinks? My treat.

You unsent a message.

You know you can't stay mad at me forever.

You unsent a message.

Come get drinks with me? I've got a cool new spot for us to check out.

You unsent a message.

I'll buy you alcohol if you promise to forgive me.

You unsent a message.

Jay groaned as she erased her message for the hundredth time. She hadn't spoken to Alice since their fight a month and a half ago. Well, it hadn't been a fight, really, more like Jay throwing a bunch of insults at Alice and then storming off. And with everything going on, Jay needed her best friend.

She knew what she had to do, but she hated doing it.

Hey, I'm sorry for what I said. Can we meet up to talk about it?

Jay locked her phone before she could rethink the entire thing. There. It was done. The ball was in Alice's court now, and if she chose to forgive her, great. And if not...

Then she had Michael.

Even if he was being a huge dick to her lately, but that was nothing new.

Ever since the phone call with Lucio, Michael had been beyond stressed. Jay had tried everything to make him feel better: sex, cooking him dinner, keeping the place clean, making him drinks, but no matter what she did, he still ripped her head off over every little indiscretion.

She hated it.

When Michael told Jay he loved her, she thought things might change, that he might soften and become a man that she wouldn't mind staying with.

But somehow, things had only become so much worse.

More controlling, more surveillance, less freedom, less love.

The desk phone rang. Jay picked it up, glancing at the caller ID to confirm who it was. "Yes, Mr. Silva?"

"Office." The line clicked.

Great. Michael was in another one of his moods again. She gathered her things and headed into the room.

Michael was of course stationed behind his desk, and didn't even glance in her direction before snapping his fingers and pointing to the drink cart.

Jay began to make him an Old Fashioned, her nerves begging her to make one for herself, but she knew that she couldn't, not unless Michael gave his permission. It was better for her to simply settle for a taste of the stirring stick, before bringing the drink over to Michael's desk.

He took it before motioning towards her back towards the door. "Go."

Jay pushed down the sting of rejection. "You don't want me in here?"

"No. Delilah and I have some business to conduct that doesn't involve you. Just be on standby if I need you." Michael finally looked up when a knock came from the door, and he permitted whoever it was to enter.

Delilah stepped in, wearing a tight white button up as usual.

But Jay didn't miss the fact that this top was a lot more sheer, to the point she could see the lace design of Delilah's bra. Her skirt was shorter, as well, or maybe just more hiked up, but either way, she was showing more leg than normal. Her heels were the most damning. A pair of red-bottom Louboutin's. Brand new, by the looks of them. Delilah shot Jay a tight but genuine smile.

Jay didn't return the sentiment.

"Hey Delilah, thanks for coming," Michael said, standing up and meeting Delilah at the couch. His eyes crinkled in the corners as he smiled at her.

Delilah nodded, setting her laptop on the coffee table in front of her. "No worries, sorry I'm late. Got stuck on the phone with a client."

"Happens," Michael said, settling into the couch with a casual air Jay hadn't seen in a few weeks.

Funny. When Jay was late because she was tied up handling *his* calls, she got her ass chewed out and a dick in her mouth. *Put it to good use.*

Michael waved his glass. "Can I have Jay make you anything?"

"No, thank you. I want to keep my wits about me while we go over this. This shit's been keeping me up at night," Delilah sighed. She gathered her hair in a ponytail, as she glanced at Jay. "Is...?"

Michael's shoulders visibly tensed, but he still wouldn't look at her. "She was just leaving."

Jay bit her tongue. Of course she was. Why would she need to be involved? She was nothing more than his—No. Lucio would *not* poison her against Michael. Michael was clearly hiding things from Delilah, like how much this was all bothering him. He needed to put up a front, and Jay needed to be supportive.

He needed her.

"Jay," Michael called, drawing her attention to him. His smile was gone, replaced by indifference. "Hold my calls. I don't want any interruptions."

She did her best not to slam the door closed behind her.

It was about two hours before there was any sign of life from Michael's office. If Jay didn't know any better, she might have thought that something scandalous was going on. But there was always a possibility. Her nostrils flared as she looked towards the door, Michael's voice carrying over.

"Thanks, Delilah. I appreciate your help."

"Like I said: you go down, we all go down with you." Delilah said as she stepped out, Michael's hand lingering on her back a second too long for Jay's liking. Her hair had been released from its ponytail, still perfectly straight. Jay had to spend hours at the salon to get hair like that. To get it the way *Michael* liked.

Delilah smiled at him. "Anything else you need from me?"

"No, that'll be it. Go grab yourself a coffee and take a load off."

Delilah nodded and headed back to her own office. Michael motioned to Jay, summoning her in.

Michael closed the door behind her, his hand never once touching her, even by accident. "Have a seat."

She did, paying careful attention to the imprints of where people had been sitting. They were spaced fairly far apart—no sign of anything having happened. Jay looked towards Michael, but he appeared just as tense as before. He had taken off his suit jacket, his gray shirt showing off the stiff muscles that worked their way through his back.

He turned around to face her again, his tie loose and top button undone. Jay's eyes quickly scanned his neck for any sign of love bites, but she saw none. That didn't mean he wasn't hiding any, though.

He came back to the couch and wrapped his arm around her. She tried not to stiffen too much at his touch.

"How much time before my next meeting?" Michael asked, taking a swig of his drink before setting it down on the table. She ignored the other two glasses that sat beside it, one with a pretty pink lipstick stain.

Jay cleared her throat. "About twenty minutes."

"Plenty of time," Michael muttered, before leaning over and bringing her in for a kiss.

She leaned away from him as much as she could. "Do you need me for something? Like, something important?"

He looked her over, and his grip on her shoulder tightened. "What?"

Jay raised her chin. "I have to get back to work. I've been fielding calls left and right for you."

"Calls?"

"Yes." She grit her teeth. "Some of the higher ups have been asking about you."

"And you didn't think to tell me?"

"You told me no interruptions, remember?" She started to stand up. "I didn't want to bother you and your precious time with *Delilah.*"

Michael pulled Jay back down by her wrist, not enough to hurt. His face darkened, a reddish tint flushing his tan. A leftover from the trip. He had taken Delilah with him, which Jay had found out later. But she didn't get to bring it up to him. They had barely spoken, really.

He snarled. "The fuck are you implying?"

"Nothing, darling," Jay said, keeping her tone light and sweet. "You and her just seem so close, is all."

Michael's fingers on her wrist tightened. "You better watch your Goddamn mouth."

She snorted. "What, you gonna throw another hissy fit? I put up with years of you hounding me about Colt, I'm not allowed to say something about you and her?"

"I've never fucked Delilah," Michael spat. "I know you were sucking Colt's dick like it was candy before I came along."

"Oh really classy of you, baby." Jay tried to stand again, but he held her wrist and pulled her back down, *hard*. Her shoulders tensed as she registered how much it hurt.

His other hand gripped her chin. "I'm warning you, Jay."

She didn't back down from his gaze. She wasn't going to this time. He loved her? He was going to prove it. "Let go of me."

"Fuck that. You want to talk about me fucking other women when you're whoring it around with every guy in this office?" He moved his hand into her hair to yank her head back. "You're going to give me what I want."

Jay struggled to keep her voice even. "Michael, you're hurting me!"

"Shut up." He used his other hand to push her to the couch, her heart pounding in her chest as he climbed over her.

She tried to push him away, but he grabbed her wrist with his free hand, using the other one to shove her shirt up.

Michael grabbed her breast, painfully squeezing it as his lips crashed onto hers. She struggled to get air, her fist slamming against his back as he moved from her breast to her skirt, pushing her thighs apart with his legs. "Stop *fighting* me."

Jay's words were muffled by his mouth still trying to overtake hers, his body crushing her. Her lungs tightened as he rutted, his dick hard and sending a wave of nausea over her. *No. No, no, no NO, NO NO!*

"I said *no!*" She got her hand free, striking him.

Michael straightened, holding his face where she had hit him. Looking wounded.

Her chest heaved, but she tried to swallow back her sobs as she caught her breath.

"No?" He looked down at her, his jaw going slack.

Jay shook her head. She had a choice. Michael wasn't taking this from her. She could do this, she could tell him—

She yelped as she was thrown from the couch, landing on the floor with a hard thud, narrowly missing the corner of the table.

Michael slowly climbed off the couch to tower over her. This wasn't like him. He had never been physical with her like this before. She was used to him being rough in bed, but this, the way he was looking at her now, was different.

"No?" Michael closed his hands into fists, the rings on his right hand glinting in the setting sun. "You think you get to tell me *no?*"

"I—"

His hand cracked across her face.

"Pain in my ass. I do everything for you and you think you get to talk back to me?" He stepped over her. "You wouldn't have shit if it wasn't for me. Don't fucking forget that. Get the fuck out."

She watched as he sat back at his desk and turned himself away from her. A warmth spread down her cheek as she got to her shaky feet and walked as calmly as she could to the door.

Some people turned to look at her, but Jay just waved them off. She made it to the bathroom to check her appearance in the mirror.

While she looked obviously shaken up, the cut wasn't so bad. It was small, just below her eye on her left cheek. Jay tore a paper towel and wetted it with cold water to staunch the bleeding.

She ignored the way her hands trembled, the way her breathing came out quick and shallow. There wasn't time for panicking. Panic meant people asking questions, which meant keeping a story straight. And Jay very well couldn't do that if her mind was racing like it was now. No. It was fine. It was an accident. It was her fault. She fell.

Damn heels, Michael had always told her to be more careful.

She needed to listen to him more often. It didn't do well for her when she didn't.

The wind pushed Jay into the bar, along with a breeze that caused everyone to turn their heads to glare at her. She dropped her eyes, shutting the door behind her.

She had spent too long in the mirror trying to make the cut on her face look like anything but. The bruising was easy—Jay knew exactly how to neutralize the colors because she had taken a while to get used to the high platforms of her pleaser heels in her early dancing days—but the scab had been a different story. Whatever, it was nothing. She had tripped, or cut herself with her nails, or some other excuse that she could come up with if Alice looked too close. With a little luck, it wouldn't even scar.

Alice was sitting at the bar, a barely touched drink in front of her. Jay sucked in a breath, and walked over, plastering on her best smile.

"Hey, sorry I'm late," she said, taking the seat next to Alice. "Couldn't get my makeup to blend right."

"No worries," Alice said. Her smile didn't reach her eyes.

The bartender came over to take Jay's order: a double margarita, salt on the rim. Alice said nothing, poking her straw around the ice in her drink.

Jay tapped her nails against the bar, then turned to Alice. "I really am sorry about what I said. It was super rude and uncalled for and I was a total bitch for doing it."

"It's whatever." Alice waved her hand, stirring her drink. "I don't even remember it."

The bartender returned with Jay's drink, and she passed him her card. "Put her drink on there for me, too."

"No, it's fine. I got it," Alice said.

"I told you drinks were on me today."

"I got this one. You can get the next one."

Jay looked her friend over, noticing now the slumped shoulders, the distant look. "Are you okay?"

"Yeah. Just a really rough day at work." Alice took a long sip.

Alice wasn't a heavy drinker. But Jay could see now that her glass wasn't anything delicate. The honey-colored liquid was nearly to the bottom, and there didn't look like there had been any mixer. "You want to talk about it?"

The only sound for a stretch was the whiny voice of some pop-star playing above them, and the din of too many people talking around them. The bar was crowded for a Wednesday. But it was fine, they could talk privately, mostly.

Alice heaved a sigh. "It was a DV case."

"DV?"

"Domestic violence."

Jay's throat tightened. "Oh."

"We've had our eye on this guy for a minute. Kept getting disturbance calls. And each time the girlfriend would come to the door, apologize, say it won't happen again. And each time it would." Alice stabbed her straw into her drink. "But this time—" she swallowed "—we get the call. And we get there and..."

Jay took Alice's hand in her own.

"God, Jay, she was unrecognizable." Tears began to stream down Alice's face. "She was lucky to still be alive, and she kept trying to say it was an accident, that he didn't mean it." She wiped her face with the back of her hand. "Can you believe that? This guy beats her so bad she might be scarred for the rest of her life, and she's *protecting* him. How can someone do that?"

The bruise on Jay's cheek throbbed. "Well, maybe it *was* an accident."

Alice's eyes widened as she looked at Jay, disbelief slowly painting over her features. "What?"

"I mean," Jay licked her lips, "maybe it was a normal fight, and things just got out of hand."

Alice slipped her hand out of Jay's. "You cannot be serious right now."

"It happens, Alice, I mean, who's to say she didn't—"

"Shut up." Alice looked disgusted, horrified, as if Jay had been the one who put that woman in the hospital. "You are not seriously defending a fucking *abuser*, are you? What the hell is wrong with you?"

"No, I'm not, I'm just trying to—"

"He beat the living shit out of her. She didn't deserve that!"

Jay's eyes darted around the space, her breathing quickening as she realized other people were beginning to stare. She tried to keep her voice low, calm. "Alice, please, don't make a scene—"

"Don't make a scene?" Alice's voice only rose. More people turned to see what was going on. "You're out here defending a fucking abuser, and I'm the one making a scene? Fuck you."

Jay sucked in a breath. "Excuse me?"

"How do you think it's okay to defend someone who is beating their partner? Do you know how fucked up that is?"

"I'm not trying to defend it! I'm trying to say that you don't always have the full story."

"What full story do I need? What possible reason does he have for putting hands on her?"

"Maybe she did something to hurt him first. Not everyone is innocent, you know."

Alice's jaw dropped. "I cannot *believe* you. Who the hell are you?"

"Ladies, please, I'm going to need to ask you to either keep it down or leave," the bartender said, clearly uncomfortable with having to address them at all.

"Don't worry about it. I'm leaving," Alice said. "I just need my card."

"Alice, wait." Jay reached out, although she wasn't too sure why. "Let me just—"

"Don't touch me. You want to defend people who beat the literal shit out of their partners, that's your business. I'm not going to sit here and listen to it." The bartender returned with Alice's check. She signed it, shaking her head. "I know you haven't always been smart, Jay, but I didn't know you were this stupid."

Something in Jay snapped. "You're the cop who's losing her fucking cool over a disagreement. Good to know I can always count on the ones in blue to shoot first and ask questions later."

One moment, Alice was sitting next to her, then the next, she was inches from Jay's face, chair crashing to the floor behind her. Alice stood so close, Jay worried that she might notice the scab. Might see that something was wrong. But Alice's eyes didn't leave Jay's. She was no longer disgusted, no longer horrified. Just resigned. "And maybe I should have. Because if I had put a bullet in that son of a bitch's head, maybe *she* wouldn't be laying in a hospital bed fighting for her life."

Jay felt her eyes fill with tears. Her cheek throbbed as her throat caught all the words that she couldn't say in that moment.

She wanted to explain. Wanted to say she was sorry.

But Alice walked away, leaving Jay to sit there in a crowded bar with too many eyes on her and no one left to care.

27

H elena wasn't sure, but somehow, Lucio had become even more unbearable. Ever since the new year started, his mood had gotten worse: he was working longer hours, and he was locked away both at home and in the office. And he had made sure to drag her in to work every single day of her winter break. She had started staying at Quinn's to limit the commute, but that just meant that Lucio was calling her into work earlier.

He said it was to keep Helena from going out, but honestly, every time she tried to even think of alcohol since the party, she wanted to vomit. Not even twenty-one and her drinking days were over. She would just have to get into hard drugs, she decided.

But she would have to settle for caffeine for now. Helena struggled to keep her eyes open as she sat at the table of the coffee shop, staring blankly out the window at the dreary February weather while Dylan grabbed their mobile orders.

He set her drink down in front of her before taking his seat with his own coffee.

"God, I needed this," Helena sighed as she took a sip of her frappuccino. Even in the cold weather, she couldn't stand hot coffee. It always melted the whipped cream too fast. She pulled her straw out to suck on the end, moaning slightly as she sucked the sugary topping.

Her eyes locked with Dylan's, whose dark skin had an even redder tint to it.

"What?" she mumbled around her straw.

Dylan shook his head quickly, sipping his coffee. He pulled it away, touching his lip and shaking his hand out as some coffee spilled on him.

"Oh, shit, are you okay?" Helena stood. "Hang on, I'll grab you some napkins."

Dylan signed his thanks as she bolted to the counter to grab something to help him clean up. Someone stepped up just as she did, Helena running square into them.

"Shit, sorry I wasn't—" she began, then froze.

Jay—wearing an atrocious, probably real fur coat—stared back, face just as shocked as Helena felt. They hadn't seen each other, hadn't spoken or texted, in months. Helena didn't know what the hell Lucio had done, but he had told Helena under no circumstances was she to have *anything* to do with Jay. But old habits died hard.

"Jay," Helena choked out, pushing back her word vomit. "Hi."

"Hello," Jay said, stepping up to the counter to put in her order.

"Wait—" Helena moved in front of her. "How are you?"

"How *am* I?" Jay crossed her arms over her chest. "The fuck do you care?"

Helena winced at Jay's icy tone. "I mean—"

Jay sneered. "I've got nothing to say to you. Now move."

Helena's shoulders slumped as Jay walked around her. She listened to Jay give her order, voice casual and sweet as she talked with the barista like nothing was wrong. Like Helena wasn't standing behind her, desperate to explain, desperate to apologize and take back what she had said. She needed Jay to understand that Helena wasn't sure if she fully believed Lucio, but if this case moved forward Jay was going to get caught in the crossfire, she was going to get hurt. Helena couldn't stand by and watch her throw her entire life away over something so stupid. There were other guys. There were other people who cared about her, people who weren't

Michael or Colt or Lucio, people who would care about her and make sure she was safe and—

"Thank you," Jay said, snapping Helena out of her thoughts.

Helena opened her mouth, ready to speak up and tell Jay exactly what she had been thinking, but stopped. A pale scar marred the deep terracotta of Jay's skin.

"Jay?" Helena called.

Jay sighed, turning around as if she was dealing with some solicitor on the street. "What?"

"How'd you get that cut?"

Jay's hand flew to her cheek.

Helena stepped forward, gently pulling Jay's hand away to see it better. "What happened?"

A subtle movement. Jay touching her tongue to the tip of her teeth, her eyes darting away from Helena's. "Cut myself shaving. I'm still learning how to use the razor. Good to see you, kid."

Helena's stomach rose into her throat. "You're lying."

Jay stopped, looking back. "Yeah, it's called a *joke*."

"How'd it happen?"

"An accident." Jay started to walk away again, but Helena stepped in front of her.

Helena knew all about accidents. She had been the victim of a few of her own, when she was younger. "An accident *how?*"

Jay rolled her eyes and brushed some of her hair away from her face. "I tripped. I gotta go."

Her sleeve shifted, just enough. Just enough for Helena to see purple and red bruising around Jay's wrist.

Helena audibly gasped.

Jay dropped her arm, her cheeks reddening.

"Jay—"

"I'm fine."

Helena shook her head slowly. "Please don't lie to me."

"Don't *lie* to you?" Jay scoffed. "Fuck off. You lied to me first, remember?"

"No, I didn't." Helena's chest tightened. "I never lied to you, I promise."

"Fucking promises. Christ, I forgot how much of a *kid* you still are."

Helena pressed her lips into a thin line, but didn't back down. She wouldn't. "Jay, if he's hitting you—"

"If who's hitting me? Do you know how ridiculous you sound?" Jay crossed her arms over her chest. "No one is hitting me. I'm fine, back the fuck off."

Helena's mind began to race. Why was Jay lying? Why was she trying to deny the bruises? Anyone with eyes could see them. They were impossible to ignore, and yet Jay was acting like it was nothing. As if she wasn't hiding more underneath that ridiculous fur coat. Something glittered out of the corner of Helena's eye.

The huge rock on Jay's finger.

Helena's voice struggled to escape her throat. "Did you get engaged?"

When Jay didn't react, Helena worried that maybe she hadn't spoken at all. But Jay's gaze fell away from Helena's.

Helena's heart dropped. "You can't be serious."

Jay's face turned a deep shade of red. "You don't get it, kid."

"Enough with the 'kid' shit," Helena cried, running her hand through her hair. "Explain to me how the hell you can get engaged to someone who's hitting you? Someone who's abusing you?"

"I already told you that he's not *hitting* me," Jay bit out, but Helena could barely hear her over the blood in her ears.

"Then what is it? Throwing you around? Spitting on you? Yelling at you? Because all those things are *abuse*. He's abusing you!"

"Michael is *not* abusing me!" Jay snapped. "You have *no* idea what you're talking about. You're just a little fucking girl, who's done nothing but rely on her daddy for everything."

"Stop," Helena whispered, wrapping her arms around herself. "You're deflecting, I know what you're—"

"You don't know *fuck* all." Jay's jaw was tight, her teeth clenched. "You only know what your fucking shithead father has told you, and we already know what you think about him. So why don't both you and him do me a favor, and get the fuck out of my life before somebody gets hurt?"

"You already are."

Jay's lips pulled back in a snarl as she turned her face away, but not before Helena noticed Jay's eyes filled with tears.

"Jay—"

A hand on Helena's shoulder stopped her. She looked over to see Dylan staring daggers at Jay.

Helena shrugged him off. "Dylan, go back to the table, I need to—"

But Jay was gone.

"Shit." Helena ran to the door, shoving it open. "Jay!"

Helena shouted at the busy streets, trying to stand on her toes to see over the sea of people. But nothing. Dylan followed her out, looking guilty.

She turned to him, her blood boiling. "Let's go."

"*Where?*"

"We're gonna get Jay out of this. Even if we have to take her kicking and screaming."

Helena didn't bother knocking as she barreled into Lucio's office. She had practically run all the way back, Dylan in tow. They didn't have time to waste. If Helena knew anything, it was that Jay needed to get out ASAP. The longer they waited, the more chances Michael had to take it one step further.

Lucio sat at his table, looking over some files with Alice. Both looked up, shocked, but Lucio's mask slowly locked back into place.

"What the hell do you think you're doing?" Lucio asked, his voice laced with irritation.

"I need to speak with you." Helena's breathing refused to steady. "Now."

"Helena, I am in the middle of a meeting," he said. She could see the vein bulging from his neck. "Leave."

"This is important."

"Whatever it is, it can wait." He glanced over at Alice, shaking his head. "You'll have to excuse her, she's—"

He stopped as Helena's phone clattered on the table, sliding over to him.

Lucio and Alice both glanced down, the screenshot of Michael's Instagram post about his and Jay's engagement clear as day on the screen. Lucio's eyes flickered up to her, the quiet rage building in him again. "What the hell are you doing?"

Alice slid the phone to herself, looking over the image. "Hold on, what is—"

"Jay and Michael got engaged," Helena said. "And—and he's hitting her. I saw—I saw the bruises, she has a scar—"

"He's what?" Alice looked between Helena and the photo. Concern. Actual, genuine, real concern flashed over Alice's features.

A spark of hope lit in Helena's chest. "He's hitting her. I saw a bruise on her wrist, Dylan—"

Helena turned around to call on Dylan, he witnessed it, he knew, he could back her up. But there was no one standing behind her. Just the open door, and the sound of Fawziyah answering the phone down the hall.

"Morton," Lucio's voice rumbled through the space, making Helena's knees wobble, "I need you to step out so I can speak to my daughter. Alone."

Alice's brows furrowed. "Lucio if—"

"Morton." Lucio cut his gaze to her. "Please. I need to speak with Helena."

Alice glanced between the two, but stood, seeing herself out. Helena remained where she was.

"Where did you see Jay?" Lucio asked, his tone the same as if he was interrogating a witness.

"At the coffee shop," Helena answered, trying to gauge him. Obviously he just wanted more information, he was probing her to know exactly how they were going to approach this, how they were going to get Jay away from Michael. And yes, Helena had messed up before, slipping with the case. But now, they could get him on *this* too, maybe they could even hold him while they were finishing the investigation for embezzlement, he would be stuck, and more importantly, Jay would be safe. "She was—"

"Did she approach you?" Lucio asked, still seated.

Helena shook her head. "No, I bumped into her, but why does that—"

"Did she threaten you?"

"Why the hell would she have threatened me?"

"Did she say anything about Michael? Was he there?"

"No!" Helena shouted, tugging at her hair. "Lucio, will you just listen to me?"

"I am listening to you. And what I'm hearing is this has nothing to do with us." Lucio shrugged, picking up a file in front of him and flipping through a few pages. "You can send Alice back in now."

It felt as if someone had sucked all the air from the room. Helena gripped the chair in front of her, trying to keep herself upright. "What?"

"Jay didn't threaten you, Michael wasn't there, so there's no problem." He waved his hand towards the door. "Dismissed."

"You cannot be serious right now." Helena breathed out a laugh, empty of humor. "He's *hitting* her, Lucio, you have to do something! You need to help her!"

"*Help* her?" Lucio shook his head in disbelief. "She's not mine to help. Why don't you go tell her friend out there to handle it?"

Helena looked towards the door. Something gnawed at her to tell Alice, to get her to try and talk some sense into Jay. But Alice's comment from their meeting still rang in her ears. *Jay's a big girl. If she wants to get involved with a guy like Michael Silva, that's her choice.*

Lucio was standing by the window now, looking out over the dome, his hands linked behind his back. Casual. Composed. Like he always was whenever Helena confronted him with an inconvenient truth.

"So you're going to let him kill her?" she asked, her voice too loud in the silent room.

Lucio heaved a sigh. "He's not going to kill her. Don't be dramatic."

"You don't know that," Helena said. "You've said it yourself, I've *heard* you say it: 'She would still be here if just one person had stepped in and said something. Because the victim was too scared to speak for herself.' Those are *your* words, Lucio."

"Look, Helena, I get involved with this, and I risk losing the case."

"You have got to be kidding me. Now all of a sudden you're worried about losing the case?" She rounded the table, pulling him to face her. She had expected annoyance. Anger. Frustration. Anything but the apathy written across his features. "You didn't care at all before when it was you against Michael. But now because he put a ring on her finger you're suddenly so worried about losing it?"

"I don't give a shit about Jay," Lucio snapped, glaring down at her. "She's never meant anything to me, the sooner you learn that the better."

The words slammed into Helena so hard she thought her heart might have stopped beating. He was lying, of course he was. She tried to coat her mouth with saliva, but it was impossible. "You don't mean that."

Lucio barked out a harsh laugh. "I do, Helena. Jay is a *boneca*, a puppet. I give her what she thinks she wants, and she plays right along. It's not my fault if she thought there was something more there."

Helena was going to be sick. This wasn't her father. Her father stood up for others, he fought for victims and people who had been wronged. Her father didn't play games like this with people; he wasn't a cold, ruthless attorney. He didn't stoop down to the level of defense attorneys who would do anything to get their client off. Prosecutors had standards. *He* had standards.

She searched his eyes, those eyes that were so similar to hers, the one that connected them, that always made people say "she looks so much like you." They didn't mean the color, she knew that. They meant the energy, the spark that he had stoked within her, nurtured and brought to a blaze, told her never to lose, even when it ended up burning him. But the fire in his eyes was gone now. All that remained was cold, dark, forest, one that if she looked too long she would forever be lost in.

Helena's voice dropped to a whisper. "This isn't you."

"It is. This is who I am, who I always have been," Lucio said, his voice deep and steady as he spoke. "You just haven't been paying attention."

"Stop." Helena's jaw was clenched so hard she thought her teeth might crack.

"Jay's made her choice."

"*Stop.*" Helena tried to cover her ears, to shake the words out of her brain where they had lodged themselves so deeply. They burrowed into her psyche, twisting themselves around his image, around the last parts of him that she thought she could still believe in. *Trust the Virgin and don't run.* She didn't believe in God, neither did Lucio. It was bullshit. He always said that if you want something done, *you* have to make it happen. Never wait for a miracle. Because miracles only happen when someone else steps in.

He would step in, she knew he would. This was all an act—he couldn't watch this happen, he had told her that. And maybe he hadn't saved Gideon, but he could save Jay, he could save her friend, if he just—

Lucio pulled Helena's hands away from her ears, and she looked at him, tears streaming down her cheeks.

The apathy remained. "Let her go."

"No!" Helena wrenched her wrists away, flying backwards and crashing into the table behind her. Papers spilled everywhere, covering the floor around her. She shook her head, the fire in her chest spreading. "I'm not letting him take Jay."

"You're not going to save her," Lucio said, his throat bobbing slightly. "You can't save people who don't want to be saved."

"Watch me." Helena turned on her heel, nearly slipping on the papers beneath her feet as she stormed out of the room.

Alice was waiting just outside of the door. She looked up at Helena, eyes slightly red. Had she been crying? Of course she had, Alice knew Jay better than anyone, they were best friends, weren't they?

The fire continued to consume Helena, burning through her thoughts. She pointed her finger at Alice. "You need to get her."

"Get *who?*" Alice asked, stepping back as Helena advanced.

"Jay! You heard me in there. Michael is *hitting* her."

Alice looked away. "I know."

"So?" Helena raised her brows. "What are you going to do about it?"

"What can I do?" Alice shrugged one shoulder, still not meeting Helena's eyes.

Helena thought she might scream. "What the *hell* do you mean? You can go over there and *arrest* Michael for domestic violence!"

"That's not how it works," Alice said.

A cold wave crashed over Helena. "What?"

"Jay needs to come forward and say that he's abusing her. She needs to have proof. If we don't have that, then my hands are tied."

"No," Helena breathed. "No, no, come on, you're her friend." She grabbed Alice's shirt, trying to get the woman to look at her. Helena's heart was beating so hard in her chest she was worried she might crack a rib. "You can convince her, you can talk to her."

"We're not friends." Alice slowly removed Helena's hands from herself. "And even if we were, she wouldn't tell the truth."

Helena's body grew weak. The world around her was swimming; she was only slightly aware of Alice saying *I'm sorry* before walking back into Lucio's office. The words were muffled, as if she were underwater. But Helena didn't feel weightless. The world plunged into darkness, she struggled to breathe as the water filled her lungs, and something wrapped itself around her. She screamed, fighting off whatever it was dragging her down, but a hand came to her face, signing against it. *"D."*

"Dylan," Helena gasped, wrapping her arms around him, burying her face in his neck. "Dylan please, we gotta do something, someone has to do something."

But Dylan didn't sign again. He just wrapped his arms around her tighter, and Helena knew. A sob, heavy and loud and real, wracked through her body. And she knew.

There was nothing she could do. Despite everything, Helena was helpless. And that was the worst feeling of all.

28

"Have you talked to Dad since your little spat?"

"Fuck him. This is all his fault in the first place."

"How is all this his fault?"

Helena kept her eyes glued on the beach that passed outside the car window, ignoring the feeling of Quinn's eyes boring into her back. They were out driving near the beach, which was currently empty outside of the occasional dog walker, or other random pedestrians enjoying the solitude. Quinn said they needed to get out of the apartment for some fresh air. They never did well with being cooped up during the winter months. But now Helena could see this was just a ploy to get her to talk about her feelings.

She traced her finger along the glass, drawing small patterns in the fog her breath made. "Because he doesn't give a shit about people. He just wants to use them for his own gain and then let them rot when he's through."

Quinn huffed. "That's not true."

"Bullshit. If he cared, he would have helped Jay."

"Hel, you know why he can't."

Helena whipped around to look at them. "No, Quinn, I really don't. Because the Lucio *I* knew helped people who were in trouble. Or at least that's what you kept telling me."

Quinn rolled their eyes. "Because he does. But this is way more complicated than you think it is. Not everything is as black and white as you want it to be."

Helena sank into her seat. "Didn't realize protecting people from their literal abusers was a gray area. I'll keep that in mind when I'm a lawyer and my client tells me how their spouse was throwing them around. 'Sorry, I can't help you. My dad taught me sometimes people deserve to get abused!'"

"Helena," Quinn chastised. "That's not funny."

"It doesn't have to be, it's true." She returned to drawing on the window. She was so sick of this shit. All she wanted to do was go home, but trying to get back to the city from here would be close to impossible. Plus, it was the middle of February, and Helena would die of pneumonia before she even got close. But it would serve Lucio right. Or maybe it wouldn't. Not like he cared about *her*, either.

"Helena," Quinn said, using that annoying tone they always would whenever they were about to lecture her.

"What?"

"You need to apologize."

She had to stop herself from putting her fist through the car window. But it was a very tempting thought. "I'm not apologizing. I didn't do anything wrong. He's the one who should apologize."

"Dad's going through a lot right now." Quinn tugged on the back of her coat, but she refused to look at them.

"*Lucio* is fine. He was fine when he was using Jay, wasn't he? What, now that he doesn't get to do that anymore he suddenly gets to be a little baby?"

"That's not what he cares about."

"Isn't it?" Helena turned back to Quinn. Their knuckles were white on the wheel. "Why else would he want to get involved with her? Face it, Quinn, this was all about getting back at Michael. That's what it's always about. He's willing to hurt whoever he can to get what he wants. He doesn't give a shit about anyone, including us."

"He's never hurt us." There was a slight hesitation in Quinn's voice, like they were leaving room for her contradiction.

"No, he's just missed out on almost all of our birthdays and graduations."

"Because he's working, Hel. To support us."

"Support us?" She laughed harshly. "When has he supported us?"

"Are you kidding?" The car accelerated. Quinn loved to drive fast, it was the whole reason they had driven to Rye in the first place. "Taking us in and putting a roof over our head, *that's* not supporting us? Putting us through therapy to make sure we could actually sleep at night? Paying for all of Gideon's medical bills when he got sick?"

"Oh yes, give him the 'Dad of the Year' award for doing the bare minimum," Helena said. "Forgive me for not being more grateful that he did what you'd been doing just fine for a decade!"

"I didn't *want* to do those things." Quinn's voice rose to match hers. "I *never* wanted to be a dad. I was a kid too, Helena, as much as you would like to try and deny that fact!"

"So you want me to say that the guy who let our brother die and who's willing to let another woman get killed is a good person? That *he's* a good dad?" Helena turned from them completely, her jaw setting. "Forget it, Quinn. Lucio hasn't protected us from shit. I wish he never would have adopted us."

The car lurched to the side, the road behind them erupting into a chorus of honks and eliciting a scream from Helena.

"What are you doing?" she screeched, looking out the back window to make sure they hadn't caused an accident.

Quinn didn't answer her. They put on their flashers, reached across her and into the glove box, and pulled out a handgun, pointing it directly at her.

Helena had never had someone point a gun at her before. Lucio didn't allow toy guns, not even ones that didn't look real. But this wasn't a toy. There was no little orange cap on the end that told her Quinn was just playing, that they were joking.

For emergencies only, Lucio had said.

He hadn't taught Helena what to do in an emergency like this one. Where the last person she could trust was looking at her like she deserved whatever came next. Like *she* was the danger.

Quinn motioned the muzzle of the gun toward the door, and Helena's heart skipped a beat. "Get out."

"Quinn, what—"

"Shut up, and get out."

She did. She kept her eyes on the gun the entire time. Her head screamed at her to run, to get back in the car, to wave someone driving by down. But she couldn't. Her heart wouldn't let her. This was her sibling, if someone saw them, who knew what they would do?

Quinn motioned her over the guardrail, keeping an eye out for someone who might be trying to pull over to see if they needed help. No one did. It was New York. People minded their own damn business, didn't make someone else's problem theirs.

Helena and Quinn walked down towards the water, both of them remaining silent. The wind was biting cold, causing inHelena's eyes to tear up as her hair whipped at her face. The only sound around them was the waves lapping at the shore, trying their best to reach them. *Say something. Talk to them. They're your sibling, this is a joke, they're taking things too far, you need to tell them.*

But Helena's mouth was sealed shut. She couldn't open it—her teeth were chattering too hard, it would make speaking impossible.

"Turn around," Quinn growled.

She did as they asked, bile rising in her throat as she saw the gun was still pointed at her.

Helena wrapped her arms around her waist, trying to find her balance in the sand. "What are you doing?"

"Doing what I should have done years ago."

"What are you talking about?"

"I'm done protecting you, Helena."

"Protecting me from *what*? From you?"

"From me. From Lucio. From your fucking selfish and self-important mindset." Quinn's fingers twitched against the side of the gun. "You want to act like everything was so perfect before Lucio came around. You want to think that I was this perfect parent. I *wasn't*. You have no idea what I went through to make sure that you and Gideon were taken care of." Their voice was emphasized by the crash of the waves. "I was a child. A fucking child. And I had to take care of two other children. Do you know what that's like? To have your entire childhood stripped away from you?

"Of course you don't. Because I *kept* you from that. You never saw what happened. You never saw what I did for work, never saw who I was out with, never saw the times where the cops brought me home. Because I didn't *let* you. I made sure you didn't see, because I didn't want you knowing what I had to do to make sure you and Gideon were taken care of. And now you want to spit in Lucio's face? He *saved* me, Helena. I'm not going back there! I'm not letting you fuck up everything."

"Quinn, what are you talking about?" Helena struggled to contain the terror that ravaged over her. "Put the gun down, you're acting completely irrational!"

"No, I've never been more rational." Quinn stepped forward. She stepped back, the waves crashing behind her, inching closer. "You have *no* idea what I've put myself through for you. You're selfish, Helena. You always have been, and you always will be."

"Quinn, please, I'm sorry!" A sob threatened to wrack her, but she bit it back, terrified it would only aggravate them further. "Please, just put the gun down, let's go home and—"

"No."

Her heart dropped.

"I'm done protecting you." Quinn's voice was low and steady as they spoke, barely audible over her blood pumping into her ears. "And Lucio's not here to do it either. You want to be on your own? This is what it's like."

"Quinn, this isn't funny. Please stop." The tears came so quick they blurred her vision.

"I'm not being funny. I'm being serious." They cocked the gun. "You get a choice here. Either kill me and save yourself, or I kill you. Three." Their finger eased onto the trigger. "Two."

"Quinn, stop!" she screamed.

"One."

Helena dove. Quinn couldn't hold their footing in the sand, both of them falling hard. Quinn grabbed a fistful of her hair, trying to pull her off. She cried out in pain as she cocked her fist back and punched them in the nose.

"Fuck!" Quinn reached for their face, blood beginning to gush.

Helena took the opportunity to grab the gun and bit their wrist until they released it. She scrambled backwards, pointing the gun at Quinn. Blood was pouring over their mouth, but that didn't stop them from coming towards her.

"Stop or I'll shoot!"

They kept advancing on her.

"Stop, Quinn!" Her hand trembled.

She screamed as they closed in on her, a foot away, the hammer clicking as she squeezed the trigger.

Quinn stopped where they were, their breathing heavy and small blood bubbles formed near their lips.

Helena was shaking and sobbing as she lowered the gun from above her head. There had been no crack, no whizz of a bullet through the air. No danger. She brought the gun back to her eye line, the orange safety staring back at her.

"That wasn't fucking funny!" She threw the gun away. "What the fuck is wrong with you?"

"Even with me threatening your life, you still couldn't pull the trigger," Quinn said. "You can't even protect yourself."

"What are you talking about?"

Quinn spat to the side, licking the blood that still remained on their teeth. "It was between me and you. And you chose me. Why?

You don't have a single shred of self-preservation, do you? You need someone to protect you because you're still a child, you're still—"

"You're still my sibling!" Helena sobbed, curling in on herself. Tears soaked her jeans, her crying loud and raw and real. Her breathing came out too heavy, too uneven. "I love you."

The waves receded, calm and quiet, now. Quinn wrapped their arms around her, resting their chin on her head. "I love you too, Hel."

She continued to sob, wrapping her arms around their chest and gripping the back of their shirt. She couldn't have done it. She had already lost her other half. She didn't need to lose any more.

Quinn pressed a kiss to her head, sighing. "But I needed you to see this."

Helena hid her face in their shirt. She wanted to block them out, she couldn't listen anymore.

"People do really fucked up things for people they love. They're willing to protect people, even those that hurt them. And they do it out of love."

She shook her head. "No."

"Yes. And it's fucked up, and wrong, and I wish it wasn't that way. But it is." Quinn brought their hand to Helena's cheek, forcing her to look at them. "I did things that hurt me for you and Gideon. And I would do it all over again, because it meant I got to keep everything that mattered to me." They swallowed, blinking rapidly. "When I met Lucio, there was a chance that wasn't going to be true for long."

Helena's eyes widened. "What?"

"I got arrested. It was my last strike." Quinn pressed their lips together. "I was seventeen, and about to be charged with solicitation."

"No, what—" Helena shook her head. The bruises, the frequent trips to the doctor, the days of missed school. Helena thought that Quinn was just constantly getting into trouble, acting out because they had been bounced around from foster home to foster home, sometimes three or four in only a few months' time. It was hard, trying to find a place to keep the three of them. So Quinn would disappear for days on end, and come back with bruises and busted lips and clothes that smelled like cigarettes and cologne and alcohol.

She always yelled at them for disappearing, for up and leaving, but no matter how many times she begged them to stay, they would go again. *I'm doing this for you guys. I'll be back soon, I promise.*

"I was, Hel." Quinn sniffled, tears wetting their own face now. "I was doing it for you, and Gideon. I was trying to save up enough money for us when I turned eighteen, so I could provide for you guys."

"But then..." Helena wiped at her face. "What about Lucio?"

"Lucio was the prosecutor for my case. He, uh, he made me an offer. I stop turning tricks, and he takes us in. *All* of us."

All. Helena remembered that day, when Lucio said he wanted all of them. Not just her, not just Gideon, not just Quinn. All of them. One almost-adult and two pre-teens who were scared of their own shadows.

"He got me out of there. Got us all out. And as much as you want to think he didn't protect us, he did." Quinn tried a smile, but winced when it moved their nose. "Because we *wanted* to be saved. We *wanted* protection."

Helena turned away from Quinn, biting her lip so hard she thought it might split. "So does Jay."

"She needs to come to that conclusion, Hel." They ran a hand over her hair. "You can't make that decision for her."

"But he's *hurting* her, Quinn. What if he..." Helena didn't want to speak the words into existence.

"She'll come around," Quinn mumbled. "She'll come to her senses and realize that she needs out. And when she does, she'll have you waiting for her."

Helena sniffled, looking back at the gun that lay a few feet away from them. The waves licked at the metal, and almost as if it could taste the bitterness, retreated. "We should get out of here."

"Yeah," Quinn said, releasing her from the hug and going to retrieve the gun. "Come on, let's go grab something to eat. My treat."

Helena wiped her nose. "I don't know if you really want to go out looking like that."

They winced as they touched their nose. "Yeah, well, that's what masks and drive-thrus are for."

29

Helena couldn't sleep. Her mind still spun about everything that had happened over the last two weeks—Jay being engaged, Lucio refusing to get involved, Helena's fight with Quinn on the beach—it was all too much for her to handle at once. So she had come crawling home, although she still wasn't speaking to Lucio. He wasn't speaking to her either, though, outside of what was absolutely necessary for work. Which was fine. She didn't need him.

She let out a loud sigh, then threw the covers off of herself. Maybe some water would help. She padded downstairs, careful to avoid the creaky steps. It was a surprise to see Lucio's office door cracked open; she had been sure he was asleep. The soft plucking of guitar strings was like a siren's call, drawing Helena in.

Lucio hummed a melody, his fingers strumming as he clumsily plucked notes. He cursed beneath his breath, trying again. Helena moved into the crack of the door, silent as she observed him.

Watching Lucio play was like seeing a jungle cat at the watering hole. There was a sense of calm as his fingers moved on the strings, his eyes half closed in concentration, his body fully relaxed over the acoustic guitar, but still ready to pounce at the slightest hint of danger.

He resumed his humming as he played a song she didn't recognize. His lips started to move, his voice a whisper, but it didn't matter. She knew his voice better than her own.

Years of him singing lullabies to her when he was sure she was already asleep, stolen moments in the kitchen when he thought he was alone, helping her through the dance at her festa de debutantes. His voice was low, comforting. The complete opposite of his courtroom voice. It was safety.

Lucio sighed, lifting his head as his gaze drifted to the door. The calm dissipated. His spine straightened, his eyes lost their dreamy look, but his smile remained. "Hey, what're you doing up?"

"I couldn't sleep." Helena opened the door more when he waved her in. "I heard you playing and wanted to come see what you were doing."

"I couldn't sleep either. I got the itch." He rested the guitar on his leg as he rubbed at his fingers. "I'm a little rusty, unfortunately."

"What was that song you were playing?"

Lucio stiffened, and she was sure she would get the same answer she always got. *Nothing.*

"My wedding song."

"I didn't recognize it." Helena waited for the dismissal, for him to tell her it was late and she needed to go to bed. They had a long day ahead of them tomorrow; he wasn't going to put up with her bad attitudehe . But instead, he motioned toward the chair in front of him. She took it.

"You were pretty young when it came out. I'm not surprised." He looked at the guitar again. "Do you want to learn?"

"Learn what?"

"How to play."

Helena sucked in a breath. Lucio had put her through years of piano lessons, saying that it would teach her discipline, but she always hated it. She never felt like it fully captured her; piano was too delicate, too typical. She didn't want to be either. "Is that okay?"

"Sure. I'll teach you a couple chords." He passed her the instrument, placing the strap over her shoulder, covered by an oversized tee shirt. One of Lucio's old band tees, from when he had been in a Pop-punk band. The black fabric was worn, some holes in it, the letting faded and almost invisible now. But it was still her favorite sleep shirt.

Helena hadn't expected the guitar to be as heavy as it was, so she was grateful that Lucio laid it gently in her lap.

She traced the curves of the guitar, her pale skin contrasted with the deep color of the wood. Her hand drifted down to the strings, plucking each one, captivated by the sounds they made.

"It'll hurt at first."

Helena looked up at him as he settled into his chair, an all black guitar now seated in his lap. Lucio passed her a small piece of plastic. A pick.

"What do you mean?"

"Your fingers. You don't have the calluses yet, and won't for a long time." He showed her his hand, the tips of his fingers reddened. "You'll need to practice and play every day to develop them."

Helena scowled. "Who says I'm even going to like this?"

He chuckled, "You're right. We'll start easy with the chords."

When he moved his fingers, Helena did her best to mirror them, but it was hard. They didn't want to move like his did; it was almost like they had a mind of their own.

Lucio helped her place them in the correct spots. "Now strum."

She did, but it came out choked and awkward, the strings catching in all the wrong places. She scowled again.

"You're curling your hand too much. You need to open yourself up." Lucio leaned back.

Helena watched his whole body release, his fingers naturally melting into the chord he had just shown her, his hand moving down the strings in one fluid motion.

She huffed, trying it again. And again, it came out stiff. "How come you're so relaxed?"

"Years of practice." As if to rub it in her face, he strummed a few chords, then fumbled one.

Helena giggled despite herself, before pressing her lips together, preparing herself for him to chastise her.

But Lucio smiled. "Told you I was rusty."

Her shoulders loosened, but she kept her back straight, concentrating on exactly where to put her fingers. They found their previous position, and she strummed. The strings vibrated like the excitement running through her.

"Yes, fihla!" He beamed back at her. "Try it again."

She did. The sound was better this time. Helena looked at him, his nod of approval clear. A swell of pride sparked in her chest.

Lucio strummed the cord again. Helena did the same. He quickly moved through a few more chords as she watched in absolute awe. She hadn't thought much about guitar, how people who played did so effortlessly. How Lucio's fingers just knew what to do, as if they had been doing it his whole life.

"Who did you learn to play guitar from?"

Lucio's face darkened. Not in anger, but with something else. Helena thought about telling him to forget it, scared that she might have ruined this moment with him, but he answered her. "My dad."

"Oh." Helena strummed the strings again. "Is he...?"

"No. He's been gone for a long time." Lucio moved his fingers and nodded to her. "This is an A chord."

She mimicked his fingers. It wasn't perfect, but a lot better than the first attempt. "You don't talk a lot about your family."

He plucked the strings one by one as he watched her alternate clumsily between the A and E chords. "Family is a strong word to use with them."

Helena pressed her lips together, concentrating. When she finally got the transition to be smoother, she asked, "What about your mom?"

"My mom?" Lucio flickered between chords, as if he was debating which one to show her next. He smiled gently. "She was everything."

"How?"

"She raised me on her own. She was beautiful, intelligent, kind, strong-willed." He strummed one chord for a few seconds. "You remind me a lot of her."

Helena ducked her head, and went back to strumming the A and E chords. Compliments from Lucio were a rare treat. She tried her best not to let it get to her, but the words echoed in her mind. *Beautiful. Intelligent. Kind. Strong-willed.*

Warmth bloomed in her chest.

"My mother took whatever life threw at her on the chin. She never shied away from a fight." His smile fell. "Which makes me wonder why she ended up with my father." His fingers moved again. "C."

She followed, strumming the chord again and again, listening to it carefully. A bright, happy sound. Helena looked up, watching Lucio. The energy radiating off of him was at complete odds with the chord that she played now. Helena bit back the question. They were enjoying themselves, she didn't need to ruin it by prying.

But she knew she might not get another chance to ask again. "Lucio?"

Lucio plucked the strings of his guitar, keeping his eyes on hers. "Yes?"

"Was he..." The words died out on her tongue.

"Abusive?" He strummed a chord different from the one that he had shown her. A mournful, deep sound that resonated through the room, reverberated off the walls and filled her being. "Yes."

Helena knew she should stop asking questions. Just enjoy the rest of the lesson. She tried to mirror the chord he had played, but hers wasn't nearly as good. His fingers moved away from it, clearly seeing that she was trying to mimic him. He went back to the A chord, and strummed, but Helena's fingers remained on the previous chord. She strummed again, forcing herself to relax. She tried closing her eyes, focusing only on the sound.

Her voice came out in a whisper, barely audible above the echoing of the chord. "Did he ever hit you?"

A new chord, this one not as heavy, but still dark. "No."

"Did he hit Michael?"

The same chord as before, the one that felt like a haunting presence in the room, that made her stomach turn and her throat constrict. She didn't like it. There was something about it that felt terrifying and real, and as she opened her eyes to look at Lucio again, she knew.

His eyes met hers. "Yes."

Her fingers remained where they were on the strings, terrified to move, as if the sound would release something. As if the spell over them would break; Lucio would turn from her, would go right back into hiding, and leave her sitting there with all these questions that she wasn't too sure that she wanted the answers to.

He plucked a string, low and resonant. "Michael was a difficult kid."

Helena mimicked it, letting it bridge the gap that was between them. "Is that why you two didn't get along?"

"No. It goes much deeper than that." He strummed again, then placed his hand over the strings, stopping the sound dead in its tracks. Unfinished. It set her teeth on edge. Lucio sighed, running his fingers over the strings but playing no sound. "The abuse didn't bring us together. It pitted us against each other."

"But, you're brothers. I thought brothers—"

"Not always, Hel," Lucio said, his eyes drifting back to the strings in front of him. "We weren't like you and Quinn, and we definitely weren't you and Gideon."

It was the first time she had heard Lucio speak his name in years. Helena swore she saw something flash in the window. But it was probably just the breeze shaking the window and moving the reflection of the lamp light. Helena plucked each of the strings, blinking rapidly. *Don't cry. Don't ask, don't cry. You don't need to know. You know enough already, it's not going to change—*

"Why did you leave?"

Lucio tilted his head, searching her face. "What?"

The words were spilling out of Helena's mouth before she could stop them. "You left. After Gideon died, you, you just, walked away. Like he never existed."

"No, Hel. I promise, that's not what happened." Lucio set his guitar down, moving to kneel in front of her. "Is that what you think I did?"

"It *is* what you did," Helena spat, but the words lacked the venom she wanted them to have, tainted by stupid tears that rolled down her cheeks too quickly. "You put me and Quinn into counseling, but you never did it yourself. You just shut yourself away in your office."

"Helena…" Lucio cooed, reaching up to cup her face.

She let him, her tears catching on his fingers. "I needed my dad and I didn't have him. You weren't *there*. I was so scared and lonely, I felt like I had to keep it together because everything around me was falling apart. I lost my twin, the one person who I could always count on, and you made it seem like you couldn't care less about him."

Lucio pulled the guitar off her, letting it fall to the ground with a loud crash, the sound of discordant notes echoing throughout the room, but Helena barely registered it as he pulled her tight to his chest.

She caved. He hadn't hugged her in so long, because she wouldn't let him. She always bristled at his touch, pushed him away, because if she did he couldn't hurt her, he couldn't make her feel like he was *actually* going to be there for her. But as her arms came up, wrapping around him and feeling the soft fabric of his tee shirt, she had never felt more safe.

"Helena, I'm so sorry." His voice shook, and she held him tighter, desperate to hold him together, because she couldn't be strong enough for both of them at that moment. "I didn't mean to. I'm so sorry."

"But you did, Lucio." She sniffled. "And I don't get it. Why didn't you care?"

"I did care. God, Helena, I cared more than you could ever possibly know." His hand cradled the back of her head. A sob wracked her body as she continued to cry. "I already lost two of my kids, to lose Gideon..." Lucio pulled back, cupping her face again. His cheeks were covered in tears, his eyes red and puffy, making the green all the more striking. "I didn't want you to see me so broken. I was trying so hard to be strong for you guys, to make you feel like everything was going to be normal again, but I couldn't. I just kept losing, and the thought of losing you, too, of something taking you away from me, my *fihla*, I couldn't handle that. And I'm *so* sorry, I'm so sorry that I made you feel for a single second that I don't love you all with my entire being, because I do, Helena. I love you so, *so* much."

Helena couldn't have hugged him tighter if she had tried. There was no way for her to express the flood of emotions that completely overwhelmed her, the way that hearing him say "I love you" and knowing that he meant it absolutely devastated her, how it seeped into her bones and lit her up and made her feel whole again. Because that's all she had ever wanted.

"I love you, too, Dad."

30

"Case number 367, the People vs. Michael Silva." The bailiff's voice echoed through the courtroom, even over the slight din of people murmuring as they waited for later arraignments.

Helena sat up in her seat straighter, her notebook clutched in her fingers. It had been a week since she had gotten the news that Michael was arrested. It had made the front page, and her entire social media feeds were flooded with videos of him. But nothing about Jay. Helena had thought about reaching out, trying to help, but Dylan had warned her against it. Now that Lucio was going to trial, it was dangerous for Helena to be seen interacting with people who Michael was close to.

So she remained silent. But once the trial was over, once Michael was behind bars, she wasn't going to hesitate. She was going to get her friend back. She was going to help.

"Luke Torres, DA, your honor," Lucio repeated for the umpteenth time that day, him and the judge exchanging a look of boredom.

"Philip Martinez, Defense Attorney, your honor," Martinez said.

Helena rolled her eyes. Martinez was infamous in the DA's office with his Giorgio Armani suits and fake, snobby accent. He was the kind of attorney guys like Michael kept on retainer, even if they didn't plan on getting caught.

The judge cleared his throat. "Mr. Martinez, your client is charged with embezzlement. How does he plead?"

"Not guilty, Your Honor," Martinez said.

Of course. Guy was too stupid to try and take a plea deal.

"Counsel?"

"No further comment, your honor," Lucio said.

"Wonderful, bail is set at seven hundred thousand. The trial will be set for June twenty-seventh."

"Your honor that amount is ridiculous!" Martinez shouted, "My client's assets are frozen. How is he supposed to afford bail?"

"Your client is a smart man, Martinez," Lucio said. "I'm sure he'll figure something out."

The gavel came down, but Martinez didn't move. Helena's brows furrowed as she glanced over at Lucio. Martinez was supposed to *leave*, why was he still standing there?

She started to lean forward, ready to ask Lucio what the hell was going on, but the bailiff spoke up before she could.

"Case number 368, the People versus Jay Sterling."

What? Helena gripped the railing in front of her, looking to Lucio for an explanation. But he kept his back to her, not betraying his stoicism. Helena's grip tightened, nails digging into the soft wood.

But her father wouldn't look at her.

"We can skip the introductions," the judge said gruffly, looking over a piece of paper. "Mr. Martinez, you're representing this client as well?"

"Yes, Your Honor," Martinez said.

"'Tampering with evidence.' How does she plead?"

Tampering with evidence? What the hell were they talking about? This had to be some bullshit. Some lie the police made up because Jay had simply been around, it couldn't be true.

"Not guilty, Your Honor."

The judge grunted. "Counsel?"

"Miss Sterling has no prior charges, Your Honor. And we were able to recover data from the laptop with no problem," Lucio said.

Helena's mind raced. What laptop? What had Jay done? Why was she arrested?

Lucio continued, "We agree to dismiss the charges against Miss Sterling."

"Great, one less thing for me to have to deal with," the judge grumbled, bringing his gavel down again. Martinez gathered his papers, and saw himself out, shooting Lucio a dirty look as he did.

"Luke?" Helena called, leaning over the barrister so he could hear her over the buzz of people around them. "What happened with Jay?"

"Nothing, Hel. It's over with." Lucio kept his back to her, pretending to sort through his papers.

"Did she try to—"

"Hel." Lucio turned around. His eyes were tired; he had been working almost around the clock the last few days in preparation for this case. "She made her choice."

The words landed, final and heavy. Helena nodded once as she sat back in her seat. So this is how it would be, then. No apologies, no explanations, no goodbyes. Only a final sinking feeling, that there was nothing else she could do.

It was over.

31

Helena hadn't seen Dylan in a few days. Well, she had *seen* him, but it felt like he was avoiding her. Which was strange, because Dylan never avoided her.

She kept trying to walk past his desk, but each time, he was buried in some kind of work that Lucio had given him. Or, at least he pretended to be. On day three, she had decided she'd had enough. Whatever it was that was bothering Dylan, he was going to talk about it.

Helena poured two cups of coffee as she breathed in deep. She could do this. Dylan was her friend, and if she had done something to piss him off, she would apologize.

She marched herself out of the kitchenette to walk over to his desk. He wasn't there, but his keys were, meaning he must not have been far off. Helena set their coffees down and sat in his chair. She lowered it so her feet could touch the ground, twisting and turning while she waited. Her eyes lazily looked over his laptop, which was unlocked. The screen was mostly blank: a notes app was pulled up in the corner with a to do list.

Helena smirked.

Of course, it was filled with tasks: go get groceries, type up some case notes, get ready for a deposition, something about sending some files.

She looked around, but seeing that Dylan still wasn't around, she added one of her own. *Buy Helena a hot chocolate.*

The message popped up before she had a chance to look away.

Michael Silva

> *Thank you for letting me know.*

Helena's mouth went dry as the message disappeared. But it remained burned behind her eyes. Michael. Michael *fucking* Silva was texting Dylan. And Dylan had clearly texted back.

There had to be an explanation. Clearly, right? There had to be some plausible reason as to why they were texting.

Helena just couldn't think of one. Her mind was completely blank, the only thing in it being Michael's words. What did Dylan tell him? What did they have to talk about? Was Michael out of prison? What about Jay, did that mean—

A hand dropped on her shoulder, turning her around.

Dylan.

He signed, his movements sharp and hard. *"What are you doing?"*

"Why is Michael Silva texting you?" Helena's voice came out quiet, and for a moment, she thought she might not have spoken. But Dylan's face let her know that she had.

"What?"

Helena stood, forcing Dylan to take a step back. She repeated her words carefully, signing along with them. "Why is Michael Silva texting you?"

"He's not texting me. I don't even have his number. I have no idea what you're talking about." Dylan tried to shut the laptop, but she stopped him.

"I saw it, Dylan. I saw it on your screen." Helena shook her head. "Why the hell is he texting you? Are you—are you talking to him behind Lucio's back?"

"No, no, I swear, that's not what it is!" Dylan rubbed his hands over his face. *"I swear, Helena, it's not what it looks like."*

"Then what is it? Because as far as I can tell, you're out here texting with the guy that Luke is trying to prosecute!"

He shushed her, his eyes cutting to the paralegals floating around them, *"Helena, please, don't shout. Look, I can't tell you why I'm texting Michael, but—"*

"I can't believe you would do this." Helena backed up, heading to the elevator. She couldn't keep looking at him. She was going to be sick. Not Dylan. Not the one person that Helena *knew*, that she could trust above all else to be honest with her. He wasn't that kind of guy, he wasn't the type to stab people in the back. "After everything Lucio's done for you?"

The world felt like it was falling apart around her. How the hell was she going to tell Lucio? The one person he had actually trusted to put on this case, above *her* even, had ratted Lucio out to his brother? Who knew what Dylan had told Michael—the entire case might have been compromised, or he might have told Michael that he could report Lucio for being his half-brother. Her mind was spiraling; she had to talk to Lucio, she had to—

Dylan caught her arm, his eyes wide and desperate. *"He knows."*

Helena's entire body went cold. "What?"

Dylan pressed his lips together, dropping his hand from Helena's arm. *"Luke knows."*

"What do you mean Luke knows? He knows that you're out here spilling secrets to Michael? How the hell would he know that? Why would he know that?"

"I'm sorry, Hel."

"What the hell are you apologizing for? What did you do?"

He didn't move.

"Dylan," she repeated. "What did you *do?*"

Helena's phone buzzed in her pocket. She almost ignored it, but something told her to check it. She pulled it out, her blood turning to ice.

Helena picked it up before she could second guess herself. "Hello?"

"Hey, Helena," Jay said, taking a shaky breath. "I need a favor. From a friend."

Epilogue

"*This is a really bad idea, Hel.*"

"*Jay has nowhere else to go.*"

"*If Luke finds out he's going to kill you.*"

"*He's a P-U-S-S-Y. He'd never get A-W-A-Y with it.*"

"Okay, as impressive as this is, I can tell that you're talking about me."

Helena shot an apologetic glance to the backseat, where Jay sat soaked to the bone, a towel wrapped around her shoulders to keep her hair from dripping too much. A freak storm had rolled through, a sudden and torrential downpour that had made the drive to get Jay a pain, but luckily Helena had been able to convince Quinn that Dylan needed to drive her home, giving her a perfect excuse to borrow Quinn's car.

Jay's brown hair had started to dry, frizzing near the crown of her head while the ends began to coil. Helena had never seen Jay's hair undone; she always had it put into braids or pressed straight. Her makeup had also run around her eyes, highlighting the deep brown. Jesus, even when she looked like she had been dunked she was still gorgeous.

"Sorry," Helena said, rubbing at the back of her neck.

"It's fine, just, fill me in?" Jay asked, looking completely out of her element in the Pink Port uniform Helena had managed to swipe.

Helena rubbed her shoulder, looking at Dylan. But he kept his eyes on the road, using one hand to sign for her to continue. "Okay, so, I wasn't entirely truthful with what I said on the phone."

Jay's smile fell. "What part?"

"The 'Lucio said it was okay for you to come stay with us' part?"

"Jesus, Hel, are you kidding me?"

"Look, it'll be fine." Helena turned around fully. "We have a guest house in the back. We'll just let Lucio know the situation, and once he's okay with it, we'll tell him that we moved you in!"

Jay sighed as she slouched in the backseat. "I was only engaged a criminal, you don't have to make me feel like one."

Helena gave her another apologetic look. "I promise, it won't be long. A week at most. And at least you've got a place to stay in the meantime."

Jay rolled her eyes as she looked out at the houses passing by.

Helena turned around, slumping in her seat. She understood why Jay felt the way she did, but it was the best Helena could do on such short notice. Besides, Lucio never would have agreed to let Jay stay had he known that she called; he was the whole reason she was in this position in the first place.

Well, not just him—Michael was a big part of this, too. Helena knew he was a controlling and abusive monster, but literally draining Jay's bank accounts was *diabolical.* Like she had never mattered to him in the first place.

Helena glanced over at Dylan, who kept his amber brown eyes on the road ahead of him. They still hadn't talked about the whole "Lucio using Dylan to text Michael about Jay's affair with Colt" thing. She didn't want to, really. She was pissed underneath it all, which is why she chose to bring him along on this whole plan. It was a roundabout way for him to reconcile with Jay, without Helena or him having to tell her exactly what happened.

And like the best friend he was, Dylan jumped into action when she needed him. He was always there for her. Which was terrifying. Michael and Colt had technically always been there for Jay, hadn't they? What was to say that Dylan wouldn't turn his back on Helena one day, or even now? He knew everything; it would be so easy for him to call Lucio right now and tell him what Helena was doing, all in the name of protecting her. Or worse, in the name of his loyalty to Lucio.

Dylan must have felt her staring, because he glanced over at her, his lips twitching.

Helena smiled back. No, Dylan wouldn't betray her. He was her friend first; even if he did work for Lucio. And while she was still pissed as hell for what he helped do to Jay, he was working on it now. He would make up for it. Helena would make sure of it.

The area became more familiar, and she looked back at Jay, noticing her eyes widened as she took in the surrounding houses.

It was a common reaction; their house was in a wealthier part of upstate where the estates were quite large. They had full lawns, both back and front, and many of them had pools. Not that it was anywhere close to swimming weather; March was still holding strong with the cold and wind.

Dylan made the familiar right turn onto their block.

Helena took a breath before turning to Jay. "Welcome to our humble abode."

Their house was huge, a mix of brick and white stone that gave it a fake charm. The front of the colonial was covered with windows, decorated with sheer curtains. Helena didn't *love* living there, mainly because of the lack of privacy, but it was where she had grown up.

Dylan threw the car into park, giving Helena one last serious look before they got out. Jay followed, holding onto her purse and the plastic bag full of her wet clothes.

"We'll cut through the house," Helena said. "Lucio's not home, so don't worry about him."

"I almost feel like it would be easier if he was," Jay mumbled, following her into the house all the same.

They walked through the kitchen, out into the backyard. The privacy fence still carried out through the back, which was good considering there was a large, inground pool.

They walked around it to the guesthouse: a small building with deep gray paneling and beautiful windows. A large sliding glass door was the main entrance, and Jay looked at Helena skeptically.

"We have curtains. You just pull them closed," Helena said as she ushered her into the house. It was tiny, but that was to be expected. It at least had the basics: a kitchen on the opposite wall with a fridge, stove, and a sink; a couch that could become a futon, and a small TV. A bathroom was at the end of the hall, a built-in closet next to it.

"We'll help you get your stuff," Helena said as she watched Jay take everything in. "Honestly, Lucio works so much and stays out so late he won't even realize you're here."

"Yeah." Jay tossed her bag on the couch.

Helena and Dylan exchanged a glance.

"I'll wait for you outside," he signed, before stepping out and closing the door behind him.

Helena turned back to Jay. "I'm sorry, I know this isn't the best living situation."

"No, I appreciate it. You've done more than enough for me." Jay sat down on the couch, placing her head in her hand. "I just don't want you getting your ass chewed out for me."

Helena shifted her weight from one foot to the other. "Don't worry about it. I'll bring out some of Quinn's leftovers for you, so you can eat."

"Thanks."

"Don't thank me just yet," Helena mumbled, walking herself out of the guest house.

Dylan was still looking at her with that stupid "this is a bad idea" face.

She glared up at him. "Shut up."

"I didn't even say anything."

"You didn't have to."

"Hel," Dylan moved in front of her. *"You need to tell Luke. Now."*

"Are you nuts?" Helena pulled him toward the house. Once they were inside, she turned back to him. "I can't tell him *now.*"

Dylan cocked a brow at her. *"So when are you going to tell him?"*

"Soon."

"Hel."

"Soon! Just, obviously not today. She needs to relax and get her head on straight first."

He began to sign something, but his phone buzzed, grabbing his attention instead. He pulled his phone from his pocket, sighing heavily as he texted whoever it was back, before signing back to her. *"Luke wants to know why the hell we're taking so long on our lunch break."*

"Tell him I wasn't feeling well," Helena said, beginning to push him towards the door. "You had to take me home."

"Now you're getting me *to lie to him?"*

"You lied to me for *months,*" Helena said. "I feel like you should be used to it by now."

Dylan stopped, turning around. *"I wasn't lying to you, I was just..."*

Helena slowly became aware of just how close they were standing. He had always been taller than her, but now...There was something about the way he was looking down at her that made her heart skip. His umber skin had lightened from the lack of sun from the winter months. He had switched up his hair recently, trading out his locs for naturally tight coils with the sides shaved, highlighting his suddenly very handsome features. She glanced at his arms, which had returned to their resting position across his chest, and she *swore* she saw the faint outline of biceps through his rain jacket. And along with that, her eyes trailed over to his neck, where she noticed his tie was ever so loose; the thought of him loosening it more was enough to—

"Hel? You okay?" Dylan signed before reaching out to touch her arm.

She tried not to let it show how her skin lit up at the contact.

"You look pale."

"Yeah, just fine," she murmured, trying to muster up enough saliva to coat her suddenly dry mouth. "Tell Lucio I wasn't feeling well."

He kept his eyes glued to her face, and she prayed he didn't notice the sudden blush creeping up her cheeks. What the hell was happening? It was *Dylan* for God's sake, her best friend. He had touched her plenty of times, looked at her all of those times; she felt perfectly fine. Why now? What the hell was happening that suddenly he was making her stomach flutter and her knees feel like jelly?

"You want me to stay?"

She bit her lip to bite back her yes, tamping down the butterflies that erupted at the way his eyes flicked down to catch the motion. "No, it's fine. I'll just go lie down."

His brows furrowed. *"You sure?"*

She scowled then shooed him out the door. "Yes, now go before Quinn starts asking questions. I'll text you later."

He rolled his eyes and waved goodbye, stepping out to walk himself back to Quinn's car. At this point, it was be a waste for him to go all the way back to work, but having him here was too much. She had a job to do, and she couldn't have him distracting her over the whole Lucio nonsense. And that was the only thing he would be distracting her with.

Acknowledgements

It only feels fair that I start by thanking my best friend, Pen. This story would not exist if it weren't for us being a couple of dumb teenagers with an internet connection and too much time on our hands. Even if it has completely changed from where we started, I hope you see the inspiration you helped create, and know that with each page, I poured my love for you into it (Even if you never read this book because it's literally full of triggers for you).

Thank you to my parents. They have no idea that I wrote this book, and they never will, but I want to thank them for always standing by me, and encouraging me to follow my dreams.

Thank you to my husband, who has been one of my biggest cheerleaders. Thank you for giving me the courage to move forward with this silly idea for a book, and always being a point of reference.

Thank you to Farrah. Without you, I literally would be lost in a sea of draft edits, spent way too much money on publishing scams, or published something that was not worthy of human consumption. You have been the best friend a girl could ask for, and thank you for guiding me in this really quite terrifying journey.

Thank you to Devin, my editor. Thank you for taking my tragic draft and breathing new life into it, showing me how to become a better writer (by, you know, using emotions and not repeating the word "eyes" over one hundred times), and how to pick myself up and brush myself off. I'm grateful to have you in my life.

Thank you to Parker, my biggest critic and my first writing friend. I cannot thank you enough for calling me out, and giving me such in-depth feedback. I'm forever in your debt.

Thank you to all my betas: J.M, Kate, Audrey, Adeline, Nicole, Katherine, and Izzy. You all were more help to me than you know, and I appreciate you all giving me honest and open feedback, even if I didn't always want to take it.

Thank you to my sensitivity reader, for putting yourself out there, helping make sure these characters feel authentic, and helping me improve my writing.

Thank you to Muhammad Waqas on Fiverr for my beautiful cover art.

Thank you to thatblank_canvas on Instagram for helping create the concept art for my first cover, and my character art.

Thank you to Morgan Teal on TikTok for my amazing dinkuses and chapter headers!

Thank you to my ARC readers. If that's you, hi! Thank you for reading this book and giving your open and honest feedback. I promised myself I wouldn't read reviews, so feel free to go tear me apart on Amazon or Goodreads or Storygraph or whatever platform you want. But if you have something positive you want to share with me, please feel free to reach out. I'd love to connect with you.

And finally, thank you, dear reader. Thank you for letting me share this story with you, and for supporting an indie author. I hope that you'll continue with me on this journey, wherever it may go, and know that we'll all come out stronger in the end.

About the author

Caroline is a wife, dog mom, and full-time lover of all things tragic. She believes that stories are powerful tools that can be used to create change, and that the curtains are never really just blue. She can often be found on long walks with her dog, or enjoying a fellow Indie Author's book.

Want to see more/be among the first to get updates on book 2? Follow Caroline below at any of the links below!

My website: https://caroline-ashfordwriting.com/

My Substack: https://substack.com/@carolineashwriting

My TikTok: https://www.tiktok.com/@caroline.ashfordwriting

www.ingramcontent.com/pod-product-compliance
Lightning Source LLC
Chambersburg PA
CBHW012027110726
47995CB00006B/1153